Caroline W. H. Dall

My First Holiday

Letters home from Colorado, Utah and California

Caroline W. H. Dall

My First Holiday
Letters home from Colorado, Utah and California

ISBN/EAN: 9783337287870

Printed in Europe, USA, Canada, Australia, Japan

Cover: Foto ©Andreas Hilbeck / pixelio.de

More available books at **www.hansebooks.com**

OR,

LETTERS HOME

FROM COLORADO, UTAH, AND CALIFORNIA.

BY

CAROLINE H. DALL.

'

Scarce hath the springtide brought the flowers,
When scarlet leaves fall through the bowers.

Japanese verses. B. H. C.

Day follows day, and still no shower of rain;
Morn after morn each thirsty blade droops down,
And every garden tint is changed to brown.

Yaka Mochi. By Basil Hall Chamberlain.

"I like a climate where the sun shines one whole day in the year, which I have not seen here." — S. W. Cheney, London, 1843.

BOSTON:

ROBERTS BROTHERS.

1881.

UNIVERSITY PRESS:
JOHN WILSON AND SON, CAMBRIDGE.

TO .

THE DEAR COUSINS,

WHO TURNED DESOLATION AND DREARINESS INTO DELIGHT,

I Dedicate this Book.

A PREFACE TO BE READ.

In the spring of 1880, several physicians in different localities agreed in thinking that I ought to take a long journey. When it was found that I could not go to Europe, California was suggested; and not only was its moderate, equal climate praised and pressed upon my consideration, but the facilities of travel were urged. I was told that I should not find the journey fatiguing, and that for a reasonable fee I should obtain devoted service and all needful accessions to comfort, — such as hot water and well kept dressing-rooms all along the way. I thought I might as well start for the moon; but it proved unexpectedly possible, and so I had seven months of unadulterated pleasure. I could not write to my friends during my rapid transit from Colorado to Utah, and from Utah to California, and up and down its length and breadth. My seven months of pleasure, however, did not bring the climate that was promised; nor did I find it easy to travel alone beyond the Rocky Mountains. On the contrary, for the first time, I found myself commanding neither attention nor respect on the ground of simple womanhood. It seemed to me that there might be invalids to whom many things that I went through would prove fatal, and that it was really desirable that travellers should know in advance that what is called the "uniform climate" of California is simply a *uniformity of change;* that each day gives variations greater than any Atlantic town can show,— and that this is true all along the coast. In this year of 1880 it was true as far back as the Calaveras grove; and the morning and evening fogs, which were heavy beyond belief from San Rafael to Los Angeles, were distinctly felt in Stockton, which last place had the finest summer climate I encountered.

I found a great many trivial things that were exceedingly interesting and wholly new,— things that it seemed to me I ought to have known before I went. I read while in the country several books concerning it which filled me with amazement, so wholly did the writers seem to be indebted to their imaginations for their facts. Among these was "Two Years in California," written by a lady who was kindly remembered by many of my friends. As an example of her statements I will offer two. In a long chapter devoted to Chinese affairs she gives an account of her visits to the joss-houses, and described them as Buddhist temples! The supposed fact is that there is not a single worshipper of Buddha in California, nor was there ever a Buddhist shrine there. I read this book after I had personally visited the joss-houses, and so incredible did it seem to me that any one should venture such statements without a shadow of foundation, that I went down to China-town again, and spent the greater part of two of my fast diminishing days in trying to ascertain where these shrines were. Again, she speaks enthusiastically of the cleanliness of Spanish houses and Spanish women. She says if the houses

in the old Spanish towns contain nothing beyond
a chair, a table, and a bed, they will at least be spotlessly clean! Now the fact is that these same houses
are proverbs of uncleanliness; and in this I take the testimony of the inhabitants, — I do not offer my own. When
I lived in Canada, the French and English traders who
brought satin and cloth for the Indian women to embroider used to have the pattern drawn on linen paper,
which was basted over the fabric. The women sewed
through the paper; otherwise their work would have been
unsalable. I had some Spanish hem-stitching done by
a Spanish woman in Santa Cruz, which was almost
worthless for the same reason.

I do not greatly blame the author I have quoted. I
doubt whether there is a civilized country on the globe
where it is so difficult to get any accurate information.
The name of a flower, the character of a stone, the
meaning of half-a-dozen hot springs grouped in a corner,
and all sorts of colors from black to golden, — these
things, however disagreeable it is not to know, everybody cannot be expected to tell; but the greatest inac-
curacy of observation and report prevails, and the
answers to persistent questions are like the old Scripture commentaries, of which Dr. Charles Lowell once
said that the human mind was sure to accept the last
with which it came in contact!

Among modern travellers Isabella Bird holds an
enviable place. For the same reason that she consents
to sacrifice artistic arrangement, and submits her reader
to the egotistic pressure of letters, I have consented to
do the same.

The following paragraph, which opens her account of Japan, would be just as applicable to my experience in California : —

"The traveller's opinion of the climate depends very much upon whether he goes thither from the east or from the west. If from Singapore, he pronounces it healthful, bracing, and delicious. If from California, damp, misty, and enervating. Then there are (as in other places) good and bad seasons, cold or mild winters, cool or hot summers, dry or wet years, and other variations. To-day has been spent in making new acquaintances, receiving many offers of help, asking questions, and receiving answers which directly contradict each other. Well, I have months to spend here, and I must begin at the alphabet, — see everything, hear everything, read everything, and delay forming opinions as long as possible."

In California, as has been seen, reading was of little avail. The country alters from month to month, and those who have written about it had a limited experience, or were mostly enthusiasts or dreamers. I have seen no account of a journey undertaken in summer like my own. There is no need to exaggerate. California has charms in plenty; but they do not always lie in plain sight, and its future will depend largely on the conscientious report of those who have eyes.

I claim accuracy for nothing I relate. These pages are only open letters to my friends : they tell how *I* saw things, and what the people said before me, or answered to my questions. I wish to give as vivid a picture as I can of the way things look in California to-day, — as Espriella went to England, and did not disdain in his inimitable way to describe the tongs that lifted the coal. ' If every detail be not true, the whole picture will be truer than if I paused to make each item so; and whoso cannot understand that mystery will be sure to misunderstand the book.

What I saw, and not what I shall think about what I saw a year or two hence, is what my friends wish to hear. It might seem as if a dinner could be had in New York that would be strangely like that in the Italian restaurant in San Francisco; but I do not think so. On the Atlantic coast the pressure of republican civilization penetrates every foreign creature to at least a trivial extent; but in California civilization has little to say about anything. The population of all the large towns seems a sort of crystallized Leadville, where the search for gold or what can be turned into gold moves gentle and simple, Spaniard and Briton, with a common fierce impulse, and which neither acts upon the nationality nor is acted upon by it. Something else comes first. It may be all very well to vote, or to speak English, but meanwhile there are the· hydraulic engines tearing out the bowels of the mountains and washing their rocky sides down into the very throat of the Golden Horn. The Spanish or French quarter is as distinct as the Chinese, yet an indescribable indifference to all stereotyped habits, to all bodily comfort, united to a lazy enjoyment of the moments as they pass, keeps every drop of New England blood tingling in the veins of one who looks on.

These people have all adopted California, however, and their fondness for the country is as fierce as that of a lion-

ess for her cubs. Object to the range of the thermometer!—you might as well accuse one neighbor of arson
and another of forgery! That you did not intend to be
personal was not to be believed! And yet, all over the
land, the dear friends who made me so welcome and so
happy would say now and then with a merry laugh, "It
is good to see some one who is satisfied with her own
home." In the midst of California fogs I told them of
the skies blue as Sorrento, which usually bend over the
hills where I write these lines. In the chill of the trade-
wind I celebrated our golden sunshine. In the heat of
the Norther, burning brown the blue lobes of the Eucalyptus, I told them of the Potomac breezes that gently
wave my oaks and walnuts. I came home the last week
in November: four weeks have passed, and I have hardly
seen the blue or felt the sunshine; the elements have
raged all around me; the snow has heaped up against the
hill-side as never before for thirty years; the tooting horn
warns the traveller of the unsteady track of countless
sleds that have hardly tried its slopes since the century
began; and gay as the Christmas shouts are we are all
heart-sick for lack of the sun. It is n't wise to write it
down. I hear you clap your hands and shout with glee
far off in the hollows of Monterey and Santa Barbara,
O friends!—while here at home the elements shriek
rudely, "Will you love this land after all? Did you say
it was good to live in? What do you think now?"

Yes, I will love it! for here we have the sweet succession of the seasons, made precious by the reiterated joys
of the world's generations. Spring, with its coy ap-

proaches, and its fountains of color and sweetness; summer, with its wealth of green and its rippling rills; autumn, with its "russet wear" and rainbowed sunsets and glowing fruit; winter, with its firesides, its vocations, and its Christmas joys. California offers a series of monotonies, and although I observed that there as here the wild-flowers knew their season, and asked no leave to be of sun or rain, yet you ate the same things all the year round, and three crops of strawberries took the flush and fragrance out of June itself.

> "The common growth of mother earth
> Suffices me, — her tears, her mirth,
> Her humblest mirth and tears."

Yet the thought of these past seven months "doth breed" in me "perpetual benedictions." As they passed they took many of those I had loved into more ideal spheres. My going was delayed by the impending death of one of the gentlest of God's children, a native of the far Northwestern Archipelago; and as I came home I walked thoughtfully between the graves of many whose hopes and purposes had been long interwoven with mine. To George Ripley, Count Pourtalès, Benjamin Peirce, Lydia Maria Child, and Lucretia Mott, in all of whom I had felt an affectionate interest for nearly a lifetime, my heart was forced to say farewell, while my feet still wandered.

> "We are such stuff
> As dreams are made of; and our little life
> Is rounded with a sleep."

If I had not been in Colorado last summer, I think I

should have taken no interest in Mrs. Jackson's new book. As far back as I can remember, stories of injustice done to the unhappy Indians have stirred my blood; and when as a child I was shown the bullets and tomahawk marks which dinted the old door at Deerfield, I only felt grieved that civilized nations should have been able to induce this simple people to carry out their own murderous plots. In Colorado I found a shameless greed for Indian territory, which accounted at once for the inroads upon the reservations and for all the massacres and atrocities recorded. When one reads the weekly reports from the mining regions, it seems as if they overflowed with gold and silver; but go into these regions, and the first thing you hear are wild reports of richer veins and grander openings covered by the Indian reservations. In the camps themselves, in the parlor of the hotel at Leadville, in the sitting-room of a small boarding-house where I finally took refuge from the untidiness of that hotel, in the cars between Leadville and Cheyenne, between Stockton and Sacramento, and later between Burlington and Quincy, I heard the same revolting story told,— how the United States should never have given these Indians such valuable land, and how the speaker had penetrated in disguise to this or that location, and had brought away superb specimens. "It was only a question of time. Nobody need think the miners would rest till the reservations were thrown open." Then samples of ore were produced and gloated over, which to well-instructed eyes showed nothing better than the usual sulphurous glare of pyrites. But if they had been pure gold, or specimens of placer earth as rich as the old deposits at Murphy's, what do our people want of them? What do they need more than they already have? In crossing from Cheyenne to Sacramento every fifteen miles shows a cluster of mineral springs, in which sulphur, iron, soda, iodine, or the like are all ready to enter on beneficent work. Why should any man covet some hidden geyser? In the same way the land wherever prospected reveals all manner of mineral possibilities. Silver, gold, iron, and copper can always be had, if "not for the asking," then certainly for the working. The Indians care little for the minerals, and quite as little for the vanished or vanishing game. But they care for their homes, for the land just subjected to cultivation, for the prospects of their descendants, and for a certain sort of education, which is broken down every time matters reach a crisis and they are compelled to remove. Here in Washington we have had anxious groups of them all winter; and one could not help wondering why they coveted knowledge, when they could not but know what successful knaves knowledge had made of white men, in and out of departments. Mrs. Jackson's spirited volume, the reading of which would make the gayest spirit heavy-hearted, sets forth half-a-dozen important facts very little known.

1. The first chapter shows us how the Indians' "right of occupancy" is a right recognized from the very beginning by all nations,—a right to be bought and sold at their own pleasure.

2. It teaches us that the Indian massacres of whites
in the early days were almost without exception either
instigated or paid for by the English, French, or American commanders.   When this was not the case, as
it was in all the raids at the time of the extension of
the settlements on the Penobscot and the Connecticut,
they were the result of the section inserted in every
treaty to this effect,— that if a white intruder crossed the
Indian lines, "the Indians may punish him as they see
fit."   This may be proved by a reference to the first
treaties with the Wyandottes and the Delawares.

3. It shows, to the great surprise of most people, that
one hundred and thirty-two thousand of our Indians are
self-supporting on their reservations, receiving not a dollar from the Government except the interest due them on
the price of their lands, or, what is the same as interest,
the annuities paid to tribes supposed to be dying out,
and to whom in consequence it has not been thought
necessary to pay the price of their lands.   It would seem
evident to the dullest apprehension that the time must
soon come when the Government will have to support
the remnants of tribes who live by hunting and fishing,
for game of all kinds will soon cease to exist in any sufficient quantity.   We have, Mrs. Jackson tells us, about
fifty-five thousand who never visit an agency, and over
whom the Government exercises no control.   One of our
surveying parties in the mountains of northwestern
Mexico lately fell in with an assembly of Indians sol-
emnly burning their dead.   The burning was attended
with sacred ceremonies, which reminded the surveyors of

certain rites practised by the Parsees; and they inquired into the meaning of the whole thing, when they saw the eye of the corpse offered to the sun on the point of a spear. "We are going back to our old gods whom we have offended," was the reply. "We have tried the white man's God, and he does not care for us. If he did, the white man would not dare to treat us ill."

4. There has seemed to be for the last half century a perverse and wilful misunderstanding of the character of the Indian tribes and the possibility of their civilization. The leading Indians are themselves aware of the change of circumstances which makes civilization desirable. If the difficulty of getting trustworthy information once excused those who have never lived on the frontier for such misunderstanding, they can take refuge in such excuse no longer. Mrs. Jackson has so industriously and faithfully gathered her facts, that he who reads running can inform himself as to the opinions of Burnet, Bonneville, Lafitau, and McKenney. How steadily the Indians improved their lands, while they met with the slightest encouragement, we may see from the fact that in 1833 their cornfields were coveted as greedily as their gold fields are in 1881. The letters and speeches of Winnemucca and others are as much to the purpose as those of the white men they confronted.

5. The history of these races shows that under a hopeful trust in the whites the Cherokees reached a point in civilization quite equal to that of any rival population. "They have adopted," says the reluctant department only three years ago, "all the forms of rep-

resentative government. They raise their own wool and cotton, and have pianos and sewing machines. They print their own laws and their own newspaper." Why not, since Sequoia invented his own alphabet?

The ninth chapter of this book is one which it is very hard to read. I do not see how a white man, who has his own vote and feels responsible for the government of his native land, can endure the reading. A woman, who sees only the moral aspect of the whole thing, and has no illegal craving for cornfields or gold fields, bows her head and tingles with shame from head to foot, as she ponders it. The worst of a great wrong, or a series of great wrongs, is that no one can ever undo it. It may be repented of, yet it remains a scar burned into the face of man or nation. But not on that account can the American people afford to pause in the work of honesty and reform. The most hopeful thing in the history of mankind is the fact, that, whenever a great wrong has been done, some great indignation sooner or later bears witness to man's outraged moral sense. Politically speaking, I have not the smallest idea who is to blame for the story which makes me blush. But behind the Democrat and the Republican alike stands human nature, which ought indignantly to disclaim the responsibility.

CAROLINE H. DALL.

Washington, Aug. 1, 1881.

MY FIRST HOLIDAY.

Denver, Col., Aug. 2, 1880. — I took New York and Boston in my way to Buffalo and Chicago on my way here, — all for good business reasons, with results by no means startling, nor especially interesting to you. I left Buffalo on the 26th, and here I am! If the Sierras are any dirtier than the "Lake Shore," I pity the prairie dogs. It thundered all that night, it seemed to me; but when, thinking it might be a dream, I asked the porter where we overtook the storm, he answered, —

"It was all along Ohio and Indiana!"

Delphic enough, that oracle, had our grandfathers been listening!

We carried along with us four or five hundred German emigrants of the best stamp. One family had a perfect stack of umbrellas of various sizes, — one for every child large enough to hold it. I had with me several loaves of berry cake, which Annie had put into my lunch-basket.

When we halted at La Porte, I went to the emigrant car, and, mustering a few words of German, asked an apple-faced woman if I might give it to the "kinder."

She looked with some suspicion on this food of the
blest, but in a few moments every child had its mouth
as full as a broad grin would allow.

At the Chicago dépôt I asked one of the men for
some small bit of information, when he answered
easily and plainly, "I do not understand what you say,"
having fortified himself with this one sentence in
advance.

At Chicago it was a treat to see how gently busy in
grave good work American women can be. There I
found Miss Martin and Miss Perry, graduates of the law
school at Ann Arbor, who more than made their expenses the very year they opened their office, and who
have the loving respect of all who know them. There
is Mrs. Bradwell, who edits the "Legal Reporter," and
Dr. Emma Gaston, who, born in Ohio, educated in
Philadelphia, and coming West from our New England Hospital for Women and Children less than three
years ago, has now already a noble place in the city
work. She holds her clinics at the Woman's Hospital,
is one of the managers of the House of Refuge, attends
on certain days at the Dispensary, and was appointed
by the city to look after the interests of a pleasant
charity called the "Floating Hospital." Far out in the
lake, beyond Lincoln Park, the city has built a pier
more than three hundred feet long. It is covered with
tents, sheds, and hammocks for countless babies and
those who care for them. For some years past the babies
of Chicago have died at a terrific rate; and now every
pleasant summer day three steamer-loads are carried
down to the pier in the early morning, where they enjoy
the lake breezes until night. A male physician paid by
the city goes down with the boat, and also a lady whom

the city appointed at Dr. Gaston's request; and these two look after their weary little bodies through the day.

One morning when I was in Dr. Gaston's office, she was summoned suddenly to the railroad dépôt. There she found two tiny creatures under five years of age, whose parents had both died of yellow fever in Memphis. Grandparents in Burlington, Michigan, were too poor or too feeble to go to them, but had sent money to bring them on. Tags were sewed to their dresses, and they were going through, — parcels by express!

Unfortunately this sort of parcel has an open mouth, and the two little ones were quite ill from the fruit and candy given them on the train.

In Chicago, too, the women edit a well supported social-science paper. I had not seen Chicago since the fire. Wonderfully has it emerged from its ashes. The superb blocks of stone stores, the new post-office and the court house, the banks and the insurance offices are covered with a florid decoration hardly to be imagined. As to the court house, the many rows of outcropping foliation can only be accounted for on the supposition that the stone blossomed of itself!

Under the eaves at the top of many massive pilasters are repeated the two figures of man and woman, as if both sides of humanity expected to have justice done within its walls. One need not criticise the anatomy : the figures bear out the general effect.

Just before I came away, I was introduced to a young woman whose story is full of interest. She came of a Cambridge family who moved to Iowa thirty years ago, where she married a lawyer of ability. He was addicted to gambling. In two years she had two little babies, and when the youngest was six weeks old he deserted her. She had always wished to study law, but no one would help her. As soon as her baby could be left she began to pick berries, holding this purpose steadily in view.

With the proceeds of the season's berries she went to the nearest large town, and took an agency for the sale of shoulder-braces. With what she earned in this way she went to Chicago and took a position as cashier; and so she has paid her way through the Chicago law school, and has been for some time employed at a fair salary by one of the best legal firms. As soon as she has mastered all the routine, she will open an office of her own. Since she began as a clerk, her oldest child and her father have died. She has brought her mother from the farm to the city, and established her and the baby out on the Boulevard. God bless her lonely and vigorous life!

While I was making my tour through the various city and county hospitals, a photographer asked me to sit for my portrait. He is making a collection of portraits and autographs which is to be sealed up and given to the city of Chicago, and Chicago is expected to give it in its turn to the Centennial Commission of 1976!

Why talk about the decay of faith? Where will this wonderful volume be in 1976; and are we at all sure that there will be a centennial commission?

I left Chicago on the Rock Island railroad at noon. How the Illinois woods have grown during the last ten years! Wonderful spikes of many-colored mints and airy pink blossoms flaunted over the prairie. The beautiful Illinois River and tall bluffs made many villages pretty. "Texas meats" were brought to us on the cars. They were "shelled out" of some nut that was a cross between the pecan and the shagbark.

I was surprised to see how wide the Mississippi is at Davenport. Between the high bluffs at Quincy it must find it rather hard to squeeze through.

My companion on the car was a Vermont woman, who has been for many years one of the foremost teachers in San Francisco. A year or two since, in company with another teacher in the Rincon public school whose health had failed under the work, she purchased a vineyard near Passadina. The two women built drying frames and sweating boxes, and last year sent six thousand pounds of good raisins to market. I shall send you a fuller account of this work some day, for I am going to the vineyards when the grapes are ripe.

Endless rolling prairies; countless herds of cattle; superb flaunting flowers; hornèd poppies, great chalices of snow, with golden centres; cactus of scarlet and yellow bloom; the *epilobium marginata*, or mountain snow; with alkaline plains that burned our eyes,— these made up the measure of the next two days.

Friday the 30th of July was a dreary day; night found us at Ogelalla in Nebraska.

Thirty-three women and children and two men used our dressing-room to-day, the latter entirely without right. Unless a party is large enough to take an entire car, ladies travelling alone will do well to heed the following facts:—

1. No palace or drawing-room cars are to be found on the overland route,— only the ordinary Pullman sleeping car, or silver palace, with the usual abuses.

2. No dining-room car goes further than Omaha; and the slow motion of cars, which is said to make dining in them so easy and agreeable, *does not now exist* on the

part of the road where they are used. I saw coffee and
soup thrown into a lady's lap, and could not hold my
own cup. The "Hotel Car," where meals are cooked
and beds are made in the same car, is a nuisance beyond
words. In spite of the promises of the company, porters
are not at leisure to obtain hot water and milk; so it is
better to provide a generous lunch basket with tea and
coffee to last till the journey's end.

3. The hand baggage is not easily managed, when the
train is full, if too heavy for yourself to lift. The fees
expected are excessive, and it seems to be the policy of
the Pullman management to force every piece through as
many hands as possible. Do not fee your porters a
single minute before you have done with them, unless
with the promise of further pay. If you do, you will be
left in the lurch.

4. Women travelling alone are airily told before starting that they go through "without change." On the
contrary, cars must be changed at Chicago, Omaha, and
Ogden. At each of these places there is several hours'
delay, and a great deal to do which involves fatigue.

5. Do not travel alone if it can be helped. If you *must*,
associate yourself on the way with another traveller to
whom your service will be as valuable as that she ren-
ders you. There is transfer of hand baggage to be paid
for at each place. One porter cannot attend to twenty
women. The white conductors are courteous but not
attentive, and never lift a parcel. The colored porters
devote themselves to men, whose boots they black, whose
coats they brush, and from whom they expect heavy
fees.

You will be told that you can telegraph from train to
train and secure your berth without trouble. Suppose

you telegraph from Chicago to Omaha; on arriving at Omaha, one would naturally suppose that she could step from one Pullman to another, or at least deposit her baggage there, while she went in search of the agent. On the contrary, she must wearily carry, or watch some strange boy carry, her baggage to the Pullman office, give in her name, and stand in file till she receives her ticket: that done she may seat herself in the car. But if at the last moment the company decide that the car she is in is not needed, she will have the whole process to go through again.

At the very point where this is most insisted on, — at Omaha or Council Bluffs, — you are also required to attend personally to the re-checking of your baggage, and to pay for any overweight. It would be perfectly easy for a clerk to manage all this, but the companies actually require you to be in two places at once; and to accomplish the re-checking you must stand in sun or rain, wholly unprotected, till all the baggage of three concentrating lines is "run off."

The lovely superintendent of the Rincon School attended to the re-checking, while I went in search of berths. My trunk happened to be the last one called, and she stood in the hot July sun just an hour and a quarter! Then, when we were seated, the agent decided to drop off our car, and I should have gone on without any berth at all, so weary was I, if it had not been for my friend's persistence.

The same day I wanted some milk, and gave my pitcher to the porter; but he came back without any. I then went into the dining-room myself, and was told that if I would pay $1.00 for a dinner I might have a glass of milk with it, but that they had none to sell. As the railroad owns land on both sides of the rails, and as it also owns every hotel, I mutely showed the printed circular on which passengers were promised every comfort required by an invalid. "Madam," retorted the clerk, "have you lived till this time, without knowing what advertisements are for?"

We stayed more than an hour at this little town called Sidney. When we resumed our journey I sat opposite the wife of a Colorado clergyman, travelling with a sick child. At the last moment she had entered the car, carrying the child and a large jug of milk, both tired and heated. The porter brought her a table, which she afterward cleared away herself. An hour after, I went to her and asked her if she would tell me where she got that milk. " I should not have tried to get any," she said, "if my little girl's life did not depend on it. I went as you did to the dining-room, and was refused. I persisted a little, as the child was really too ill to go into the dining-room, but it was of no use. I saw a restaurant on the street, and went there; but they had sold the last drop hours' ago. They directed me to a milliner's shop, three or four blocks away, where fresh milk was kept. So I went on slowly with the child, and got back in time!"

The alkaline plains have begun, and it must be remembered that milk is often twenty-five cents a quart, and always difficult to get; also that there are too many women travelling alone for all to be waited on. But it is easy to see what should be done. Everything belongs to the two companies, and one word from headquarters would remedy the evil.

On the 31st of July I rose very early, as the only possible way to get my bath. I found the porter in the ladies' dressing-room, where he certainly did not belong.

In a few moments, however, he left it in fair order. It was about five in the morning when I went to the rear for fresh air. Deep ultramarine drifts of cloud were stranded in a golden sea. A man and a boy from Western Pennsylvania got off in the neighborhood of Central City. The man owned five thousand head of cattle or thereabout. Afar off was a low frame house; nearer, two houses built of sods: a chimney smoked in each, and each had two frame windows and a door. These houses must be very warm, and would look pretty with their well rounded tops covered with vines. The drovers who live in them had already gone out to the herd. Soon I saw on the horizon a pair of antelopes; then a prairie-dog village, with one white-bellied creature on guard, who scuttled away like a kangaroo. I do not in the least know the names of the flowers I see.

At Cheyenne the cars stopped directly in front of the hotel, where a good dinner could be had for one dollar. I decided to dine, as I was obliged to wait two hours for the train to Denver, and my porter in the Pullman assured me that if I did so, the porter of the hotel would carry my bags to the Denver train without charge. What happened? I paid the porter of the Pullman fifty cents for conveying my movable traps to the hotel. I paid one dollar for my dinner, and another fifty cents to the porter for putting them on the Denver train, — two dollars in all, which there was really no need to spend. In the hotel no dressing-room was open, and I was indebted to the courtesy of a permanent boarder for a chance to wash my hands. The mountain view from the second story of the house, however, was cheaply paid for at that rate. It was delicious on the other hand to follow with kindling eyes the level of the illimitable plain.

Between Cheyenne and Denver we saw a grand gey-ser of dust, and a great many little whirls of the same sort off on the horizon. The cattle and the pretty gray jackasses fled before it. Then came irrigated fields, and finally the magnificent Rocky Mountain range. Lift the White Mountains into the air, multiply their length by five, and you will have some idea how the Rockies look from Long Mountain to Pike's Peak. I was surprised to see no signs of snow, except a scratchy white line here and there, which I afterwards found indicated a ravine five or six hundred feet wide and perhaps a thousand in depth. Greeley, in the valley of *Cache La Poudre*, was the first irrigated town I saw. It is a tem-perance town, checked off by sloughs and ditches, and its green wheat-fields and orchards made a charming contrast to the great stretches of short gray buffalo grass, which looked as if they had been sprinkled with salt.

As we neared Denver, the "Transfer Express" made his appearance; and, as it was growing late and dark, I asked him to take charge of my hand baggage. He de-clined. "There was a conductor and an omnibus to take me to the house; I should have no trouble." Before we ran up to the dépôt, the conductor dropped off the train, leaving me in the hands of the brakeman. When we stopped, the brakeman peremptorily refused to touch my bags. With a good deal of reluctance I left all my wraps and bags in the car, went out into the dark space, and hired a man to go back with me and take them to the omnibus, which was only prevented by our united shouts from driving away before we could enter it. That my reluctance was wholly justifiable the event showed. I was the last passenger dropped. When we reached Campa Street there was only one man on the

box, who refused to leave his horses; and unable to lift
my bags, as a strong man could have done in a moment, I called in the assistance of a chance-passer. In
the transfer, one of my most valuable possessions, — a
finely made umbrella, intended to serve also as an alpen-
stock, — finally disappeared.

All the way to Cheyenne the ascent, though gradual, is
decided; and there we are exactly as far above the sea as
on the summit of Mount Washington. From Cheyenne
to Denver we slide down a thousand feet; but the "continuance in upper air" had a decided effect, and I
reached the city feeling fresher than for many months.

My first view of the Rocky Mountains, all along the
way, was a great disappointment. Pike's Peak, it is
true, is 14,400 feet above the sea; but if you see it from
a plain which is itself lifted 6,500, it is but little higher
than Mount Washington, and what difference there is
the eye cannot detect. It is the wide extent of the
range, and the exhilaration of the air, which first rouses
the spectator.

Denver, August 3, 1880.— Dr. Avery's house is full
of friends; so she has a pleasant little room for me
on the opposite corner. When I got up this morning she was showering her beautiful lawn, herself
as fresh and dewy as any rose that blossoms upon
it. Together we have driven about the town, and
I sat a long time in the doctor's carriage on Capital
Hill, watching the magnificent mountains, well masked
in volatile clouds, which changed position and color
every moment. All at once Pike's Peak showed itself,
a cone of glowing amethyst. This does not mean that
it looked purple; it was to all intents and purposes

translucent. At Mrs. Scott's I found Mrs. Wilson, whose husband is stationed at Leadville, on the U. S. Survey. With her was a lady from Ouray, who seemed thoroughly to love her mountain home, and taunted my fancy with her vigorous outlines of lofty perpendicular cliffs, romantic gulches, and cascades dripping from the skies. I had come so far, urged simply by my love for my friend; but I am not to go back "till I have seen Colorado,"— so the doctor decides. This is the land of many-colored cacti, of the Euphorbia, of the Epilobium augustifolium,—hard words, which I would not use if any pretty familiar ones would tell the story, but which represent an amount of grace and color and capricious floral charm, of which words fail to give any idea.

The streets of Denver are made beautiful by buildings of volcanic limestone, brought here from the Foot Hills, some thirty-five miles away. It will command a price when its beauty is known. All tints glow through its creamy base, from rose color to bluish gray, and the sunlight modifies the tender effect every moment.

Jackson, the photographer, who was such an important adjunct to Hayden's Survey, has established a studio here; and I spent an hour or two to-day looking over his superb pictures of the cañons.

I hope other people have clearer ideas of Denver than I had before I came to it. Although it is nearly as high as Mount Washington, and only fifteen miles east of the Foot Hills, the city lies in a basin so slightly tilted toward the west that it seems absolutely flat. The citizens have planted the streets with trees, so thickly set that it looks at a little distance like a young forest; and nowhere within the street lines do you get, in the summer, even a limited mountain view, unless you try to cross a square. It is the natural centre of all the excursions to be made, and has in straggling, unkempt business streets some very excellent stores. Above it is the great level bluff, called Capitol Hill, whose roads are cut through the disintegrated granite of the mountains, and are as hard as Nahant Beach. Here a few houses have been built. There are many lovely places in Denver, and one very excellent hotel,— the Windsor,— which all my foreign friends unite in praising. As to other houses, we must recollect, when we hear them praised, what sort of accommodations the old residents would be likely to find sufficient. What a Western man calls "a good hotel" cannot be expected to suit the denizens of the Fifth Avenue. I saw fine skins, stuffed figures, and furs of unheard of creatures in many of the shops. Coyotes, wild-cats, and foxes glared at me. Lying in full sight were poor attempts at painting the superb "lilies of the field," beautiful iridescent fragments of peacock pyrites, long crystals of the newly discovered "Celestine" (a sort of quartz of heavenly blue), agates from the hills, and "fulgurites." These last are long tubes of vitrified sand, glazed within, which are said to be formed by the lightning when it penetrates a sand-bank. These are valued at $25 each. "Conversations about Common Things" may now begin: "Who was the first glass-maker?"—"Fulgur." Beside these lay fossil fish from Green River. There are three varieties, none more than five inches long. They are involved in laminated limestone, and split so as to show skeletons, not scales.

This afternoon came news from Mrs. W. Her husband has telegraphed her, and she will go to Leadville to-morrow. I promise to stay with her two or three

days, if, at the end of that time, she will go on with me
to Colorado Springs.

August 4, 1880. — With well-supplied luncheon baskets, we took the cars for the South Park Road. We did
not know it, but it happened to be the very first day
the South Park train had run into Leadville; and, indeed, this road itself was started less than two years
ago. When I left the main line of travel at Cheyenne,
I went south a hundred miles to Denver. From Denver
to Leadville I go southwest on a narrow gauge road,
one hundred and fifty more; and as we took fourteen
hours to make the distance, it enabled me to see the
country fairly well.

When the engineers first entered the Platte Cañon,
which traverses the South Park, not only had no vehicle
ever passed through it, but no Alpine climber had
attempted it; no trapper's imagination had suggested
the possibility of a trail. There were few places where
the banks of the river were not precipitous cliffs,
stretching heavenward for a thousand feet. For twenty
miles the road goes over a rolling prairie, with little
farms thrifty and pleasant in the summer sun, but grew-
some enough, I'll warrant, when the snow begins to fall.
The surveyors gave up the theodolite for triangulation
and stadia-hairs; while nitro-glycerine did duty for
shovel and pick. In a dozen places, at least, they made
a new channel for the river, that the old channel might
serve as a bed for the railway. Cuts forty feet deep
were made through solid granite. Walls which cannot
be distinguished from the everlasting hills were reared
to defend the road. Men were lowered from five hundred to a thousand feet, by ropes, to drill the holes to

which they attached the platforms upon which they
were to work. The road crosses the river several times.
It is a succession of curves. More than once I looked
directly out of the window near which I sat into the windows of the cars behind. Two miles of this road it cost
$32,000 to build; and the cheapest mile cost $4,000.

This miraculous engineering is to the credit of a Mr.
Eicholtz; and very proud he is of his work. The road
runs under narrow, projecting ledges, by the side of
the turbulent Platte River. Its surroundings have a
cool, green look. Spires and pinnacles of red granite
rise here and there. At one point the grade is 137 feet
to a mile; at Kenosha, seventy-six miles from Denver,
the road ascends the mountain spirally at a grade of 185
feet. At first we entered a wide grassy vale, with a
perfectly clear view of the whole "Continental Divide."
Not one traveller in a thousand sees this. The view is
often limited to the nearest Foot Hills. A thrill of delight passed through me at the first glimpse of this
magnificent *mesa*. At the mouth of the cañon we came
upon mining sheds, and men were at work fifty feet
above us, digging a ditch to irrigate the cliffs.

The river is a series of rapids. Forty miles out we
came upon a little camp. Curious dome-like rocks and
spires, thick-set as those of the Cathedral at Milan, rise
a thousand to fifteen hundred feet above us,— it does
not matter which; for I have already learned that in Nature as in mathematics there is a point at which mensu-
ration passes human perception, and can be appreciated
only by the Infinite. Some of the Foot Hills are crowned
with groves, and in the grass a tiny scarlet flower be-
trays, by its fine color, the character of the soil. Pentstemons, pink, purple, scarlet, crimson, make lines of

living light athwart the grass. Every now and then
there is a low opening into the hillside, like a door or a
fire-place. The jambs are stoned up, and overhead a
slab of heavy granite makes a sort of mantel, and holds
up the crumbling shaft. The hills and the moraine at
the foot of them are covered with a net-work of dead
branches, which has a curious effect. Then the valley
opens to a park-like glade, and snowy tents of invalids
offer lovely suggestions of summer life. It is all so green,
and so sweet with the breath of pines. The angles of
the hills open wide. An elegant city carriage with two
prancing horses held by the lightest traces dances across
our path. The open stretches into enamelled meads. I
half expect to meet Persephone. Primroses, purple
vetch, zinnia, and nodding sunflowers half hide and half
parade their charms; painted-cup quivers like a flame.
At Kenosha the mountain is 10,200 feet above the sea.
We wind up 185 feet to the mile. The sight is still a
new one. A valley gracious as Paradise and noiseless as
the night opens from a bend in the river five hundred
feet below. Gay teams with four horses catch a glimpse
of us, and wave through the silence white banners of
cheer. Delicious white lilies with speckled hearts,
scarlet honeysuckles and cranberry blossoms, with bells
twice as long as those which grow in New England,
tantalize us as we fly past. The South Park opens as
we descend. The whole chain of mountains stretches
across the eastern side. It seems only flecked with
snow, but the white specks cover acres of ground, and
are from five to eight hundred feet deep. Near us the
yarrow blooms bitter-sweet, as on my eastern hills.
Pike's Peak is cut into the sky, as if by intaglio. Everywhere beyond the Mississippi we encounter "parks."

Sometimes they are vast extents of geysers, of eccentric rocky spires, or frowning cliffs, as in the valley of the Yellowstone. Sometimes they are green glades, spangled with flowers, and showing perennial drought in dwindling trees. South Park is a cup-like plain, set within mighty walls, and some thirty miles by sixty in extent. Its rim is dappled by hills that in the winter lift their heads out of the snow, from three to five thousand feet above the sea. The South Platte crosses the Park. This and the trout-brooks are full of fish, the coverts teem with small game, and from the cliffs the sheep, elk, and deer eye the sportsman placidly.

We stop in the wilderness. Far away is a miner's shanty. As a second-class passenger drops off, with a dozen hand parcels which his late companions toss toward him, a tidy wife, leading a little child by each hand, comes to meet him, while two or three larger boys race on before, each striving to be the first to grasp a bundle. It is a pretty sight. Life's brightest pinnacle is touched here, far below the summit of Cathedral Rock. Mounds of moraine begin to rise abruptly. I see the Buffalo Peak, and recognize the lumbering likeness. Here we come to what has been until lately the end of the freighting road. The long trains of mules and wagons, coupled two together, follow a single driver over the natural road of the ravines, and are so picturesque that it is pleasant to encounter them. The profits of the teamsters are said to be very large. The men live with their mules, and are almost as brutal. I have long since made up my mind that there is no sin necessarily connected with the habit of swearing. Coarseness there must be, but no intentional wrong against Deity itself if a man does not know what Deity is. To some unknown power these men address imprecations which are not only terrific, but which are perfectly unintelligible to the listener. Like the Negroes of Bambarra, they neither talk nor want anybody to talk to them, and answer without lifting their eyes when busy among the teams. All along the way they travel the air is scented with dead horses and littered with broken wagons.

Here are platforms still heaped with bullion. The wagons which brought food will take this away. If it stood here for a year it would be safe, for it is too heavy for a thief to lift.

Out of the side of the mountain, without preface or apology, darts a volume of water. It is as thick as a man's body, and widens into a trout-creek, to run the next nine miles. You cannot put a pin between the fish. One man caught thirty-four before breakfast to-day with no more delay than transferring them from the stream to his bucket involved. Then come groves of piñole, looking like a ragged old apple-orchard, capital for firewood, and bearing under the scales of its cones a kernel the size of an acorn, sweet and tender, such as they grind into flour for bread in Sweden. The volcanic limestone which pleased me so much with its soft tints in Denver yields $35 worth of silver to the ton, and was used by the Mexicans three hundred years ago. It looks as clean as if cut to-day. No sort of moss or lichen will cling to it; and this cannot be due to the dryness of the climate, but to the indestructible character of the stone. Parasites grow on other stones, and on all the old tree trunks. Ten miles from Buena Vista a cliff of white chalk makes a most unexpected appearance, and rises two thousand feet. Wherever the mountains are cut you see the granite disintegrating. They are everywhere so shaky and full of fissures that it seems as if any great convulsion might prostrate the whole range; and yet in the sunset light where Harvard, Princeton, and Yale wall out the valley of the Arkansas, how solid and indomitable they look! A little way back is Weston, a deserted mining camp, where they have been opening graves to remove the dead to a cemetery. There thirty-seven bodies lay as they died, "in their boots;" and two who had killed each other in a fierce quarrel were found in the same box!

As I dwelt almost without hope on this sad story, gazing absently at the dark ledge full of the crevices in which such graves are made, a burst of sunlight kindled a distant peak lying far back of all the rest, and brought it into sudden life and beauty. So may a diviner light kindle some day the darkest recesses of the darkest human hearts, and rebuke our coward thoughts!

My companions to-day were three gentlemen from Cincinnati. Two of them were superintendents of the Adams Express, and the other had charge of the local telegraph line. They got me a campstool, set me out on the rear platform, told me stories, and gathered me flowers all day. The car was clean, the porter attentive, and the day passed like a festival.

Our arrival after dark at Leadville was unfortunate. Much as I wished to see the place, — and I did wish to see it, not for its own sake, but as a type of other places, passed and passing, — I would not have gone to it alone. When I joined Mrs. W. it did not occur to either of us that we might not find quarters together. As her husband was a resident, our plan seemed very simple.

But this was the first attempt the cars had made to run into the town. It was the darkest of dark nights,

not a lantern on the platform, no dépôt as yet in existence. We were hurried into an old-fashioned stage-
coach, without step or ladder, treading in the blackness
over broken joists, carpenters' débris, and protruding
sleepers. It is best to forget how I found my way in:
I believe it was over the shoulders of men. Then Mr.
W. made himself known by his voice; but our telegram
had not reached him, and I was obliged to go alone to a
hotel, while he took his wife to a small room he had
hired near the Survey. It is not worth while to say
anything about the hotel. Fortunately I wanted nothing to eat.

Leadville, Aug. 5. 1880. — I wrote some letters and
took them to the post before breakfast. What a villanous crowd I pushed through! Not a woman to be seen.
The street is fuller than Broadway seen as you look down
to the Battery from Grace Church, for Leadville is the
base of supply for all the Gulches. I made a vain attempt to drink a vile poison called coffee, and to eat some
mountain trout embedded each in a pasty sarcophagus.
Then went to the front window and leaned over the
rail of the balcony to watch the crowd in the main
street until the W's. came for me. I did not feel par-
ticularly ill, and strange to say, although I had found
my pillow drenched with blood, it made hardly any impression upon me; and so great was the excitement
created by my novel circumstances, that I wholly forgot
the probability of illness in an altitude of eleven thousand feet.

A surging mass of villanous faces swayed up and
down before me. If there were faces that were only
coarse or rude, they did not mitigate the impression.

Two policemen were murdered last week, and yet the one in front of me was not afraid of the two men astride their asses whom he was seeking to separate and arrest. Gentle-looking men on superb horses dashed by now and then. Half-a-dozen women walked quietly by, as if to a day's work. There was not one here last year. There are a great many loiterers, although more than a thousand have gone away since the failure of the little Pittsburgh and the Chrysolite. Broad hats; broader backs astride well stuffed saddle-bags; Mexican ponchos, shooting boots; bells jangling on the necks of mules, used as a warning when they enter a narrow pass; a string of pack-horses or pretty gray jacks, and at last a man on horseback with three or four led mules, entirely hidden by their packs, consisting of feather beds, furniture, and cooking-stoves!

By and by a little child of four years old or so, in a knitted cloak of shaded crimson wool, in a delicate lace cap lined with a crimson silk which told of some far-off home, came slowly down the street. Her little hand rested on the neck of a lovely young burro of soft gray color, as graceful as an antelope. She leaned against the creature and walked steadily through the crowd. Now and then the animal paused in a way which suggested its native obstinacy. She lifted her hand, gave it a little hit behind with a fairy fist, and moved on through the always parting crowd. I fancy there was a servant close behind, but the crowd was so dense no one could distinguish him. She might have been the —

"Heavenly Una, with her milk white lamb."

One is not apt to think of the old warriors, scarred in the cause of freedom, as likely to go crazy over gold

nuggets, or placer diggings.   Yet I had heard that Asa
Hutchinson was here, and that while his wife rode on
horseback from one mine to another, Asa had opened
a boarding house, where a few travellers could get
rooms, and a great many travellers and residents were
supplied with wholesome meals.   I had made up my
mind that the horrible food and terrible untidiness of
the hotel could not be endured for even another day;
so as soon as my friends came I went in search of Asa.
I saw from afar the broad-brimmed hat and large snowy
collar folded down, and in a few moments a cheery
voice shouted, " Mother! here is an old comrade in want
of a room."   The house is in close proximity to a livery-
stable and a marble-yard, and has nothing attractive
about it.   Here however I speedily engaged a room, which
was, as Dickens said, " so many feet short by so many feet
narrow," at a dollar and a half a day, in exchange for
abominations at the hotel for four dollars; and here, as
long as I stayed, I found the very best of food, whatever
else I missed.   There are many sources of illness in
Leadville which a stranger would not suspect, — among
them the absolute want of drainage and the putrid condition of the water, which is kept in hogsheads filled at
discretion.

A servant went back with me to the hotel to bring
away my hand-bags.   Entering without warning I found
the chambermaid searching my drawers, and did not
realize till a long time after that she had appropriated
some toilet conveniences.   We then went to inquire
about Mosquito Pass, which I was very anxious to cross,
as it gives the same view of the Rocky Mountains that
Thorn Mountain beyond Jackson does of the White
Hills.   But I could make no arrangement.   The stage-

coach goes daily over it toward Fairplay, and it almost
always encounters rain, snow, or hail. There is only
one chance in a thousand of the view I wanted. This
coach would take me to meet the return mail, but only
one of these vehicles would be covered, and I dared not
risk a storm at twelve thousand feet above the sea in
an open team. We then took a carriage with a driver
to "see the town."

Leadville lies in a narrow valley, without any view of
the hills, which rise steeply all about it. It was first
known to story as California Gulch. To the south rise
Carbonate and Freyer hills; and in these are all the
great mines. It is upon one of these hills that the
traveller should seek a shelter if he would avoid illness.

With eight thousand residents, and a floating population of thirty thousand, Leadville, at queer shifts to as-
sume the appearance of a town, is in reality only a con-
geries of mining camps running out upon the side-hills
with one long street as a centre. If the shanties had
been log-cabins covered with creepers, the effect might
have been pretty at a distance, in spite of filth, of excre-
tions animate and inanimate, of tin cans and hoop skirts;
but the houses are built of bright yellow planks, which
keep marvellously fresh in the clear mountain air, and
their chimneys terminate in a small cask or a rusty
stove-pipe.

The three or four trading-streets are a mile in length,
along which parapets of painted boards help the wretched
one-floored shops to put on airs of two-storeyed grandeur.
At right angles with these is Chestnut Street, where
livery-stables, gambling hells, brothels, and well-lighted
dance-houses, without screen or curtain, cluster and

throw their lurid gleams across the street at night. From this nucleus spurs of similar character and proportion shoot out sharply upon the hills, or widen into clusters, as a smelting house, a new strike, or a lifting crane may suggest. There is no drainage, a plenty of water of late, pure in itself, but kept in most places in such a way as to turn it fetid. Countless children swarm through the streets, with no better playthings than a tin can or a stray jack. Yet in the midst of all this you find here and there a tidy woman, or a lovely babe, telling of hopes long delayed or better things forsaken.

Our driver was a boy under twenty, who came from Iowa, and made three dollars a day in the smelt-house, till he nearly died of the poisonous fumes. Now he drives for the "Livery" until he is well enough to go back. He seemed frank and pure. As we drove up Freyer Hill to get a general view of the town, we came across another lad of the same age, — George Hagars, of Hagarstown, Maryland. He was in miner's rig, but leaned across our vehicle with the easy slouch that only a Southron knows, told us where to go, and gave us an introduction to the foreman of the "Robert E. Lee," a certain George M., hailing last from Washington.

Our carriage drove in and out among dry stumps and rubbish as we went ; but with brave persistence the sunflower, the gillia, and the painted cup nodded all along our way. The "Robert E. Lee" is called the richest silver mine in the world. The large bucket is moved by a powerful steam-engine, and pours a river of water down the sweep. Then a smaller pail brings up the clay-colored ore, which is dried and sent to the smelter. Fifty thousand dollars lay in one muddy pile. In Peru, the bars of galena are counted and covered. Here they lie for days along the railway ; there is nothing to prevent theft but the difficulty of transportation.

M. went to the Paris Exposition as an attaché of the Governor of Arizona. The position was a sinecure, and he availed himself of it to travel two years in Europe without any definite aim. He was a cultivated and intelligent but very wild-looking fellow, and I have little doubt that drinking had forced him to a frontier life. We went with our driver to the smelting houses, and brought away some rich bits of ore; but I had been giddy for some time, and could not get out of the carriage. Before our early dinner was over I was as ill as my worst enemy could desire. There was no one to do anything for me, and various people came in and out of my room, saw me suffer, and went away without a word. At last I bribed a Swedish servant-girl, who was very ill herself, to sit with me until the W.'s came to devise an excursion for to-morrow. Mrs. W. undressed me, and her husband went for brandy. (I advise the next traveller who needs it to go to a dram-shop and not to a druggist's.) If I lay perfectly still I could keep my consciousness, but any attempt to go up the low stairs which led from my room deprived me of it. My condition decided the direction of our excursion. There was no doubt I was suffering from the altitude; at the Twin Lakes I should be five hundred feet lower, and it was thought a day spent there would enable me to start for Colorado Springs, where I should speedily recover.

August 6, 1880.— How I dressed this morning is as much a mystery as how I got into the stage-coach on

Wednesday night. My poor Swede had something to do with it. When Mr. W. drove up to the door to see if I was able to start, I agreed to try. It is said to be eighteen miles to the Lakes. We went a long way over the arid plain, strewn with the filth first of the town and then of the camps, with dead horses innumerable, and charcoal kilns. When I first saw how bare the hills were, I forgot that a furnace was the necessary consequence of a "strike," and wide-spread dreariness the next step to the furnace. Somewhere hidden away there must be trees, for the fires still burn. At one of the fords we met a charcoal wagon. The driver was pouring water over his coal. It had been thrown into the wagon before it was cool, and he had already lost eight or ten bushels. Strings of mules, pack-horses, strollers with poncho and sombrero could not beguile my senses altogether. The awful odors of decaying flesh upon that dreary road I shall never forget.

At last we came in sight of the Lakes. They lie serene under the hills, the soft clouds and golden sunlight flitting over their bosoms, as if there were no such place as Leadville in the world. Each covers about a square mile, and they are connected by a rapid feeder. A few board shanties put up by squatters supply creature comforts to the little camp. Near the oldest of these, Mary Hallock Foote and her husband had taken a log cabin, but she was not well enough to see me. The best "claim" here lies in a bullet, and that must yield to the miner's strike. These "Twins" are the remnant of a great glacial sea, and the Foot Hills are moraines superbly marked and shaded a little by yellow pines, piñoles, and cotton-wood. We crossed over to the new house, built by a Stahler family from Pennsylvania, migrating with broad strides from Pittsburg to Colorado through twenty-five years of married life. Rain fell, and they made us welcome. We had already taken out our horses and lunched by the lake. The water was delicious; we drank it under the pines, the hills looking down, and through my giddy brain shimmered the thought of Ullswater. I had asked for a lunch, as I should be away over dinner; and it would be a pity to omit stating that when my parcel was opened it contained precisely one doughnut and one sandwich! It was fortunate my friends were better supplied.

If I had only been properly informed, I need not have gone back to Leadville to start at the ghostly hour of 3.30 to-morrow morning. Had I brought my valise I could have driven to Granite from the Lakes to-night, and taken the cars there after an 8 o'clock breakfast. As we went over to the Lakes the dust had settled on us an inch deep. The rain laid it; and, as we returned, the wind carried away the odor of the dead horses. We encountered drunken drivers, quarrelling ranchmen, and, on the verge of the town, policemen, risking life and limb as they wrested firearms from the hands of drunken brawlers. I shall never forget this drive. The landscape, a little dreary, was all on a large, grand scale; lines were interminable, distances immeasurable, and at the Lakes themselves the mountains do not rise as steeply as the photographs represent, but have a protecting air, as in Westmoreland or at Lake George. They were covered with gay orange and red lichens, and the gnarled piñoles gave them a domestic look. There were no birds, — indeed I have been struck by the absence of animal life ever since I left Illinois. The gopher and the prairie dog, and a sort of squirrel, skip-

ping from mound to mound, form the only exception ;
and these are not very plenty. We re-entered Leadville
over the •crest of the hills, meeting two funerals on
the way, and passing many smelting-houses, with their
stacks of charcoal and heaps of slag. The many funerals have a depressing effect, as the miners themselves
confess. It seems to me that I have not looked up once
without seeing one.

Leadville is doomed. Such a town can exist but a
very short time at the best. Its life began as a placer
digging, until some wise fellow recognized in the rejected
waste of the old washing something which looked like
iron ore. Then within two years five thousand shafts
were sunk, of which perhaps fifty have paid. It is said
that six millions of dollars in small grains of gold were
taken in a few years from the old washings of California
Gulch. An honest, hard-working set of men carried this
six millions east ; and the gamblers in mining stocks
and "prospectors" who have succeeded them are a
wholly different set. Nothing that life has to offer
would be cheaply purchased to me by six years residence in Leadville. I never saw a kitchen in which I
would not rather serve my time.

There were two superintendents of education here
lately, and one was, as I suppose, insane. They quar-
relled, carried their revolvers into the school-room, fought
before the children, and the sane man was finally driven
out before an axe in the madman's hand. Insanity is
not much worse than ignorance, and when the city
superintendent was put into confinement the county
superintendent did not get on. Colorado University
keeps its eye on these lawless outposts. It appointed a
new professor, and sent him here to see what he could

do. God speed him! This is the Unitarian's proper work. Why is he not about it? I am afraid the spirit of self-sacrifice has died out of our wealthy church. Doing as one pleases, by running a popular city charity, is not as some people think a work of disinterested benevolence.

This week the manager of a circus, having sent off his vans, was preparing to follow in his cart. He had $8000 in silver, and was carefully stowing it away when two ill-looking fellows harnessed his horses, sprang up in front, and drove him and his treasure away. Murder as well as theft would have followed; but the axle-tree fortunately broke at the first hill, and the men made their escape before the mounted police could get up with them. Mrs. Astor's diamonds would stand a poor chance here.

Leadville newspapers are vile beyond conception. Vice appears to be accepted by them all as a creditable fact; and by vice I mean licentiousness, gambling, and drinking. If a community could live that permitted murder and rapine, the newspapers would accept those also; but there are limits for gods and men. Any one coming here should bring twice the money which would seem necessary. He will be cheated and overcharged at every turn.

My illness made me curious about the height of this place. This valley lies ten thousand five hundred feet above the sea; the highest of the Rocky Mountains rises over fourteen thousand feet; the Alps fifteen thousand; and the Himálas twenty-three. I do not suppose I should live if I ascended Pike's Peak. As I dared not undress to-night, I lay on the sofa in the parlor and listened to the mining talk of some New York capitalists, whom a gang of scurvy-looking fellows had been following and coaxing all day, as the manner of mining towns is. I had not been in town an hour before some persons came to me to talk about mines, for it is naturally enough supposed that any decent people who come here must intend to invest. They went away disgusted when they found that I was curious only about education and morals. What I heard to-night was as instructive as what I saw on Chestnut Street. I was greatly shocked to see the effect of the town life on women of good standing and average character. I heard a young man tell his mother, that, owing to the forgetfulness of a customer, he had an opportunity to overcharge to the extent of sixty dollars on a piece of work. And this woman, whom I had known for years and always supposed respectable, coolly advised him to do it. " The customer must look out for himself," she said. " If you do it for him, and those who are like him, you will never earn your living." And so little moral consciousness did she show in the whole matter, that if she should read this page she will never imagine that it refers to herself.

Leadville, through Pueblo to Colorado Springs, August 7, 1880. — My landlady bade me good-by when she went to bed last night, and I was given to understand that I must open the door for myself this morning. I asked her to leave some milk and crackers on the diningroom table, and did not undress. At three o'clock I called my faithful Swede, and asked her to light the lamps in the long passages, that I might find my way through the hall. Of her own kind heart she began to dress, when there came a thundering knock at the door.

The dépôt was not a mile away, and why I should be
called at half-past three to go to cars that did not start
till ten minutes after five, I was unable to guess. It
was now only three, and I had not taken my milk. It
was decided that Mrs. W. should remain with her husband for a month, and I had no companion or advice;
still, I absolutely refused to start then, and the man
drove off after other passengers, and when he came back
I was ready. I went out under the stars, with a faint
rim of light showing the horizon, and was shaken up
rudely over the frozen ruts till I reached the spot where
a dépôt should be. I found there a crowd of people
standing on boards so thickly covered with frost that it
seemed impossible it should not be snow. At first I
walked stupidly back and forth to keep myself from
freezing. At last I saw a young wife, with a baby not
two months old, crouching from pure weariness on the
cold plank. I went to the cars, but they were fast
locked. I next piled up my bags and shawls on the
platform of the car, and insisted on her sitting upon
them. Then I waked up the guardian of the South
Park train, who was snoring by his puffing engine, and
begged him to put her into his own train; but he had no
key. After an hour and a quarter — at fifteen minutes
past five — our cars were opened, and we all crowded
into the "Horton Coach," where there was a fire. The
hour for starting had come, and neither conductor nor
brakeman appeared. The engineer whistled furiously;
the passengers swore; some went home; others only de-
claimed. For me, as the hours wore on, I was appalled
by my physical suffering, and knew not what to do.
The father of the baby — a young civil engineer — at
last took pity on me and brought me a glass of good

Philadelphia lager, which I think saved my life. There was a space during which I was hardly conscious.

Exactly at five minutes past seven, just two hours late, the conductor appeared, looking somewhat shame-faced; and the train started. No explanation of this great outrage was ever offered, except that a rattling fellow on the train, evidently one of the conductor's sort, asserted that he had found both the men in a gambling hell winning at kino. "Couldn't leave when he was winning, you know," continued the fellow, and asserted that the conductor was so great a pet of the company that he might do as he pleased. This story is only worth telling as significant of the time and place, and I will finish it here. In the afternoon the general manager of the road came into the car. Before that time, in spite of terrified remonstrances from white-haired men, we had been whirled through the Royal Gorge of the Arkansas at the rate of thirty-six miles an hour, on a narrow gauge road; and when we reached Pueblo on time, we had made up the whole of the lost two hours. This was now told to the manager; and I was asked by Mr. L., of the New York "Tribune," if I would not write a plain statement of it to Jay Gould; but I declined.

Never was there a more disgusting car than that in which we made this journey; and our dressing-room was in the possession of a few men attached to tobacco pipes for the whole day.

I was delighted with the opening of the road. Except that it was on a grander scale, it made me think of the interval before Moat Mountain, at North Conway. Sunrise is the time to see the "Continental Divide." Western light leaves its huge masses in shadow. The

morning rays picked out the rocky summits; clematis
wound and blossomed round their base. We passed
near the California Gulch, out of which so much money
was washed in the shape of pretty little golden beans.
Along the way many small shafts plunged into the moraine. Delicate lights and shadows of purple, blue, and
rosy brown, touched with the tender green of the "quaking aspen," sped over the rocks; great boulders rose out
of the midst of the broad river. The valley is more open
and sunny and yet more jagged than that from which
the cañon of the La Platte opens. It sweeps straight
forward for a hundred miles, and where it falls into
the plain it moves through a cañon whose walls are a
marvel for sheer depth. There is something inspiring
in the slopes which rise westward six thousand feet
toward the mountains. In a lovely open, walled in
by four mighty crags, the wide river turns. The summits seem ready to crumble. The road is paved with
the red sand from their disintegrated surface. A peak
rises athwart the pass. A moment more and we are on
the moraine, with the Divide reared like a wall against
the western sky. Green, purple, gray are its shadows.
I did not enjoy this cañon as I did that of the La Platte,
although it is far grander, — partly because the speed at
which our delinquent ran the cars kept us startled and
anxious, and prevented deliberate gazing; and partly on
account of the character of the soil, which makes it impossible to go to the rear. The dust of the detestable
Lake Shore was never worse. The walls of the cañon
were already finer than any I had seen, but so perpendicular as to be very difficult to observe. A sidelong
glance won nothing. The lights were more and more
mellow on the grand old hills. At South Arkansas an

omnibus was waiting to take people to Gunnison and
Ouray. It would not have seemed more out of place in
Heaven! More trees, more moraine, and then came
some hot springs with rude arrangements for bathing. On
some of the prairie-dog hills sat the companion owl, and
he bowed twice, in a knowing kind of way, to whoever
approached, as much as to say, "It's between you and
me." Then the cliffs contracted. Only at intervals did
we get the superb mountain view. The rocks changed
from granite to slate, or something slaty, and then once
more to limestone.

The La Platte was partly a leafy ravine: not a leaf
breaks the front of the Royal Gorge. It was a positive
pain to rush through it at such a rate; and if the speed
had not destroyed all pleasure, the terror of the passengers would have done so. As we rocked from side to side
of the open observation car, the mighty walls which rose
bare for two thousand feet seemed to be heated red-hot,
and to burn the air. There is nothing lovely about the
midday glare, but much that is frightful. We have
rushed through eight miles of this, but have not turned
sharp corners as on the La Platte, nor once seen our engine at right angles with our train: there was not the
same kind of care required in guiding the train as in
the South Park. At Black Hawk on the Georgetown
Road, where I am not going, the cars do not attempt to
turn. They ascend the side of the mountain by a series
of zigzags, backing a mile after the first move, then
moving forward, and then backing again, and gaining a
few miles in height at each move. Miss Seward, who
has been round the world and through the ghauts of
Bombay, thinks the zigzag at Black Hawk, the loop at
Kenosha, and this tunnelling of the Royal Gorge the

three most wonderful railway achievements in the world. Cacti perk up here and there as we come out into the valley, and at Cañon City the penitentiary, built of an arid stone in an arid waste, has a sixteenth-century Mexican look which puzzles me.

We pass it at a distance and come on grass, cotton-wood trees, and bulrushes for the first time. Immense thunder-clouds arise and contend above. There is vivid lightning, and on the southern horizon two great dust spouts whirl like dancing dervishes. We watch their convolutions. The quaking asps which flourish at the very limit of vegetation begin to soften the red rocks.

Just here I fancy I am coming on a Pueblo town. I am startled. I think I can see how the ladders lean. I see the trap-doors, and the open windows,—almost a lattice. We come near; we pass it: it is a "*wash out.*" The lozenge-shaped windows which remind us of Oriental ruins in the far Punjaub are made by swallows who have plastered their muddy nests in friendly juxtaposition upon the face of the cliff. A "washout" is a cliff of sandstone rising directly out of the moraine. Floods have washed or waters have purled all the friable portions away, leaving columns, towers, and pinnacles fit for the proudest feudal lord. Some stolen beauty must be hidden in these fastnesses. From the very walls of the castle itself this boulder, strayed half way down the slope, has surely fallen. In another moment we shall hear the clarion, and the still massive walls will bustle with men and arms! This is the work of the imagination, but it is work which we repeat daily, hourly: we cheat ourselves over and over again. Now that I have seen these wide-spread remains, I perfectly understand what suggestions they offered to the primitive inhabitants. In such a country the cliff-builder and the rocky town are a natural result. Stupid indeed would the savage be, who did not accept Nature's hint to secure shelter!

Next an immense arid waste, where even the sage-brush will not grow. Only cacti gasp out a parched life between the mimic towns. Then we come upon a long range of towers and walls, whose cornices are dark, and which slope back as if to invite the lazy giants of Abou Simbel. The guide-books call these "Egyptian Tombs." Hundreds of them lie across the plain, and look in the distance like ruined cities.

Somewhere along here the delinquent brakeman brought me wild convolvuli, their snowy petals rosy at the heart. They brought quick tears to my eyes, so often had I gathered them with my husband and children in a New England home.

About an hour before we reached Pueblo, rain began to fall and the car to leak. Heavy thunder, vivid lightning, mingled rain and hail tormented the passengers when they went out to dinner. It was fortunate that I was on the dry side of the car, which leaked badly, for I had been expressly told that I should never need a waterproof, and I was not properly protected. We waited for the Eastern train, and then ran out five or six miles, when we were signalled by a scout, and told that the road was badly washed a little beyond; so we backed into Pueblo and waited four hours.

While we were rushing through the gorge this morning and the terror-stricken passengers were entreating the conductor to pause, the man said doggedly: "The company expect me to make my time." I turned quickly and said: "That would be a very fair excuse, if they did not also expect you to start on time."

The town is a mile away. While we waited in the dreary-looking open space surrounded by a few eating-houses, which constitutes the Pueblo station, there was a good deal of irritable talk about the morning's delay. I felt a little annoyed that everybody grumbled about inconvenience, and nobody seemed to see the moral failure of the company; so I spoke up to that effect, and turned the conversation as soon as I could, by asking some people who had just entered the train about hotels at Colorado Springs. This attracted the attention of a gentleman, who stepped up and asked permission to be of service when we arrived, telling me, what I never should have dreamed, that Colorado Springs, known all over the country as a most desirable resort for invalids, had not a single comfortable hotel. The names of two had been given me, but on inquiry I found that they were both in the same hands. It was partly the talk about the train, partly I suppose the signs of extreme illness, that attracted him.

As we had come down from Leadville we had gained four thousand feet; and some of my worst symptoms abating, I had leisure to meditate on what I had suffered. I was perfectly willing to pay the price of this strange experience, and was now glad to talk over the mining towns with my pleasant companion. In a Leadville paper, which he held, I read how a party of police had gone to the very bed of a bad woman to worm out of her the secret of her lover's hiding. I had known the same thing to be done in Boston with less excuse, but there the daily paper would not have gloated over the details. In a few moments we had found each other out. The gentleman was President Tenney, of Colorado College, the author of "Coronation" and other pleasant books; and I was a friendly critic with whom he had been in correspondence, although we had never seen each other's faces.

We continued to run through meadows and cotton-wood groves, streaked with washouts, until we reached the Springs. These washouts had quite a different character from those between Cañon City and Pueblo. They looked still more like the erections of man, a mound being often crowned by what looked like a fortress; or a long wall would run across the plain for miles, as if it enclosed a Roman town. When we reached the part of the road which had just been repaired for us, we saw washouts in the soft soil, occasioned by the morning's tempest, exactly like those that lifted themselves in rocky strength above.

There was a pleasant little village bustle when we reached the station at the Springs. Some one came to meet my companion, and told him that his wife and servant were both ill. He was himself bringing home from Leadville a clergyman sick with fever, for whom both nurse and physician had to be provided. He insisted, however, on putting me into the omnibus and sending me as his guest to the hotel, where I was to wait in the sitting-room until he came to take me to better quarters.

The first thing which I saw in Colorado Springs was a mole-hill, crowned by a flag-staff rising out of the plain, which I was told stood for the height of Mount Washington of the White Hills. Then a double rainbow, which might have drunk in all the alkali of the plain it was so bright in color, climbed a cloud to the zenith, and finally hung there, a mere thread of light burned into a thunderous vapor. The President came back at last. Diffi-

culties had multiplied in connection with his sick friend;
so I was only too glad to relieve him by remaining in
the hotel for the night. There was, however, no room
in the building I had entered. I walked a couple of
blocks till we came to the old "Crawford," under the
charge of the same proprietors. Here I was shown into
a large room, which might have been perfectly comfortable if any "woman's wit" had had to do with it. As
it was, a petticoat and a shawl had to do duty for curtains at the wide windows, which looked out on not
merely the superb outline of Pike's Peak, but on a
much frequented highway. The bed was perfectly clean,
but large holes had been burned through the spread and
blanket. The carpet was well swept, but full of holes;
and wherever one occurred it was held fast by a forth-
putting and close-set circle of zinc nails. I learned
long ago that I must not travel in out-of-the-way places
without toilet covers and table cloths of my own. So
some "turkey red" plaid came out of the depths of my
bag to do duty on the very untidy furniture. Then I
made interest with a fat boy who served as chambermaid, and got a "carrier" full of water, and four towels,
each about four inches square! With a night's sleep,
and such a bath as these would secure, I hoped to anni-
hilate the remnant of my suffering.

Colorado Springs, Sunday, August 8, 1880.— Never
shall I forget the view of the mountains which
greeted my waking eyes, as I roused from a refreshing
sleep, having wholly forgotten the miseries of extreme
altitude. Breakfast was brought to my room; but I
think the strongest appetite would have quailed before it. I drank a glass of sour milk, and had re-

course to Dr. Avery's lunch basket, where some crackers and some delightful crab-apple marmalade still looked inviting. I wrote several letters, carried them a few blocks to the post-office, and then went to the piazza of the Springs Hotel, which I left last night. It was Sunday, but no one would have guessed it. Groups of people were seated all about. A pretty antelope ran up and down the steps. Gay riding parties formed for the day. The lofty peaks of the Divide were stretched out before me, mantled in tender rose-color, purple, and brown. I drank some water from the iron springs, and made some talk with some people from Kansas; but the lady probably did not approve of me, for she took a chair and turned her back full upon me.

My kind friend soon arrived to tell me he had found pleasant rooms and board for me on the other side of the town; and almost immediately a carriage drove up and Mr. J. came to take me for a long drive. Soon after we started we took in a gentleman from New York, connected with the "Tribune." Then we picked up Miss S., who was spending the summer with her father, Judge R., and took her to church. There was no time to go to my new rooms. We drove directly out upon the mesa, a high table-land, in this instance skirted by that spur of the Rocky Mountains to which Pike's Peak belongs, and by the Spanish Hills. Never shall I forget this drive. If the day was not made in Heaven, nothing better ever can be made there; and the holiness of a saint's life could hardly lift one further above all care and misery than the purity of the air, the glow of the sunshine, or the refulgence of the sapphire vault it filled. The bluffs hid the strange peaks of the "Garden of the Gods."

Although this is in some respects the best month to visit Colorado, I was too late for the immense variety of the spring flowers; but there were more than I had ever seen before on so elevated a site, and they were of great size and intense color. Half-a-dozen varieties of sunflower and hawkweed pertly threw back the sunshine, as if they said, "*We* have gold enough;" tall spires of pentstemon, of all the colors from blue through purple to crimson, and hornèd poppies, flaunting great white banners, were to be seen on every side.

We were bound to Cheyenne Cañon. Not a soul did we meet on the wide expanse until we came to a sort of shed at the entrance of the cañon, where milk and beer are sold. There was a gate beyond, behind which horses could be tethered. Here were a woman and child. We paid ten cents, and walked on for more than a mile. This cañon is hidden in the gulches of Cheyenne Mountain. It twists and turns like the stream, which once cut a fierce way through the rocks that shut it in, and which now purls and murmurs as quietly as a trout-brook in a narrow channel at the bottom. This is said to be one of the wildest gorges in the Rocky Mountains, with walls rising in places to two thousand two hundred feet, with only a dangerous footpath between. Nothing so mighty appeared in that part of it which I saw on this sweet summer morning.

We left Mr. J. lying on the grass, as he was not well enough to climb with us, and went a forty-five minutes' walk up the stream, which we crossed half-a-dozen times. Its walls, from six to eight hundred feet high, are crowded with tortured pinnacles of red sandstone, in the style in which the gods of Colo-

rado are supposed to delight. At last I sat down on
the trunk of a tree, in a spot which reminded me so
much of my old Sunday haunt on Goat Island that I
could hardly believe I was not there. A sudden turn
in the rock brought us under a fall of two hundred feet,
taken in three leaps. There is only a trickling drip
now, but in the spring it is a foaming torrent; and if
the guide-books are to be believed, there are many more
further in. It was green and delightful all the way,
tapestried with hanging cresses and curling mosses. It
is an easy and most lovely walk. If the red sandstone
peaks would only change to granite, one might think it
a White Mountain glen. The proportions are the same,
although the dimensions may be much greater; and it is
proportion, *not* size, which the eye takes in. I cannot
judge of wells or walls out here.

When some of us had drunk lemonade, and some of
us milk, our friend rose from the grass, where he had
lain "under the weather" in one golden, sunshiny sense,
and also in another not so inspiring. Then he took us
over the beautiful mesa, with its broad sea-like expanse,
bordered in the far distance with a deep line of ocean-
blue. We met people with berries in their hands:
they glowed like rubies in the sun. We went to the
lovely home of "H. H.,"—a quaint juxtaposition of four
rooms and a hall, with what looked like an old porch
made into an alcove for books. Nothing could be prettier. I wondered what she was doing far away as I
washed the hands that had been pulling mosses, in the
deep basin that sometimes receives her own. Every
honest soul must bless her for the attempt to right the
Ponca wrongs and stir the sense of justice in the
national heart, which now takes her away from this

charming spot. There are few houses in the world which have such a magnificent range in view as that which·meets the eye from her porches.

Judge R. had most kindly invited me to dine. His daughter had seen my husband in India; and, in almost the saddest moment of my life, I had met the charming lady who is now his wife. There were seven of us at table, and seven is a divine number. The conversation was brilliant. One of the company went to lie down just after the soup, and begged us to remember all the bright things that were said. I wish I could do it; but it were as easy to offer the sparkle of the champagne that was served. The Inniskillen lawsuit brought up Ben Butler and his continual impertinences. At one time, before a certain judge who shall be nameless, Ben took the judge's work out of his hands, and proceeded to sum up the case from his own point of view.

The judge interrupted: "Mr. Butler, what am I here for?"

"Indeed, Judge," retorted Butler insolently, "that is something I never could find out."

Our New York friend thought it was a pity that Butler had not had Judge Shaw to deal with on this occasion. It was Judge Shaw's wise and manly habit occasionally to put in a word to restore the equanimity of a flustered witness, so as to facilitate the course of justice. He once did this for one of Butler's witnesses, and then turning to the counsel told him to proceed. Ben took no notice; the command was repeated, and then the irritated judge exclaimed, —

"What are you waiting for, Mr. Butler?"

"Only to see if any one else in the room has anything to say," Ben retorted with aplomb.

"Apologize, or go to prison !" said the judge sternly.

Butler disclaimed, but the judge was obstinate; and apologize he did.

The anecdotes are public, so I do not betray my host when I repeat them; moreover, the day was one of the brightest of my life, and so forgive me, you who know, if I seem to speak when I should be silent.

Our dinner consisted of seven courses : —

1. Turtle soup, — with lemon and hard-boiled eggs.
2. Boiled lamb, — with green peas, potatoes, and caper sauce.
3. A salad of lettuce or tomato, — with mayonnaise.
4. Broiled birds, — with mushrooms.
5. Raspberries and cream.
6. Roman punch and sponge cake.
7. Peaches, pears, plums, grapes, and two kinds of wine.

I have given this bill of fare for a reason. It was what was offered by well bred people, who certainly had not more than two house servants, as an informal Sunday dinner, in a town which had not a civilized hotel, although perhaps something near to one might be found at Manitou, three miles away. The meal was perfect in preparation and serving, and it was as grateful to me as the sunshine itself. It is curious to think of, — served in a little town of four thousand inhabitants, which is in reality a temperance colony, where a title to land is forfeited the moment a glass of liquor is sold. The great modern system of "canning" has made as great a change in the American *cuisine* as the telegraph and the telephone have wrought in commerce and the market. All things are possible at all times now, as we see here in a town not five years old.

We went out on the piazza after dinner to take our

coffee. Judge R. drew my attention to the "herder" who had just brought home his cow. He was a bright Spanish-looking boy, on horseback, swinging a lasso. He comes every morning for the cow, and takes it with a dozen more to the fields. He watches it all day and brings it home at night, for a dollar a month. A poor neighbor earns a daily quart of milk by feeding it and milking it in the shed.

It was so pleasant to talk, and to see about me all the charms of civilized life, that I forgot my manners and stayed to tea without being asked; then Judge and Mrs. R. walked home with me, on or rather *out* of their way to church. Home is now the pleasant room at Mrs. W.'s handsome house which President Tenney has provided. The house has lately been built by the widow of Mr. W., of Springfield, Illinois. He was one of Abram Lincoln's pall-bearers, — one of the "neighbors and loving friends" who followed his body to its last rest. Until she replaces the capital which she expended in building, Mrs. W. consents to let her rooms; and these are so superior that it is a great blessing she is willing to do so.

Colorado Springs, Aug. 9. — Another public benefactor is Miss Warren, who, two doors away from Mrs. W., accommodates a few lodgers, and supplies the best of table board for a large neighborhood. Miss Warren is one of a family of sisters who came out here from the neighborhood of Boston, in search of health. I hope she will not soon be the only one, for all are gone but two. They did not seek the mountains soon enough.

I suppose the necessity of providing generously for those she loved induced Miss Warren to begin this work. I wish she could be persuaded to open a hotel. She does well and thoroughly all that she personally undertakes, and is never hurried or harried by her work,— a New England woman of whom it is easy to feel proud. The breakfast was a luxury. Clean, well laid, delightful; and as I went in and out in search of it the fifteen thousand feet of Pike's Peak lifted dun and purple shadows athwart the sky. Of course I knew that I could not climb it, and I knew it with the same regret that I felt when I found that I must not go to the Mountain of the Holy Cross at Leadville; but the delicious air and the inspiring mountain ranges lifted this regret far out of the region of fretfulness.

Soon after breakfast Mrs. R. came for me, and we started for Glen Eyrie,—so called from an eagle's nest on one of the cliffs that wall it in. This glen opens about half a mile to the north of the Garden of the Gods. As we drove over the mesa, its sea-like aspect was still further impressed upon me. Below Manitou and the Garden there was once a mighty arm of a primeval sea, which has left its traces in fossil beds of shell-fish; and the meadow which it once covered still looks strangely like a salt marsh, from which the ocean has this moment retreated. How exquisite were the drifting colors on the mountains, — the quivering lights and shadows on this earthy sea! Our glen is only the beginning of a small cañon, and the Ute Pass is beyond the house. It is a pity this glen was ever separated from the Garden of the Gods, for it contains some of the most remarkable of the formations which have made the Garden famous.

The carriage-road winds for a while through a lane bordered with forest trees, till we come to a rustic lodge; then through hedges of cotton-wood tangled with clematis and wild rose-bushes, covered with crimson hips, until we break into the amphitheatre in which the house of General Palmer stands. Upon the lawn are mighty relics of a primeval time. There is the *major domo*, an obelisk which is two hundred feet high, and leans like the tower of Pisa, — a square mass which looks like a castle on the Rhine or a fortress at Agra, a half-vitrified rock, which echoes the musical note it utters when it is struck ; and quite near the house is what Mrs. Palmer calls the " five toes of Atlas," whose immense red body lies leagues away, under the rocky ledge he so presumptuously tried to lift. This is a pretty Kindergarten way of teaching her children mythology. The five toes are. five mighty red rocks, gradually sloping from the first to the 'last in line, and spreading slightly. Pines and evergreens of varied sort grow out and about, contrasting prettily with the warm reds and shining white of the rocky walls.

The charm of the glen and the character of the house remind me of many a like spot on the Essex coast. The house is built on a hospitable scale about a huge central chimney.

Our friends rose from the piazza to welcome us, and led us into the entrance hall, which is intended to resemble that of an English hunting-lodge. Its huge mantel is of the gnarled and twisted boughs of the cotton-wood and red cedar. Knots from the same tree-trunks are set as a sort of a basket bracket above, and the hearth is an unfinished slab of fossil clams. At the foot of the stairway is a gigantic candlestick made of twisted boughs. Heads of mountain sheep and bison are nailed to the walls, and their skins lie under foot. The dining-room, library, and parlor which open into the

hall are full of bric-a-brac, tastefully arranged. Among
the things in the dining-room were two of the most
finely wrought flasks from Cashmere ; they were of solid
silver encrusted with gold. Our hostess was in keeping
with the scene. As if she had walked out of an old
portrait with the flasks in her hand, she stood before us.
She wore a close-fitting morning robe of flowered tapestry threaded with gold, over which hung a priestly
cassock of black silk with hanging sleeves, lined and
corded with crimson. Her beautiful hair was fluffed
out till it appeared like a head-dress. Up and down
the bank a huge shepherd dog tossed and tumbled two
quaintly dressed children. The mixture of associated
ideas started by all these things seemed to daze me.
I stood half stupid, thinking how little while ago it
would have been impossible to bring hither flasks of
gold, wondering what the Venetian maiden thought of
the bison, and whether a war-whoop would ever echo
again from the mighty organ stone !   •

We drove away round some fenced fields and so on
into the Garden of the Gods. All the way the shrub
oak, which is such an ugly dry thing that we call it
"scrub" in New England, made delicious verdure, with
leaves as glossy as those of the microphyllum. Before us
rose the lofty rocks which are called the "Gates,"— three
hundred and thirty feet high, by seven hundred long !
Red as ochre they rise ; but out of the red sand at their
feet springs a wall of white sandstone concreted with
snowy lime. The Jurassic confronts the Triassic ! Even
Agassiz asked wondering, "How ever came it here ?"
Certainly never until fire and water joined hands in a
way fit to crumble the everlasting hills ! The eccentricities of this park are well known. It contains about

sixty acres, and boasts a very silly name. " Playground
of the Titans" might suit it better. It looks a little
like a garden, with paths winding here and there.
These are well sanded by disintegrating hills, bordered
by Colorado bloom, and partly shaded by pine, cotton-
wood, and a dwarf oak. No green clings to any stone in
this State. Here the rocks look like lounging men,
sleeping bear or buffalo, Turks' heads, and cockerels. At
one place we saw a jack-rabbit with its long ears laid
back; and next a dainty parrot on a stone perch as
round as an osier. From hence we drove on to Manitou,
a true Swiss village. Here I tasted springs of soda and
iron. Pretty park-like glades open from the rustic way.
Grace Greenwood's empty cottage nestles near it. Monument Mountain, covered with fantastic figures in stone,
is between us and the sky, and its lovely park, like a
vale of paradise, is half way up. A trail which rises
three thousand feet in three miles leads up to it, and
twenty-five hundred of these feet are made in two miles!
I hated to leave the piney sweetness, the long-reaching
woody paths, the alcoves of living green, which would
be the dearest of homes if snow and maelstrom never
befell. The old village of Colorado City, built on the
site of the camps of Benton and Frémont, lay in our
homeward way. It looked dull enough. The old capitol building, a disreputable frame affair, is falling to
pieces. Its life was too brief for dignified decay.

At dinner I was surprised to meet two friends from
Buffalo, — one on her way to join the gold-diggers, the
other caring for a sick son. She brought him here in
what she thought a curable stage of consumption, only to
see him fall ill of diphtheria at once. He tells me, like
Mr. W., that the sage-brush consists of such solid alkali

that it can hardly be called vegetable, and that if it be taken in season it is always an infallible remedy for the mountain fever. It is only necessary to steep it in cold water.

After dinner I went with Mrs. S. to the curiosity shop. There were a few fine crystals and furs, but I saw what pleased me better, — a living cinnamon bear, a magnificent mountain lion, and two wildcats. I wondered at the patience with which they trod their great cages. At the same place I bought some large crystals of celestine, which has just been discovered here. It is clear and blue as the sky.

Before we went home we called at the studio of Alice Stuart, whose water-color portraits of Colorado flowers are quite famous. I was amazed at the great variety she could show me, as well as at her steady improvement in the work. She had a class of ladies painting, and painting well; but I felt a sort of angry impatience that they were not sketching Pike's Peak in oil, instead of puttering over pentstemons and mentzelias. Then President Tenney came to take me to drive. He seemed a good deal worn by the care of his sick friend and the pressure of committee meetings.

Colorado Springs is regularly laid out in squares. It has wide avenues, well set with beautiful trees, along which irrigating trenches run, with feeders leading into every garden. But there is something wrong. Diphtheria and scarlet fever are at work here, in an atmosphere which, if men were as wise as they are presumptuous, need never have been tainted by either. We drove out by the college, which is built of the tender-tinted stone I saw first in Denver. The college does not need large buildings. It works on

a sort of University plan, sending out its teachers on a
broad humanitarian basis. President Tenney lives nearly
opposite, on Cascade Avenue. A broad, irrigating
stream flows down this avenue, dropping a foot or two
here and there, with a cool murmur of content. The
road lies along the base of the Divide, and all the houses
face the mountain ranges. Just under the college
walls a little rabbit started up; too innocent of human
ways to be frightened, it let the President drive round
and round it, and we soon after treated a lark in the
same way. The latter wore a white cravat with a black
edge, and very stiffly starched. I wish I could have
heard it sing.

We drove to Austin's Bluff. We ascended by a
heart-breaking and carriage-breaking road, shaded by
yellow pines. The proprietor of a big sheep-ranch
bought this bluff in order to preserve the timber. A
thunder-cloud had been gathering for some time. Now
and then it spit spitefully in our faces, but it seemed to
be bloated with wind, which constantly escaped with
complaining voice to the shelter of the pines. How
they bent and answered pitifully,— moaning and mur-
muring till the whole air echoed at last to a mighty
rushing call! The road had been so badly washed that
even the horse was nervous, and we lost a good deal of
the expected calm pleasure of our drive. Often the horse
lapped his feet over each other to keep his footing. To
the North rose the Divide, nearly eight thousand feet
high. Away at the South, where a grove of trees marks
the course of the river are the Sierra Mojada and
the Spanish Peaks; eastward the sea-like plain. The
clouds were strangely lighted. The loneliness, delicious
at first, soon grew oppressive, and we darted over the

mesa, under scattering monitory drops, looking off one hundred and sixty miles.

A sudden death within the circle of my friends changed so many of my plans that I should have left this afternoon, only Miss W. proposed an excursion to the Cheyenne Mountain, for which I consented to stay.

Aug. 10, 1880. — I am going away laden with treasures. Among the most curious is a granite tube concreted with lime, which I took from a twig on Austin's Bluff; except that it is not glazed internally, it is precisely like a short *fulgurite*. For some reason that I do not know, Miss W.'s excursion dropped through. Mrs. S. was the one faithful friend who set me on my way. The train ran slowly off, through meadows washed out in such a way as to suggest the more serious work in stone near Cañon City. The plains were verdant for Colorado, and old donjons and castle walls seemed to surmount every mound. The seats are very narrow, and at some inconvenience to myself I made room for a little damsel of sixteen, travelling alone. She wanted a pencil, and I furnished it; she got into trouble about her baggage checks, and I straightened the matter out; she was thirsty, and I lent her my cup: but she put my pencil in her pocket, and at Denver station walked away at the first glimpse of a friend without so much as saying "Good night!"

Yet she belonged to the same generation as President Tenney's little maid of seven, who, when I made my farewell call this morning, mixed me a glass of lemonade without orders, and brought it, saying sweetly, "Taste it; it's so cool it will do you good."

When the omnibus reached my boarding place I

found it dark and silent. From the opposite corner came shouts, and I saw waving hands. Dr. Avery cried, "Welcome home!" and I found that my landlady had taken herself away in my absence, and that Dr. Avery's servant had kindly moved all my possessions into her lovely home. There I gratefully sat down, only to be surprised in a few moments by a vision of one of my friends from the Springs, supposed to be too ill to travel.

· As I journeyed through the plains to-day I was occupied a good deal with my own thoughts; and these thoughts, in spite of my pleasure in the mere fact of living in this sunshine and delicious air, in spite of the kindness of most generous friends, were very sad. In the first place, I am greatly impressed by the want of all proper sanitary regulations wherever I go. The irrigation made necessary by the dry climate has its own dangers. The slope of the flumes or irrigating vats, and the distribution of the water over private property must be watched, or stagnant pools will appear, and disease follow. Denver is regularly laid out, looks green and brisk and pretty; but its business streets are very dirty, and there are many inexplicable bad odors in the lower sections. Everybody in Denver declares it is perfectly healthy, but as soon as you reach the next town you are told, and I think truly, that it is riddled with typhoid fever. My dear friend lives here because the sun shines; but I have seen "clouds and thick darkness," yes, even drops of rain, every afternoon! Why should that young lad sicken with diphtheria, and why should scarlet fever flaunt through the streets in Colorado Springs? It is a very small place, in the purest air and finest climate in the world; and yet I cannot call it healthy! Somebody is very much to blame.

But worse than this is the moral malaria which pervades this whole mining community ; for Denver is only a base of supply for the mining towns, as Leadville is only a base for the camps about it, — and with the fortunes of the miners it must rise or fall.

I have been an unintentional listener to all sorts of talks ever since I crossed the Mississippi, and everywhere I have found a fearful "lust of gold." Everywhere they talk of the Indian reservation as if it were richer in gold than any other part of the country. Again and again I have heard miners say that they have gone privately to locations within it and brought away bits of ore. They deride the slowness of the Government; they insist that if it does not move they will go with pistols in their hands to prosecute this greedy search. I have been amazed at the openness with which all this has been said, and my heart has sickened over the stories of treachery and wrong. Nor is there the least reason to think that the Reservations offer anything better than these men now have. The simple fact that they are shut out from some special ridge or placer sets them to dreaming about it.

Aug. 14, 1880. — My last day in Denver was devoted to gathering in some of Jackson's fine photographs, and buying some delicate fossils from Green River. These consist of little fish about six inches long, of several species. They lie in a cream-colored stone which is called Green River *shale.* This splits in thin layers, of the most fragile sort, showing the anatomy of the fish or insects it holds. These seem to be printed on it rather than imbedded in it, and must be packed with great care. Parts of this rock are saturated with petro-

leum, like the "Stink-stone" of western New York;
and during the building of the railway the rock took
fire and burned for days, — "a pillar of fire" by night.
I have stayed in Denver longer than I intended, that I
might recover perfectly before going among strangers.
Mrs. W. and myself both contracted in Leadville an
ulceration of the throat and lips, which has yielded
very slowly. It was thought to be due to the arsenical
fumes of the smelting furnaces.

I left the house about 6 o'clock this morning, with
reluctant steps. Colorado has been only a dream of
beauty. I was well provided with bread, marmalade,
and Crosse & Blackwell's potted meats. The road
through Central Colorado to the junction, running parallel with that from Cheyenne to Denver, by which I
came, seems much more attractive than that. It runs
along the edge of the "World's hunting-grounds," where
elk, deer, antelope, and bear tempt English gentlemen to
linger year after year. It also leads through the heart of
the wheat fields and the mining regions. On all sides of
us swept solitary horsemen on the most superb horses.
Drovers and herders, clinging with their knees to any
part of the creature they might happen to hit, seemed
to trust to the swaying Spanish "lope," as if a fall were
unheard of. Up and down the abrupt gaps the animals
struggled like cats, while they swept over the plain as
easily as leaves fly before the wind.

"H. H." says somewhere that Rotterdam is a great
deal wetter than Venice, because it pretends to be dry
land. So I thought to-day that some of the towns we
passed in the clear cool morning were a good deal
browner than they would have been if they had not pretended to be green!

Walled bluffs cut the mountain range midway, as we
sped south. Cleoma, pentstemon, blue, purple, and rose
color, sunflowers and euphorbia, scarlet painted-cups,
and escholtzia embroidered the meadows, and the transparent banner of the hornèd poppy still waves over gay
beds of mountain pink, — and they call it too late for
flowers!

Every now and then little door-ways showed themselves on the hillside, but here the mining is quiet. It
is an industry. The prairie cannot be turned into a
gambling hell like Leadville. At Ralston the blue
peaks lift themselves above a soft, gray, wave-like expanse of meadow, while afar off the great Divide or
table land, held up by the central hills, showed a distance purple as that of ocean. From it Alexander, had
he strayed so far, might have seen *two* worlds to conquer. Is there any other State, I wonder, where a
single glance will take in a whole country? Branches
of the creeping Platte cross and recross the way. The
lark rises, soft and lovely in color, his throat muffled in
black and white: he has sixteen different songs, and I
have not heard one of them! Here leaps a saucy
jack-rabbit with such long ears! The thistles show
bunches of purple splendor as large as my fist, and on
them dance, not butterflies, but blackbirds by the score!
Bulrushes show themselves at last, and I perceive the
sweet odors of a farm-yard; about it piles of the soft-
tinted stone I saw in Denver. These blocks, just cut
from the quarry, are not cleaner than the churches which
the Spaniards built of the same stone three hundred
years ago. Never did I see such contrasts in the color
of the soil as here, — red, blue, yellow, and brown appear.
What would a child born here think if he saw the words

"earth color," or "earthy?" What a limited experience has given birth to our literary phrases! Fortunate for the poets that literature began where the courses of the season exist!

Lovely are the orchards of Longmont and Loveland. Estes Park, somewhat off the road to the left, is a little wonder of Nature's landscape-gardening set in a cup, rimmed by snow-capped mountains. Fort Collins is well irrigated and well planted; and, chief wonder of all, we saw here green fields, surrounded by white fences. Apricots were plenty and delicious.

All over the fields, wherever there is a hollow or a little runnel in which water can hide, flowers tell the dewy secret; and we see that the ribbon fashion in gardening had a freer and far lovelier prototype in Nature. Hornèd poppies, which I saw in Southern Colorado five or six inches across, are not much bigger than a sixpence here, — which seems to imply that the water has harvest work to do. There is fine red sand in the water-courses, and great banks of soda, or some boracic deposit. Hundreds of dead horses — that horror of the mining regions — curse the plains. The raven who taught Cain how to bury Abel ought to come here and instruct the miners! Dark clouds were gathering while I wondered at it all, and when I got to Hazard a tempest of rain and hail was driving across the station. For once a porter gave ready and pleasant service. There was not a moment to spare. "Without money and without price," I and my baggage were hurried about five hundred feet across the platform, from one train to the other, and I entered the Pullman drenched! And this is the road over which I was forbidden to carry an umbrella or a water-proof!

I am now once more on the main line of travel, on the way from Cheyenne to Ogden. The cars are themselves cleaner than those I left a fortnight ago, but the dressing-room is very untidy. Now that I understand that I have neither courtesy nor cleanliness to expect, it is all very easy to bear.

I found a young girl in the car, living with one of the " shepherd kings " at Cheyenne. She came out for a visit seven years ago, and has never gone back. Until to-day she had never entered a car since her arrival, but has almost lived on horseback. She was on her way to Laramie, and I learned with pleasant surprise that the "shepherd king" she spoke of was the son of an old neighbor of my own in Boston, — a lady well known now in the great charities of New York City. It does not seem longer ago than yesterday, that, a child when she was a bride, I carried her flowers and verses on her wedding morning.

I lent the young woman my button hook ; I " found the place " in my guide for an old lady in the corner, and got out my medicines for a case of cholera morbus in the next section, — reflecting all the while what a comfort it was to know how to travel.

The rain increased. It was so heavy that for the first time I was glad I was not in a coach. The settlers think the rainfall increases on the plains every year. As I watched, a double rainbow made its appearance in the northeast. Both bows were almost complete circles cut slightly by the horizon. Within the interior and finer bow the cloud was almost white, but the space enclosed between the two was black with storm. A sudden flush of light which filled the air made me turn. The sun was sinking in a golden bath. From the ocean of splendor rose a long blue cliff of cloud, and above it the mackerel sky was fretted with gold. I knew as I looked for the first time what suggested certain wonderful decorations to the Japs.

Sunday, Aug. 14, 1880. — In spite of rules the porter kept possession of the dressing-room, while I waited for it. If the company choose to allow him this privilege, why does he not take the gentlemen's room? I suspect it is because he knows that men would not stand it.

The piles of contorted rock which form the hills along our way are capped with tent-like roofs; out of them rise walls of red and green shale, and mimic castles crown the summits of these walls. I got out of the cars at Green River, where people who are not wise enough to carry their lunch baskets are invited to breakfast. I found no good fossils. It is better to buy in the towns.

Geologically considered this is a most wonderful region. The color of the river is *verde antique*, like the mass of the Niagara river below the whirlpool, and the color is imparted by that of the green marl through which it flows. There are ludicrous forms beetling from the cliffs. One giant of eld dropped a club here, eight hundred feet long; and another has set down his teapot, about six hundred feet in diameter, with such force that no one has yet been found to lift it. Here not only the pretty little fresh-water fish, but flies and bugs are safely laid away for us in the fresh cream-colored beds; and close by, but a little to the north, Professor Marsh found his three-toed horse, the Areodon, and the great Titanotherium with a jaw four feet long. Big as this creature may have been, he failed to escape the miseries of modern life; for not far off enormous mosquitoes were caught napping in stone, and gigantic fleas and cockroaches had as good a chance at his toe-nails as if he had been a passenger in a modern East Indiaman. These things are found in a succession of *buttes*, which look like ruined cities, and are being rapidly washed into the plain by snow and storm. To the south is the cañon of the Colorado, where Major Powell encountered and conquered greater dangers than he fought at Shiloh.

A lonely sand-hill crane stamped round an enclosure in front of the eating-house. He was called a stork, and imparted a Parisian air to the locality! The old woman who waked up her husband one morning in this neighborhood, to look at a " petrified Solomon's temple," was not quite so absurd as she seemed. " David's Tower " stands here as square and solid as it does on the walls of Zion.

The red cliffs and rifts in the soil were fringed with unknown purple bloom after we passed Piedmont. These flowers have never been named, but is there another country in the world where there would be no popular name for them? The Indians had a name, I feel sure. Here is a snow-shed on a ridge of the Uintahs twenty-seven hundred feet long.

A little northwest of Hilliard are two whole mountains of sulphur, nearly pure. It is as inexhaustible as the solid gold, and suggests the region which ought to underlie the fire-ridden plain. The thin laminæ of the " candle earth," or fossil paraffine, which are found at Green River, make a bolder appearance in the valley of the Wasatch, and some of it took fire and burned for days when the workmen were busy on the road. Here this may possibly be only clay saturated with oil; but in Southern Utah it looks like cannel coal, and can be

moulded by the fingers like putty. Now clinging to the
second step of the rear platform I enter Echo Cañon.
Almost on a level with the mightiest peaks of the Wasatch at first, we dart down to the bottom of the valley.
It is five thousand nine hundred and seventy-four feet
above the level of the sea, with mighty walls panelled
and buttressed in gray and red stretching eight hundred
feet toward the sky.   Castle Rock on one of these walls
has open casements and an arched doorway, which gives
us a momentary glimpse of the blue sky over its wide
courts.   The swallow, primeval mason, has cut the oriel
windows and fretted the cornices.   Indeed, it seems as
if in the millions of years that passed after these heights
were lifted, Nature herself began to sigh for a human
presence, and undertook to give a home-like look to
these great valleys.   At one spot, before open portals, a
tremendous sphinx lies couchant, mourning the loss of
her head-dress.   The columns of the temple behind her
are red, capped with gray.   Suddenly you come on
yellow sandstone, and the gorge narrows.

This is where the Mormons once intrenched themselves.   The town of Echo itself shows signs of life.
Farming lands appear.   The red sandstone is graciously
hidden by waving green, and a cliff of conglomerate juts
out.   Beyond Echo, rounded terraced cones of red rock
rise like battlements, and take that name.   Then
"Witches in Waterproof," somewhat worse for wear,
watch over a narrow pass.   A good deal of landscape
rock, etched by the artist we know as Dendrite, is found
here and further along by the "Devil's Slide."   To the
south are two mighty ledges of granite eight hundred
feet above us.   From the summit to the base of one of
these run two parallel ridges of rock.   They start fifty

feet out of the side of the mountain, about twenty feet apart. As you see them from the road, it looks as if some anxious ogress had walled in a coast for His Satanic Majesty, who seems to have scorched his way from top to bottom.

A little further on, in Weber Cañon, the front of a wholly inaccessible cliff is fretted with hollows and flutings, said to be made by the mountain wind on the principle of the sand-blast. That principle was first applied to the arts and made useful to mankind at the suggestion of Old Ocean: how long before this the mountains knew the story, Hindu architecture seems to me to proclaim emphatically. In the deepest of these hollows countless eagles build within the range of the traveller's eye, yet far beyond the possibility of his interference.

At Peterson an immense gap opens in the mountains. The Sweetwater plunges madly by, as if it would cut the hills in twain. A comparatively low ledge heads it off, and turns it sharply to the north. Defeated again, it makes a perfect right angle, cuts its way to the left behind the opposing ledge, and rushes into the great Salt Lake basin, — a wonder to the eye and a puzzle to my pen!

Here we see the mountains, which rise as islands from the waters of the lake, and the loveliness born of daily rural toil replaces the majesty of Nature. Devil's Slide, Devil's Gap, Devil's Gate! — three of the most wonderful things upon our road. Is it not strange how men always invent a demon to account for any material marvel? Moran can never exaggerate the red and yellow of this region; Nature will always be too much for him. We pass out of these mighty ruins, millions of years old, and not yet tender enough to win mosses or men to their bosom, set all over still with beacons of flaming color! Joyfully we glide into the green valley of the Weber, to find luxuriant Mormon ranches stretching as far as we can see. Like a garden they glow with flowers. Tall hollyhocks, which tell in rosy color of the habit of the forsaken English home, fence in the fields of corn,— delicious oasis in our alkaline desert! The sweetness of new-mown hay floats on the still air, and far too soon we drift into the station, and with the usual inconveniences and disappointments find our way across the platform, and wait for the train to Salt Lake. What strange groups of Mormon people surrounded me while I waited! Many had been to Ogden for a day's shopping, as Brooklyn people go over to New York, and were waiting for the last train. There were stunted and crippled youths, flimsy attempts at finery, and a good deal going on which would have exasperated Brigham Young. Some of the women were returning with their babies from long journeys, and one man at least welcomed his wife fondly.

Into the car I went, almost the only gentile. How critical the Mormon problem has now become may be gathered from the fact that in this car, crowded with men, women, and children, I heard no theme started save the domestic relations or discomforts of those in whom the speakers were interested. The heavy purple range of hills which walls in the valley at Ogden, a spur of the Wasatch, seemed so near and so peculiar that I thought I must be mistaken about it. I asked what hills they were of all the people round about, but no one knew!

In the whole number of more than forty persons I

saw only one instance where the man and the woman seemed to talk to each other, as if they truly "kept company." These were newly married, and their first baby was in the arms first of one and then the other, — handed round, as somebody says, as if it were something good to eat. They, too, talked of a young friend's unhappy marriage. All the faces in the car looked full of care. Some seemed unhappy, and a jealous or suspicious look was stamped on every face. This opinion must not be supposed to be the result of my prepossessions. I did not realize that the people about me would be Mormons until I was surprised into admitting it.

The wind blew violently as we scudded away south between rural homes trimly kept and set in small farmsteads, with every appearance of comfort. Very far superior they must be to anything their owners have ever possessed in the far-off regions of their birth. A tender sunset sky, flushed with rose color, hung behind the hills. Then the darkness fell, and, except that there was more courtesy toward me as a woman than I have encountered anywhere, my arrival was just what it might be in any town of the same size.

At the hotel I was surprised to find a "set basin" in my chamber; and after various attempts to air out the odors, I was obliged to ask for a room in which this convenience did not exist. After sending out the letters of introduction which had led me to come to Utah now, instead of waiting until my return in the autumn, I went down to supper. In the dining-room I found two delightful English people just come in from a drive. Captain B. was quite lately of Her Majesty's Fourth Dragoon Guards. He is on his way back from a two-years' tour round the world, in which his wife has been his companion. He already talks of returning after a twelvemonth, to hunt elk and bear in the North Park. They have been to Thibet and the Sandwich Islands; have slept in tents and on the ground. They have followed Isabella Bird everywhere, and could tell me a great deal about my belovèd Lady Duff Gordon. Miss Bird makes herself dear and regretted everywhere. The story of her life in the Sierras is no fiction. The hunters, the miners, and the desperadoes know her name, and speak of her with affection. The wise newspapers which accuse her of writing about things she never saw would be afraid to repeat such charges, I think, after a talk with those who have known her.

In Egypt Captain B. had lodged in Lady Gordon's quarters and employed her servants, in whom she had stimulated a wild enthusiasm of love. When I spoke of the mystery of her lonely life there, I gathered that the exasperations of her illness were such as to make it the pleasantest life not only for her, but for those who loved her. I did not ask a second question. Long ago I knew that one petition must be forever stricken out of my litany, — " From sudden death, good Lord deliver me!" In the present state of society there is no mercy to elderly people like sudden death. The time seems to have gone by, when the young can be patient with the eccentricities that illness, sorrow, or age may develop in those who have loved them best.

Salt Lake, Monday, Aug. 16, 1880. — As soon as I rose, I sent a note to the B.'s asking them to join me in a drive. I had no response to my notes of introduction, and supposed that the gentlemen to whom they were addressed must be out of town.

We took an open barouche, with a bright driver who tried to make up by talking for the paucity of the sights.

I was much struck on the train last night by the languid, unhealthy look of the children who ran back and forth, and what seemed the lack of strong health in most of the young men. I also saw more cripples than I should have seen in any of our large towns, in the same number of hours. Speaking of this thoughtfully to Mrs. B., who arrived in time to attend service in the Tabernacle, she replied at once: "This is not an American town, nor are these American people. These are my country-people, not yours. In their former homes their lives were inconceivably low, and passed in an utter absence of comfort. I know, for I have seen them where they originate. Denizens of a Christian land, polygamy was not a degradation to them, but a step upward in the social scale. Before they became Mormons these people might have sold their wives in the market-place, or have exchanged them with each other. ·They would only have followed in the footsteps of all their people. Those of them who are not Welsh and Cornish miners are Scandinavians, — Jutlanders, or Finlanders."

I quote this reply with great satisfaction; for every hour that I linger confirms this judgment. It is evident that the Mormon people regard their numerous wives as so many servants, and estimate their children in a way that reminds me of our New England ancestry, who, faithful husbands each to a single wife, still talked of a son "born to me, prized at seventy-five pounds sterling," or of a daughter as equal to fifty.

One of the bystanders said that the original band of

Mormons were a puny race, but that their children raised in Western air and freedom were stalwart. This may apply to the rural regions; it does not to Salt Lake or Ogden. The present feeble physical condition of many grows out of an entire ignorance of physical and sanitary laws. Here, as at Denver and Colorado Springs, I began to hear at once of diphtheria and typhoid malaria. Excusable in cities, where it is difficult for wise municipal management to follow fast enough on the increase of population, this is utterly inexcusable and unendurable here. The irrigation of Salt Lake City, which has wrought superb results as regards harvests of wheat, tons of hay, and the most exquisite fruit and vegetables ever seen, is not perfect, and threatens serious danger. It does not always surmount the inevitable obstacles of decaying sluices or changes of grade, and forms many stagnant pools; while in what they call the lower part of the town the water fairly oozes out of the soil. The garbage of the houses lies in unhealthy heaps about them, and the drainage is on the surface.

'We passed first the beautiful houses and gardens of the Walker Brothers, who own the well-kept hotel, and are apostate Mormons,—men who might, even five years ago, have been hurried to quick death but for the presence of Federal authority. These houses might belong to gentlemen anywhere. Upon the green lawns the sprinklers were set, and above them rose, in strange unsuitableness, the grotesque trees and shrubs of Southern and semi-tropical Utah. These things are only native to a soil where grass does not grow, and both lawns and plants brought back the memory of the Hunnewell place at Wellesley, and some of the Centennial achievements at Germantown.

Then came lovely irrigated farms, with fields of wheat such as no Eastern farmer sees, even in his dreams. Certain portions of these were pointed out as church property, tithes of rich men's possessions. In order to get a full understanding of the great amphitheatre in which the city is built, to get a glimpse of the circular sweep of the hills, and reach the spot whence the Mormons first saw their promised land, we drove out to the penitentiary, where we watered our horses. While this was done, I made a rapid inspection of the jail. It is a small, neatly kept building of yellow brick, manned by Federal officers. Of the forty inmates not one is a woman. The thirsty soil cries out all around for the spade, and for these forty men not an hour's work is provided! Is reform possible to idleness? Irrigating ditches could be dug to advantage for miles and miles throughout the territory. In the grand mountain pass through which the Mormons entered the valley there is now a great lager-beer brewery. A few trees make an excuse for as many tables and chairs, and a cabinet of minerals in a shed near by turns speculative minds to the great lottery of mining, which Brigham Young had the excellent good sense to frown upon. ·

We got out of the carriage here and tasted the lager, which proved rather bitter. I have heard that the word "lager" is not recognized in Germany; but I can hardly believe it, as it was introduced here by German-born brewers. The word means a store-house; and, when applied to beer, indicates a kind which must not be used until it is seasoned, any more than new wine. As we sat talking about it there flashed again into my mind a dream which I had lately, and which is worth telling, because it shows upon what obscure clews the mind, when not preoccupied, can act: preoccupation in our waking hours is strong enough to blot out their existence. A friend asked me just before I left Buffalo what a *prawlong* was. She is curious in confectionery; and in an old book she had found this word, but could get no explanation of it. I thought it out in all the languages I knew, and I tried to guess what word a clumsy Britisher could mispronounce into *prawlong*. I did not see through it at all, when two or three nights ago, at least three weeks after the question had been asked, I heard a voice say in my sleep, "Prawlongs?— oh, that is pralines; the last syllable was nasal once. Before the Academy made gender a matter of euphony, a *pralin* was a burnt almond." I woke instantly and wrote it down, for the whole impression was so slight that I should have lost it before morning!

Out of just such habits of the mind, only when applied to more important themes, the old faith in miracles and oracles arose: and no wonder, for at first it seems impossible to account for such action.

Near us as we sat, but a little lower, outside the brewery yard, is Mount Ensign, the "Mount of Prophecy." From a spur of the mountain rises a sort of oral crown, which may be one hundred and fifty feet high. Here Brigham Young asserted that he received the intimation that the valley was to become the site of a great people. And here I have no doubt that he did receive it, for he was a man of insight, sufficient to foresee possibilities, and of energies equal to the undertaking. Only a very dull mind need have been impervious to the hint.

At Camp Douglass, where comfortable looking buildings are erected of a reddish stone, I saw Indian captives digging ditches in charge of a United States officer.

They belonged to that half-civilized cross which may be defined as neither man nor Indian.

An extensive view of Salt Lake, with the valley and the surrounding mountains, is obtained between the brewery and the camp. I despair of giving you any idea of its beauty, although you have visited many lakes. Lake Huron, if seen at all from a height, is like the ocean; the lakes of Central New York are on too small a scale. This sheet of silver glows in the sun, surrounded by snow-capped ranges; and floating on its bosom are mighty island peaks like those which surround Ullswater. It gives the impression of a vast expanse, hardly broken by these mighty upheavals. It shows no alkaline desolation; its rosy orchards give no hint of apples of Sodom.

As we drove back into the town we went first to Temple Block, an enclosure of ten acres, surrounded by a high wall. This contains the Tabernacle, the Assembly room, and the New Temple. The Tabernacle can be used only in summer, as the expense of lighting and heating it would be so enormous that the money has never been provided. For winter use, when the audiences are necessarily much smaller, the Assembly room was built. This looks like a cheap Masonic Temple. Very odd frescos, prophetic pictures of other temples and cities, are painted in sepia upon the ceiling, reminding one of nothing so much as George Washington Custis's ambitious attempts at Arlington. Some workmen were coolly eating their lunch within the altar rail, and when we went in they were vehemently discussing a trifle of Church discipline. A very narrow-minded set they looked.

East of Temple Block a large number of buildings are enclosed in a curious and very heavily buttressed wall of stone. These are the Tithing offices with their spacious courts, the Emigration office, and the old residence of Brigham Young. Looked at in a certain direction, the gable windows of the President's house suggested the popular name of the "Dove Cot." I counted ten in one row. These buildings are all of the color of adobe, and a section of the heavily buttressed walls shows a pyramidal structure; they are three or four feet thick at the bottom, and about eighteen inches at the top. Whatever Brigham Young undertook he did thoroughly well; there was no "jobbing" under his administration. Wages, which to all men emigrants consist simply of shelter and rations from the Tithing house, offer few temptations to a cheat, while the certainty of an immediate employment sufficient to secure physical comfort was an incentive to emigration that many Governments would do well to furnish. In distributing new-comers Brigham was very wise. It often happened that the new emigrant came out expecting to work for a friend; but when this was not possible he was sent to a bishop having charge of a diocese in which some of his country-people could be found, which did much to check the homesickness of the Scandinavians.

Directly opposite Brigham Young's own door a large arch is thrown across State Street, surmounted by a spread eagle. It was impossible not to ask what it meant. Our driver replied that it was originally erected as a sort of toll gate, through which all the hay was brought in from the meadows. Every third load was seized as the property of the church, and driven into the Tithing yard. If this was true, it must have been when the pastures were held in common, as they used to be in some of the Connecticut River towns. It is so no longer. Now a faithful disciple is expected to surrender one tenth of his crop; and it must be said that even if a large part of the tithes does go to dignitaries and bishops, yet not only are these hard working men to whom the church gives no other pay, but the tithes support the new emigrants, the poor and sick, and pay the expenses of church and temple building. All this seems to have been honestly intended and thoroughly carried out at first; but since the President's death, and for some time before, the great increase of population, and increase in the number of municipal, state, and church cares, have interfered with it a good deal.

I went to look at Brigham Young's grave. The Mormon graves upon these arid slopes are strangely neglected. Their condition indicates what every face I met repeated, — the low mental character and absence of spirituality in the population. An effort seems to have been made here to enclose, in separate sections, ground that has been too carelessly kept. Farthest from the road a square lot contains the body of Brigham Young. A neat iron rail encloses the grave, but no attempt has yet been made to erect a monument, or even inscribe his name above the spot. Just below, to my right, rose the chimney of the cottage where his first wife, the mother of John W. Young, still lives. As I knew something of the history of that woman, I looked with pathetic interest at the gently curling smoke which rose from it. She has never hesitated to say that with polygamy the iron entered her soul; but her confidence in her husband was perfect, and she truly accepted it as the Lord's own way of weaning "Latter-day Saints" from the things of earth!

As I wished to see something of the women, we went

to the office of "The Woman's Exponent," very well edited by Mrs. Emmeline B. Wells, one of the wives of the Councillor D. H. Wells. This councillor is distinguished among polygamists as having had seven wives and, I think, thirty-six children, who have all lived harmoniously and prosperously together. Mrs. Emmeline had gone out of town on business, and left affairs in the hands of one of her "nieces," — that is, one of her husband's daughters by another wife. This was an intelligent young woman, with a graceful air, but a delicate, pallid look, and I should think a little under thirty. I was very glad to talk with her, because her family are always named as the principal supporters of polygamy.

If the councillor's looks do not belie him, he is a sincere and unbending fanatic, who still believes in the "Avenger of Blood." In his family he is kind and firm, and has that sort of shrewdness which has enabled him to choose as his wives women who could live peacefully together.

Of the seven wives, two live happily with the mother of the young lady before me, the four others constituting a separate household. When any questions were asked about their relations, her mother always replied that she had lived so long with these women that they seemed to her like her sisters.

"And how do you feel toward all these brothers and sisters?" I asked. "Of course I like the children of my own mother the best," she replied; "but I like them all." She acknowledged that none of the young women were in favor of polygamy, and that they preferred to marry gentiles. "What would your own father say to you if you were to do that?" I asked. "He never interferes; he expects us to please ourselves," she replied. "Two of my sisters have married gentiles."

My English friends then spoke of the polyandrous tribes in Thibet which they had just visited. The men are mountaineers; few women are born among them, and these few have it all their own way! Mrs. B. had visited one woman who had sixteen husbands. When one of these returns from the chase, the man in possession leaves, and the order and time of this is probably arranged beforehand. The women are light-hearted and gay; they do not care for their children at all, but these are much petted and caressed by the men, each one of whom seems to know and believe in his own. Miss Wells evidently forgot herself in listening, and when Mrs. B. paused, and I said, " That condition of things implies to me a very much deeper state of spiritual degradation than polygamy," she turned eagerly to me saying, " I think so too," — not in the least aware of the admission she made. She did not resent my implication; nay, I am sure that she herself felt polygamy to be degradation, but not necessarily of so personal a nature as polyandry.

After dinner Professor Newbury, whom I was most glad to find here, took us to Barfoot's Museum, — Barfoot being a greater curiosity than any on his own shelves. He was an Englishman from a manufacturing district, and reminds me of the naturalists developed under most discouraging circumstances, and described by Mrs. Gaskell in " Mary Barton."

Very crowded, very untidy, and very unscientific were his dusty little rooms; but they were not devoid of interest. Besides the ordinary array of minerals, there was a strange apron embroidered in silver and gold by Queen Elizabeth of England, — one of the treasures Brigham Young had brought over! There was a panel

portrait of Calvin painted by Holbein, and close beside
it the boat in which Kit Carson first tested the waters
of Salt Lake!

Beautiful ores of copper and salt, dead scorpions and
tarantulas decoyed us to an inner room, where a great
live hornéd owl scolded at us. In the next case was a
prairie dog, with his two attendant owls. I was much
interested when I was greeted by both the latter with
the elaborate Turveydrop courtesy of which I had heard.
Both bowed as soon as I approached, and not only bowed
but half courtesied; and although some persons assert
that this is a timid attempt to see in broad day, the
thing has never been explained: it may be only one
of the queer mimetic occurrences constantly to be met
in the animal world. Here too I saw for the first time
a new product of the smelting furnace, containing a re-
crystallization of pure iron and copper, with the deep
blue glory of lapis lazuli; here too the mineral wax, or
candle grease, which I first saw at Green River, was exhibited in masses weighing fifty pounds.

Later I went in search of the persons attached to the
Congregational Church and Academy, to whom I had
letters; but with the exception of the Rev. Edward Benner, they were all out of town. With his pretty wife
I went to call on several Mormon women; and especially
on a woman who was a teacher in the family of Brigham Young, who is an apostate, and who with her husband was obliged to hide from the "Avenger of Blood,"
in the days when there were no United States troops to
protect apostates.

This Salt Lake Academy is one of the out-lying missions of the "Colorado College." It is unsectarian, and
founded on the idea of the best New England Acade-

mies. It has a four-years' course of study, and is intended to prepare teachers for destitute communities. No
attempt is made to bias the church connections of pupils, but a decided religious influence is exerted. I regard this and similar institutions at the West, where
gratuitous instruction is afforded, as the most hopeful
thing in Western life. I was much pleased, after talking
over the whole Mormon problem with Mr. Benner,
to hear him say that if the Mormons would renounce a
few radical errors, he had no desire to force them to
change the name of their church.

After this I went with Mrs. Captain B., who is preparing to leave to-morrow, to buy stores at the shop of
the Z. C. M. I., or Zions Co-operating Mercantile Institution, — a really noble shop, fit for the largest Eastern
city, and kept with beautiful cleanliness. It contained
everything from spring-seat wagons to apricots, sugar-
plums, and boot-laces.

Mrs. B. says that Miss Bird is a sweet, capable, unpretending, middle-aged person, everywhere liked, and the
very last to be suspected of the daring things she has
done. She is also acquainted with Dr. Garrett Anderson,
and spoke with enthusiasm of her lady-like manners,
pleasant house, and professional success.

She said she never should forget her first view of
Dickens, who came to dine with her sister-in-law with
an artificial rose pinned into his coat. I think a good
many Englishmen might do the same thing; but Mrs. B.
was educated on the Continent, and has well disciplined
ideas. The first time I ever saw Dickens he was in the
street, wearing a green coat and a scarlet-velvet waist-
coat, with a shining gold chain attached to his eye-glass !
I thought he must be color-blind, a subject to which my

attention had been directed by my grandfather, who had
a constant struggle with a friend who always insisted
on buying scarlet cloth when he was sent for bottle-
green, as the scarlet always came of finer quality!

Mrs. B. had met Sir Edward Lytton at Nice, with
whiskers nicely curled, and wearing eye-glasses attached
to his gold chain, as well as a huge vinaigrette. He
was writing that lovely story, "What will he do with
it?" at the time, and used to come down from his room
and coax her cousin's maid to stitch the sheets together
for him! She evidently thought it altogether wisest not
to make the acquaintance of literary lions.

Salt Lake City, Tuesday, Aug. 17, 1880. —While I was
waiting for Mr. Benner this morning and looking over
the magazines, a man from Illinois, interested in mines,
came in. He was far more of a heathen than any Mormon. He brought a most beautiful specimen of Galena
embedded in feldspar, which was colored bright green
with copper. Mr. Benner showed me a letter from an
apostate. This man had helped the mission to lease
some rooms in which to start their school. This being
suspected, the son of one of the bishops had set upon
him, and beaten him badly. He had come to the mission with his coat torn to pieces, and now wrote to
caution Mr. Benner as to the time and way of opening
the school; but promised to stand by him boldly whenever it was done. Mr. Benner confirms what Miss Wells
said yesterday of the growing disinclination of the
young girls to marry Mormons. It causes much irri-
tation. A pleasant young superintendent of a mine
here was lately introduced to a Miss C., daughter of
one of the wealthiest Mormons. He was invited to

visit her, and kindly received by the family. This had happened several times, when he was set upon one night as he went in the dark to the dépôt, seized and held by several young Mormons, while two others beat him nearly to death.

Mr. B. asserts of Young that he was selfish and crafty, that he loved power, and was both obscene and cruel. I do not in the least wish to defend Brigham Young, but I wish to account for him; and no man ever won the influence and effected the results visible in Utah by such traits alone. Many proofs exist that he could be considerate and tender; and obscene words, or those counted such in his Tabernacle addresses, may have been chiefly very plain talk addressed to men of very low intelligence and base natures. It has been charged against him that he pointed out pregnant women in church, and adjured other women to emulate them; but we must remember that these women had been long trained to consider this condition a mark of God's special favor, and Brigham's emphatic course was not merely the result of state exigency, but, as he often declared, of a wholesome disgust of the practices in our own large cities. If a New England Doctor of Divinity found it necessary to preach three successive Sundays in Boston upon this subject, we need not reproach Brigham Young. The sort of talk complained of may have seemed very necessary to him when he found the agents of Madame Restell at work among his people, or when he wished to impress on them the sacredness of child-bearing. We must not pass judgment upon him as if he had been talking to educated people, or even to the most ignorant of the people to be found in our country towns. A single glimpse of any congregation gathered in Salt Lake City reveals the source of his power. All his energy, all his plain speaking, was required to penetrate the dense nature of the people with whom he had to deal. So far as I could understand, the women honored him; and I know one thing greatly to his credit in his dealing with his own household. A friend of my own travelling in Utah, a very accomplished physician, was summoned on arrival at the hotel by Brigham himself to attend on one of his wives, who was in great danger after the delivery of a child. A note which was waiting had been left some hours before, and my friend went to the Dove Cote in great anxiety lest the delay might have cost the woman her life. He had been struck by the clear statement of symptoms in Brigham Young's note. What was his amazement on arrival to find the President himself in attendance on the woman; her hips had been raised, ice applied and stimulants given, very much as he himself would have ordered. When he afterward spoke to the President about this, the latter said that he had found it necessary to study medicine, as only very inferior physicians were willing to settle in Utah, and that their character was often such that he did not trust his women with them. He added, that partly to obviate this he had induced some of the brightest young Mormon women to go to the Woman's College in Philadelphia to study medicine; and it happened that I was afterward present when two of these young women graduated creditably.

There is no doubt, according to the testimony of both Wells and Taylor, that at least five hundred persons were once immolated who were about to recant. Brigham fully understood that the absolute authority of his church must be established in the beginning, even if it

were by a "reign of terror;" and he must also have
known that many of his converts would be dangerous
citizens under any reign less absolute than his own.
That out of this enforced control a far higher development has arisen than any one could expect is God's mercy.
Our Illinois heathen here broke into the conversation
to say, that, "to one who has seen the whole, it looks as
if a nation of giants had been born of pigmies."

We went next to the Tithing House, inside the buttressed wall of which I have spoken. Here, within
separate courts devoted to different articles, the faithful
are supposed to devote one tenth of what they raise or
receive to the support of the church. Loads of hay
were driven into one yard. Some new spring-carriages
stood under a shed. There was a long row of vegetable
cellars opening by hatches under a sort of porch; in this
were rooms with counters which looked like the obscure
shops in the suburbs of great cities, such as one might
find at Haarlem or South Boston. Counters were set
a little way within the doors. At each was a man with
an account book, who wrote down what was received.
I saw a whole side of beef delivered at one counter,
while a woman laid down a dozen eggs on another. A
poor widow brought her mite in the shape of a can of
milk; and another, wearing a yoke such as the Chinese
use to carry burdens, brought in two slices of liver!

It is openly said that the delicacies go to the authorities, while the coarse food goes to the workmen on the
temple. If this be true, would it be different in any
Christian land we know?

I cannot conceive anything lower than the faces I
saw in these tithing yards. They belong to an order of
persons who, recognizing the church as the author of all

the good they have ever known, would not hesitate 'to commit any crime which it ordained.

We went next to the Tabernacle, a photograph of which can be obtained in any large town. It is unlike any building on earth, unless it be the great skin-sheds or tents under which the Tartars sometimes aggregate. It looks like a large oval mushroom, and has an humble homelike air which invites the poor worshipper. The walls are five feet thick. It is a great elliptical amphitheatre within. The organ and apostles' seats are at the same end. Two large covered barrels in front of and below these were said to hold the sacramental water, brought from the highest hills. The Mormons claim that the organ is the second largest in the country, and was made and set up by themselves: I had always understood that Hook's men went out to do it.

It is curious that Brigham Young should have devised anything like this building. The ovoid is two hundred and fifty feet long by one hundred and fifty broad. The height of the dome is sixty-two feet. At the time of our visit a screen of sage-brush had been erected across the entire end behind the organ, and wherever it was visible it was ornamented with sunflowers. The pungent odor of the sage was evident the moment we entered. The whole roof was decorated with long wreaths of cedar, hung with the most delicate exactness, and with a fitness which I should like to see imitated in higher quarters. From the front of the gallery hung baskets filled with cedar and simple forms of paper flowers. The people had just been celebrating the fiftieth anniversary of the opening of Mormon prophecy.

The architecture is impressive, because so unpretending and so vast. Twelve thousand persons have been seated under this brooding roof, and it is asserted to be a miraculous success as regards its acoustic properties. A pin dropped into the sexton's hat was distinctly heard to fall two hundred feet away, and a whisper at the desk was audible at the most extreme distances. Of course such a property gives an immense advantage to a preacher, for he may use successfully the same tones that he uses in conversation. It impresses the true Mormon believer with great awe, as he thinks this quality was granted in direct answer to prayer.

We went from this strange place to the New Temple. As I passed down the aisle, Mr. Benner handed me a child's paper picked up from one of the seats. I read it through, and, with the exception of expressions of formal allegiance to the Mormon Church, found it much freer from objection than most Christian papers. I copy the following words from it:—

"Children, remember this: You cannot be Latter Day Saints, unless God is with you through 'His Holy Spirit;' you cannot maintain the Gospel, and love it, unless the spirit of that Gospel, the Holy Spirit, rests upon you; you cannot dwell happily with Saints unless you love what they love. The spirit of Babylon will not dwell with the spirit of God. Children, you must know that Mormons receive you as a gift from God, the very best thing he can give. Among the Gentiles thousands despise this gift. They do not regard children as a blessing; they look upon them as an expensive, cumbersome burden, of which they must rid themselves in order to live in luxury. This is a wicked state of things which we hope you will never know anything about."

The value of the teaching in the first clause depends upon the idea entertained of God. Fortunately this church can no longer control that. Their body is too large; and railways, telephones, and phonographs have already brought them into too close contact with the nineteenth century. As soon as they get money, the people send their children away to the best schools, — of course they are not Mormon schools; returning, they bring with them the best books. In many respects Brigham Young "builded better than he knew." It is a pleasure to see how thoroughly he made his people work; and that they yielded to his urgency shows the best side of the old feudal system in force here. Brigham was "Lord of the Keep."

The marvellous structure called the New Temple was begun twenty-seven years ago; it has already cost three millions. It is not the policy of the church to finish it. The new converts who arrive without any settled plan are put to this work. Beside their wages in rations or money, which are always low, they are taught to expect especial spiritual gifts and "a robe of glory" in return for their labor. Very few are employed at once. It is astonishing how skilful they soon become, religious enthusiasm stimulating whatever intelligence they possess. This building will be devoted to the sacraments and ceremonies of their faith. It is built of the finest white gneiss from the Cotton-wood Cañon. It is one hundred and eighty-six feet long by ninety-nine broad, within. The walls are eight feet thick, and the towers are to be two hundred and twenty-five feet high. Each polished step of the stairway is said to cost one thousand dollars before it is laid in its place. Persons are not generally allowed to enter it, but I carried a talisman which availed. The crypt beneath it resembles that under the capitol at

7

Washington; the columns are equally short and thick.
When I had climbed to the battlements a superb view
was spread out before me. As I gazed over the fruitful plain and caught the silver glimmer of the lake beneath the snow-capped mountains, and remembered the
humble workmen patiently waiting for "Endowment
Robes," which are to be theirs if they live until this
New Temple is finished, my eyes filled with tears! In
what painful ways must God educate these children!
Why need we despise them as we do? It is so easy to
be deceived, and to deceive ourselves!

From hence we went to the grave of Heber Kimball.
He was a strong but thoroughly crafty and base man,
whose only merit seems to have been his loyalty to his
leader; and this loyalty had power to bring a shower of
tears to Brigham Young's eyes when Heber died. About
his stately monument the obscure graves of his many
wives are grouped in a way which is highly significant
of the Mormon idea. Close to them I picked the brilliant
orange blossom of a mallow which was new to me. A
drearier spot never was seen. The lovely flower was
hardly visible before I gathered it, and seemed to me
emblematic of the higher life which is yet to be born of
this bewildered church. As we went up to it we passed
a little cottage, where an aged woman was sprinkling a
few dusty plants with a hose. "It is hard work to keep
them alive," I said with sympathy, for I wanted to speak
to her. "It is, indeed," she answered; "but we remember
when we had no water,"—and her tone was one of deep-
felt gratitude. This was one of the widows not yet
gathered into the shade of Heber's obelisk.

We now went to the office of the Board of Emigration. I really desired to inquire into the statistics of

this Board, but far more did I desire an excuse for an
interview with some Mormon officer to whom I could
speak about the *insanitary* condition of the town, and
the large death-rate of the little children. Mr. Anderson, the secretary, has a pleasant face, but is himself
evidently overworked; he has lately had repeated attacks of falling sickness. He took us into an inner
office and left us for a few moments. We employed the
time in looking at the portraits with which the walls
are hung. Taylor was a fine, resolute-looking man, of a
more cordial make than Young himself. Wells's face is
that of a narrow fanatic. How came all those sensible,
kind-hearted women to love him? It is he who still
believes in the "atoning and avenging by blood," with
which of late the United States bayonet has sternly interfered. His face is almost the exact counterpart of that
of an eminent Free-Religionist, who would feel basely
insulted by the suggestion. I felt perfectly familiar with
every line of his thin lips. While we sat talking with the
secretary, one of his subordinates took occasion to come
back and forth through the room several times, on some
pretence. He gazed at us with scowling suspicion.
Every time he went out he left the door open, and as
often the secretary rose and shut it with silent care.

The Board still receives about 2,800 emigrants between April and October of every year. It neither
seeks nor assists American converts. These emigrants
are chiefly Welsh, Cornish, or Scandinavian. The latter
are Jutlanders or Finlanders, and some come from obscure mountain towns in Norway. To the question
whether these men improved their physical condition by
coming, the secretary answered candidly that the greater
number undoubtedly did. Then followed numerous an-

ccdotes, vouched for by my gentile companions, showing that the converts themselves hardly knew how great
the gain was until they tried to resume the old life. A
woman from Wales came over with her husband, under
a distinct promise that she should return if she were
not contented, — a promise Young usually found it
safe to make. The man's health failed, and the wife
remained with him thirteen years. During the last
years of his life a second wife was "sealed to him,"
chiefly that his first wife might be able to command
proper assistance in nursing him. As soon as possible
after the man's death means were provided to restore
the first wife to her early home, which still smiled on
her in her dreams. The second wife, as a true Mor-
man, of course inherited all the effects.

Not long after, the second wife married again; and
in a few months the first appeared, a suppliant at her
door. She had not known how to endure the hardships
of the Welsh life she had sighed after. The newly
married pair built her a little cot in one corner of their
garden, where she still lives.

I asked Mr. Anderson how the new-comers were dis-
posed of, and whether paupers existed. He said that
most of the emigrants were bound to special localities,
where they had friends. If without money to buy a
home, they were immediately provided with work. If
this were not possible in Salt Lake City, they were scattered the day after their arrival. Those wholly without
means were set about Government work and supported
by the tithes. There are no paupers. All who are
really poor are secretly assisted by the bishops.

When I brought forward my main business, Mr. Anderson was much interested. He said with a sort of

despair, "We are so ignorant in all these matters!"
He fully admitted the truth of what I thought I had
seen. I told him it was useless for me to try to rouse a
large community like that at Denver, in any time a traveller had at command; nor would I speak to him now if
the needful changes required any great outlay of money.
My list of evils consisted of, —

1. Foul air.
2. Imperfect drainage.
3. Stagnant water on the outskirts.
4. Accumulations of filth.
5. The introduction of the Chinese into closely built
squares.

In a town like Salt Lake City there were simple
domestic remedies for most of these evils, and it
was certainly competent to the church to employ
new-comers in removing filth and altering drainage,
while the municipal authorities could oblige the Chinese to live according to the laws of civilized human
beings. Mr. Anderson listened with great interest,
and explained the position of his own bedrooms that
I might show him how to ventilate them without direct draught. He then begged me to remain to a
meeting of the City Council to be held the next night,
that I might repeat what I had said to the men in power;
but this I could not promise to do.

He then desired me to go over the "Amelia Palace"
with him; for he said Brigham Young had meant to
make that a perfect building, and he would like to see
if I would object to its water supply as I did to that
of my hotel.

This building, containing one hundred and thirteen
rooms, looks like a modern sea-side villa. It is a bur-

den to the church which owns it, and Brigham himself called it the "President's Folly." President Taylor has been asked to live in it, but refuses. The secretary thought it would have to be opened as a hotel. "Was it not intended for Brigham's favorite wife?" I asked, and the secretary laughed. "No," said he; "President Young was not much in the habit of talking about his plans, and the people thought what they pleased. The true name of the building is the 'The Regardo House.' After the trouble at Nauvoo, Colonel Kane, of Philadelphia, stood Brigham Young's friend with the United States. Some years afterward he came on to visit Salt Lake City. There was no good hotel, nor was there in the whole town a house in which the President was willing to receive him. He was much mortified, and at once laid the plan of this building, in which he hoped to entertain strangers."

I went over this "Palace" with great interest, giving, as I was asked to do, especial attention to the plumbing. For this I was the better fitted that I had recently examined the plumbing of several large State institutions in Central New York. I wish I could ever expect to see another house as carefully built as this Regardo. The hall and stairway were grained and painted on the wall in a fashion of Brigham's own, which he had found so serviceable that he wished to perpetuate it. The ceilings were lofty, and the whole aspect grave.

All the walnut for the doors and panels was dried by a fire which was kept burning and watched, night and day, for months; and up to this time it has stood the test, — not a crack has appeared, not a joint has gaped. There is a rounded moulding between every floor and the surbase above, which, besides covering any possible shrinkage, would prevent furniture from touching the wall. The cornices and pillars, with their capitals, in the elegant reception-rooms are toned in tender colors and touched in gilt. All the hinges, pulleys, and locks show evidence of superior care. I never saw window casings so exquisitely fitted anywhere, except at Mount Vernon. The plumbing was done under Brigham's own eye, and every pipe well trapped, in the best fashion of four years ago. After all, the fashion is of less importance than the thoroughness of the work. The simplest device, which leaves least room for error or ignorant interference, will always be the best. It would be impossible to use the house for a private family ; it would require too many servants, and it is evident Brigham intended it for a hotel. I left it with an increased respect for his general ability. It is heated by steam, and the bath-rooms and kitchen ranges are the finest that could be obtained. It was built by Mormons ; and if these men instruct others in their ways, they will be of great service to the industry of the Western country. When we came out, Mr. Anderson said again : "We are very ignorant of sanitary science. I wish you could stay and tell us more about it."

I wished very much to see Orson Pratt, who is now the church historian ; so we went on to his office, where we found two elderly men and a pleasant young girl copying old records. Mr. Pratt was out of town. Suspicious looks were turned upon us at first, but they soon cleared away before my evident interest. They showed us the Book of Mormon translated into nine languages, — English, Welsh, French, German, Swedish, Norwegian, Danish, Italian, and, most marvellous of all, into Hindostanee! This last translation

was made by a Scandinavian resident in Hindostan, a Dr.
Meik. The character of his immigrants led Brigham
Young to consider the difficulties of spelling the English
language, and he not only devised a new phonetic alphabet, but printed the Book of Mormon in it. Of course it
did no good, and is so much dead matter on their shelves.
With that frank acknowledgment a copy was presented
to each of us.

As I ran over the shelves, I was astonished to
take down a bound but manuscript volume, containing the personal diary or autobiography of Brigham
Young! I opened it eagerly. Surely this man's life is
as well worthy of study as that of Napoleon Bonaparte!
The first entry examined comprised instructions to his
agents in foreign countries. It was written in the time
of the Crimean war, and the agents in Constantinople
were told intelligently how to provide for, take care of,
and distribute the missionaries which Brigham sent out.
In Calcutta the agent was instructed to send his missionaries up country, before a certain season of the year, to
avoid all risk of fever. I wish some Christian powers I
know were as considerate!

The last entry I read was characteristic. " I have been
talking with certain strangers," it ran, "concerning inspiration. INSPIRATION IS COMMON SENSE!" This last
clause was dashed off in large black letters and under-
scored. This remark may be registered among the rarest;
and as it evidently expressed his private convictions we
can easily see how he came to look on himself as
inspired. It was a claim such people may be easily
led to make.

I heard to-day of Mrs. C., for many years an apostate,
who has only just left Salt Lake. She was afraid to do

it until the United States were ready to protect her.
There is no doubt in my own mind that the disintegra-
tion of the Mormon body politic has begun. The disintegrating forces are five :—

1. The tithing system.
2. The greed of certain officials.
3. Underpaid official work.
4. Educational advantages.
5. Polygamy.

1. The Scandinavians will not yield to the demand for
tithes, and under the eye of the United States the church
cannot enforce payment by violence. The Northman
counts every dollar his own, and keeps a tight grip on it.

2. Of those who have innocently and willingly paid
tithes, many are now aroused every year by seeing that
the priests and not the community are benefited by the
sacrifice. This is not the vaunted idea at the bottom of
an ideal commonwealth.

3. The officers employed by the church are not paid
as well as they should be in money. This leads to dissatisfaction, to efforts to earn in some outside fashion,
which result in overwork and alienation, as well as the
failure of health in the most valuable men. It leads to
"prospecting" and gambling in stocks, which Young would
not permit.

4. The generation born upon the soil feel the need of
education, and are quick to see the difference between
themselves and other American citizens. They are determined to learn, and the education of their children
nurtures independence of thought, which soon begets
resistance to church claims. Mormons send their children to the best schools they can reach, no matter who
keeps them.

5. One of the first results of outside education is practical. It is the refusal of the young women to marry polygamists. They encourage attentions outside their own church in the hope of escape, and many now marry gentiles. It is perfectly well understood among themselves that the overthrow of polygamy is only a question of a few years. The thirst for wealth, which the railroad and contact with modern society at school and college has imparted, is a powerful influence in this direction.

Perhaps no one in the United States thought the presence of the Mormon church on its soil a greater disgrace than I did before I went to Utah. I always felt keenly about it, and thought that the United States ought to interfere with its polygamous habit. But actual contact with the evil has changed my position in many ways. Before I reached Salt Lake, my interest in behalf of the people was strongly roused by what I had heard said against them. The military, the miners, the rapacious and greedy of every sort covet their fruitful soil and charming valley, as they do the hunting grounds of the Indians. Unconsciously, the religious and moral part of the community are playing into the hands of a parcel of swindlers. If the President could have gone among them as I did, or if any of our leading statesmen would take the trouble to do it, they would discover the truth. So long as the Chinese are permitted to remain in California a separate community, worshipping idols, practising polygamy, putting diseased infants to death, and burying their sick and dying in unwholesome fetid dens in the bowels of the earth, so long the Mormon church has a right to demand supremacy in its own jurisdiction.

As to polygamy, its stronghold is in the emigrants of low character who come over afresh every year. It seems to me that the United States may interfere so far as to forbid polygamous marriage to future immigrants; to forbid United States offices to men who are polygamists; and to refuse to receive as a territorial representative any man who practises it. If a man is intelligent enough to understand in a wide sense the business interests of his country, he can be made to see that polygamy does not mean the greatest happiness to the greatest number. Even this I would not have the United States do, until it is prepared to take the same steps with regard to the Chinese. But if the Government were to take any more active ground, — if it were to deprive women married for years of position and support; if it were to declare scores of children illegitimate, — then it would have, and it would deserve to have, all Utah in arms against it. Gentle, gradual measures the people are prepared for. Their young men and women show their consciousness of the evil by refraining from any admission that they are Mormons when they are away from home, and by ceasing to defend the institution. Let the whole past stand, interfere solely to protect the future, and polygamy will die a natural death, strangled by the nineteenth century, — a death which may seem violent, but *is* most natural. The moment we see that these people never were American citizens, that they were far more degraded than any class we know, and that the Mormon church even with this drawback has really led them on and up, and made decent citizens out of turbulent animals, the whole question changes its aspect, and the predicament becomes endurable. I think one such missionary as those which Colorado Col-

lege sustains here of more avail than all the acts of
Congress or battalions of soldiers.

I made an attempt to see the hot springs, but the
heavy showers which have followed me all the way prevented, and it was raining when I went to take the cars
for Ogden. Until I came here I did not know that
there are two bathing stations on Salt Lake, within
an hour's railway ride of the city, and that trains run
out to these, morning and evening. Among the
Mormons, going to bathe seems to be a sort of church
duty; and I have no doubt that Brigham Young used
all his influence to strengthen the feeling for sanitary reasons. I had been much disappointed not to
avail myself of one of these trains, and now fortune
favored me. A large party had come out from Ogden
to bathe, and our train, running for some distance in
sight of the lake, backed down to it to take this party
home. I was much surprised to see how little evidence
the shores gave of the rapid evaporation, and how beautiful are the mountains which rise from its bosom. If it
had an outlet, of course Salt Lake would be as fresh as
the mountain rills which feed it.

I am in love with the whole Wasatch range. Professor
Newbury wished me to stay longer and go down the valley to Juab. He says I should see the finest mountain
scenery in the world, the Swiss Alps being nothing to it.
When I return it will be too late; after the snow falls it
would not be a safe journey.

There was a torrent of rain falling when I reached Ogden. I had quite a long distance to go, with three pieces of
hand baggage. I could not persuade a porter to touch
them, unless I would leave them exposed on the platform
at his discretion. I hired a boy to lift two, and then in-

sisted on the shelter of a smoking car for myself and my baggage, until a gentleman from Brooklyn procured my berth ticket. The three colored porters could not have been more disobliging if they had been three fiends. So absurd are the regulations, that the gentleman in question was compelled to go back and forth four times in the pelting storm before he could get my ticket. These regulations are nowhere posted.

En route from Ogden to Reno, Aug. 18, 1880. — I have passed my last night in the cars. I did not find the bed on my silver-palace car as good as that on the Union Pacific. No one should travel this road without a large air-pillow. I was up an hour before the porter would relinquish that use of the dressing-room which the regulations forbid, but which I have so far found a constant thing. Last evening we ran a long way by the side of Salt Lake; it gleamed like silver in the moonlight which succeeded the storm. When I began to look out this morning we were running into Elko, which is full of hot springs, out of which it expects to make a fortune. But any spot in this desert may do the same, for no space twenty miles square can be found which is not full of springs supposed to be medicinal. Next we ran through the Five Mile Cañon, — chiefly remarkable for the odd, earthy figures into which it is worn. It looks not in the least like rock, but like an immense fortification of adobe crumbled by time. At Twelve Mile Cañon, a brilliant yellow lichen began to cover the cliffs. It is the first growth I have seen on the rocks, and colors the landscape in a most picturesque way. " Palisades " is half-way down this last cañon, and its perpen-

dicular walls — a good deal like the Palisades on the
Hudson to the eye — rise on both sides to the height
of eight hundred feet, making a very narrow gorge,
in which nestles a population of about two hundred
souls.

A curious scene met my eye as the train trundled in.
A group of erect, dark-skinned men in bright blankets
were gesticulating violently around a water-trough.
The centre of interest was made by two camels busily
engaged in filling their private water bottles. The yellow soil made me rub my eyes, and wonder if I were
really in Arabia Petraea. A little further on, the cars
of a travelling circus dissipated the illusion but did not
disturb the pretty picture. About the platform crowded
a number of Indian women, ready to show their fat
little pappooses in their standing cribs for "two bits
apiece!"

We dined at Humboldt, where the mountains began
to close around us, and where the perseverance of a
woman has made an oasis in the desert. The house
stands in the midst of vast burning plains, a rocky
bluff not far off only intensifying the arid glare. But
it also stands on a lawn green as emerald, dotted with
fruit-trees and stretching out into hay-fields which are
worth more than a mine. A fountain sparkles in the
centre of the lawn; a pond full of trout flashes out of
the blue grass. Three hundred bushels of potatoes
have been taken from an acre of this farm. Eighteen
tons of alfalfa have been garnered at once from the
lot behind the house, and it is cut from five to seven
times a year!

The proprietor has lived here many years. For about
three months in the summer his family come to him

from San Francisco. At last his wife insisted that if this were to be his home, it should be made a pleasant one. Her husband had plenty of money, but he did not wish to spend it in the mountains. Very likely it would have gone in solitaire ear-rings for each of the girls in San Francisco. She insisted, — and this little paradise grew up, as pleasant as it is profitable, and famous all along the road. For half a century to come, every traveller will bless her woman's wit.

Now we are in the desert in earnest. The black sand streams down the bare hills, and streaks the white plains. Volcanic signs appear everywhere. Hot springs are on one side; on the other, saline deposits glitter on the surface. On the horizon the brown mountains look as if they were quilted down or caught in, as mattresses are. A great many low-looking Chinamen come round and chatter in a tongue whose flat, round sounds are so little broken by consonants that one hardly feels as if it were articulate speech. Then we come to the Truckee River, named for an old Indian follower of General Frémont. We begin to perceive that there are three kinds of sage. The tall brush furnishes fuel for the campers and the engines at the mills. Cattle grow fat on the white sage, which is almost pure alkali; and the sheep are so fond of that which grows close to the plain that the ranchmen call it "clover." It was nine at night when we reached Reno. Circulars had been distributed through the cars, saying that the hotel had just started, and that the proprietor would be glad of any suggestions which would enable him to meet the public demand. I found a clean supper-table and good food, if I except the tea and coffee. The bed-chamber was the cleanest I have seen since I left home.

Reno to San Francisco, Aug. 19, 1880. — When I paid
my bill this morning, I said to the landlord, in pursu-
ance of the purpose of his circular, that I was an invalid,
and that I should not have dared to sleep here if I
had known that I should have found no bell in my
room. "If you expect to entertain women and children," I said, "you ought to put bells into a few of your
rooms." The man looked up at me steadily for a moment, and then said rudely, "*I'm* running this hotel!"
"Yes," I replied, "but I understood that you wished to
run it in the interest of the passengers." Another look
and the words, "We runs this place to suit ourselves!"

I stayed over night at Reno to get a good view of the
Sierras, and by taking the morning Express from Virginia City saved at least two hours of time. I wish
some one had been honest enough to tell me that no
good view could be had unless I was on horseback.
Before we got to Reno we ran for miles between snow
fences erected to break the force of the storms on the
plains. But here we begin to run through tunnels and
snow-sheds, some of which have sharp-pointed roofs
like a Swiss châlet; while others, clinging to the side of
the rocks, are in truth sheds only, whose pitch is on
occasion only a continuance of the mountain slide down
which the avalanche thunders.

We began our day's journey by sitting for three
hours on the steps of the rear platform, watching
the rapids of the Truckee River and scenery exceedingly like the cañon of Still River in West Virginia. It was like the White Mountain valleys and
intervals also, but abounded in flowers of many colors
and kinds, some of which grow in New England.
The rock is distinctly basaltic. Here begin our forty

miles of dreary sheds. "Observation gaps" are cut out here and there, which tantalize us with glimpses of beauty that we may not see. There is very little snow on any of the mountains this year, so that element of landscape effect is lost. Purple pyramids and jagged cliffs break the horizon when we pause to look back. The road-bed is cut through granite. Not all our dangers are surmounted when we are well defended from the avalanche: at short intervals the sides and roof of the snow-sheds are of corrugated iron to defend the road from forest fires, which are quite as fatal. We get glimpses of Donner Lake, two thousand feet below us. A snowy range of mountains shuts it in on one side; green fields and fir trees shadow it. Yesterday near White Plains we passed the perfectly dry bed of what was last year a lake thirty-five miles long by sixteen wide! The water has been diverted for irrigation. The sight of its deserted basin increased the scepticism which I always feel when immense periods are assigned by scientists to account for comparatively trivial changes.[1] I have seen Table Rock break away in one year to an extent accorded to a century.

At the summit, two hundred and forty-four miles from San Francisco, we are surrounded by peaks which rise ten thousand feet; but their aspect is not dreary, as it was at Leadville. There are a great many fir trees; and the houses of immigrants and miners, grown brown with years, are hung with vines, morning glories, and blossoming honeysuckles, which give them a pretty home-like air. There were many of these in Blue Cañon.

---

[1] "The Past in the Present," by Dr. Arthur Mitchell, shows that this scepticism is legitimate in archæological as well as ethnological matters.

This is the limit of the winter snow, and here the road falls rapidly one hundred and sixteen feet to the mile.

Dutch Flat, a German mining town, about two hundred miles from San Francisco, has a tidy, quiet, business-like look, in great contrast to the slovenly Colorado towns. It is older than most mining towns, having been settled in 1851. The gold mines are now worked in the hydraulic fashion, by water-power which the cutting of the railway diverted.

Cape Horn is the name of a curve made by the railway two thousand feet above the river, where the first foothold was obtained by men let down by ropes from the cliffs above. It is not very impressive to one fresh from the greater wonders of the Colorado roads. The red soil begins to remind me of the clay between Baltimore and Washington. A pretty young bride from Salt Lake City helped to make the day endurable. It is the only thoroughly uncomfortable day I have had since I started. The thermometer has been above 100. The tops of the seats scorch, and our clothes feel hot to us as we move in them. Here the live oaks begin to be hung with moss, as in Beaufort, South Carolina.

There is fever and ague in Sacramento. It is an attractive-looking town as we approach it, with all its avenues well shaded. Here we have been much annoyed by the train regulations. There is no sleeping car. Those of us who do not wish to go out to dine must remain in the hot car, which is locked tight at both ends, the closed doors shutting off the only possible air. No refreshments were brought into the car; and in the midst of this hot noon, with both doors locked so that we could not go out on the platform, the Irishman in charge proceeded to sweep the woollen carpet!

We have had an odd passenger in this car. He was brought in by the porter of the Silver Palace at Ogden, very much excited by the double annoyance of heavy rain and delay in getting his berth. He had a companion, and the first night he talked in a loud tone, which kept everybody awake, about the wickedness of the Pilgrim fathers, who, coming across the Atlantic to escape persecution, persecuted the Quakers in turn, whipping them at the "cart's tail," and so forth. In vain a mild man in the next berth represented that this was a common form of punishment everywhere at the time. He continued to rave, reviling Plymouth for the guilt of Massachusetts Bay, till we were all weary. This morning, as we dropped down the valley of the Truckee, we were driven out upon the platform by the violence of the man, who raved still further about the early days of San Francisco. He asserted that he was one of those employed by the old Vigilance Committee, and held himself ready to shoot any man who asked him forty dollars a barrel for flour when his children were hungry! He insisted that men had no more right to the soil under their feet than to the sea over which their vessels sailed! He would murder anybody who claimed the soil over his mine! This man had been a miner at first, but was evidently now a property-owner. His lips had the same thin cut that I remarked in a Mormon who believed in the "atonement of blood."

When the people came out from dinner, we began to run down from Sacramento to the sea. I had been much astonished at the short time it took to pass through the Sierras, and I was entirely unprepared for the breath of sea air that now played about my temples, for the tender green meadows, the market-gardens, the salt marshes, and

the impressive forms of the mighty Coast Range amid
which we glided down to the shore.   When we crossed
the river at Benicia, it was delightful to drink in the
salt air, and I was still bewildered by the delicious verdure of the Mormon ranches through which we descended.   At Oakland my first sight was of my daughter, with her hands full of flowers.   The Golden Gate
gleamed ruddy through a tender haze.   I got an indefinite impression of a superb western sky, seen through
the cliffs which wall it in.

If I had known that this was the only glimpse of its
beauty which I should ever have, I should have looked
more carefully.   "A fog closed over it," I wrote that
night.   What was there that the fog did *not* close over
in the next two months ?

San Francisco, Aug. 20, 1880.—Nettie took me out over
the hills in one of the cable cars, a method of ascending
the sharp bluffs which our horses refused to ascend last
night.   The wind was fresh.   There was something marvellously bleak in the aspect of the thickly crowded gray
houses and warehouses packed together on the hills,
with neither lawns nor trees visible, — the trees being
exactly the color of the houses, they are so laden with
dust.   The houses are mostly of wood, with "balloon
frames," which are said to stand the earthquakes best.
Many of the warehouses are of stone.   I was struck by
the lovely views of the ocean which opened at every
cross-street.   When I came into my daughter's parlor
last night, I sat down in a bay window which commanded a view of the harbor, over which the starlight
fell, and which was lighted beside by the thousand
lamps of the city and those attached to the vessels in

the harbor. It was a scene of transcendent beauty. Never shall I forget it. The islands of Alcatraz and Yerba Buena rose from the silver surface of the water, where shifting lights and deepest shadows hover. It was a scene from fairyland.

My rooms are bright with lovely flowers, sent by my friend Mrs. D. before I came.

Aug. 22. — A great many houses here look dreary without and charming within. I think I can never have talked over San Francisco with any one who has been here, for the whole appearance of the town is a surprise to me. Its three hills rise bare and sharp, at an angle which horses, unless especially trained, absolutely refuse to undertake. I took a hack on my arrival to avoid added weariness, but the last two blocks I had to climb, while the hackman trudged heavily behind with my bags. To meet this difficulty the "cable tramway," which has attracted a great deal of attention abroad, was invented. A large steel cable is sunk in a trench midway between the rails. This cable turns round drums at each end of the road. The conductor holds a lever, at the end of which is a grip or clamp which seizes this cable. By the use of a break which relaxes this "grip," it is possible to stop at the intersecting streets. The cable is moved by a steam-engine at one end of the line. This system is about to be tried in Chicago, where they do not need it. It could easily be applied to such cities as Gibraltar and La Valette.

From Mrs. Davis's room in one corner of the Palace Hotel you see the whole city rise picturesquely from the water, and it looks more like a fortified rock in the Mediterranean Sea than anything else I can think of.

To-day I went to a pleasant home where Miss Cleveland and two other teachers from New England live together.   Its back window gave a charming glimpse of flowers and vines.   I also tried to do some simple shopping, but the prices of goods were enormous, and their quality poor; so I hesitated.   I was much struck by the depressed air of the tradesmen.   At the East trade has revived, and there is general prosperity.   Here the times are "bad."   It is said that the commercial tone of San Francisco has never been sound, nor its financial policy liberal; and this has influenced the tone and policy of the whole State.   All the towns have been divided into rings, monopolizing and crushing as seemed to suit the leaders.   In some senses San Francisco is still little else than an old mining port, in which the ignorant, unscrupulous, lawless class opposed to all decency and order still have their way.   The rough element in a mining community is something which neither Boston nor New York knows anything about.

Gambling in mines and stocks, and all operations of uncertain tendency, affect the character of the banks, and prevent the people at large from realizing that the whole country is rousing from a sleep full of bad dreams. San Francisco is said to have lost a large section of its population; and it must lose more, because the decay of some of the older enterprises leaves a large population unemployed.

August 27. — Already several lunches have been offered me; and at a lunch in one of the most elegant houses here eight entrées appeared.   First, the strongest and best of beef tea, sipped from elegant Haviland cups. Then melons, cool but neither sweet nor rich as I have supposed I should find them here. Third, fried oysters with coleslaw, followed by chicken with green peas and cauliflower. This was succeeded by tomato and lettuce, served with a delicious mayonnaise. Coffee and cake, ice-cream, and finally conserves of the most delicious crystallized fruits, and sherry. All the concomitants of a good dinner, except the power of choosing, and lingering over what is chosen, until hunger is satisfied. I always go home hungry from a table where the waiter brings round a single dish at a time.

At these lunches, of course, I have seen only ladies, and they have talked in a way which can be found in all cities, but which in Boston or Washington would not be used by ladies with whom I should be thrown. Of course there are exceptions to this, but I speak of the general impression received. A New England woman said to me the day after I arrived, that she had never lived anywhere where it seemed to her the women were so intelligent, and took such pains to cultivate themselves, as in California. She lived in San José; and as I thought it hardly likely that this town would be very superior, I took occasion later to inquire where she had lived previous to her marriage. I found it was one of the small interior towns in Maine. When an opinion is very positively pronounced, it is well to find out how wide an experience goes to its make-up.

To-day I went the rounds of the Chinese stores, in search of a few articles I wanted. I do not know how to deal with the almond-eyed Celestials, and soon gave it up. They are very indifferent; they do not urge one to buy, nor do they ever lower their prices.

On Sunday I had some shrimp salad served in a mould. It looked exactly like the marble the Italians call "vermicelli," but tasted very pleasantly. To-day I ate an olla-podrida, made of crabs and vegetables, well seasoned with red pepper and garlic. This was delicious, and was followed by a dessert of fresh figs, skinned and cut up in sugar and cream. I think the sugar and cream constituted the whole attraction. The figs themselves have no decided flavor until they begin to dry upon the trees.

After lunch we went to the Mechanics' Fair in the Mission Street building. As this is the season of the trade winds, the ornamental trees here are kept as tight-rigged as a ship in a storm. I saw several trimmed cypresses from fifteen to twenty feet high, with all their young limbs braced tightly to their trunks. On the lower floor of the Mission Street building we had the usual exhibition of manufactures and inventions. The prettiest thing was the garden ornamented with tropical trees, orchids, ferns, and vases of cut flowers. Then came the marvellous exhibition of cereals, sent by Professor Hilgard from California University; another of grasses, and still another of seedling fruits. Figs, nectarines, grapes, plums, and wonderful boxes of raisins were the chief attractions. Many of these things, especially the University cereals, were described as raised without irrigation. What that will mean I shall know when I see the Professor. There were, of course, superb minerals. A great many things were exhibited cut from the shell called Abalone, or Venus's Ear. The lovely colors and shades of the shell are skilfully adapted to the objects represented, as was evident in the figures of birds and fishes. But these articles are very expensive; for which there is no excuse that I know, except that the polishing is done by hand. Three dozen buttons would have cost me thirty-six dollars! and I saw nothing pretty under ten or fifteen.

There were sleeve-buttons and stocking-balls of the beautiful woods of California, and others from the Sandwich Islands. Among them the sweet-scented Mina Loa, which always makes me a little sick, with its under odor of castor oil! Of pictures I saw only one I cared to look at a second time, and that was "The Lady of Shalott," by Anna Lea. Among the photographs I was chiefly interested in some of Taber's, representing the giant cacti and terrific wash-outs of Arizona. Some practical joker had marked the latter "Prehistoric Ruins."

The sun has not shone since I arrived until to-day. It is clear overhead, but the bay is covered by a fog, which makes the Golden Gate invisible.

At the risk of repetition, I must try and draw a picture of this strange city. No one who has never seen it can imagine its bleak aspect. Imagine a three-pointed rock rising from an ocean, hid in black and envious fogs. Across these summits, lifted by almost perpendicular ascents, the intersecting streets strike like huge steps, by which they must be climbed. If I look down when half way up the hill, or if I look across from the upper windows of the Palace Hotel, I seem to see a city built of stone, with outworks and door-yards that befit a fortification. No green thing flaunts on the air. The houses crowd upon one another. They are so foreshortened as to show no spacious areas, though there are many. All the accessories are absorbed by the rock itself. A few dismal-looking trees of a stone color, with their branches tied down, may be seen. Down in the close streets the atmosphere is like that of other large cities; but climb to the crest of a hill, where you can catch the full force of the trade-wind, and it seems to stop your very breath. The hills — Rincon, Telegraph, and Russian — rise about

three hundred feet above the Bay. Although the houses
are built of wood for safety, they are cut and finished as if
made of stone, and have that effect in all the better streets.
California Street is crowned by two houses which look so
exactly like huge fortresses that they give that character to the whole town. The flinty rock, which makes
the heart of the three hills, is hidden out of sight by
heaps of loose sand, which change their places every day
at the instance of the Pacific winds. The sand was
a source of great annoyance and suffering until it became possible to pave the principal streets. These are
now as clean as any in Boston or New York; but the moment one goes beyond the city limit the old annoyance
is felt, and the fleas that abide in the sand are not more
active than every hopping, skipping particle of it. I was
told not to bring black silk or velvet here. The advice was as absurd as it would be in regard to New York
or Washington; but according to my usual foolish fashion, I believed what I was told, and followed it to my
own great inconvenience.

San Francisco feels poor for the first time. As this is
quite evident to the stranger, it must be still more so to
the people themselves. There is a shabby assortment of
goods in many of the best shops, and superfluities are
lower in price than necessaries, because of the hard
times.

I am told that the most finely decorated rooms in
the city are the bar-rooms. San Francisco is not so
unlike Leadville as one might, at first think. It is so
very orderly, that one is suspicious of what lies under
the *evident* visible surface. I went into a jeweller's
shop, largely patronized by the doubtful class of women.
Its ceiling is adorned with frescos, representing houris,

odalisques, and dancing girls of the size of life. They wear coronets, bracelets, and girdles of the richest jewels, which glow in the gaslight, and are removed every night.

Dupont Street, just below me on the hill, is devoted to " strange women," who remind me of Solomon's wearisome experience every moment. What I saw there is far, far worse than anything I ever saw among the Mormons ; for this is evidence of fearfully disordered life, while polygamy at the worst is only a mistaken, or perhaps it would be better to say an anachronistic, *order*. No woman goes through Dupont Street who can avoid it ; but it is frequently necessary. It is close to the busiest portion of the city for obvious reasons.

The first time I came through it ignorantly, and this is what I saw. A row of small tidy houses, just one room wide. This one room was entered directly from the street. Opposite the entrance was a door opening into a kitchen or dining-room, with a servants' attic above. At the side of the entrance door was always one large window, with green Venetian blinds outside. That first night these blinds were tied together with scarlet cords, leaving a space about four inches wide. The rooms behind were well lighted with gas. The windows were within fourteen inches of the floor, and just about where a woman's waist would come when she was standing ; a bar crossed the open window-space cushioned in velvet or brocade, and deeply fringed. There were from ten to fifteen of these houses, and of course as many bars ; and over every one of them a woman leaned. In every case she looked healthy and clean, was perhaps more than commonly pretty, and had a quiet face : with no look of shame, no air of brazen impudence, to betray

her. When I passed the first time, leaning on a gentleman's arm, I heard more than once the words, "Come
in, darling, come in!" But even that did not rouse my
suspicions, so different was the whole air of the locality
from anything I saw in the five years which I devoted
to what people smother under the name of "the social
problem."

Among this score of women, only one was at all occupied. *She* was a pretty blond creature, with fresh
cheeks and a sweet innocent look, quietly sewing.
Whatever may have been the reason, these women
looked more healthy and more serene than the average
woman of respectability.

Imagine my surprise, then, when I walked the next
day in full daylight through the street. These women
were chattering French to each other and their servants. Several of the rooms were thrown open, and in
one of them an upholsterer was at work. The interiors
were neat, and had a home-like, pleasant look. Each
room was a bedroom, and on each open door was a silver
plate bearing the occupant's name, — "Mlle. Therese,"
"Mlle. Adrienne," and so on. There were but two English names, — "Miss Annie" and "Miss Harriet." The
houses were evidently built for this bad use; but in regard to their occupants our women's theories must fall
to the ground.

When long ago I had occasion to think and write on
this subject, I sought the almost daily counsel of my
friend Dr. E. H. Clarke. As I now looked and listened,
I remembered what he once said to me, when relating
to me his own experience as a physician among the
grisettes of Paris : "You must not judge these women
by your Puritan standard. They take up this life as an

avocation. They come up to Paris to earn a dowry, and go back to the country to lead honest village lives as married women. This life is no more shameful to them than the buying and selling of goods. So long as they can continue to regard it in that way, it will degrade them less than the women who pursue it against their consciences."

This was said by a man who led the purest life, and who cherished the noblest aspirations for his kind. No depraved or tawdry taste, no disease, disorder, or drunkenness bore witness to the life led on Dupont Street, if one may judge after many inspections, any more than paint showed, as one might expect, on the fresh faces. Was it of such women as these that Dr. Clarke spoke?

"She lieth in wait for her prey, and increaseth transgression among men."

"And they departed, and she bound a scarlet line in the window."

"And when Jehu was come, Jezebel painted her face, and tired her head, and looked out of a window."

How these words of Scripture flashed into my mind, especially as I saw, day after day, that the "scarlet line" was sometimes changed two or three times in one day, and that the various colors used to tie the blinds were evidently signals hung out for special persons!

If I follow Dupont Street across California down the hill to the north, I enter Chinatown. Here a similar class of women, with painted faces, with henna-tipped eyelids, gummed hair, and jewelled ears, walk about the streets. If they show neither shame nor impudence, it is in this case because the soul has been dead in them and their forbears for centuries; and if a few are young and pretty, the greater part are fear-

fully diseased.   San Francisco people have a great deal
to say about the "strange women" in Chinatown, not
a word about Dupont Street, where the little houses
are built and owned by respectable church members,
who do not wish to know where their rent comes from!
When the Californian is willing to enact and enforce
one righteous law for the Mongol and the Anglo-Saxon,
the Chinese problem will be easily dealt with.

Another strange feature of this strange city, which is
so quiet and orderly in comparison with what it once
was that its inhabitants no longer know it to be strange,
is the open bar-rooms, half-a-dozen of which I pass
every day on the principal retail streets.   The bar is
set up in what would be the first floor of a house, only
the entire wall is knocked away, and the pavement is
carried over the line the wall once made, so that one
may say the sidewalk has gone into "retreat."   Here,
sheltered from sun or storm, the proprietor offers all
sorts of drinks; and if one watches the faces of those
who go in and out, it is clear that drunkenness is considered no disgrace.   I have never expressed an opinion
here on the subject of temperance; but I have asked
many questions of those who drink as well as of those
who do not.   Every one asserts the vice to be a growing
one.   I do not believe in pledges as an efficient means of
reform.   I do not think we shall ever have a temperate
community till we have a community reared under the
law of perfect self-control; but as I walk through these
streets I see an "open way to hell,"—positive instruction
in lawlessness administered at every corner.   As I have
seen boys of twelve drinking at these bars, I am told
that boys of the same age are investigating the mys-
teries of Dupont Street!

The loan shops are an attractive feature of San Francisco. They are so because this is a cosmopolitan port, so that curios and jewelry from all parts of the world find their way into them. On one window-sill are tiger claws mounted by slender fingers on the banks of the Ganges; Japanese crystals which Merlin would have coveted for his mirror, gold bracelets from Abyssinia, and silver peacocks from Mexico. One can hardly buy these things, low as the prices often are; for they have passed from base men to baser women, and come to the pawnbroker at the end of a life no one would like to think of. I often pause and look into these windows because of the odd character of the things exhibited. Then "Uncle Harris" pops out of his retreat like a big spider: "Something you want to buy? Come in, ma'am, come in! we've a variety to show." But I believe I would rather go to a far worse place.

In a shop on Montgomery Street the other day I saw two very interesting things. One was a double oak-leaf of pure gold, attached to a fragment of quartz, from the "Big Oak Flat." The leaf was fretted all over with almost invisible bubbles, and it was hard to believe it a freak of Nature. It has ninety dollars' worth of gold in it, and was priced at $250. The other was a mass of crystal from Fusiyàn, eight inches high, three broad, and as many thick. It was also a freak of Nature,—a dragon rampant, to which the Japanese artist had fastened silver claws. It was priced at $200, and the owner asserted that it had not been cut; but that I hardly believe.

Chinatown must have a chapter by itself. As I look north from my lofty window, half way up California Street, I look down over a city of roofs. These are all flat, with narrow parapets. The lowest part of each roof seems to be in the centre. Some of them are surrounded by frail fences; but on most of them, whether hotels or houses, there are frailer sheds, where the Chinaman who does the washing for the family plants himself. On one of the parapets is a row of buckets, which at this distance look like ink-bottles; and every morning the launder may be seen carrying his linen through the whole row. A Chinaman has not the smallest idea of cleansing clothes, unless he has been taught by some capable housekeeper, and kept at it long enough to fix the habit. He steeps his clothes in a solution of lime ; he dips them into an acid to destroy the lime; he carries them rapidly from one of the ink-bottles to the other in the third place for a " rinse," then for a " blue ;" and finally he "gums" them in some mysterious manner best known to himself. When he comes to iron them, he appears to use them very often instead of his handkerchief, — which explains the streaks on the wrong side of his work !

On Sundays the roofs are full of these creatures, getting up their own garments, —chiefly blue jean and white cotton. They have, among the poorer classes, so few changes of clothing that they often take off for this wash everything but their slippers and a single pair of drawers. They give the streets a very foreign look, as they patter about with a long yoke over their shoulders, from each end of which is suspended an inverted cone of a basket holding fruit and vegetables, or a bag of flour. I can imagine that when this was a mining community it was worth while to have the Chinese come over to do the washing ; but many of the best citizens do not employ them, and after a little experience I felt as if I could not. One of my kindest friends sent me the colored woman employed by herself. The second week I left a message with the chambermaid for this laundress, desiring her to fold some articles in a particular way, as they were going to be packed and sent East. To this she retorted, " I have been washing too many years to take lessons," and went off without the clothes !

Professor Marsh, of Yale College, and several English men whom I had met in Colorado are here, buying old Japanese bronzes to take home. One of the latter was quite wild over some gold and silver cherry blossoms a fine artist had dropped all over the hilt of an old sword. I have been looking for abalones again ; but the best shells are evidently sent to London and New York, and are cheaper there, where they are polished by machinery, than here, where it is all hand-work, and each shell takes an entire day. I think before the business troubles of San Francisco are over, the people will find it necessary to make change accurately. They must use the one-cent coin, and cease to regard " two bits" or ten-cent pieces as equal to a quarter. I have been told here that " two bits " and " two dimes " were equivalent terms, and in buying fruit at the street stalls on all the corners I have tried experiments to test this. About half the time the dimes were taken ; but they were frequently refused, and I was glad of it, for it is a shiftless, dishonest way of proceeding. For my own part, I do not like to spend five cents where one will do, nor one when I ought to spend five.

I have just wandered all round the fortified residences of Mrs. Mark Hopkins and Governor Stanford on the summit of the hill, getting such an impression of bare rockiness as I never had in my life before.

Aug. 28, 1880. — After loitering around the shop windows a while, I went down to the wholesale warehouses to look at some Siberian goat-skins. They are floor-rugs, and about the same color as the Siberian squirrel-skins, but of course much larger and coarser. They are brought over in the Japanese mail-service, and I have never seen them at the East.

After dinner I went to Red Man's Hall to see what the Women's Social Science Association was about. If I had been at home, the single line appended to the advertisement, "No gentlemen admitted," would have been sufficient to keep me away; for I do not believe that any good work of any kind will ever be done by one sex alone. The business was very loosely transacted. Dr. Sawtelle read a very good paper on "Ventilation and Drainage." It was debated; and I thought the debate showed very little real thought on the subject. Mrs. Stowe proposed a committee to take steps toward incorporation, in order that the Association might hold property. She wishes to buy a silk ranch, and open on it an industry for women and children. The majority of those present were opposed to this; and there was really no need of discussing it at that time, as no money seemed to be ready. Whether it was a good thing to do I am not yet qualified to judge, but it is not the proper work of a social science association; and so I said. The Association very kindly invited me to address them; and when I found it necessary to decline, voted to put aside their usual business at a moment's notice, should I ever find it possible to do so. If this body of women will be frank and forbearing with each other, as men are trained to be by constant friction, they can do an immense amount of good. The danger is that those who disapprove of any advocated measure, lacking courage to say so, will drop out of the work. Several of the ladies claimed me as old friends, or friends of my son. In some way or other the labor question was broached, and I had to hear a great deal of the rant against capital which distinguishes most of the political gatherings in California. That certainly cannot be claimed as original woman's work, and it made me heart-sick to hear it.

The meeting over I found myself the centre of a cordial group; and strangest of all was the sweet, loving voice of a white-haired woman, who came forward with outstretched hands and said: "I have not heard your voice for thirty-four years, and I knew it the moment you spoke!" I shall have to think whether that is a compliment or not. It seems to me that my voice ought to have grown sweeter and fuller beyond all recognition in these many years. This lady belonged to my free classes in Dr. Peabody's church at Portsmouth, N. H. Since I saw her she has travelled around the world on her own earnings. She lives in Berkeley, with her aged father, and her learning is spoken of with respect wherever she is known. She is now a governess. Happy the children who are in daily contact with the hopeful, aspiring spirit of Harriet Stevens! Her eyes are as merry and as bright as they were in her girlhood.

What a very small world our old earth is after all!

Sunday, August 29. — Very much do I regret the impossibility of going to church and Sunday-school every Sunday. Mr. Stebbins's sermons are too good to miss. Berkeley, the seat of California University, where I have at least one good friend, is I suppose an extension of

Oakland, which is inside the Golden Gate and exactly opposite San Francisco, on the Bay. At the mouth of the Bay, on the very Gate itself, lies San Francisco; and the little watering-place of Saucelito is just across to the north, as Oakland is to the east. The Bay stretches north and south of these central points, which may be not inaptly described as the clasps of its girdle. The water-front of San Francisco lies to the north and east. West of it are several miles of dreary driving through the sand to the Pacific and the Cliff House, within sight of whose windows, if it ever *is* clear, the seals slip up and down the rocks. Market Street, California Street, and their parallels go south from the Bay and climb the sharp hills, already described, on their way. Montgomery and Kearney streets, with their parallels, terrace off the hills at every block. Anything more beautiful than the view of this harbor from these hills I do not believe the world holds, — that is, if the fog would only lift so one could see it! Beautiful it always must be in parts, but I have only seen it once, — on the night of my arrival, when every mast was hung with lamps, and the serene heaven bent like a crown of light over it all. To the south the Bay melts from the sight like the sea itself; to the north we look across Saucelito Bay to Angel Island, owned by the Government and covered by barracks and parade grounds. It shows a finely made road, and if there ever should be a clear sky I mean to try it. Alcatraz is nearer to you in the same line, and is a solid rock of not many acres, crowned by a heavy fortress. All the water used upon it must be carried to it; and here is the fog-bell. The whole Bay is dotted with islands and fringed with hills, — among which Mount Diablo to the east, behind Oakland, and Tamalpais to the north, beyond Saucelito, are the finest, and always in cloud or sunshine make part of the landscape. It is said that no mountain of the same height in the world shows a view so fine of mountain sea, and valley as Mount Diablo; but not one in five hundred of those who climb it find their reward!

The name of Tamalpais has puzzled me very much; none of the inhabitants could give any account of it. It is one of the finest of the coast hills, and its majestic outline is everywhere to be seen. It is two thousand six hundred feet above the sea, and varies its light costume of shadow and cloud with every passing moment. In the history of Marin County, in which Tamalpais is situated, two accounts are given of the origin of the name. In old Aztec, as in most of the Romaic languages, *pais* or *pays* (pronounced *pice*) means country. *Tamal* was the Aztec word for a primitive dumpling of corn-meal wrapped round a bit of meat and boiled in a corn-husk. If this be the true origin, the name of Dumpling Land or Tamal Pais probably designated the shape of the hill. Others attribute the name to the Nicasio Indians, with whom *Tamal* means coast and *pais* mountain; from which we have the very name we confer naturally on the whole range.

I have said nothing of the tiny little island half way between San Francisco and Oakland, and still called Yerba Buena. The city of San Francisco, as we know it, is not yet forty years old; but when the location was first occupied by a Franciscan mission which afterward gave its name to it, the good Fathers called the island Yerba Buena, in honor of a fragrant and tonic mint which grew there, and which cured the prevailing agues and the "miners' fever," so far, at least, as the latter was a fever of the flesh! When the first movement was made toward the present city in 1835, this name was transferred to it; but I believe it was not used after the first six or eight years.

We started at half-past ten for Berkeley, and crossed the ferry to Oakland in a boat full of Sunday excursionists with their baskets. This boat is large and splendid beyond any mere ferry-boat that I ever saw, and it is kept in excellent order. The morning was lovely, but a black curtain hung over the Golden Gate, and many gray draperies fell from the sky to the sea. It was clear enough to give me partial visions of Tamalpais, and showed lovely opaline effects under the Coast Range. It seemed to me, as I crossed this bay, that the water was deeper than on the Atlantic shore. Calm as it looked, I felt throughout the long roll of the sleepy Pacific. At Oakland we took the steam cars, for although Berkeley, the village in which the University is situated, is within the Oakland limits, it is five miles at least from the ferry. Many of the suburbs of San Francisco are beautiful, but they are too far away; and beautiful as the Bay is, magnificent as are its boats, a business man must be very tired of a trip which costs between two and three hours daily. I think the future should see a railway bridge connecting San Francisco with Goat Island, and that again with Oakland. All the railway trains I have found west of the Mississippi move at so slow a rate as to be tormenting. With a double track and proper speed, Chicago need not be more than three days' journey from San Francisco. A rapid train from San Francisco across the Bay would shorten distances immensely between home and shop.

Oakland is named for the oak groves which adorn it, and its streets are well shaded. We had a delicious

view of the Bay all the way. Our visit was to our friend
the Secretary of the University, Professor Stearns, — a
man whose rare gifts as a naturalist and artist make one
regret that the principal clerical work of a great public
institution should fall to his lot. He is living in a small
house which he has lately built, surrounded by a flower
garden. No one can imagine the number of flowers which
one plant will produce in California until he has seen it.
These flowers, superb as they may be, would never recon-
cile me to the absence of grass. The gardens produce
upon me the same dreary effect which I once experienced
in Charleston, S. C., where a century plant or a cactus,
springing from the dry soil, seemed a decoration best
suited to the City of Desolation. In front of one of the
houses which we passed, where there was a fine lawn,
produced by costly irrigation, I saw a beautiful Norfolk
Island pine. It had broad, palm-like leaves, every one
of which was a branch. The principal streets of Berkeley
are set with eucalyptus or blue gum, — that curious Australian tree, as prodigal of blessings as the cocoa-palm.
It is heteromorphous; has round leaves when young, and
lanceolate when old, square stems at one time and round
at another, which give it a queer look. The Monterey
cypress is to be seen everywhere. It is a noble tree,
with branches growing in shelves like those of the Cedar
of Lebanon. In six years it shows a diameter of thirteen
inches. If one is rich enough to buy water, one may
have any amount of trees and turf here. There is also
a way of bordering flower-beds with a very green little moss, which takes away the dreary look; but few
people practise it. The wild-flowers, which I saw on
the scorched plain as I walked about, were the golden
escholtzia or California poppy, a gigantic scarlet pimper-

nel, staring boldly at the dry sky, wild-turnip and mustard, and a lovely little yellow thistle.

After lunch we walked up to Professor Hilgard's. He has charge of the chemical agricultural department of the University, and sent the excellent collection of cereals grown without irrigation to the Fair, of which I have already spoken. His pretty house stands in a wilderness of flowers, perking up in the gayest and most confused manner from the dry soil. The magnolia grandiflora was showing snowy buds. An Eastern horticulturist would go wild over the wealth of carnations springing from one root; and as for roses and fuchsias, the splendid color of their petals buries out of sight everything like a green leaf.

After we left the house we walked through the University grounds. There are now several handsome buildings erected, which I shall visit on some working day. They stand proudly on terraced slopes overlooking the Bay; and the lofty mountains beyond. In the hollows of the slopes tower groves of live oak. The terraces have a promenade and a carriage drive, whence we may look over Tamalpais, inspect the ridgy streets of this Western Tri-mountain, or count through the shifting lights of the Golden Gate the comatose pulse of the Pacific. These terraces are planted with a gigantic dew plant, which binds the soil. No corporation in the world could afford to irrigate so many acres. The dew plant drinks deep of the heavy fogs; it is a dark bluish green. The grounds are beautifully laid out. The green-houses are fine, and many Australian 'plants, beside the gum tree, are growing well, especially great numbers of gay-blossoming climbers. Our walk was frequently impeded by a disagreeable creature called *tar-weed*. It undertook to smear our skirts as we went, and prevent us from shaking off the dust they gathered.

After my walk, Mr. Stearns took me to his study, and showed me some beautiful sketches and the specimens he is at present working up. Several varieties of cuttle-fish were there. He says I can find them in the old mar-ket near the Bay, with tentacles more than six feet long. The tentacles are eaten, not only by the Chinese, but by all Europeans, and are gelatinous like the nape of the hal-ibut. The creatures have a horny beak like a parrot. He showed me a very interesting Aztec terra-cotta and a ver-rillia seven feet long, preserved in glycerine in a long glass tube. The glycerine was as clear as the glass itself; it had been given him by Agassiz. There were many others of the species no larger than threads. He is now working up a beautiful extinct helix from the very end of the Si-erra Nevada. He thinks it lived in rock crevices, and is a good instance of transformation compelled by environ-ment, of which naturalists do not take sufficient account.

Professor Stearns reinforces my convictions as to the mistakes geologists fall into in deciding the lapse of time required for great changes. He saw the denuda-tion of ten years occur in three days last season in a cañon near the coast.

As we went home in the cars we took up the excur-sionists of the morning at a place called Shell Mound. They were not disorderly, when we consider that they were all more or less drunk. One fellow staggered into the car brandishing a bottle full of whiskey, whose praises he sang all the way to town.

August 30. — I had a talk to-day with Mr. L., who has been here seven years, concerning the Chinamen.

Their filthy underground dens were described. Mr. L. spoke of their treachery, of the murder of a white man known to him in this neighborhood, three Chinamen 'lying in wait for him at night on his own stairs. He told of a lady among his friends, who lately dismissed her cook for stealing, and was nearly murdered by him only a week or two ago. A German broker present described the subterranean horror called "The Last Chance," where the old and the diseased are carried to die without food or medicine. They lie in their coffins, which are set around the place like bunks.

I said that from my own observation I should consider the Chinese orderly, but not clean. Mr. L. said that was the fact, and that he could tell stories of their filthiness which would not be believed. He alluded to the dirty ways in the laundries. Mrs. L.'s sister had a Chinaman for five years. When he wanted to go back to China, he brought another to take his place, and remained to teach him. During that time he was detected in an attempt to break into Mrs. L.'s room at midnight, and was put into the penitentiary for stealing her jewels. This sort of talk may be hardly worth repeating, but Mr. L. takes no interest in politics or the labor question; is not a householder; and it was curious to see how exactly his observations tallied with those of more prejudiced men. I have been told several times that a Chinaman, however honest *in* your service, feels at liberty to steal the moment his contract is terminated.

I meant to have spoken yesterday of a fine Japanese ivory shown me by Mr. Stearns. It represents two monkeys devouring a man. It is only a skeleton which they clutch between them. One has torn out the heart, the other devours the brain. All these figures rest on a large human skull! It looked a little like a satirical jest aimed at the Darwinians.

August 31. — This afternoon I went with my cousin to San Rafael. This is a little town to the north of Oakland, with a ferry of its own. It is just an hour from the city, and I think in Marin County, under Tamalpais; but as I cannot find it on any of my maps I may be mistaken. When I first arrived in San Francisco, I went to a leading bookstore bearing a well-known name, for a guide-book. It was not until I had paid for it and taken it home, that I discovered it was nine years old and incorrect in every particular relating to the Yosemite, for which I had especially purchased it! As the salesman refused to take it back, the cheat reminded me of another incident of my journey which I believe I have never told you. Between Chicago and Omaha — just as I met Miss Cleveland — I inquired on the cars for a "Guide across the Continent." I had examined one in a bookshop at a dollar and a half the day before. One was brought me in the car, and the price named as $2.25, the salesman asserting that it was of a new edition of increased value. I had every reason to believe that I had previously seen the new edition; so I asked leave to examine it. I kept it some time, and was much puzzled by the omission of the title-page which should have shown the date. The lad asserted that it was all right; so I finally paid the two dollars and twenty-five cents. In a few moments I saw Miss Cleveland reading one like it, and I asked with an apology if she would tell me where she bought it. "On this car," she replied. "And what did you give for it?" — "A dollar and a half." When my friend took her paper cutter and pressed back the leaves in my copy it was evident that the title-page had been carefully cut out. In a few moments I had an opportunity to ask the name of the pedler of the conductor. I wrote it down carefully, and then said to the conductor : "Go to this book-agent and tell him that unless he refunds me seventy-five cents, I shall denounce him immediately to this company, who do not tolerate any cheats." After an explanation the conductor went off; and in a few moments I had my money back, and was listening to all sorts of lying protestations, which I quickly checked. In spite of such experiences I have bought a good many maps, and found them very unsatisfactory.

San Rafael seems to be a good deal in the hands of a Mr. Colman, who plants avenues of eucalyptus, cypress, and other trees. It contains five or six hundred families, whose heads are in business in San Francisco, and has no poor population whatever. It nestles under Tamalpais, which, being high enough to bathe in the clouds, keeps green and beautiful all the year, while all the other hills are brown and dry. My cousin's little daughter was waiting in the pony phaeton to take me to the house. This is surrounded by a quarter of an acre of lawn as green as possible, and starred with the loveliest flowers. The piazza is covered with passion flowers. But, alas, the lawn was wet! The children may not roll on it, nor their elders play croquet. Dear stayers at home, remember your blessings!

I enjoyed the trip over the Bay as usual, although it was half veiled in fog. My cousin called it a very clear evening! I believe all the people are so used to the fog that they do not see it if there is a ray of sun overhead.

For myself I was never weary of longing for one clear glimpse of the beautiful water, with its fortressed rocks, its rim of mountains, and the opaline splendor which the sunset throws across it.

San Rafael, September 1.—This morning I had a delicious drive in the pony phaeton with Mrs. F. We went back and forth among the hills, of which only Tamalpais is fresh and dewy. These are very steep, and lovely valleys filled with live-oak are to be seen on all sides. One ravine looked so much like New England in November that it made the tears start. There are beautiful country seats, with turf green as emerald within their gates,—as great a contrast to the burnt sod without as heaven would be to hell. This is a country in which only rich people can enjoy themselves. It was intensely hot, but I did not realize it we moved so slowly. After we came down from the hills we went about the town and looked at the pretty places, — at the avenues of acacia, blue gum, cypress, and oak. The finest lawn we saw was a Mr. Cook's; but why have green grass, at the cost of a fortune, if you cannot walk on it or sit on it? Very beautiful ferns abound here in the spring. The mosquitoes are very thick, unused to human flesh, and so light that you can kill them with a touch.

September 2.—We started early to go back to San Francisco. All the way over, my cousin was saying how delightfully *clear* it was, and I was thinking how the heavy fog spoiled all things! Not that the fog has not a beauty of its own, but I could see *that* on the Atlantic coast.

I have been taking steps to go to Portland, and have been offered passes on the steamer with the Presidential party; but I think I shall hardly have time to see the whole of California itself.

This afternoon I went to Mrs. H. D.'s rooms to hear Mrs. Williams — the daughter of James, the novelist — give an analysis of " Romeo and Juliet." I was a good deal amused when she said that as it was Romeo's impatience which brought the story to a tragic end, so his weakness of character would have made it a greater tragedy still if the pair had survived and lived together ! The heroic character of Shakspeare's women and the non-heroic character of his men was further commented on. It was all very bright. .

The female school-teachers of San Francisco interest me very much. I have had a long talk with two of them to-day. I think them superior to most of those in similar positions in Boston or Providence.

I keep trying experiments with the fruit at the street corners, but none of it is luscious. However fair it looks, it has a thin, watery character. Earlier in the season I should have found the mango apple from Acapulco and dried plantain served up in corn-husks. Now I find the citrons, oranges, lemons, and limes; but, with the exception of the limes, all seem to me of coarse fibre and inferior flavor. There are many figs ; and when they are skinned and cut up, and eaten with sugar and cream, they are agreeable. So are most things ! Olives, almonds, raisins, prunes, and dates abound ; but I defer speaking of them until I have seen them growing.

San Francisco, September 3. — I have been exploring the south side of the town to find the Rincon school. As I passed up Third Street I went through a perfect arcade of loan-shops of the second class, quite as entertaining

in their way as those on Kearney Street, and quite as
characteristic. Here the sailors' sweethearts deposit rare
shells, carvings from the Sandwich Islands, idols from
the Burmese sea, and walrus tusks from the whalers.
One is continually reminded of the close proximity of
San Francisco to the regions of myrrh and frankincense.
It was only after an hour's hard walking that I found
the steep steps which lead to the bridge across First
Street, on Harrison Avenue, and climbed to the Vassar
Street entrance of the Rincon school. This bridge is a
testimony to the municipal destruction of Rincon Hill, in
total disregard of the rights of property-owners. Very
many such interferences we have to lament in Washington.

The gate into the yard was locked, on account of various
small thefts which have occurred ; but after much ringing
a little girl appeared, and led me to a pleasant office on
the second floor, where I found Miss Cleveland. The
room was neatly carpeted, had a useful little library,
and all the papers were arranged in the orderly way
which one expects of a sensible woman. Her assistant
is a Miss Stowell, who came from Deerfield, Mass., and
knew me and my traditions. She is a well instructed
Unitarian. I heard some recitations in grammar and
arithmetic, and listened to some good music. There is
excellent discipline in the school. The children are plain
and clean in their dress, a very great and pleasant contrast to our Boston school-children, who dress too much.
"What could the daughters of our lords wear more ?"
asked poor Lady Amberley, when I took her through the
Irish school on South Street. Every room in the Rincon
is clean and well ventilated, and bears witness to the influence of New England. When we went back to the

office, a child who had been degraded for falsehood came there to talk the matter out. She had not the smallest sense of shame, and was not in the least annoyed by my presence. I was much struck by the grieved and serious manner of the teacher throughout the interview. The present School Board is undertaking an economical reform, which begins by cutting down the salaries of the best teachers, and has roused very serious opposition. The teachers appealed to the Legislature, who decided in their behalf ; but the Board refused to obey, and appealed from the decision. There is probably need of economy in all State and municipal expenses ; but this is not the place where it should first be felt.

After dinner, N. and I took the Geary Street cars to the Park,—the Golden Gate Park,—a delicious tract of turf and flowers redeemed from sand-dunes and desert, which may well be the pride of San Francisco. We had been told that carriages would meet us at the gate of the Park, but this proved a mistake. We therefore walked on to the Conservatory, where we found a lovely show of flowers. I have never seen more orchids together in my life, nor a greater variety of bright-leaved plants. A great many different colored leaves were found springing from one root. I saw the coleus in bloom,—a delicate purple spike, which looked oddly coming out of the heart of beet-red leaves. There were oranges and bananas growing, and a very great variety of begonias. I saw for the first time one of the enormous monumental cacti of Arizona, —a pillar of green standing twenty feet high, grooved by vertical rows of spines, and crowned by a capital of white blossoms in which each flower looked like a Cape jessamine. If the Greeks had access to any such things amid the Libyan sands, there was no occasion to

invent orders of architecture. I am told here that in
the old Ophir and Mexican mines there is a world of
fungi that counterfeit everything known or imagined.
Some of them are ten feet high, and look like sheeted
ghosts. Others look like snowy owls or bearded goats,
and they are so white that they seem as if cut out of
marble. Great bunches of what looks like snow-white
hair drip from the branches, and soft pulpy snow-white
masses form on the levels, which seem to arise from
some of the deposits made when the mines were worked.
Sometimes one of these fungi lifts a rock weighing a
hundred pounds three or four feet into the air. On the
highest levels, where the air is driest, these fungi are of
a more delicate make. They look like twisted rams' horns,
or the bunches of white paper which are hung in the
Shinto temples to catch and detain the sun-god. Sometimes a single stem seems to blossom into a thousand
lilies, and nothing has been found in these mines which
resembles the fungi of the outer world.

One of the most interesting things to a traveller on
this Western slope is the mimetic or prophetic character
of natural objects. The stone wonders of the parks in Colorado suggest as much as the fungi of Ophir, but they certainly rose to the surface before the world was peopled.

In the tank of the Conservatory a blue lotus had just
come to perfection, and a pink one promised to do so
in a few days. The green-house has three domes; under
one of them the palms were growing, under another,
our common balsams or touch-me-nots lifted their frail
stems, hung with "jewels" of every color. The whole
park is surrounded with magnificent roads, made of the
disintegrated surface of the mountains, which make the
causeways delightful all the way from Colorado. They

are said to be as fine as the famous shell roads of New Orleans. Within the park they are bordered — for it is hardly more as yet — by the most delicious verdure, the sod being formed of a fine trefoil. Walking back to a dummy which connects with the Geary Street road, and regaining that, we found a carriage in which we swept onward to the Cliff House. We started in a pale sunshine, which was more cold than clear, and went on in one of the heaviest fogs I ever encountered. At first it rolled over the open dunes like solid balls of cotton. Then it took on a brown color, and settled into all the hollows, where it might to all appearances have been cut in slices and broiled for breakfast.

We swept between vast sand-hills and plains, covered with sage-brush, with a vast array of lupin, yarrow, yellow thistle, and the like. Anything drearier even in sunshine it would be impossible to conceive; and yet even to-day a few slant beams would now and then deck the shifting heaps with a sort of iridescent golden glow. When we reached the Cliff House, the seal rocks were invisible, and the animals themselves had retired to the sacred privacy which the weather made desirable. Our garments were soaked; and, as my daughter is subject to chills, I got out of the carriage and went in search of some stimulant. I finally found a private parlor, where I rang a bell and ordered two glasses of lager. For these two glasses we paid the modest sum of fifty cents: but that was surely better than a fit of illness.

We drove a long way by the sea. It was a bold thing to undertake to make a park out of pure sand; but at any cost it must be considered a delight and a privilege to contrive an ocean park, with beaches and sea-lions! Near the water grows a dark glossy hibiscus,

which had crimson blossoms two months ago; and about
the time that they sold lilacs for ten cents a bunch the
bristly cactus put out along the shore a dull red bloom.
I am not so much impressed by a foreign look to the
vegetation as I expected to be; but everywhere I find
the eucalyptus or blue gum of Australia both striking
and ugly. It has, however, a most refreshing pine-like
odor, with a drooping air. It is an evergreen. The
first year's leaves are obovoid, of an ashy blue color.
The older leaves are long and narrow, and of a
dark glossy green. Two branches often cross each
other, which look as if they could not belong to the
same tree, the longest leaves being not less than twelve
inches. The bark is very thin and of a light reddish
yellow, smooth as that of the sycamore; but soon de-
taching itself as the tree ages, in long ghostly strips,
which make it in my opinion entirely unfit for a lawn.
It has a wonderful power of condensing the moisture
in the air; and this, when not a drop of rain falls, will
run down the long funnel-like leaves until it stands in
pools, or forms a small rivulet at the foot of the tree.
The fruit is like an acorn cup, full of tiny seeds. Sixteen years ago some blue gums were set out in Oakland,
looking a good deal like a field of cabbage; these are now
nearly seventy feet high, and some of them at one foot
above the ground measure three and a half feet in circumference! This rapid growth and the condensing power
would alone make the tree very valuable in a dry, bare
country like California on the coast; but it is also good
fire-wood. It is full of an aromatic oil of great medicinal
and artistic value, whose uses are hardly yet understood.
It absorbs malarial influence, deadens bad odors, and is
considered to stand as high as the cocoa-nut in its use-

fulness to mankind. The fine Japanese photographs which took the gold medal at Vienna, in 1873, were set with the gum of the eucalyptus.

As we drew near the Gerry Street exit from the park on our return, we came into a wealth of gaily blooming borders, flowering shrubs, and emerald turf of which I can give no idea. It is overwhelming! I do not know that I have seen a single flower in California which I have not seen before, but the luxuriance of their bloom cannot be imagined by those who have not seen it. Hedges of fuschia divide the front door-yards; roses nod from the eaves. A wall of geraniums fifteen feet high now and then compels one to stare. The gardens are a tangle of superb color. And yet I have not been, and shall not go, to Santa Rosa, — the most luxuriant place on the northern coast.

September 4. — To-day I went to the several markets, which are very fine, but do not impress me with any great wonder. The arrangement of articles is not so good as at the East, and I did not see nor have I yet tasted one ripe tomato among thousands. Figs and grapes abound. I was sent out here to eat grapes, but I have not yet eaten any. They are sour and watery, and do not tempt me. When I criticise them, my friends suggest a new kind; but the new kind has the same fault. The meats are cleaned and skewered to suit the taste of all countries except America! There seemed to be a hundred kinds of sausages and brawn; and many kinds of unknown cheese, hard and soft, sound and rotten, spoke their own praises in detestable odors of one kind or another. The cool climate prevents the fish-market from being as disgusting as I have often found it, but I observe that the poultry is generally sold alive as at Washington, — a troublesome practice for which there is certainly no excuse here.

Mr. Stearns met us at the old market, and went off with me on a raid for odd creatures. My octopus looked so queer when I saw it, that I think I should hardly have known it without his help. The body, with its upstart eyes and parrot beak, is so small that the tentacles falling from it in a bunch, and about seven feet long, looked like so many ropes of human flesh. The little cups upon them were large enough for easy examination. Small oysters to-day are six bits (or seventy-five cents) a hundred, which would about fill a pint measure ! Large ones are fifty cents a dozen. Shrimps are abundant, eerie-looking creatures that they are ! Craw-fish are " devilish," as Pet Marjorie would say; in earnest, they have a wicked look. The fish-market is not a good one. The smelts and anchovies are fine, but the larger fish are not inviting to one who knows Gloucester Bay.

I also went to the Coast Survey to look at all sorts of charts of this region, but I did not find those in charge of the office able to explain them.

Once or twice to-day I have been told that something " costs a cent." It is a good sign. Poverty, or perhaps I should say *reverse*, is teaching this people a much-needed lesson.

This afternoon I went to Woodward's Gardens. They were given to the city by Mr. R. B. Woodward in 1860, and it is claimed that the whole income has been used to add to the attractions. These Gardens consist of two great parks, lying on different sides of a road, and connected by an underground tunnel. On one side is a beautiful garden, a museum, and a great pond for geese

and ducks, besides some cranes and a big cormorant, who
is a nasty, greedy fellow that vomits his food all over
the rocks, as if it were on purpose to disgust little boys
with greediness.   It is so dry in San Francisco that anything green is delightful, and people make picnics in this
garden.   I did not wait for the concert, but went to see
the seals and sea-lions fed.   As I went out I saw a tiny
green paroquet and two little houses full of a hundred
little white mice, which ran in and out the doors and windows, up ladders and over each other's backs.   The seals
are ugly creatures, Charlie.   You would never think it;
but if mamma can show you a leech, they look just like
that, only so big!   If not, you must think of a bolster
made of black leather, pinched so as to look like a head
at one end, and with four fins or flippers that the seal
uses for feet, and which look as if they had been cut out
of India rubber.   In the head is a pair of soft, pretty
eyes.   They tumble off the rocks with a great splash, and
bark like dogs.   They swim on their sides, and when they
eat anything it protrudes all along the passage through
the body, exactly as if they were snakes.   Professor
Henry says that there are four museums here, all classi-
fied and well arranged, but I had not time to examine.
There is a fine menagerie.   There are vast conservatories
and a rotating zoögraphicon, which undertakes to show
the physical geography and the animal and vegetable
fauna of the world, in eight rotating sections, and does it
fairly well.   There is an Art Gallery and there are eight
marble statues outside in the grounds, and if these are
not remarkable they have a very pleasing effect.   On one
side of the tunnel are verdant retreats and the great audience hall; on the other, a great playground for the children, with swings, goat carriages, camels, and donkeys

for them to ride, and little boats on a pond. In a gallery which looks down on this gay place are all the cages of the menagerie and a tower with a camera. Besides showing us the usual moving pictures, this camera revealed the monkeys combing their babies' hair, the seals plunging, and even the white mice skipping over each other. There is also a skating rink; and so well is the whole place managed that no accident has occurred within these grounds during the whole twenty years since they were opened, and the children of the middle classes are often left here for a whole day without a protector. There are stands for the sale of fruit and candies, as well as for all sorts of drinks.

On May Day all this was opened for a festival. The children carried or bought their lunch, and played with bright birds, such as cockatoos, parrots, and pheasants. There were two May poles with red, white, and blue ribbons, and round these and the happy little queen danced a hundred little fairies, dressed in bright colors to imitate May flowers. Nowhere have I seen so orderly a crowd as in this pretty place; but our own adventures will best display its charms. The ordinary afternoon performance was half over when we arrived, but in the pavilion we saw incredible feats on the flying bars by Mons. Loyal. Then a coarse Irish fellow sang a mad or drunken song in a way to amuse those who do not know what a sad and serious matter a drunken frolic is. Then the " Great Dyllur," whoever he may be, sang the " Mc-Carthy's Party," of which I brought away the important fact that " seventeen were present !" The show was ended by a comic pantomime called " Covers for Three," in which all the company appeared. There was a young girl and her mother ; the latter sent her to the ironing

board when she wanted to play the harp. But then a
series of lovers came in and had a word to say about it.
One jealous fellow tormented all the rest, who were one
after the other covered up like furniture and finally detected. The girl appreciated this young demon's sharp-
ness, for she finally accepted him. There were many
comic points, but nothing bad; on the whole the thing
was cleaner than could be expected.

There was a good concert after this; but I pursued
white mice and bigger creatures, and finally the zoögraphicon, which was capital, although I am sure the same
snowy peak in it officiated alternately as three separate
mountains and an iceberg! There is the most magnificent aquarium I ever beheld, but I hardly enjoyed it
I wanted Willis and Charlie so much. You go down
into a subterranean grotto, entirely surrounded by great
glass tanks, green as the sea and as clear as light. I
think they are about four feet high, and open to the air
and sunshine at the top. The light passes through the
water and shows every object clearly. It is as if you
were in an enchanted bubble at the bottom of the ocean.
All sorts of fish are to be found in the tanks. The salt
water ripples through them all the time, and the creatures are healthy and vigorous and most beautiful to
see. We began with cray-fish, and went on to sharks
and sturgeon. Trout, tom-cod, and salmon were all
active and undisturbed by our prying gaze.

When we came out we went to the Exotic Gardens, whose products we had seen at the fair. There
are fine conservatories and a tropical garden, which is
probably kept up in winter but looked forlorn enough
to-day.

A Résumé.

Sept. 4, 1880. — What would my darlings like to hear
of all this wonderful journey that I have taken ? Shall
I tell them of the Egyptian lotus blooming in the Calu-
met River, and sold by children in Chicago streets ?
Who dropped the seed just there and in the Rouge, and
nowhere else in this wide land ? How is it possible to
tell of it, and not recall the Egyptian head-dresses and
calm Osirian face of the finest Peruvian terra-cottas, to
be seen to best advantage in the museum at Ithaca, or
in the superb collection of Walter Evans at New Ro-
chelle ? Shall I talk about the great pillared cacti of
Arizona, rising fifteen and twenty feet, whose snowy
capitals are alive with fragrance and beauty ? Shall I
tell how the five stone toes of Atlas, protruding from
the soil of Glen Eyrie, are nothing less than just such
cacti turned to stone, or how the whole country is filled
with mimetic ruins, Egyptian tombs, like those at Abou
Simbel, with visionary giants leaning back like Ramses ;
old castles of the Rhine, with arches and portcullis,
with mighty walled cities or fortresses a thousand feet
up in the air, for which the country finds no grander
name than "wash-outs" ? Shall I tell how the de-
creasing herds of antelope still flash across the plains ;
how the bison are no longer seen, although their heads
are nailed to many a frontier wall; how the lazy Indian still loiters around "the track," and shows her
pappoose gladly for two bits ; while away in mountain
fastnesses, not out of sight of the mountain coach, the
wild-cat and the mountain lion still dispute the pass
with the rattlesnake ?

Shall I tell how I saw a little child pass though one

of the wildest and wickedest crowds in Leadville, leaning on the shoulder of her tiny jackass, whom she half-
caressed and half-punished with her baby hand; or how,
in the "Garden of the Gods," a snowy rampart from the
Jura springs suddenly from the soil, and confronts the
bloody sandstone of the Trias, with mysterious significance?   Or shall I tell them how we climbed the Sierras, and with jaded eyes saw Lake Donner two thousand
feet below, and at last gladly caught the first sea-breeze
at Sacramento, and floated down by its broad waters,
till the white bosom of the mighty Pacific shone and
throbbed for us beyond the Golden Gate?

Shall I tell how the rocky steeps of San Francisco
rise over hills too perpendicular for horses, with a climate whose coolness veils a burning heat, whose summer
warmth scarce hides the winter's breath?   Will they
hear how, when I ask a question on the street in
English, it is answered in a dozen different tongues;
how the marvels of all lands lie in the windows of
pawnbrokers shops; and how the pleasantest place I
have seen since I left home is the Grammar School on
Rincon Hill, where Miss Cleveland and Miss Stowell,
with their score of assistants, preside in the old New
England way, and half cheated me into believing I had
not crossed the Rockies at all?   From my window I
look down over Chinatown, where there is hidden the
terrible traditionary refuse of a past faith and a past
civilization, taking forms unintelligible to any but the
student of Aristophanes.   Among the coolies who trot
by, smoking opium twisted in brown paper, and on a
yoke across their shoulders carrying baskets of fruit,
vegetables, or meats, there is a worse slavery than that
our Civil War has hardly yet exterminated.   I am

not so afraid of the leper who drags his weary length
along, a little behind, as of the legacy which Chinatown, — yes, Chinatown, — even when broken up, de-
molished, and *burned clean*, is yet to bequeath to this
Western coast.

For the fortnight that I have been here, the sun has
never once risen or set. He finds such a heavy breakfast of Pacific fog that it takes him all day to devour it,
and the meal is followed by such throes of indigestion
that he dare not lift his head from its gloomy sheets.
Yet the market is full of peaches and pears, and plums
and grapes, of nectarines and apricots, of figs purple and
figs white; so there is a sun somewhere and he shines!
Do all these things *taste* good? Not a bit of it. They
bewilder the eye with their lovely colors; but one northern peach is worth them all, and is a better hint of the
infinite love and beauty. And there are less lovely
things in the market. There are shrimps, those ghosts
of shell-fish who bear the same relation to crabs and
lobsters that May-flies do to the devil's darning-needle.
There are cray-fish, with a wicked, uncanny look; and
since not only the Chinese, but all the foreign residents
eat them, there are *cuttle-fish*, whose tentacles drop
down from their small bodies like ropes of flesh, with
polyp-like blossoms all along. I saw one this morning
with six arms, dropping down nearly seven feet each in
length! And all the years our respected fellow-citizens
have been breakfasting on these gelatinous curiosities,
our scientific friends across the water have been gravely
wondering whether Victor Hugo did not *invent* the
devil-fish! And that reminds me to say that one thing
a traveller must learn on this Western trip, — and that is
greatly to distrust the definite conclusions of scientific

men. No one who has seen a sudden storm undo the
work of a century, an alkaline plain turn into a hay-
field in one short month, or a lake thirty-five miles long
by sixteen wide drained by a year's irrigation, can feel
at all sure that into scientific chronology all the conditions have been entered.

Yesterday I went to see the wonderful park which California has made out of six square miles of sand-dunes.
I went to get my first view of the Pacific and the rocks
where the seals still clamber; but on the way the fog
which the trade-winds bring shut me in. This afternoon I was carried off to Woodward's Gardens, not knowing in the least what I was to see. Glad indeed was I
that I went, for nowhere in the world can one see so
much for "two bits." It occupies two blocks of land, —
one, a pretty verdant slope of landscape gardening; the
other, supplied with swings for children, goat carriages
and donkey drives, zoölogical dens and a camera. There
are four museums, menageries, and conservatories, an
art gallery, and a vast audience hall. It was impossible
to see all these things in one afternoon; and I went to
the regular entertainment, which was half over before I
arrived. My part of it began with incredible feats by
a flying acrobat, who always did what he undertook,
but did it so clumsily that he kept me in perpetual
terror. He was followed by a Rose Julian, who went
through posturing feats in so little clothing that I could
not have endured it if she had looked in the least like
a woman; but she was only a tangle of legs and arms
which seemed to change places, and might have belonged
to a cuttle-fish. The saddest sight of all was a dear
little child not six years old, who danced skilfully to a
tambourine, but with a pale face which told what she

had suffered in learning. Comic songs and a comic pantomine were followed by a concert; but all these I left to go in search of something which delighted me extremely. I mean the subterranean aquarium, in which all sorts of fishes and shell-fish live in great tanks of sea-water, some dozens of which are set into the walls of a dark grotto. You see the fishes just as they see each other, vivid with iridescent color, darting with graceful play of fins or tails, half-transparent and altogether lovely. Aladdin must have inspired the whole thing.

Sept. 5, 1880. — I heard Mr. Peabody preach this morning, and this afternoon I went up to the San Dolores Mission. It was built by Junipero Serra of adobes, and dedicated Oct. 9, 1776. It was here that he erected a cross, and gave to the port the name of San Francisco. Some of the outbuildings still linger, and wherever the mission churches are found, the schoolhouses, tanneries, and workshops attached to them give them the air of a picturesque hamlet in old Spain.

The adobe wall is covered with white stucco or "rough cast." The church is long and narrow. The lower half of the wall shows several short, thick, white columns, and above in the gable are three open arches in which are three bells, one larger than the others. They have quite a Moorish look, and are very sweet in tone. As the church was not open, we went in through the priest's house. On the right as I entered was an extraordinary fresco painted on broad sheets of cartridge paper fastened to the wall in squares like patchwork, and representing the baptism of some Indian converts. There are three shrines beside that of the Virgin, all decorated in crimson and gold, and with three or four figures carved in wood, each of which represents one of the heroes of the Franciscan or Jesuit order. One was the great Las Casas himself.

Outside, the roof is covered with long red tiles, looking like bits of split cinnamon lapped over each other, as Bret Harte once said. Inside, the roof is painted so as to suggest the same thing.

There is a very large graveyard attached to this mission, well filled with the unmarked graves of two thousand Indians, whose names, however, are said to be written in the "Book of Life" and in the early records of the church. On the side opposite the strange fresco the doors and windows of the old church open into this garden of graves. It is overcrowded and badly kept, but is a tropical wilderness of flowers. A superb old damask rose brought from Spain by the monks has the size of an apple-tree, and nods over half the tombs and into the open door of the church. The periwinkle sends up sprays of purple and green to the height of three feet, and its flowers are as large as our morning glory.

There are two remarkable monuments. A white marble obelisk erected to the memory of the first governor of Alta California, and another to the honor of a wretch who was put to death in the Plaza during the reign of "The Vigilantes," for several murders and a host of minor atrocities. It was erected by "many friends" who undoubtedly ought to have shared his fate. The flowery vistas of the old place are still charming, and the decorations of the walls are interesting because they were the work of the Indians themselves.

There is a story to-day about malarial fever at Portland, which makes it most unlikely that N. would dare to go there with me. Mr. Dall's illness will probably make it impossible.

We called on Mr. Peabody this evening, and he urges me to go to Santa Barbara on my return from Los Angeles for the sake of the little church. I saw too, for the first time, the son of my friend Starr King. It is not often that a boy inherits so much love.

Sept. 6, 1880. — After many delays and disappointments Mr. W. came to-day to tell me that the special officer who takes visitors to Chinatown was ready to wait upon me. If I had known the town as well this morning as I do to-night I need not have sought for him.

A little before the hour officer Duffield named, I went with Mr. W. to the Pine Street joss-house. This is so much cleaner than those I saw afterward, that I think it must have been erected by the best class of the people, who still hold to the early faith. The better classes, that is the more educated classes of the Chinese nation, seem to have no faith of any sort. In my opinion contact with the Western world has done both Chinese and Japanese great injury in this respect. Both nations, who are the very opposite of scientific by constitution, now affect a scorn of all worship, and seem to think it only one manifestation of superstitious ignorance.

You enter the joss-house from the street by an ordinary door. Behind this, two enormous paper lanterns hang in a perfectly bare hall. Beyond, we crossed an open court-yard between houses. The walls on each side of it were hung with parallelograms of red paper covered with Chinese characters. These are the "accounts" of the worshippers, though for what they are supposed to owe money I could not learn. If the temple is, as is said, a refuge for the sick, that may explain this tax-list.

Winding round the temple itself by a narrow bricked

passage, we enter it on the side. The State faith
in its purity did not provide for any priest, but the
corruptions of the last ten centuries have introduced
an attendant to whom it is common to apply the
word. The first room I entered was a sort of vestry
intended for his use, and filled with supplies for the
temple service. The air was fragrant with sandal-wood.
Painted paper cylinders about the size of a candle, filled
with sandal-wood dust, were burning before the altar.
On each side of the temple as you enter it are hung immense mottoes or prayers, in crimson and gold. Every
ones knows how the inscription on the side of a stick
of India ink looks. Magnify it a hundred times, and
make it crimson where it is black, and you have the effect
of these mottoes before you: they hang from the ceiling
also. The long narrow room was divided into two or
three courts by screens of carved wood, wrought in panels
and reaching half-way up, as well as by banners mounted
upon this, as if it were a balustrade. From the roof
hang pretty gay-colored lanterns. The shrine was arranged much like a Catholic shrine, only the deity was
some canonized ruler or hero whom I found it impossible to recognize.

The panels of the carved screens which were next the
floor were old and very beautiful, and so were some of the
panels of lacquer and gold, and the falling lambrequins of
old embroidery; but the only very odd or striking thing
was the image of the Dog Fo, with his scarlet mouth and
tongue. This was everywhere repeated. There were two
before each altar; and on a sort of chancel rail, with a dog
in the centre, there was on each side a great square candlestick of cloisonné. In these were what our guide called
"candles," but in a Chinese shop I afterward saw carved

wood colored and gilded in the same way, with only a tin cup set in the top to hold oil and a taper. These cost five dollars a pair. The true candles are immensely thick, carved in the wax itself, and so costly as only to be used on grand occasions. The crowning ornament which holds the cup is a dragon's head. When I asked the "priest" who the god upon the shrine was, I could get no intelligible answer. Several solar radiations in heavy gilt convinced me that it was essentially a State shrine. "He one God, same as Jesus Christ," was the steady reply to all questions!

Mr. Duffield served on police duty in the Chinese quarter for seven years and a half; he is appealed to by the Chinese themselves when they want protection. He can take you to their gambling saloons, to the lowest form of lodging houses, where men push themselves feet foremost into their "pigeon holes," and into the subterranean labyrinths which I could enter only by putting on a man's dress, and where I would not go if he would take me. I did not find, however, that this man knew anything about the State worship or the Buddhist shrines, nor could he give any name to what he saw. For that reason I have been forced to do a good deal of hard work myself, of which I offer you the results.

I suppose you may have seen some notices of the wonderful lectures of Terrien de Lacouperie in London last summer, which seem to indicate that the Chinese, the Chaldean, and perhaps the Egyptian are only offshoots of one original stock, which believed in one God, and from which the different nations separated at different eras, carrying with them the distinctive characteristics of the time at which each started out for itself.

The most remarkable and touching thing about the

11

Chinese religion is the fact, which may be considered proven, that this people has worshipped one God for at least five thousand years. This monotheism encountered two dangers from the very beginning. First, the idolatries which naturally grow out of the worship of the sun, moon, and stars, which worship has left traces in their ideagraphs or primitive hieroglyphs; and, second, the system of divination, which shows itself also in the primitives. If it were not for the evidences thus offered, it would almost seem as if the Chinese people must have started from their Akkad home before the worship of the one God had seriously degenerated. It is very extraordinary that the Chinese have been able to keep monotheism (the prominent element of the State religion) from the beginning until now; and in his last work Dr. Legge shows this conclusively from the ancient hieroglyphic characters, without knowing apparently anything about the conclusions of Lacouperie. Yet his own lectures must have been delivered before the Presbyterian College in London while those of Lacouperie were passing through the press. In this way Dr. Legge has vindicated fully the personal use which he makes of the Chinese "heaven" in his translation of the Chinese classics, — a use which has elicited some criticism.

The Chinese themselves are ignorant of the origin of many of their own customs and the meaning of much of their own literature. Dr. Legge cannot explain why the Emperor must sacrifice to the "six honored ones," after offering his tribute to the "one god;" but Lacouperie finds six inferior gods at Susa, directly after the chief deity; and it was not only the Emperor Shun, but the magnates of Babylonia, who received provincial princes with the title of "pastors."

Dr. Legge emphasizes the fact that only the Emperor of the Chinese in all the nation worshipped the Supreme Being, and believes that the fact that the people were forbidden to worship was fruitful of evil; but it does not seem to have occurred to him that the leader of the "hundred families," or the first emigrants into China, might possibly have been a priest, who was accustomed to consider the solstitial sacrifice one of the functions of his caste, and that the prohibition might have been a matter of prudence in the beginning, — a sincere effort to keep the original people to a simple faith. Lacouperie finds a sort of hieroglyphic dictionary in the Yh King, which so puzzled Confucius, accompanied apparently by a vast amount of archæological information, — information which we are now as certain to possess within a few years as we were of the contents of the Egyptian stele, from the moment that we had mastered the Rosetta stone.

I am very sorry that the great Egyptologist, Goodwin, died so soon after he went to China. I wanted him to find in the old mathematical and divining books, which have an evident relation to similar things in Egypt, a common key to the origin of the two nations, and an indication of the intellectual advancement of the people from which both must have been an offshoot. The numeric formalism of both countries is the same; and the cuneiform characters may have had an origin in that "cone" which stands for generative power in all the three nations, but not usually, as Lacouperie suggests, for the "generator of fire." While records were considered sacred, the making of them fell naturally into the hands of the priests; and nothing was more likely than the obscuring of hieroglyphics by the use of arbitrary symbols in the

place of lines, in proportion as motives of cabalistic se-
crecy prevailed over the instincts of pure religion.

Yao divided his country into twelve provinces, and of
their limits, productions, and manufactures the Yh will
some day furnish an account.   His system was only the
duodenary feudal system in vogue at Susa.   The "Chief
of the Four Mountains" in China seems to reproduce
the "King of the Four Regions," one of the titles of the
Chaldean sovereign; and the signs for the four points of
the compass are the same in Chinese and Akkadian.   If
Professor Sayer's "oblique-eyed population of Babylon"
are soon to be proven close kindred to the Chinese, it
seems rather hard that Baron Bunsen could not have
lived to see what he so fully predicted.

The Japanese are also an "oblique-eyed population,"
and whatever tends to explain the origin of the Chinese
will partially explain the rise of this more intellectual
and artistic people.   I cannot help thinking of this when
I find the religion of both nations called "the way," the
monarchs of both peoples sun or heaven descended, and
the Emperor of China offering his great sacrifices at the
solstitial periods, while the sacred mirror in the shrine
at Isè is only the emblem of the Sun-God's approach
after the winter solstice.   The secondary deities of both
nations are found in the forces of Nature, and the reli-
gions have been corrupted equally and at about the same
period by Buddhist influences.

A stranger in San Francisco, who has some pre-con-
ceived ideas of the simplicity of the State religion,—meaning by that the religion of the ancients which Confucius
"transmitted," — and who thinks to find in the worship of
"ancestors" only a simple and ancient service in keeping with a reverent and conservative life, would find

himself somewhat puzzled if he entered a joss-house or attended a funeral. There is no one to tell him that not only has the old State religion been somewhat corrupted, but that in its ardor for organization the Celestial Empire has really affiliated with the impish Tao-ists.

When we find that close beside the primitive symbol of *Ti*—the one absolute God—there are two others pronounced *shi* and *shǎn*, which refer to spirits in general, and which are almost if not quite as old, we see how easily the superstitions inherent in polytheistic worship would make their way with a people forbidden to pray to the one God for themselves.

In spite of Professor Tiele's positive assertion, Dr. Legge refuses to recognize pure animism, or a preponderating tendency to fetichism, in the State religion of Confucius. He finds in the early faith a true religion, for which it is evident that he is liberal enough to feel a sincere respect. At twenty-two hundred years before Christ he finds the Emperor Shun worshipping every fifth year in the "four quarters" of the country, in a fashion which again reminds us of Chaldea, and which Dr. Legge insists was a pure worship of God, attended by a sacrificial recognition of the inferior powers supposed to be instruments of the divine government. There was a worship of God for all, but the ruler of the State was its sole voice, — and a worship of ancestors for all, the head of each family officiating.

In houses and temples, those familiar with Chinese customs will remember certain white tablets about the shape of an ordinary tomb-stone, but of various sizes. Upon these is written the character *shǎn chǎ*, which means the "seat of the soul," and perhaps the name and age of the departed. This is set up before the worshipper in "ancestral" service, and fixes his attention

as the abode of the spirit. The first prayer invokes the
spirit; the last "escorts it on its departure." When the
worship is over, this little bit of wood is no more sacred
than any other. These tablets were sometimes carried
to the field of battle, as the ark of the Israelites was
brought into the camp. During the dynasty of Chan a
living descendant of the same name took the place of
the tablet, as the vehicle of the ancestral spirit. This
change probably originated in a truly spiritual perception
of the thing desired; but it was only a fashion, and passed
away. Those of us who have had the great privilege of
praying with Theodore Parker, and remember how he
bowed in spirit before the "Father and Mother" of us
all, not knowing in what other way to express his sense
of the divine tenderness, cannot fail to be interested to
know that the same transcendental ruler of the Chan
dynasty called God the "father and mother" of creatures, as the Emperor was the "father and mother" of
his people!

The Emperor, worshipping for his race, made his offerings at the summer and winter solstice. These offerings were tributes of love and duty merely, and neither
propitiatory nor vicarious, but attended with music and
dancing from the beginning; and the period of observ-
ance naturally connects them with the original sun-
worship of Central Asia.

It seems, too, as if the "bull" had a good deal to do
with this solstitial service, for seven hundred years before Christ a court poet wrote, —

"In autumn comes the autumnal rite
　　With bulls, whose horns in summer bright
　　Were capped with care, — one of them white."

"And, see, they place the goblet full,
　　In figure fashioned as a bull."

From the first the Chinese seem to have held the goodness of human nature as a tenet; and Dr. Legge admits that Mencius anticipated the statements of Butler, and that two hundred years before Moses was born T'ang ascended the throne and proclaimed the essential goodness of human nature. That the Chinese believed in immortality he admits; but Confucius did not encourage precise views of a subject he did not himself understand. Dr. Legge points out very emphatically that the Emperor cannot be called a "high priest," since there are no priests in China. It does not seem to have occurred to him that the first ruler might have wished to abolish a priestly class as Moses certainly did, and yet that in his own person he might have furnished an historic precedent for the priestly functions of the emperor.

It will be clear to you that, with all its openness to deterioration, the popular ancestral worship could never be responsible for what I have found in California. It could not explain the figures in the temples, the propitiations of the evil one, or the sale of amulets; neither could Buddhism pure and simple. I was therefore compelled to investigate the perplexing subject of Taoism. Well was it for me that just as the necessity arose I was able to control Dr. Legge's last publication, to talk with Basil Hall Chamberlain, and to read the appendix to Miss Bird's "Letters from Japan."

In China Tao-ism is the name of a very transcendental philosophy of which Lao-tsze was the chief exponent. This is as mystic as Kant or Concord could desire. It is also the name of a very low order of worship,—a polytheistic religion of which this same philosopher is the chief god; a religion sustained by magic and incan-

tations, in which the worship of evil forces and a belief
in transmigration are united to a faith in purgatory and
hell, and which last is painted on the temple walls in
an apartment called by foreigners "The Chamber of
Horrors."

It will seem to you that this is hard enough to understand, but it is made still harder by the.fact that this
worship has for the last thousand years put on many
of the external shows of Buddhism. Dr. Legge himself does not seem to understand how this system
of magic could have arisen from a super-spiritual
philosophy; but it seems to me a very simple thing.
Such a philosophy entrusted to wholly ignorant people,
to whom it is by its nature unintelligible, naturally
degenerates into precisely this. What can a Chinese coolie make of a philosopher who wants him "to
taste without knowing the flavor"? What can he
think of a leader who says, "The common people are
full of discrimination : I alone have none,"—or who tells
him that he does not know the name of the mother of
all things, but will call her "the Way"?

To all the other puzzles is added the fact that the
Tao-ists are acknowledged by the State as the disciples
of Confucius are ; and it is a common saying that "whatever disorder afflicts the empire, the Changs and the
Kings have no occasion to be disturbed," — the Changs
being the leaders of the Tao-ists.

Since A. D. 1015 the chief of the Tao-ists has had
large tracts of land near Lung-hu, which were granted
as a perpetual endowment.

It was not till after the beginning of the Christian
era that the philosophy degenerated into a system of
magic, although a great deal of superstition is evident

in the writings of the Tao-ist philosopher, Lieh-tsze, three centuries before it.

You will remember that when I entered the joss-house in Pine Street I found there three seated images. It is the only spot I have found which has reminded me of a Buddhist temple, but the attendant asserted that it was not Buddhist, and pointing to the chief figure, he asserted that it was "all the same as" my Jesus! These three figures I now find to be the "Three Holy Ones of the Tao-ists." The chief of the three who is "all the same as Jesus" is Lao-tsze himself. The next is "Hin Hwang," a magician of the Chang family, who takes charge of all earthly affairs; and the third is Chaos or Confusion, and I do not think it is at all strange that he should be worshipped in this category!

It was probably about the year 65 that the influences of Buddhism took hold of a loose bundle of superstitions, and helped to precipitate from them this definite form. Confucius saw the whole thing coming, and said, like St. Paul, "Respect the spirits and keep aloof from them." In spite of the assertion that there are no priests in China, the Chang family hold a predominant relation to the Tao-ists and wear upon their heads a sort of badge made of wood, which Dr. Legge calls the "yellow top." Every one of this family is a magician; and it was one of them who came to the assistance of the Emperor and filled the stage with wraiths and half invisible creatures, in the play which I saw at the "Gold Cinnamon Garden."[1] The presence of inferior deputies of this family can alone account for the sale of amulets and charms in San Francisco. The dread of spirits is both the Chinaman's nightmare and his waking horror, and

[1] See p. 373-379.

by pandering to this the "yellow tops" maintain their sway. They teach a belief in three souls, — one which clings to the corpse ; one in the ancestral tablet ; and one which passes into purgatory. An account of this purgatory may be found in "Strange Stories from a Chinese Studio," by Herbert A. Giles, published in London only this year. The purgatory involves trans-migration, and in it bones are beaten, bodies scorched, flesh is scalded with hot oil, and tongues are pulled out! The whole list of horrors has a very Magian sound. If by repentance a creature escapes punish-ment, by five virtuous acts it earns a reward ; if it be a woman, she shall be born as a man ! Is there not some innocent crime one might commit to escape that ?

The mystical words of Lao-tsze, as Dr. Legge says, conducted this forlorn people to the brink of a great prospect, where they looked down upon a sea of mist. I think Julien was quite right when he wrote of the Tao, "Il est un être confus." It was never infinite, but sadly limited by the weakness and dim-sightedness of its prophet. For, after all, we must judge of the real power of a philosophy or a religion by its concrete results.

The deity whom I commonly found enthroned in the joss-house was Kar Quon ; but none of the educated Chinese know about him. Kwang Kung, the Chinese Mars, is evidently quite another person. I found in the temples offerings of food on wooden trays, and what the Japs call *gohei*,— slender rods fringed with white paper, intended in Japan to attract the rays of the Divine Sun. I could not find out their supposed use in San Francisco.

The god is supposed to be in the temple ; the wor-shipper claps his hands to "attract his attention !" but there is no service. He buys long paper tubes filled with the sweet dust of the sandal-wood, and burns them before the images. The Dog Fo is everywhere a creature who seems to be propitiated. At the funerals the living and the dead are supposed to eat together, although the visible food is sold again for strangers to eat. The tablets in *this* case *are* fetiches, for a lamp is kept burning before each as long as the bereaved relative can pay for it. Gilded paper is scattered at the funerals to propitiate the devil.

One anomaly I cannot understand. In Japan the number of household gods is almost infinite, and in every house there is a " god shelf," which we should probably translate " altar" if we respected the faith. On it is a temple, a tablet, the household gods, oblations of food and flowers, and a burning lamp. Something like this is to be found in many Chinese homes in San Francisco; and why? Dr. Legge does not allude to any such custom.

I do not undertake to go into the philosophy of Lao-tsze; that you can easily read up for yourself. But until this last little book of Dr. Legge's was issued, it was almost impossible to find out anything about this system of magic. The Chinese in San Francisco show a great dread of death. They do not like to be in a house where death occurs. If they foresee it they will leave the best employer. They expect it to be averted by charms and prayers, and will entreat their employers to have recourse to them when the physician fails. I suppose no rational account of this could be given; but I never saw it alluded to.

From the City Hall we went through the famous Plaza, where in the early days so many pronunciamentos were made, and so many executions took place. It is now a

pretty city square, with trees, fountains, and an iron rail,
which last we may suppose to typify the decent restraints
of law.   The old Post-office and other buildings which
surround it now swarm with Chinamen, who make everything untenantable by any other nationality.   Duffield took us first to a joss-house, but it was not so
neat or attractive as the one I have described.   He asserted that from the time these shrines are first erected
they are never cleaned.   I felt it necessary to raise my
dress from the floor, but the beautiful marble stairways
of the Capitol are far more untidy.   As we passed
through the streets we were the objects of undisguised
curiosity, freely indulged.   The men were dirty and
wretched beyond conception, and swarmed from narrow
alleys hardly ten feet broad, where they crouched cooking or eating in doorways.   On one street we stopped
before a stall, where the officer informed me that everything exposed for sale was stolen.   He took up what
looked like a cheap fan, opened it, and displayed a long
knife which could easily deal a fatal blow.   Laws against
the wearing of arms might be easily evaded by this fan
in a workman's belt.

A great many bright-looking girls of ten or twelve
were running about the streets.   These do all the drudg-
ery of the quarter, and are in training for prostitution
if attractive enough.   They are sold when quite young
for two hundred dollars or more, and later for four hundred.   Prostitutes crossed our path at every step.   Some
of them in quite common clothes had their hair so superbly dressed as to attract my attention.   It was bound
and fastened with elegant daggers or bodkins.   I believe
the hair is dressed only once a week.   Miss Bird thinks
the uvario japonica is used to clean and dress the hair;

but here it is a bandoline made from a Sapinda, popularly called soap-wort. It glazes the hair to the point
of brittleness and would certainly break it all up if the
Chinese women lay on soft pillows as we do. Now and
then one of these women passed us, swollen with disease
or devoured with ulceration. I saw one case of elephantiasis, which I might not have guessed had I not seen it
before, and one or two of evident leprosy. The whole
population, as I moved among it, gave me an extraordinary conviction of great physical depression and general disease. At last we came to the joss-house of one
of the commercial companies. This special company
claims to be a sort of masonic society, but is actually an
association working for the mutual protection of thieves
and assassins. The Chinaman whom Duffield called to
guide me through it is a man who is supposed to be a
frequent assassin, and who committed two murders in a
street brawl a few weeks ago. He is out of prison on
three thousand dollars bail, and evidently has no idea of
suffering for his crime.

On the first floor was a sort of trading-room with mottoes on the wall, a silk panel bearing the picture of the
usual demi-god, attended by two women. I made a fresh
attempt to get at the name, but in vain. On the next
floor was a joss-house, and here I repeated my question.
The murderer shook his head and said, "He good man; he
die; take care of you, me, and all folks not bad;" but I
suspected it was just the other way, and was told afterward that this was a place where the "dangerous classes" sought protection for their misdeeds. As the murderer spoke he drew his finger across his throat with a
disagreeable guzzle, which perhaps indicated that this
was the god of the assassin. A piazza built out from

this room gave us a fine view of the Bay. Banners, paper lanterns, and pots of flowers made it look exactly like a piazza on a tea-tray.

We went next to the Jackson Street joss-house, the oldest in the city. In the outer room we found three shrines exactly like that I have described, except that these were much more splendid in decoration: gold and vermilion blazed everywhere.

Behind the large central figure of the "good man" was a long, narrow room with a shrine at each end, but without any screens. Here the women come to worship. At the lower end of this room was a very plain shrine with the usual deity, attended by a large Dog Fo covered with crimped paper or crape, made to resemble curled hair, — a most curious toy. At the upper end was the image of a truly fine-looking woman. On the dirty floor, half-way between the two, was a cheap tablet of white card-board, with a taper burning before it. This was the remnant of a late funeral service. To this place, after the funeral, the women related to a dead Chinaman come to have a sort of mass said for his soul. They are clad in white, and execute a sort of dance, leaving the taper alight when they go away.

This mass never costs less than forty dollars. Fortunately the attendant was able to tell me the story of the woman on the shrine. She is Kwanyin, goddess of mercy, and was the child of poor parents who lived three thousand seven hundred years ago. Her family wished to sell her to a lover, which meant prostitution, and she refused to go. They beat her cruelly. She took refuge with the Emperor, who, finding her divinely beautiful, married her. According to Chinese etiquette, when she, an inferior, was raised to the throne, all her family should have been beheaded to guard against possible disgrace. But she forgave them all the cruel wrong to which they had been a party, and pleaded against the custom, until the Emperor found for each one a position of trust.

This is the only place where women can worship publicly. The joss-houses are very small, for there is no "hour of prayer" and no congregation. Each worshipper goes when he feels the need. Some extra fine sandal-dust tapers were given me here, and a square of silk paper with a gilded centre, which represents a prayer, — or, as some say, the money paid for a prayer.

Next we went to a Chinese market, where we saw bushels of dried fish so small that each looked like a silver thread, and many less pleasant things. There was something that resembled bunches of slender string beans about fourteen inches long, growing from one common stem; a long root that looked precisely like a string of small sausages washed with gamboge, for it was girt in at regular intervals; and there was one sweet, pure-looking vegetable, white as the driven snow, five or six inches in diameter and as long as one's forearm, which I instinctively called a radish! The Japanese call the food prepared from it *daikon;* and it is even more offensive to the untrained nostril than the vilest *sauer-kraut.* Miss Bird calls it, as I did, *Raphanus Sativus;* but the botanists do not accept the name, and think it some other *Raphanus.* The root is dried and also pickled in brine filled with bran, which of course occasions fermentation. When it has lain in this three months it is taken out and stewed, the odor driving every civilized being out of the house. Whoever has ever left the last radish of the spring too long in a glass

of water can guess what this odor is like. I saw the Li
Chi and the bacchantic nut, which looks like a goat's
head with two long horns, which is sometimes called
"sea-chestnut." Then there were ʼqueer little bricks
of a bright-yellow color stamped in India ink, with the
maker's name in large letters. These are a sort of muffin made of beans boiled to a stiff paste, with sugar and
Carrageen moss! At the far end of the shop, where all
these abominations were to be bought, was a rough
counter at which half-a-dozen Celestials were stolidly
eating with chop-sticks, every mouthful bearing witness
to great manual dexterity.

On one side of this street was a three-storeyed building, with as many piazzas gaily decorated in colors and
with paper lanterns. It was a restaurant. We entered
through a vile baker's shop, entirely open to the street
on the front side. Round cakes, weighing each almost
a pound, covered the counters on every side. They
looked like a very plump Chater's muffin, and contained
chopped fat and curry. On the next floor was a very
bare eating-room for the common customer, and above
that another, with finely carved ebony chairs and small
richly wrought tea-tables with marble tops, such as we
often put into our drawing-rooms. Cheap pictures in
crape adorned the recesses, where hard couches were
spread with carpets and pillows, that the guests may
retire to smoke opium. Different qualities of tea, from
the finest "mandarin" down to leaves which have been
twice dried, are served on these three floors.

We went next to a butcher's, where we saw a whole
hog prepared for roasting. This is baked slowly in a
sort of stone well, heated from above and below, having a cover for coals like our old Dutch oven, only of

course much larger. In the doorway sat a man eating soup out of three different bowls with one pair of chopsticks, and we all stood and looked at him till he laughed! I had never thought of him as human until that moment! He bore the inspection in a shame-faced but good-humored way. In the cellar-ways we saw groups of gamblers, with unimaginable horrors in their rear. I never shall forget the narrow alleys which I threaded amid a crowd of silent figures. The stealthiness of the Chinese makes him unendurable; I would rather every joint bend with the report of a cannon.

I went into some shops. My disposition to purchase was thwarted by the fact that the traders could not even talk "pigeon English"! I bought a box, some harlequins, and some women's hairpins of opaque glass, handsomely cut in imitation of jade. Things were sold at fancy prices. They have a bulb for sale, which is I think the narcissus. They call it the "New Year's lily," and it bears the same relation to their New Year that the holly does to our Christmas. To offer it to a friend is to say, "Good luck, and a happy New Year!" A rich man died and left three sons. The two older cheated the younger and gave him no share of the money, only a rocky farm. It would yield nothing; and, while sorely troubled, the lad fell asleep and dreamed that the "Great Heaven" had taken pity on him. He was told to go out in the morning and dig for gold. He found no gold, only thousands upon thousands of little bulbs, which sold readily and brought him "good luck."

We made two calls this afternoon,—one on Miss O. at Mr. B.'s, where we saw some very rare and beautiful articles from Japan; among them an immense incense-burner from an old Buddhist temple, which bore the

crest of both the Mikado and the Tycoon, which is
something I never saw before. The other was on Mrs.
A., one of my son's old friends, the widow of our late
minister to China.

Her story is another proof of the inadequate protection
afforded to women by our Government. Her husband
made a Roman Catholic his executor, without understanding that he was a Jesuit. This man appropriated
all her ready money, and applied to the courts for leave
to sell the real estate. Then Mrs. A. interposed ; leave
was not granted. Mr. A.'s private secretary sold the
most valuable personal property and cheated her out of
the proceeds. As she cannot yet sell her real estate she
is extremely poor, and cannot even go home to her Eastern friends.

In the evening I went to the public meeting of the
Academy of Sciences. The building in which the Academy meets is dirty, dreary, and forlorn, — enough to put
a wet blanket on the most shining light. There were a
great many interesting things told, but every member
apparently spoke with the greatest reluctance and without the slightest interest in what he was saying.

There was something about California pines, a paper
about ray and cuttle fish, and an acknowledgment of
the reception of a piece of bees-wax from Sitka, —
part of the cargo of a Japanese vessel wrecked there
in 1833. Three survivors of this wreck were picked
up by the Hudson Bay Company and carried to
China. They were refused permission to return to
Japan by the Government, to whom their destitute
condition was referred. Having been adopted by Gutz-
laff they finally made their way in disguise to a small,
uninhabited Japanese island, through a part of Siberia ;

and, pleading a wreck, were taken off by some fishermen.
By keeping silence over their adventures, they probably
eluded the death penalty pronounced at that time on all
travelled Japs!

San Francisco, Sept. 8, 1880. — "And he wist not
that his face shone!" — these were the words which
flashed across my mind as I turned away from Starr
King's church last Saturday. If anything can recon-
cile the human soul to sharp and unusual sorrows, it
must be the consciousness that it has so responded to
the divine touch as to become in an unwonted degree
the medium of divine power to other bereaved or har-
assed creatures. It is in this way that the hearts of a
parish come truly near to its minister, and a foundation
is honestly laid for the kingdom of God on earth. In the
Sunday-school room I found about three hundred souls,
counting teachers and children; and their faces seemed
so homelike that I half fancied myself in Boston while
I spoke to them. The superintendent, Mr. Murdoch,
was once a pupil in our old Indiana Place Chapel.

A quarter of a century ago, before Mr. Hayward had
left any money to the India mission, and at intervals
ever since, I have heard a great deal said about the folly
of sending preachers to the heathen, and the great need
of money for "home missions." I wonder where the
"home mission" is. Is it in my neighbor's kitchen, at
Five Points, among the negroes of the exodus, or among
the untaught "white trash" still roaming the highlands
of our Southern States?

Not much is doing in these directions by Unitarians;
yet as I have come across the continent my very soul
cries out bitterly, "If my people really believe, why do

they not send out their prophets to take possession of the land?" Where are you, young men, who ought to be filling these Western pulpits? After the magnificent opening which Starr King made for you here, the truth should have risen new-born on these Western shores! When I say "pulpit," I do not mean a massive structure of wood and drapery, but simply a place to preach, — a place which would widen before a young man's powerful plea until it might embrace a bishopric.

We all of us heard a while ago that Rev. E. P. Tenney, the author of "Coronation," had been made President of Colorado College. Because of *his* associations, we were inclined to think it must be a Congregational institution; but on examination we find that it is simply *Christian*, asking no doctrinal pledges on the part of any one connected with it. What it is doing, in an absolutely silent way, here in the West, none of us have guessed. It is entering all the empty vineyards, while we stand talking. When the Faculty find a field untilled, they look about for a person who is qualified to do the work needed. As soon as he can be reached, he is created a professor of the college, salaried, and sent to his work. In many ways the liberal thinker has a better chance to reach the lowest scale of humanity than the evangelical preacher. Why is he not awake to his opportunity?

Few of our people, I think, know what manner of man the Leadville miner is. Last year at this time, it is said, not a woman had ever been seen in the streets of that direful place. Now a few, connected by blood or interest with what is going on there, may be traced on their isolated path. And yet if a few *could* go, for higher reasons, who would understand the whole thing!

I could tell terrible stories of poisonous fumes from the smelting furnaces, of barrels of drinking water standing in the sun till they go putrid, of drains that do not exist, or which exist only to poison a well or a sleeping-room; but if I could take any dear New England woman into the balcony of the Clarendon House, and let her look down upon the great human tide that streams through the Leadville Street, she would not be there thirty minutes before she would know that a far more dangerous current than any I have named sets down that lofty valley, ten thousand feet above the sea, and that nowhere in our broad land can her own children wholly escape its influence. Let her go out into Chestnut Street after dark, and look into the windows of the bar-rooms, gambling hells, and dance saloons. What goes on in such places is everywhere else curtained in from the prying eyes of night itself. Here the bright light streams out from their horrid precincts, to tempt by a cheerful ray whatever young lad or lass may lean against the pane.

If I were a young man, able to endure the exposures of life, and able to raise a small sum among friends who would trust me, I would go straight to Leadville. I would build a clean shanty close to the main street. I would keep its little enclosure free from the disgusting litter that taints the town, and at night I would have hot coffee and a biscuit, and a few pleasant pictures and a good paper or book, ready for any one who should come.

There the wedge should enter. A little step forward was taken the other day, when four prominent traders signed a pledge to close their places of business on Sundays, and so to rescue a few hours for quietness.

Whoever violates this pledge is to give two hundred dollars for the benefit of the town.

"Inspiration is common-sense," wrote Brigham Young in his autobiography, which I held in my hand the other day. Taking these words for a text, how much a Unitarian might do for his people! Is there not a noble field for the Church there? He who would go must be young enough to be enthusiastic, and old enough to know where to seek the instruction which will make him wise in practical matters. All the needs of life can be satisfied here at less expense than in the Eastern States, and a hay-field is as good as a gold-mine. If all Christians had taught what they professed to believe as earnestly as Brigham Young did, there would not have been much room in the world for the fanatic, the polygamist, or the avenger of blood. But, thank God! men must grow as well as trees, and even in Salt Lake valley and San Francisco streets the old ligatures will burst.

At the Art school, under Virgil Williams, I find good drawings and excellent models, but unfortunately the school will not be in session while I am here. I was shown also a fine full-length figure of a woman, which was found in a rural drinking saloon out here, and is supposed to be by Rubens. Whoever painted it, painted it well, and it is evidently very old.

The best picture shop here is kept by Mr. Morris. He imports many very costly *genre* pictures, and shows very good California work, especially in the direction of flower-painting in oils. A little picture of an old grandmother reciting Mother Goose, and another of a mother picking out the stories from the old tiles about a mantelpiece pleased me. Mr. Morris went with me to see Bradford's pictures. They all represent the same scenes under the midnight sun, and the lurid mixture of red and blue in them was not pleasant. I should like to see one of them by itself against a neutral tinted wall. Pictures often put each other out.

Then I went to Mission Street in search of articles made of California woods. After I had gone to bed, there came a telegram from Dr. Buckel asking me to assist at Mrs. Hayes's reception at Oakland. We had already exchanged three or four messages on the subject, on account of the uncertainty of the Presidential plan. I was much struck by the thoughtful kindness with which Dr. Buckel followed the matter up.

San Francisco, Sept. 9, 1880.—Very early this morning we went through crowded streets to Oakland. We met Senator and Mrs. Sargent on the ferry-boat. As our message gave us absolutely no directions for the day, we thought it best to go to Mrs. Sherman's with the Sargents, and try to find Dr. Buckel. It was like meeting an old friend to see Mrs. Sherman,— she is so like our dear Mrs. S., in Buffalo. We were received with the kindest courtesy, and Mr. Sherman walked with us to the Doctor's little house. There another friend of Dr. Tyng's — Dr. Follansbie — received us, and did all she could to make us comfortable. After a light lunch, it was suggested that as we had been invited to go back to the Shermans, we had better go and get a glimpse of the procession. The ladies of the President's party were lunching there; and, in the pleasant company of Mrs. Hayes, Miss Rachel Sherman, Mrs. Audenried, Mrs. Hewin, and Mrs. Mitchel, we soon forgot all about processions. This lunch was a real, thoughtful kind-

ness on the part of Mrs. Sherman, since it enabled
the ladies to rest quietly before going on to the reception.

This reception was given by the Ebell Society of
Oakland.   There was once, as I understand, a certain
Dr. Ebell here, who was in the habit of taking parties
of young ladies to Europe.   They often found themselves unprepared to enjoy what they saw; and, in
accordance with a wish of his, societies were formed
for study, all through the State, to which his name was
given.   The Ebell Society of Oakland holds a monthly
meeting at which papers are read.   I believe it owes a
good deal to Dr. Buckel; and, as I suppose, it is the
best specimen of woman's work in California.   I very
much regret that it will hold no regular meeting during
my stay.   I find it everywhere spoken of with interest
and pride, and I hoped Dr. Buckel would call a special
meeting for my benefit; but the State Fair, and the
uncertain and delayed reception to Mrs. Hayes com-
plicated matters so that she thought it impossible.   The
separate members I shall meet to-day.

Private carriages met us at Mrs. Sherman's to take
the party to Mrs. Hewes's, where the reception occurs.   One was most generously provided for myself
and my daughter; and it carried us to a house, the con-
ventional London suburban villa, situated in limited
grounds, which slope, however, to the very edge of Lake
Merritt.   There are half-a-dozen pleasant rooms on the
first floor of this house connecting with one another;
and on the second, a picture gallery and library.   The
front hall was furnished in a charming way, with
chairs gracefully made of the horns and skin of the
Siberian goat.   The walls of all the rooms were covered

with copies of the old masters. I do not suppose
the reception was held at this house because it was
the most elegant in Oakland, but because Mrs. H.
is a member of the Ebell Society, and because the
family feel a sincere interest in the work Mrs. Hayes
is doing. The society had decorated the whole house
in the most charming way with flowers and ferns, carefully toned to the general effect. The hour that elapsed
before the guests arrived was spent in looking at the
flowers, the pictures, and the lovely Swiss view at the
back of the house.

My heart warmed more than ever to Mrs. Hayes, as,
wearied with her long journey, and in the deep mourning dress she wears for her only brother, she went from
one room to another, listening and enjoying with *genuine* interest. This is what has won the heart of the
people. She is not *civil*, but cordial; not *attentive*, but
interested. She was first received by her invalid hostess, and then we all went through the library to the
upper piazza. Fresh as she was from Lake Tahoe,
Lake Merritt could not have seemed imposing to Mrs.
Hayes; but to me it was truly lovely. The green turf
sloped to the water's edge. Live oak and maple trees
were in the foreground, and beyond the still lake rose
the lofty peaks of the coast range.

It suggested Switzerland, with an altogether lovely
effect. I believe Lake Merritt is an artificial lake, but
if it was made for commercial reasons it certainly adds
greatly to the charms of Oakland. On the lower piazza
an elegant collation was laid; but, as the party had
lunched at Mrs. Sherman's, all further refreshment was
declined. After this was once said not a motion was
made toward the beautifully-laid table; and this rare

good breeding pleased me. In a bend of the piazza a magnificent pyramid of fruit had been erected. Grapes drooped from its edge, and melons, peaches, plums, and pears mingled their superb colors in the pile. But no one disturbed them. So far, I have eaten less fruit in California than I ever ate in the same number of days. Reason, that the fruit which goes to market seems made for the eye only.

When the whole thing was about half over, I was drawn away from a pleasant talk and stroll with Miss Sherman into a comparatively unoccupied room, and introduced to about fifty people, half of them being gentlemen connected with the university at Berkeley.

After all was done we drove back to Dr. Buckel's. On account of the State Fair and the presence of Mrs. Hayes a great many active and interesting women were in town. Many of them, I suppose, are corresponding members of the Ebell Society. For this reason Dr. Buckel and her friends offered me a reception at the Blake House this evening, and there I met most pleasantly about sixty ladies. Almost every subject of interest to women was brought up, and every woman present seemed to have her own special work. Representative women were there from distant parts of the State; and among those who came over from San Francisco was Miss Emma Marwedel, who brought letters to me in Boston when she first came from Europe, and who has now a charming Kindergarten on Franklin Street. Several gentlemen were present, and teased us very kindly about our schemes. I have seldom been in an assembly that pleased me more. It was like many that were held in Boston thirty years ago, but its like could hardly be found there now. Its atmosphere did not so much in-

dicate what was intellectual or literary as common sense,
practical ability, and wise activity.

A Mrs. Condit, engaged as a missionary in the Chinese
quarter, offered to take me into the Chinese homes, and
I do hope I shall have time to go.

The sun and the moon have dropped perpendicular
rays upon us almost every day for a week, but not once
have I been able to see across the Bay.

Sept. 10, 1880. — I went to-day to the rooms of the
Olympic Club. This consists of four hundred of the
finest young men in town, most of whom have bodies
so finely developed that it is a pleasure to look at
them. I am also told that these young men are among
the most "fashionable," but as they are not allowed one
drop of wine or beer I have to pause over the statement. The rooms are the very best. Everything is
provided toward gymnastic exercises, and no drinking or gambling is allowed on the premises. Drawing-rooms, reading-rooms, billiard-rooms, dressing-rooms,
and bathing-rooms seem to revolve about the great
gymnastic hall. The bathing-rooms are adapted to the
supposed or real needs of gymnasts, and have showers
and douches that may be used on every part of the
body.

To-night I went again to the Mechanics' Fair, as I had
some purchases to make. The evening was far gone
when music and bells announced the arrival of the very
uncertain Presidential party, whom no one now expected.
Poor Miss Marvædel was in despair. She had at first
been promised by some very unwise official that Mrs.
Hayes should certainly visit her pretty Kindergarten.
Inspired by that hope, some one wrote some verses of

greeting for the brightest little girl to recite to Mrs. Hayes, and every child prepared a specimen of her work, which was tied into a fanciful little book. Imagine the despair of the children, when, after all this, they were coolly told that "Mrs. Hayes would have no time for Kindergartens!"

Miss Marwedel has her section at the Fair, and the unwise but tender heart of somebody inclined him to promise that Mrs. Hayes should certainly pause there to speak to Miss Emma and receive the children's book. It was very soon apparent that even this would not happen; so I tucked my bewildered little friend under my arm and hurried away to the Tropical Garden, where Mrs. Hayes was looking at fountains in crimson, orange, and purple light. As soon as the procession moved on I took the little book from its timid and speechless possessor and put it into Mrs. Hayes's hand. I did think my Presidentess an angel when she smiled and responded. But "Oh, what a bold woman!" was all the reward that I got from my overwhelmed little Belgian!

Sept. 11, 1880.—I went this afternoon to the rooms of the Chinese consul; but he had gone home to prepare for General McDowell's Presidential reception. The vice-consul, in an elegant drapery of black velvet, purple brocade, and white silk, pooh-poohed the whole matter of the religion of the Chinese, about which I went to inquire. He said they worshipped stick or stone, — anything, anybody! To which I replied indignantly that it was quite evident that he never entered their temples; for in all the joss-houses in San Francisco it was quite clear that only one hero was worshipped. I asked him why his people were so unwilling to answer very simple questions about their customs. To which he replied that they had no ideas ! I asked him why it was necessary for sensible people to talk to them in "pigeon English," and he said again, "They have no ideas." Say, "Light fire, other room," and a man will go and do it; tell him to take up the kindling and go into the other room and light a fire, and he will stand still bewildered. The connecting links of a sentence mean nothing to him. It is not uncommon for a Chinese to say to a new mistress, without the slightest intentional disrespect, "You talkee too much !" They know most of the words which communicate facts.

I am much struck by the inarticulate character of their tongue. The vice-consul thought Mr. Bee would give me an interpreter when I come back from the South.

I then went to the Protestant Episcopal Mission, where the native teacher gave me the name of Kar Quon as that of the popular deity. The joss-houses look far more like Roman Catholic shrines than Buddhist temples, but there is no doubt that they are simply Tao-ist as they exist to-day.

We went to the theatre which the Presidential party attended, to see Niñon. The house is small and gaily decorated. The acting was very fine, but the play most unfortunately chosen, if the object were to refresh the travelling party. It was a story of Marat and the French Revolution, and more than once the stage was filled by a blood-thirsty mob, which was altogether too well presented.

Sept. 12, 1880. — A sermon full of vital power from Dr. Stebbins. As I came home I passed many groups

of much painted Chinese women standing at a street
corner under the charge of two old men. As I stood
looking at them, I thought what a pleasant family story
I could have imagined of these young creatures, if there
had been no one to tell me that these men were two
" procurers " advertising their last arrivals at the street
corners.

A Résumé.

The things to be found in the markets of San Francisco are very different from what one expects to find.
The piled-up figs and grapes, apples, peaches, pears,
and nectarines, which scent the air and fill the eye
with beautiful color, do not tempt the Eastern palate,
accustomed to concentrated sweets and sours. They
tell me I must go South to find out what California
fruit really is, and I am going, but without much
hope.

As the people of all nations congregate here, some
dish from every other gets to each one's table. I ought
to have said before, that fruit is quite as dear as it is at
the East, only of a different sort. We have no figs nor
rare grapes, and our plums do not grow as large ; but we
give as large a bulk of the fruit we do grow for the same
price. The fish-market is a poor one, and not nicely
kept. An Eastern purchaser on his first arrival will
waste a good deal of time in looking for a neater place.
Vegetables and fruit are all picked too early. I have
been frequenting the market for a month, and have
never yet seen a ripe tomato. The meats are very inferior to those in the Eastern stalls. These things are
not said captiously, but to comfort those who fancy
everything good can be found in California, from a gold

nugget to a "golden drop." I have seen no new vegetable, unless the artichoke be one.

The horrors of the Chinese market I do not know how
to describe. I have not seen rats or mice exposed for sale,
but far more repulsive articles, consisting of the entrails
of many creatures. Beside that, and far worse, is the
disgusting odor of their meat, for they do not like it fresh;
and every article of food is as fat as possible. Nothing
that can have nutriment in it is despised by them, and
the terribly diseased condition of their common people
may be one of the results. Many things they bring from
China, — dried snails, a dozen kinds of tiny dried fish,
cakes of spawn, and so on. They make a sort of meat-pie
by the thousand, which ought to have been described in
Dante's "Inferno." It would nauseate Lucifer himself;
and yet it looks, when first baked, like an innocent egg-
muffin. There are radishes which are as white as snow,
and weigh about three pounds each, — the only attractive things I saw. They cut these in slices for a salad.
There are black nuts which ought to be sacred to Bac-
chus, for they look exactly like a ram's head and
horns. There are also enormous cucumbers and egg-
plants.

In the shops where all these things are sold they cut
up whole hogs, or split them open, flatten them out as
we do a prairie-hen, and cook them whole in a circular
furnace, built of stone or adobe. When baked they are
almost as brittle as a stick of candy, but they are not
burned. The Chinese have the reputation of being a
cleanly people, but they are not so. They are orderly,
and have been so for untold ages, and the whole character of their government sustains this characteristic;
but the common people are filthy beyond belief. I

should not dare to tell what I have seen. The confidence of the European races in Chinese cleanliness grows out of the Chinese imitativeness, which makes them — when no stronger motive intervenes — do exactly as they have been taught. It was necessary to say this, because both filthy habits and orderly ways are very conspicuous in the markets of which I speak. These consist of the lower story of an ordinary house with the front wall knocked out. In the doorway are the sample baskets, strings of unmentionables, and odors unendurable. Imagine, too, a floor which was never washed. Half-way back are the furnace, the baker's oven, or the chopping-block, as the case may be. The workmen swarm like bees, and run over each other like ants. If they were Irishmen they would quarrel, and nothing would be done; but the Chinaman follows his own path in silence, and order is the result. Across the top of the room is a board with seats; and here, in the very presence of all that is offensive, as many as can sit are eating with their chop-sticks. The place is so crowded you can hardly get to the stairs.

To-day has been Sunday. There was a military review this morning, and all the unclean are abroad. When I came home from church I was invited to dine with a friend's family at the Italian restaurant. As a matter of curiosity, perhaps an account of the meal is worth giving. The cost is "four bits," or fifty cents to each person. Not much is spent on service. The dining-room is on the level of the street. Long tables covered with coarse gray-looking cloths run through it, of the quality that a shop-girl or merchant's clerk would expect at the East. Nothing has been spent on mirrors or chandeliers, and the floor cannot be clean, and is not.

When we entered, the room was nearly full of men, women, and children, chattering in all conceivable tongues. If I did not hear Hebrew, some of those sharp-nosed, sleek-haired, dark men with pointed beards could certainly speak it. Before us — a party of five — was a square table, with a stiff napkin for each and a somewhat sticky knife and fork. The castor, Worcester-shire, mustard, and pickle jars were in the centre, and looked clean. A goblet filled with ice was given to each of us, and two bottles of good California claret set down. For the " four bits " each person was served with eight *entrèes*, — they could hardly be called courses : —

1. Salad and bread.
2. Soup.
3. Fish, or mussels.
4. Vermicelli.
5. Chicken-stew, with oyster patties.
6. Fried cream, or beef, mutton, or veal.
7. Dessert, — whipped cream, pie, and a strip of pastry, on one plate.
8. Coffee, black, or with cream and sugar, and with peach brandy or " kisch."

The salad was made of shrimps, crabs, lobster, or po-tato. It was served neatly on two crisp leaves of let-tuce, and Delmonico never seasoned it better. The bread was French and perfectly acid. The soup was tomato, chicken, or *bouillon*. I tried the *bouillon*, and found myself served with a pint-bowl of amber-colored liquid, which would have been improved by boiling down seven eighths. My friends took tomato and found no fault. For the third course a large platter of mus-sels, hot from the fire, was served to each one of us

which we were expected to open and eat with our fingers.
They were about one fourth the size of those on Massachusetts coasts, and very sweet.   The next course proved
in my case the *piece de resistance*.   It was a good-sized
plate of vermicelli, well-cooked, and dressed with beef
gravy, seasoned with cheese, Worcestershire, and tomato.   It looked and tasted good; and, as I was very much
afraid I should not get enough dinner out of my eight
entrèes, I devoted myself to this.   Then came chicken
stew with oyster patties.   This dish looked nice, and
was fit for the ordinary stomach, but would prove unsuited to any delicate digestion.   The chicken had certainly taken too much exercise.   It was a very gymnast
of a chicken, but it served to flavor a stew of cymlins
or summer-squash, and tomatoes cut in slices in a rich
gravy.   An oyster patty was put on the same plate
when the stew was served, and this was made in the
ordinary pastry-cook's fashion, — each patty containing
two or three of the invisible California oysters "smothered in cream," like Anacreon's pomegranates.   We
were next asked whether we would have "fried cream,"
or a plate of beef, mutton, or veal, with the usual vegetables.   We said "fried cream," because we did not
know what it was.   A platter heaped with what looked
like slender rice croquettes was then brought, flaming
with brandy, and a bottle of peach-brandy or "kīsch"
was set down beside it.   This dish is well worth intro-
ducing to Northern tables.   A nicely-made "Italian
cream," shaped in a "brick," is cut into pieces of a solid
sort, which are dipped in oil and then sprinkled thickly
with cracker-crumbs.   They are piled neatly on a dish,
peach-brandy poured all over them and set on fire.
The cream is browned to the consumer's taste, the quan-

tity of brandy not being limited. Of course the alcohol
is consumed, and only a very delicate flavor remains,
the cream not being melted as it would be if set on the
fire. At dessert, whipped cream, custard pies, and pies
made of green-apple marmalade, as well as slender slips
of pastry to eat with the cream, were put on one plate
for each. Coffee was served black, or with cream and
sugar, for each of us, — well-made Central American
coffee, not the finest Mocha. Then one of the gentlemen took a saucer full of lumps of sugar, which he filled
with "kisch," and set it on fire. This burned until a
light-brown syrup succeeded, — not in the least like that
produced by French brandy. Of this, two or three tea-
spoonfuls were put in each cup. The alcohol is wholly
consumed, and what remains is pure flavor. It does
not improve the black coffee, but gives a delicate bitter-
almond taste to that served with cream. This may be
agreeable when an ordinary berry is used. Nothing
can improve Mocha.

I have described this dinner so minutely in order
to show what can be had for fifty cents. For myself
I should prefer four courses, with a larger proportion
of soap and water.

In spite of all the wealth in California, one is often
struck with the absence of refinement on great occasions. At one of the most elegant entertainments I
have seen here, a superb pyramid of fruit was piled in
the centre of the table. At the last moment, apparently, the grapes seemed likely to break with their own
weight, and two or three newspapers were insinuated
beneath, plainly evident to the guests at the supper!
The "blood of the grape" would have been a much less
offensive sight.

We went through the Chinese quarter as we returned from dinner. The Chinese never put up a curtain; and through the broad low windows of their shops, all with brilliantly lighted interiors, it was quite pleasant to watch their performances. In the barbers' shops the men were having their queues braided, and their eyes, noses, and ears cleaned out with a padded probe, while little children played round their feet. They were as indifferent to our inspection as if they had been slugs on a garden wall.

Sept. 13, 1880.—I went to-day to see Mrs. ——, simply to look at her jewels. I had warned her before that I should come, and I am sure it gave her pleasure to see how they pleased me. Diamonds she has and to spare, with many other wonderful things; but in these days diamonds are not startling. What did startle me into so strange a proceeding, were two magnificent rings, each worthy to be a king's ransom. One is a blue turquoise, about half an inch in length and a third of an inch wide. And when I write blue, I do not mean bluish gray or green, but something as blue as the heaven itself. The other was a pink pearl of about the same size, vivid as the heart of a damask rose, and creamed all over in the most perfect way. Both stones were set in a circlet of diamonds. Her husband has a passion for rings, and these were two of his gifts. I looked at them, as I might at a star or a cloud, with simple delight.

I was invited to a crab supper, which I enjoyed; but not even the shell-fish here have the full flavor of the Atlantic shore. The Pacific ocean itself is deficient in salt.

San Francisco to Stockton, Sept. 14, 1880. — To-day we started for Stockton, and in preparing we encountered another little episode of travel entirely unsuited to a civilized community. I was sent to an office under the Palace Hotel, to get tickets and checks. There were two clerks in attendance, who said that tickets used to be sold there, but were now only sold at the ferry; that the express would not undertake to check baggage at the house, unless I went down in advance and bought my tickets, which was all right enough, — so away I went. Leaving the office, I turned to say, " Be sure you send the checks ; there are two trunks to go." " Oh," said the clerk, " the man will have a dozen, checks, and you must be ready at half-past two."

About twelve o'clock, before we were fully packed, the " express " appeared and demanded our baggage. He had no check, and refused to give any receipt for the articles ; so, much disappointed, I sent him away. A neighbor passing at the time volunteered to send a carriage, which I allowed. The hour passed, and Mr. W. was despatched on the same errand again. When the carriage came, it refused to take the trunks, which were only large valises, although it had been warned. I insisted ; and, after all, we barely caught the train. Because we went as far as Lathrop on our through tickets to Los Angeles, and bought a way-ticket from Lathrop to Stockton, the road would only check our luggage to Lathrop, which we reached after dark, thus adding most unnecessarily to our small perplexities.

We moved through a very level country, with marshes or the Bay itself to the northeast, strange as that will sound. The Coast Range was between us and the sea. They were threshing wheat by steam on several ranches.

I did not like to see them. Bucolics bid fair to be impossible to the poet who comes after the nineteenth century. Now and then a pleasant homestead appeared. High hedges shut lawns of emerald away from the brown waste.

Certainly the "Father of Lies" must have settled California, for no one can speak the truth here even by accident! Instead of the three hours we were promised, we soon saw that it would be five before we should reach Stockton; and my daughter was faint with hunger. At Lathrop, Cousin Will appeared; and after we got into the Stockton cars things went smoothly enough. We drove from the dépôt to the house in the clear light of the moon, and I found that my spirits had risen with the fog. Four dogs, and a lovely woman clad in white came out to meet us, as we entered a house spotlessly kept.

A supper of fruit, ham, eggs, potatoes, bread, and delicious coffee was soon set before us, followed by a second course of ice-cream and cake.

Sept. 15, 1880.—Early this morning I went out into the grounds. I am afraid I never can call anything a *garden*, which has neither a grass plat nor one green-bordered bed. Beds can easily be bordered by dew plants here, but few persons seem to think of it. This house stands in a clump of live-oak, quite a distance in from the road. Never did Eastern mortal see so beautiful an oleander as stands by the gate. It is more than twelve feet high, has many stems, and the flowers are double, of the color of a damask rose, and they fill the air with sweetness. The live-oaks are covered with ivy to their topmost boughs. Jessamine covers the porch, where pretty potted plants are in bloom, and hanging baskets swing. By looking at some hedges I discovered, much to my amazement, that what is sometimes called a "scrub oak" here, is really a sort of holly! There is a very curious ailanthus here, covered with beautiful pods. It has no disagreeable odor when in bloom. The flowering maple shades the house, and the delicate pepper tree adds everywhere its lines of fragile grace. The pepper tree is the most delicious thing in California. It looks like an acacia. I have heard that in India it requires a support like a vine. Here it forms a strong but slender trunk that has the gently swaying character of our white birch. The foliage is of a delicate green, the blossom almost invisible, for I have not observed it, while the bright scarlet fruit hangs in graceful bunches after the manner of grapes. This tree holds such a place in the tree world as the maribou does in the world of feathers.

I already feel the climate of Stockton the most agreeable I have encountered since I crossed the mountains. One of the torments of the San Francisco climate lies in the fact that you cannot go out early or late without a winter wrap; and if I start for an excursion between the hours of eleven and three, when the thermometer is close on eighty, I must carry an oppressive shawl in reserve. Here one does not feel the change till darkness falls, but there is no pleasant sitting out on the beautiful porch even here. "Come in, you will catch the rheumatism!" is Cousin Will's cry, as soon as the sun disappears. In the early morning, however, I found it delicious; and I puzzled my brains over some common double balsams, or touch-me-nots, growing in pots. I remember seeing some in the conservatory at the park.

What a funny freak of the climate, if it refuses to grow balsams !

We went out to drive soon after breakfast, and passed through the pretty cemetery, where in the Italian style the Monterey cypresses are trimmed so slenderly as to look like tall sentinels. There are many of them around each lot, and they remind me of the tall cactus on the plains. I hear to-day that this cactus is most useful. It is full of threads, which are made into cordage ; and when it begins to grow, the Mexicans cut it off, scoop out the trunk, and as the sap accumulates pour it into pails. It is distilled into *aqua ardiente*. After the growth ceases the root is boiled, and a more delicate sort of liquor distilled from that.

Stockton is well planted with trees. It is a wide plain, dizzy with windmills which control the irrigation. It is surrounded by sloughs, pronounced *slews*. There are a great many New England-like houses, very tidily kept.

A Mr. Weber, an original proprietor here, who was probably insane and certainly very eccentric, gave all the land for the Catholic cemetery and the convent-school. We encountered three small-pox flags as we drove about, and saw the enormous loads of wheat from every part of the adjacent country driven to the already teeming warehouses. Five or six powerful horses were attached to each load. The streets are so quiet that it does not look like a busy town. It is however a base of supply and a wheat centre.

We went to the Asylum and brought the wife of the superintendent home to lunch. She is a charming wo-. man, full of pluck. When she arrived in San Francisco thirty years ago a policeman said to her, " Madam, why did you come ? There is not a decent woman in the State !"—"There is certainly one, now I have got here," was her quick reply.

During her stay we talked of really delightful things. She left us at three o' clock; and as the day was quite hot, although the feel of the icy trade-wind was perceptible under the torrid glow, we rested until Cousin Will brought his friend Mr. C. home to dinner. The latter is full of information and pleasant talk, for he has been here since the State first had a name.

He said it did him good to hear me describe Leadville. He had always wanted one woman to know what a hell California was when he first saw it, and I had described it. When I spoke of the little child leaning against her burro, he went on to say that before ever a woman had set foot here the circuses and strolling theatres came. Everybody went to them, because there was neither society, books, magazines, nor papers. In each troop was a little child, a "California Pet." Nothing ever came so near the heart of the men. When they called her back to the stage they would shower it with gold.

Stockton, Sept. 16, 1880. — Early this morning we took a carriage and drove over to the Insane Asylum, of which Dr. George A. Shurtleff is superintendent. He originally came out here to practise his profession, and when his wife joined him they opened a private boarding house, as much for the comfort of sundry gentle friends as their own advantage.

I believe I went through all the wards, with the exception of the "*Filthy*" male ward; and that I forgot those was due to the satisfaction I felt in the general aspect of things and the charms of the surroundings. I never saw so clean an establishment. The purity of the air is not merely due to the management, but is largely the result of a climate which will allow doors and windows to be kept open all the time. The floors are made of Oregon pine, and they are spotless. So is the surbase of the wainscot; and that means more. In the *"Filthy"* female ward not an odor was perceptible. Never have I seen a sweeter room than one which holds women as helpless as new-born babies. I talked with many of them. A great many nations are represented here. I saw Malays, Lascars, Chinese, Spaniards, Mexicans, half-breeds, Indians, and Chilians! Poor things!

Dr. Shurtleff says that intemperance is the exciting cause of insanity in this State to a greater extent than anywhere in the world. I never saw a finer laundry. There are no regular religious services, but Catholic priests come often to patients of that communion.

We went through the beautiful grounds, and in the vineyards plucked "mission grapes," which I always inquire for, because I am told they are the finest table grape in California, and were brought from Spain by the Franciscans. Half a ton of them are given to the patients here daily, but I did not find a sweet one. I observe that the leaves are allowed to grow over this fruit in California in a way that I never saw anywhere else. I suppose it is on account of the fog, which is perceptible though not heavy even here. In the garden there are five or six century plants in bloom. I am told that the real reason why this name was given to the aloe is that it will live a century if in a climate which does not permit it to bloom. It dies as soon as it has attended to the duty of perpetuation, and the blossoming occurs in its fifth or sixth year, if it has a rapid growth.

The blossom-stalk shoots up from the centre at the rate of fourteen inches a day, and to the height of thirty to thirty-five feet. Branches issue from it on every side, so as to form a sort of pyramid of greenish-yellow flowers, which well sheltered will keep in bloom for two or three months. This flower-stem is cut off if the natives want to make *pulque*, and the juice of the leaves, which lathers well with salt and fresh water alike, is pressed into cakes and used for soap. There were a good many nuts on these stalks, but I could not get one of full size. The castor-oil plant rose everywhere in princely beauty, all its spiked fruit crimson and shaped like the berries of the sumach. The crape myrtle is everywhere, in delicate pink or white. Two cork-elm trees planted in a sheltered court sixteen years ago are now sixty feet high!

The male ward is covered with an immense ivy in which hundreds of rats have made their nests, and which just now looks rather dilapidated. Before it was cut it stood four feet out from the wall. When the doctor lost one hundred chickens in a night, he thought it best to investigate! After his first attempt at poisoning, more than two hundred rats came to the chicken-house in one night for water and died there.

This afternoon I drove sixteen miles to Waterloo and back, in about an hour and a half! What a delightful rush it was through balmy air, perfumed by figs, grapes, and wheat! Lovely little homes surrounded by vines and fig-trees rose everywhere. Empty wheat teams crept all along the road. In every instance the driver was lying intoxicated across the bottom, and the five or six horses or mules were moving at their own pace. A fine pair of mules had lost their driver altogether, and dragged their empty wagon back and forth in front of us till they swamped themselves and it in a ditch beside the road. The farmers and tavern-keepers spread wheat straw deep all over the road about their premises to keep down the dust.

When we got home I went out in a lovely, rosy sunset to see my cousin milk,— a thing he always does himself because he does not like to trust his patent milking tubes to any other hand. The little nickel tubes are put one into each teat. These are attached to rubber pipes, which all unite below in one vent. As soon as these are firmly and gently inserted, their weight draws down the milk; and all the milker has to do is to strip the cow at the last. It was quite new to me.

Stockton, Sept. 17, 1880.— I have really packed up for the big trees, and have given up the Yo Semite. I have letters from India which make me anxious, and I have no news from my banker as I expected; so I dare not go. I have a good imagination. Huge photographs have made me familiar with every turn in the valley; and I have seen so many cañons that I shall not miss anything but immeasurable dimensions. So I try to console myself, and wonder that I do not feel more disappointed. After breakfast I went to see the artificial ice made, with which Stockton is supplied. I daresay I have forgotten to tell you that I have missed ice greatly in San Francisco. It has only been offered to me once; and the wealthiest persons seem to prefer to do without it.

It is possible to make the artificial ice twelve inches thick, but they do not wait for this. It is usually cut at six inches. An engine exhausts the air from hollow tubes which run round the ice tanks. Then

a preparation of ether rushes in, and by rapid evaporation condenses the water. The ether is condensed
again in its turn, and the waste is so slight that the
manufacture costs very little.

In the neighborhood of the river everything looked
green, and the air was heavy with the odor of wheat.
We walked through the immense warehouses holding
eighteen thousand tons of wheat each. The railway
cars were trundling away, reeking with grain; wagons
were unloading on the square. Even the outside
porches of the warehouses were packed to the ceiling.
It was easy to guess at the character of each farmer
by the way in which his wagon was packed.

Next we drove to the paper mill, and I got specimens
of paper made of wheat straw, such as the "Bulletin"
is printed on. No wonder it cracks when one turns
the leaf.

Last of all we went to a fruit garden, kept by De
Costa, a Portuguese, married to an English woman,
whose mother, a Mrs. Lyley, began to cultivate this
spot just thirty years ago. Here we saw what sitting "under one's own fig tree" might come to mean.
Mighty trees, twenty-five years old, and beautiful for
shade and fruit, environed the modest dwelling and
perfumed all the air. Thirty-five hundred pounds were
sold from the largest of these trees last year. There is
a large orchard of white and purple figs attached to the
place, and now bearing their third crop. There are
wonderful peaches, plums, and pomegranates, and a
vineyard which has given me my first conception of
California grapes.

They loaded us with fruit, more than we could carry
away; and finally brought dried figs for me to carry to

the Calaveras to-morrow. These were purple, and had
been half dried on the tree, until they had just the
taste of the best imported fruit. It was delicious, a
thousand times better than that of the ripe fig fresh
from the tree. De Costa thinks the purple fig the
richest. The first crop of the Smyrna white is as
good as can be grown. The second is worth less, which
means that it turns acid because it ripens under too
hot a sun.

Stockton, Sept. 18, 1880.— Never shall I forget the
luncheon basket with which Cousin Minnie sent me off
this morning. It was heavier than the valise which
held my clothes, and much to my surprise was certainly needed at every point on the way. The train
carried me toward Milton, through vast fields of golden
stubble, where sunshine would have lingered even had
the rain been falling. Do I not remember the wonderful grove in Michigan through which I once
travelled in heavy rain, and never realized it was not
glowing sun ?

There are seven varieties of small-leaved oaks on
these plains. The foliage is very dark. Immense
trees are scattered along the margins of the wheat
fields. Here and there the plough had lately turned
up a rich black soil. I saw, too, a strange "header"
wagon, with one side so much lower than the other
that the reaper tosses the grain into it easily. Beautiful stacks of grain or straw were on every side. The
certainty of dry weather cheers the farmer while he
cuts and stores his wheat. The straw was stacked in
a long oval, of a bulk which suggests the fruitful year.
This straw was once burned. It now goes to the paper-

maker and in a year like this for what it costs to carry it. It would be quite as well to lay it down on the dusty highways and bind in the clay. Sun-flowers and the purple spires of the musk-weed were the only blossoms that I saw. A short mullein, which bears a faded cream-colored flower, blotched the ground all over, each plant starring it in dusty state and with a very odd effect.

Dreary wastes! At last at Peters, where we tarried for wood, upland slopes began to hint at mountains. A moraine pushed out under the foot of one, as though there had been glaciers before the lava burst through. Then a few dingy, shelf-like "wash-outs" showed themselves, looking, in color and form, as the woody fungi which grow out of old stumps would do if they were magnified. Trees were few; and many cracks in the soil seemed to tell of transitory torrents. Hill-tops soon spread at a wider angle. When we were over, pine forests hung with grapes appeared, and manzanitas, called also by the Spaniards the parsley-leaved hawthorne. These were hung with clusters of small crabs as big as a rose pip, but not yet ripe. Through these and the cedars fell Rock Creek, purling and babbling, and now and then rushing madly over a crag. A mighty rapid it must be after the rains. Out of the water and out of the hill-side great black tombstones of trap spring up, and in the very bed of the stream large masses of a green stone like serpentine. Scarlet and yellow mosses "tricked out" the slabs, as a coach-maker would say. The soil was red with iron, and clayey.

At times the dust hid the nearest horse's head. I was alone in a coach meant for nine, for "the season" was over, and I played a good game at battledore and shuttlecock with silent partners. At last we took up a returned miner and the proprietor. We were crossing Bear Mountain, one of the spurs of the Sierras. I did not like to part from Rock Creek, it seemed so like a stream in the White Mountains, except that here granite is changed to trap, and the whole scene has a wider angle, and the inexpressibly mighty character which belongs to the Rocky Mountains. We were about 2,300 feet above the sea. There were plantations of figs and grapes trained in rocky hollows, but no houses visible. Thousands of sheep strayed up and down the tossed and rugged slope to the creek. They are sheared twice a year, in May and October. Layers of slate thrust themselves edgewise through the soil, painted with gay lichens. We came to a point called the Reservoir, where there is an artificial lake, covering 1,300 acres, for the use of the miners at North Hill. Here were flocks of sheep, mighty enough to haunt Bo-Peep through all the ages. They are penned at night, but never sheltered in the day.

At last I heard one of the men behind me say, " I suppose that lady won't submit to smoking, so we must have a chew." The " lady " kept a safe silence,—she had hardly had a breath of pure air since she entered the State, and she thought it best to make the most of this opportunity.

Our road now lay through a vast ranch, — a privilege granted that the farmer may get his mail a little sooner. There was a cluster of houses, — one prettily shaded with vines and trees, one other with a chimney outside, Virginia fashion. A mighty farm-yard, dusty with a thousand hoofs, opened here. Groups of lovely gray jacks stood about the huge barn, and some fine horses. Black pigs, as clean as the horses, were skipping gaily about, and poking each other in the ribs.

After we had cleared the gate, in the midst of a vast field we saw a neatly enclosed lot, where crape myrtle and oleanders bloomed radiant in rose-color and white, while a few white stones rose here and there. It was a graveyard, and belonged to the ranch we had left. How clear before my eyes rose such another enclosure,— on the dear old homestead in New Hampshire,— where roses and cypress-trees nod through the rails !

Then we drew near "a lodge in the vast wilderness " a mile further on. It was a "whisky mill," the driver said. In front of it stood a blind fiddler. We took him up, and I learned afterward that his youth had been violent and wicked; but up here in the hills people do not discuss each other's failings as freely as over the tea-tables of San Francisco. Some trouble brought on by his excesses was not well understood by the oculist in San Francisco. He bears his blindness cheerily, lives round among the neighbors, and gets a new suit of clothes from the stage company, for which he once drove, whenever he needs it. He seems a favorite, and earns his pin — or perhaps I should say his button — money by his fiddle.

"Give me my cheese box," he says, as he clambers in and reaches out his hand for his fiddle.

Then he shouts to the man in the whisky mill, " Poison the next fellow who comes along, only be sure you kill him !"

Then in answer to the driver,—

" I was a jolly Mexican last night, and a jolly Dutchman the night before."

14

"And you will be a jolly Chilian to-night, if one of them wants the fiddle ?"

"To be sure."

"Did they plank down well ?"

"Yes ; business don't go on long without the 'collaterals,' you bet."

Soon we came to Gibson's, in the midst of a paradise of trees. Everything was clean ; but I knew I had a better dinner in my basket than Gibson could give me; so I ate it sitting on the piazza, in the divine, golden air, with an Italian sky above me. In my bottle of coffee were three pats of butter, each as large as a nutmeg, mute witnesses to the purity of Minnie's cream.

There is a great reach of mimetic apple-orchards all about. I saw no bird but the wood-pecker, and he was busy boring holes in the trunks of the imitative live-oaks, and sticking them full of acorns till they looked as if they were embossed. When I said this, the men began to talk of the blue-bird, of the California canary, and a lark with a few sweet notes quite unlike the bird of sixteen songs who soars in Colorado.

Beyond Gibson's we climbed a second spur. We lost the trades altogether, and came into a cool mountain breeze. The driver, who was a braggart and had large stories to tell of *his* horses and *his* coaches, said suddenly, "There are some quail, George ;" and at my very ear a gun went off. Mr. Madison shot two, and the coach was detained for him to find and pick them up. A little way on, a team stopped to tell us that Senter, the shopman at Murphy's, had been thrown by his horse and run away with. Here Mr. Madison's wife and son came to meet him in a carry-all, drawn by two beautiful grays; and as the coach was late, and I the only passenger, and Mr. Madison the proprietor, I was transferred to it, and bowled rapidly along the lovely road they call the " Grade." This is a turnpike between Stanislaus and Calaveras; and, besides resting me very much, this change saved me an hour of time. Never was there a lovelier mountain ride. A hill covered with trees, vineyards, and sugar-pines rose to the left; a brook rippled on my right, hid by clambering vines. Ledges of snowy-white peeped out from the trees. Mr. Madison said these were of lava, and that a great stream of it — white, gray, and rose-color — fills what is known as the " Dead River " bed and underlies the ridge on which the " Big Trees " stand.

I was delighted with the delicate, tender way in which the proprietor's family spoke to each other, and much surprised at the evidences of general reading and self-culture.

The lava beds are at right angles with the courses of the living rivers. Mighty pines completed my bewilderment. Mr. Madison said that these were sugar-pines, whose cones are twenty-four inches long. They are tapped like maples, and from between the sap and the heartwood exudes a sweet substance severely drastic, which the Indians used as medicine. Botanically speaking, I guess this to be the *Pinus Lambertiana.* Some of its trunks are twenty feet in diameter and two hundred feet high. The trees stand singly, with almost no branches for more than one hundred and twenty-five feet. The seeds are often roasted or made into bread. They have a sweet, oily taste, and Europeans assert that they relieve various affections of the kidneys. There is a very prevalent idea that the sweet character of the exudation is due to the partial charring of the trees. But this is probably a notion. Those who live among them disdain the story.

We soon rolled into Murphy's, a pretty green oasis in this mountain wilderness, and I was instantly transferred to a coach with four horses; and I supposed I was to continue my journey alone, after the shuttlecock fashion. Before we got out of town, however, the driver saw a child in the road, and shouted out : " Hollo, Hatty ! I'd forgotten you !" and we turned out of our course to a side street, where we took in trunks and the said little girl, daughter of the landlord at the Big Trees, and entitled I suppose to her passage.

Between Murphy's and the Big Trees we rose two thousand four hundred feet. A good part of the way the road was hardly visible, being a mere wheel-track under a mighty forest, for we were climbing the Sierra itself. I was obliged to cling with both hands to the coach, and hardly thought I should reach the end of my journey alive. Very glad was I that my daughter had not come with me, as I wished. She would not have been able to bear the journey itself, nor the changes of temperature, nor the start for home at three o'clock in the morning, which I must take.

After the moon rose, and the great trunks of the sugar-pines were silvered, the whole scene took on a majesty beyond words. God grant I may never lose the memory of it ! The surplus water of the Union Tanks made as sweet music as a heaven-born brook.

A vast saw-mill takes up five hundred acres in the very heart of this timber. The sight of it went through me like a knife ! One by one the monarchs of the soil are falling. I am glad that I came before it should be too late. Is there anywhere else in the world such a forest as this? It is soon to be only a memory, and if there are others, they too will perish!

We carried the mail into several ranches, shouting through the still night as we went. We rushed over bridges which had neither beams nor rails. We nearly ran over a Chinaman from the saw-mill while we shouted out the news that Senter was dying. He carried a plank over his shoulders, with an odd-looking Chinese bundle tied to one end, while his fingers played with the other as if it were a twig of ozier.

Mark Twain should describe all this if I could get hold of him. Every moment I expected to be thrown out and killed, but I declared to myself that I would at least have a good time before it happened. My driver is a character. His father, a Mr. C. in Wisconsin, taught Mrs. Maxwell how to stuff and preserve skins; and he was full of anecdote about her. He had lived near neighbor to Ole Bull, and could not do his work in the stable when Ole took to playing. He does not like California, and is going East, which means — to Colorado! I was amused to hear him say, as he riddled the dust on the horses' backs with his whip, that he would like to get to a " clean place " to die ! I had something of the same feeling myself. He knew the scientific names of most of the trees, and distinguished them easily. Both drivers to-day asserted that intemperance is on the increase throughout the country, and neither of them drank a drop.

So, jerking, bouncing, pommelling, and chattering, we dashed round the base of the hill. It cannot happen to many people to make this journey under the harvest moon, and my cup was full to the brim as we rushed be-

tween the two "Sentinels," not a whit more striking figures than the giant pines through which I had already
passed, and up to the door of the long, low, white, com-
fortable-looking hotel. How fragrant and soft the air
through which we drove !

A dozen whisks assailed me, — before, behind, above,
below; but, alas! the dust was a "deposit," and would
budge for no one's striving. I hardly waited to throw
off my cloak before I went out with Mr. Sperry in search
of the white ghosts that haunt the grove. The moon
rode full and superb in the sky. I hoped that the
gaunt branches of the naked "mother of the forest"
would turn to silver under her witching beams. I had,
too, a feeling that I ought to walk a few miles to throw
off the effect of the severe bruises I had received.

This last benefit I fully realized, and also the wonderful night-walk through columns of a temple Atlas might
have reared to sustain the heavenly dome, set with a
thousand points of light. The "mother of the forest,"
however, seemed to resent my impertinent curiosity, and
steadily refused to show the stately form which, shorn
of its natural clothing, stood naked in the night. The
trees bent before her and held her in their sacred
shadow. The malice of Diana was foiled.

Calaveras Grove, Sunday, Sept. 19, 1880.—I ought to
say that I found a comfortable bed here, but uneatable
food and a very untidy room. My morning bath took
so long that it was after eight before I could go out to
the trees. Then I took a guide-book and followed the
path alone.

The only way in which any one could get a true
idea of a tree taller than Bunker Hill monument

would be to see it standing alone. If the Vandals who
bored through the trunk which forms the floor of the
little dancing-hall had cleared a space for it instead,
they would have deserved well of mankind. But, alas!
over three hundred feet high and ninety-two in circumference, it rose direct to heaven, with such vertical
accuracy that, after the trunk was wholly divided, it
would not fall. When it was finally lowered, in true
California — or rather mining-gulch — fashion, a billiard-
room and a bar-room were built upon it. I was amazed
at the number of fallen trees. Five of the prostrate
trunks are ascended by ladders of from twenty to thirty
steps erected at their sides! Their twisted roots still
cling to and burrow in the earth. Those that are broken
bristle defiantly; but draw near, and each bristle may
be from eight to eighteen inches in thickness. The
same Vandals who sawed or bored through the sound
trunk which was first levelled, deprived the poor
"mother of the forest" of her bark, and this was
afterward destroyed by fire,— I think at Sydenham.
She is 327 feet high and, without her bark, 78 feet in
circumference. The sun touched her white limbs with
light this morning. It was as if the filial guard, which
had shut out the cold rays of the prying moon, opened
to let the genial sunshine bathe her dishonored form.

A great many estimates are given of the size of these
trees. It is easy to say that the tree is measured at the
ground, and again at six and twelve feet above it; but,
in point of fact, no one ever finds the foot of a tree.
Each is surrounded by a mound, consisting of the accumulations of centuries; and above this the tree is so
heavily buttressed as greatly to exaggerate the figure.
If the tree grow naturally from a single germ, it will

be no more than gracefully strengthened at the base, and then rise like a mighty column to heaven, every perpendicular line channelling the trunk, as an architect might do. It will stand so true that if sundered horizontally it could not fall. There are eight of the largest trees so formed, and their glowing trunks might be the jasper colonnades of the heavenly Jerusalem.

But most of these trees appear to be composite. From one fallen cone two or three tiny threads have started, blending into one as they grew. That one thread should be a little stronger than the others occasions first abnormal buttresses at the base, and then a twist in the whole column, with a sort of Byzantine effect, all the lines swerving round the tree. It is impossible for the human eye to take in the height with one glance, unless at a distance of sixty or seventy feet; and this is seldom attainable. This is as true of the sugar-pines as of the sequoia. To stand at the foot of one of these trees and try to let the eye pierce the heavens with its shaft, is like no other experience on earth. There comes with it an intense sense of Almighty power and presence, and a sort of sacred awe when one thinks of the ages that have passed since the fire was kindled which has killed some of these trees and scarred so many. Some people think the Indians kindled it; but, if so, what Indians?

Close to the charred trunks are others, centuries old, which are not harmed. Many of the fallen trees were felled by fire which must have burned more than seven hundred years ago. What could have put out a forest fire strong enough to eat out the heart of a sequoia for more than ninety feet? Within the memory of living men, a small sequoia was accidentally set on fire. It was not killed, although its red heart was eaten out; and yet every tree within forty feet of it was charred, and no man could breathe the air of the grove!

The foliage of the youngest and healthiest trees is oddly disproportioned to their size. The branches come out at from one hundred to a hundred and fifty feet above the ground; and they never look huge, although they are so, as the fallen giants show. The leaves are like those of the cedar; but, instead of being flat, they are round, spurred all about at first, and perfectly smooth only when quite mature. The rosy bark, soft as velvet to the touch, and marked with silver furrows, was an entire surprise to me.

In among these trees are sugar-pines two hundred and seventy-five feet high, and from nine to eleven in diameter; and to say that these do not look large, is to say something very emphatic about the whole grove. Still, this Calaveras grove does not impress the imagination with dreams of a primeval forest, owing to its thin foliage. I have little doubt that if I stood in Windsor Forest, or in the Bois de Boulogne, or on the skirts of the Black Forest, I should be far more deeply moved by the ancient oaks and beeches, simply because they are not so tall, and the circumference of widely sheltering foliage is added to that of the trunk.

It was through three miles of forest, consisting of the pines which I have described, that I came up here last night. Nothing I have found here impresses me like this drive, crossed by the fantastic shadows the weird moon compelled.

Some of the guide-books say that it is nonsense

to suppose that any of these trees ever reached the height of four hundred and fifty feet. But why ? In Australia, the eucalyptus does this often, and it is a very rapidly growing tree. Some of the fallen sequoias, which are sound for three hundred feet, have still a deep furrow to show where their proud summits once lay. In some of these furrows trees two centuries old are growing. In one, a horseman may ride far and not lift his head above the surface of the soil. The fallen "Hercules" is a good illustration of what I said about the twist in the trunks. Before he fell he stooped earthward for sixty feet at an angle, which some of us remember in the old Greek marbles.

The "Pride of the Forest," "The Hermit," "The Nightingale," and "The Forest Beauty" fill the eye and the soul in a way I cannot describe. I must omit writing of some superb trees, because they have names which would eat out the heart of any description. To think of being compelled to bow one's head in wondering awe before a tree named for a man who did not fail to be a traitor for lack of the desire ; or before another, named for one the thought of whom flushes every woman's cheek with shame ! It does not seem an accident that the tablet which bears this last name has burst asunder with the recent growth of the mighty trunk. Some day perhaps it will fall.

A beautiful group of three trees in perfect line is called " The Graces." The " Pioneer's Cabin " has room for two old " settles " in its hollow trunk, and a chimney through which the stars shine. The " God of fire," however, was not satisfied with these slender accommodations. Seventy feet away in a still living tree, two hundred and seventy-five feet high and seventeen in diameter, he has hollowed out a chimney ninety feet in height, and cut away a window seventy feet above ground, to add fury to the draught.

Just here I came upon the fallen trunk of "The Monarch of the Forest." Centuries ago it fell. Its bark is gone, and much of the exterior wood. It is sound at heart; but it struck against another tree in falling, and both were shivered, so the upper half of the tree long since disappeared. The furrow it once filled is still visible, and full of flowers. The acrid juice of the sequoia prevents insects from feeding on it. I never in my life was in a wood where there was so little life. Nothing seemed to live in the dead trees, but ninety feet from the ground I saw many bees' nests. The fall of these trees is pathetic. If one strikes a rock or another tree, no matter how small, its own weight shivers it,— imparting significance to the most trivial obstacle.

So is it with man himself.

I walked through the empty bowels of the " Father of the Forest." Two hundred feet one may follow the outline, after the three hundred feet of trunk still exist-ent has been explored. It is a hundred and twelve feet in circumference at the base, and about fifty where we lose sight of it. A man on horseback, perhaps two, could ride through it. Out of the dead trunk spring tender flowers, and because a never failing spring is at its root green vines and young trees start from the crevices.

As I wandered languidly toward the house, weary of the strain on my feelings, some young men who had been trying to measure the trees, and had found their

strings too short, plied me with questions. They were
not wasting their day of rest. The dead trees shone
with the golden touch of the lichen; a piney sweetness loaded the air; some little children in a camp
close by were laughing and crowing. It was easy to
believe that God is good.

This mammoth grove fills a small valley near the
headwaters of the San Antonio, in Calaveras County.
It still contains ninety-three of the large old trees, and
many young ones, on which I wish they would begin
to try experiments to decide the manner of their
growth. I have no objection to thinking these trees
fifteen hundred years old, but I do not; and on my
suggesting the idea, I find scientific men here not dis-
inclined to think that they may make wood faster than
has been supposed.

The grove of sugar-pines, in which the trees stand, is
more wonderful than they. I think the elliptical walk
which leads through this is perhaps a mile and a half
long.

In the South Park Grove, to which I should have
gone on horseback if I had found Mr. Belden here,
there are 1,380 trees. One, still alive, has a space
capable of containing sixteen horsemen. The groves
are not so uncommon as has been believed. Eleven
have been explored, and hundreds more may exist
unseen of men.

Mine host is kind and intelligent, but he has not yet
learned what the public want in a house like this. I
have been the only guest, and have been offered at
dinner four different roasts and three sorts of vegetables, no one well cooked! The bread might have been
good, but was spoiled by the rancid butter used on the

pans. Bread and milk, with a good cup of tea, might satisfy anybody; but this feast of Tantalus is costly and uneatable.

I wrote two hours in the heat of the day, and then went through the grove for the third time to strengthen my impressions, and to collect cones, bark, and foliage.

At the last moment, Mr. Belden arrived. He has been hunting near the summit of the Sierra with three friends. The latter will go down with me, laden with quail and trout. One of the proprietors has been with them, and will drive us down to Murphy's with four fresh horses. We shall make good time, and sleep there to-night.

Later, the coach was detained while Mr. Belden showed me some flowers he had gathered on the summit, some of them blooming in the snow. He generously shared his specimens with me. We took a road to the right, on leaving the "Sentinels," not nearly so attractive as that by which I ascended under the light of the moon. The road was intolerable. We dragged over prostrate trunks and uncovered roots. The forest seemed tame. The only lovely thing as we dashed through was a narrow valley, or bit of interval, occupied by a Mr. Dunbar as a ranch. It was as green as emerald, about six miles long and half a mile wide.

At the half-way house my companions all "took a drink," except one ranchman who held the horses. Cold water was brought for him and me. He came from Walpole, N. H., and Mr. P. from Charlemont. P. has a son going to Denver. I was amused to see the whole party receive as news a very garbled account of poor Senter's accident, of which we had brought the first tidings. A moment's reflection would have shown them that there could have been no later word.

At Murphy's, Senter was reported "out of danger." Mr. Garfield's son had a tin-can full of tiny chipmunks, a quarter of the size of ours at home. He amuses himself by digging tarantula nests out of the bank. These are made of clay, glazed inside, and have a close-fitting cover with a perfect hinge, and a sort of staple into which Mrs. Spider thrusts a leg when she wishes to decline company. The boys cut these out of the bank, when the spider opens the door and departs. They do not harm her, and she does not resent this perplexing interference.

At Murphy's we found excellent food and clean rooms, which last the mosquitoes enjoyed as well as ourselves. The bread, the baked beans, the salad, the salt fish dressed with cream, as well as the tea and coffee, were all delicately prepared and most grateful to one starved atom of humanity.

Murphy's to Stockton, Sept. 20, 1880. — I rose at half-past two this morning. The landlord refused to furnish me with hot water before starting; so, much against my will, I breakfasted on cold chicken and cracker crumbs steeped in brandy. A true temperance reform will never be practical till people understand the need many people have of internal stimulation. Hot water will often supply it sufficiently; but at present, unfortunately, it is easier to carry a flask of brandy than to command hot water.

There was a good deal of delay in starting. Saturday the load was so *light* that I was taken into the proprietor's private carriage, and the coach sent

round a longer way to collect the mail. This morning
it was so *heavy* that the same course was adopted. A
buckboard went for the mail, to join us at Aldersville;
and we went down the Grade. As we went past the
house, Mr. S. pointed out Douglass's Flat behind it,
where from a little placer or valley surface, scarce
half-a-mile wide and two miles long, more than ten
millions in gold have been taken out! He said all this
money had been honestly earned by men who worked
hard until they secured a competence, and went East
to invest it. All this gold was taken out in small bean-
shaped nodules. When they got down so low that
water showed itself, it could no longer be profitably
worked. A ranchman from Sonora was in the coach.
He said that in ploughing his own farm he got from
two to three ounces of gold a day, without at all intend-
ing it; and that near him men were constantly working
where bits were washed out as large as a watermelon
seed, but pure and polished. They had found two hundred and fifty dollars worth in one lump, and chopped
it up!

And now a more glorious gold glimmered in the sky.
Rose-color and ashes of roses mingled and shot through
the gold. All the blue was flecked with gauzy white,
the full moon hanging like a sphere of impalpable mist.
In such soft glory as I had never seen in California I
sat on Gibson's porch taking a second breakfast of fruit
and pure spring water, while the rest were eating hot
meats within. When we started again I got up on the
box with the driver and a young girl who came in
from Aldersville on the buckboard. Quail were on all
sides of us, innocent of a gun, — running, flying, sidling
towards a covert. One side-hill swarmed with magpies.

A bird as large as a pigeon ran across the road; they said it was the meadow lark, with "a few sweet notes."

The young girl began to talk. "The girls were living out. Webb hired them out and took their money. If her father did that she would n't stand it."

"He needs it, don't he?" said the driver.

"I suppose so; but I would n't stand it."

"*You* are eighteen," said the driver.

I then asked a few questions, and found that this girl's father was a ranchman at Copperopolis. She had taken a first-class certificate at fifteen, had gone to the State Normal School at San José, and at eighteen had begun to teach. She is now twenty, and earns one hundred dollars a month for the six months the school lasts. I was not only shocked by her free ways with the driver, which I do not describe because I could not describe them without giving a false impression, but by her very untidy dress. It was not only a soiled, but a ragged "best dress" put into common wear. A clean calico — skirt and sacque — costs so little and looks so fresh! She boards at T.'s ranch. As we drove in at the gate Mrs. T. stood there with the mail in her hand, — a bright woman speaking with a sweet, clear voice. The young teacher, who had been away to spend Sunday, got off here. She had still a mile to walk to reach her pupils, and, as she said, felt much more like going to bed! At the beginning of the term she had registered forty-five pupils, but "only fifteen held on."

"Did the girl come?" she asked of Mrs. T.

"Yes, she has come and gone," was the placid reply.

"Why, in the world!" — began the teacher.

"Nobody knows why," returned Mrs. T. "Colonel, do you know of a girl to take care of children? I have a good Chinaman."

"I might," replied the colonel, who was also the stage-driver, oracularly; and we rolled away.

Ranchwomen have their troubles it appears. The colonel said that all the young girls found the ranches too dull, and would not stay at home if they could earn money in any other way. I asked if they put by any money. "They hardly can," he answered; "a teacher must dress well!" I remembered what I had just seen, and wondered if he were quizzing me.

The sun was very hot, and at the Reservoir I got inside the stage again. I can give no idea of the bad road or the hard coach. The Sonora coach drove up at the moment. There were twenty passengers on her, with their baggage; and we had not enough to keep us steady, but flew about like so many tortured shuttle-cocks.

"I should think you would be glad to take some of those people," I said to the driver.

"I don't think I shall," he answered rudely; and it soon came out that this coach was an opposition to our older line. We were both a little short of time, and when "Sonora" stopped to let a passenger gather some grapes, we drove rapidly by, got out of her dust, and as soon as we had distanced her taunted her by loitering through the "water waste," which crossed the road like a river, to "set our wheel-tires."

I wish I could give you any idea of the amount of partridge and quail which I saw on this journey. They seemed to be in thousands; they were so tame that they ran under our wheels. The gray rocks turned brown under their pretty backs, and they kept the stubble in constant motion by their flight through the fields.

In our coach was a man so far gone with consumption that I dreaded the end every moment. When we reached the cars at Milton, he was lifted out more dead than alive. I slept all the way from Milton to Stock-ton, so I shall not reiterate my observations on the scenery. There dear Cousin Will met me, and took me and the trout home. As soon as I had had my bath I be-gan to write to you. Mrs. S. came as jolly as ever, and was utterly amazed that I had borne the journey at all. It has certainly relieved the local congestion.

I found my mirror garlanded with wonderful grapes from the De Costas. I cannot say one word for their taste, when I remember the same sorts in our Ashton grapery.

Stockton to Los Angeles, Sept. 21, 1880. — I should never have got my early breakfast, if dear Minnie her-self had not risen with the dawn, a pure incarnation of something much better than Venus! When it was over we walked about six blocks to the slough, and, treading daintily over a catamaran, got into a small row-boat, where we sat stiffly erect.

The sloughs, or slews, of Stockton and its neighbor-hood are a delta formed by the ancient drainage of pre-historic seas, at the time the Coast Range was lifted. So distinct are all the fluvial marks that it is easy to im-agine the Coast Range still dripping with water; and the Rocky Mountains themselves are only a still older coast range, as their clam beds and oyster flats show. The mysterious thing about it all is, that the whole looks so recent, — no parasites, no tender grass or herbs covering the scars or clothing the naked limbs of either " lift."

I hear people say that this is because the air is so

dry; but it is rather to be traced to the sulphurous and alkaline elements in the soil uplifted. We rowed down the slough some three miles to a fruit ranch on an island, owned by an old Scotchman named Crozier, and called " Rough and Ready." The surface was untroubled, except when a small steamer crossed our path and sent us tossing. It was precisely like a grand canal. The object of the excursion was to show me what cultivation could accomplish in this locality. This island of sixteen hundred acres was once a mere tuli swamp. It is now a forest of apple, peach, pear, plum, and fig trees, a tangle of every kind of grape, with a bewildering resemblance to the English Coteswold.

Two fig trees, about twenty years old, completely shade Mr. Crozier's little home. He is a bachelor, and a deacon of the Presbyterian church; and the winter storms are never heavy enough to prevent him from rowing down to Stockton to his Sunday work. We strolled under the trees a long way, until we came to the steam-engine which irrigates the whole. A little beyond this we went through a hedge and into a field, where we had a fine view of the tuli swamp. This is, I suppose, an aboriginal word, since no European language acknowledges it. It designates a tall reed, out of which people tried to make paper at one time. It is now used principally by the nursery men, who pack their young trees in it for market. The swamp made me think of Lake Sirbonensis and Pharaoh's sunken chariots. Sportsmen with heavy boots often find themselves entangled.

Turning back we travelled through plantations of pepper, tomato, and sweet pepper, which latter is a sort of cross between the sharp pepper and the tomato, across great vineyards to the other side of the island, and so round to the house again. We brought in many wild-flowers, and found an evening primrose about four feet high, covered with pure golden bloom! Each corolla was at least two and a half inches in diameter. While we rested under his fig trees, in a wholly delicious air such as I have felt nowhere else, Crozier went into his vineyard and brought back a bushel basket of grapes for us to lunch upon. I am sorry to say that after I had tasted them they tempted me no longer with their lovely glow of jewelled color. Nettie sat binding her bouquet; her flowers were crimson, purple, orange, yellow, scarlet, and blue, — all nameless so far as the party could tell. We floated back, and found it hard to say farewell to Mr. C., from whom we parted in the bows of the catamaran.

After lunch I drove once more to the cemetery to take a last look at its green sentinels, which remind me very much of those in Mr. Hunnewell's garden at Wellesley. They seem suitable at the graveside.

Will came home early, bringing great bunches of new sorts of grapes for me to taste or carry away. I can see that I disgust them all by my lack of faith in the vineyards.

After an early dinner, during which we sat with our sweet cousins for the last time, Will went with us to the Southern train. It is not often that so much of my soul goes into my kisses as went into those with which we parted.

A woman who had a child with the whooping cough pressed near us at the dépôt. When at last we made our way into the sleeping-car at Lathrop, there was no lower berth for either of us. To protect N. from the contagion

I hurried her into an upper berth and sat up two hours waiting for a man to come in from the smoking-car who was said to prefer his pipe to his pillow. Finally a fellow-passenger went in search of him, and, after unwinding several fathoms of red tape, returned with the man's orders to the consequential porter that the berth should be made up for me. For the first time in my life I felt indebted to tobacco! But not a step would the porter stir until he had the berth ticket, so away went my friend again. This useful person and Mr. Lockhart will leave us at Mohavè. After four days and nights of travel and "camping out" they are to "prospect a mine" in "Dead Man's Valley." What cheerful names our miners give their haunts! We have also a young woman going to her husband in Nevada. She doesn't know where to find him, but seems to have plenty of friends; has just paid $4.65 extra on one of her trunks, and will send the other by freight. Her ticket, including her berth, has cost her $25.50 for the five hundred miles to Los Angeles! One would think her trunk might go too. Surely the Eastern roads might exclaim like the German landlady in H. H.'s story: "Oh, I have been much fool! No more I give good chicken!" Under my daughter's berth slept an English miner's wife with two healthy babies, both in arms. She had been down in the city to await the advent of the younger and was on her way back to the mines.

A French Jewess with four children and a servant were on the road to Los Angeles. All had magnificent black eyes, but were otherwise six as ugly mortals as ever lighted on the planet. The oldest child, a girl of eleven, was frightfully ugly, and always dragging about a baby of two years almost as big as herself. She was so fond of him that her whole face overflowed with loveliness whenever she took him, in spite of her twisted mouth and bad skin.

I rose at five and made my toilet without much comfort in a dirty dressing-room. All night the glowing full moon had shown us only a succession of rough alkaline plains, as bare as the desert at Humboldt of everything except a few tufts of sage-brush. Now the Coast Range came in view, looking fresh from the swirl of raging waters. Then tufts of demoralized yucca starred the plain. Finally we ran into the bowels of the earth, passing through tunnel after tunnel till at last we reached the wonderful loop in the Tehachapian spur, and climbed it spirally. We penetrated it by tunnel, and then, making a complete revolution, crossed the summit over the roof of the tunnel.

For twenty miles the grade here is one hundred and sixteen feet to a mile, and it is claimed that not only a greater difficulty is conquered here than at Cape Horn on the Central Pacific, but that it is conquered by work of unsurpassed excellence. The road over the Styrian Alps from Vienna to Trieste is a little like it, but even there the road has no occasion to " climb its own back." The cañon of the creek is most picturesque, but there are no words wherewith to describe the individualities of these oft-repeated wonders.

Soon after we passed the lake of the same name. It is now only a long, narrow bed of salt, which is dug out and used for everything except the curing of meat. As the road turned and twisted among the hills, the sun was first on one side of us and then on the other. As my daughter's berth was on the opposite side of the car from mine, I had an understanding with my friend from

"Dead Man's Valley" that I might use either seat, as
the sun made necessary. This outraged the porter's
sense of propriety. Having had a night's rest he thought
I ought to confine myself to my daughter's seat. Finding me quietly impervious to his hints, he walked over
to N. and asked if I was any relation to Captain Dall.

"Which Captain Dall?" said N., for we all understand
that two or three white-haired Swedes of this name have
made themselves well known as pioneers in the naviga-
tion of the West coast, as well as my son.

"Why, Captain Bill, or Captain John, or any of 'em!"
impatiently returned my lord. "Not the least," said N.
"I thought so," responded the porter in a loud voice and
with a satisfied chuckle. "Them is such *experienced*
travellers they'd never think of taking a gentleman's
place all day and all night too!"

"Dead Man's Valley" got its name from a party of emigrants who wandered into it in the early days, and could
never find their way out. It is four hundred feet *below*
the level of the sea! At Mohavè the mountains open
to a wider placer, spotted by frequent mining shafts and
as many yucca palms, — awkward, straggling pillars of
tawny gray. Here our miners left us. To the east are
conical summits of the loveliest shape, floating in a sea
of mist.

There had not been a drop of rain for seven months, and
every grain of sand seemed alive. Far away a Chinaman's
picturesque wash, consisting of blouses of scarlet and
blue cotton, was stretched along a line. It seemed as if
the clothes might turn to flame. This Mohavè palm —
which is really a sort of yucca — is very fibrous, and used
to be sent to a Boston paper-mill, but proved too brittle for use. There is also all along this road an abund-

ance of *yucca gloriosa* and *yucca filamentosa*, — the latter
the lovely panicle of moon-fed blossoms which Margaret
Fuller immortalized at Jamaica Plain. Its fullest bloom
and sweetest odors greet only the full moon. Farther
south it grows to fifteen feet in height, and twelve hundred blossoms have been found on a single stalk. I wish
Margaret had seen it. When she delighted in Manitou-
lin Island, she little knew what worlds were left to conquer. How strange it seems that she not only never
saw, but never even heard of the hills and cañons I have
seen to-day! On the summit of Tehachapi there is a
salt lake. A little beyond, at Cameron, the road goes
through a crack made by an earthquake; and at Lancas-
ter, through a cut of chalky-looking rock brought up by
an earthquake in 1868, half-buried trees are to be seen,
and the traces of the shock may be discovered for miles
along the road. Deer and bear are plentiful here.

Now came a ledge of rocks with streaks of white;
then oak glades and bees. Cacti broke out along
the hills, which are washed out queerly like those
in Colorado. The summit is harder than the slope.
The rain has washed away the latter, and left a row
of conical chimney caps. At one place the head
of a sphinx protruded from the soil. A part of
the shoulder showed itself. More tunnels, then a
semicircle of hills, — low, sharp, and overlapping one
another like the card-houses our children build on the
dinner-table at night. Everything looked green. . We
pierced the Coast Range by a tunnel a mile and a half
long. The plain opened. Again I saw the showy
leaves of the euphorbia and the group of sunny, golden
flowers that rose like beams of light from the mesa of
Colorado.

Between the hills the Mission of San Fernando rises
surrounded by a grove of orange trees. At the little
town the cars paused. Vast walls of prickly pear rose
beside the way. They had a dark, dull, red blossom,
set thick on the edges of the platter-shaped leaves. The
Indians use the leaves to eat from. Further on, large
fruit which tastes like a mango, or sub-acid pear, replaced the fallen flowers. The mountains became majestic, and below them I saw what looked like the
channel of a dead river. I smelled salt air, — an odor
which has not reached me before on this coast. We
rolled into Los Angeles, and while I was gathering up
my parcels I felt a tap on my shoulder, and both bags
were taken out of my hand.

It was Mr. Severance, who asserted that he recognized
my back hair! Across the road Mrs. S. sits in her carriage, and in a moment more we were whirled away to
the boarding-house our friends had taken for us. Then
they went back to take home Mr. and Mrs. L. with their
baby. These last have been at Monica all summer.

We passed old adobe houses, without glass; sometimes without shutters. They were bare; and, although
in ruins, not a spear of grass or leaf of creeper seems
ever to have grown upon them. I shall never believe it
is because the air is dry, for everything which I possess
of steel or silver tarnishes in the heavy fog, which leaves
nightly pools of water on roof and terrace on every part
of the coast. Before the Severances left, I found that
I must probably give up my long stay at Los Angeles.
The boats go to Santa Barbara only once in five days.
The first one goes on Friday, the 24th; the next on the
Wednesday following. It was a great disappointment;
but after we were left alone, N. and I decided that we

must go on Friday. We lunched, made a hurried toilet, and sent for a carriage. We drove first through Childs's fruit ranch,—a perfectly level orchard with wide carriage roads. Pears, apples, peaches, plums, and grapes were growing with encouraging profusion. I wanted to see if the pretty things tasted as fine as they looked, and the gardener brought me his arms full. They had a bright, sweet flavor, better than I had expected to find it; but the apples evidently knew they were not at home. I saw almost no weeds; the few the gardener called such were very lovely flowers!

At Wolfstill's orange ranch, of two hundred acres, we saw immense avenues of orange trees more than twenty years old. We got out of the carriage to look at them, as they had just ploughed up the avenues. From the older part of this grove Wolfstill claims to have netted twenty thousand dollars only last year. He has beside almonds, olives, figs, grapes, lemons, and limes, as well as younger orange groves.

Wolfstill lives in a very unpretending house, and is only a workingman. After taking a general view of the town, we were struck by the small, mean-looking houses and large gardens; by all manner of superb climbers, blossoming in scarlet, blue, purple, rose-color, and gold; and by Monterey cypresses trimmed into hedges, cones, pyramids, pineapples, peacocks, and the like, in the old stiff Italian way.

I have often wondered where the home of the bees is. Since I tasted the honey of Hymettus, which is stimulating and tonic because the honey is derived from the blossoms of the thyme, I have wondered why the "bee masters" so seldom make any attempt to decide the character of the crop. This would be easily done by the vegetation placed within reach. Before I came into the Southern counties, I heard a great deal about honey made of orange blossoms; but when I got to Los Angeles, no one knew anything about it. And I am inclined to believe that the finest honey is only that which is made near clover fields, or when the greatest variety of blossoms are out.

I was much astonished to be told that land good for nothing else was good for bees, which are glad to rob the white sage, the sumac, and a thousand nameless things which bloom in the gulches of the hills. The bees begin to work about the middle of April; and in May the keepers begin to take honey once in ten days. I give these particulars without knowing whether they differ from those in other localities.

In 1853, a Mrs. Shelton is said to have carried two hives into Santa Clara County. One of her hives was sold in San Francisco for one hundred and fifty dollars! The next year, honey for one dollar a pound; and very grateful it was to a population that had neither butter, nor apple sauce, nor maple sugar. All the bees in California are said to have come of this stock. Six years ago the State had hardly enough for its own need. In 1877 there were only twenty-two ranches, where there are now five hundred; and last year several ship-loads were sent out of the country. There are said to be two hundred thousand hives in the Southern counties and a crop of at least three million pounds is expected.

Before going home we drove to the height from which Frémont once commanded the city, when, at the time of the Mexican invasion, he aided Stockton to secure the country to the United States. The old breastworks command a wide view of the town and the mountains. Far away on the Western horizon, under fast gathering fogs, a line of light indicated the Pacific. I had expected to be much nearer to it.

Los Angeles, Sept. 23, 1880.—We had just started for a photographer's, when we met Mr. Severance and the carriage. Thinking it very likely that we should decide to go to-morrow, they had come in all ready for a picnic; and so without a word we were off.

We went first to the San Gabriel Mission, out over the half-desert road to the foot-hills on the right of the town. Hundreds of tiny squirrels, who seemed far more like prairie dogs, lifted bushy tails over their backs and flitted away to their holes.

The hills are brown, rising out of a dry plain; but their outlines are broad, and give an indescribable sense of freedom. At last we struck the main street of San Gabriel, and came upon the usual mixed population,— Spanish, Indian, Negro, and Chinese. The aristocratic adobe houses, which were built for the early Spaniards, are now the wash-houses of the Chinese. We passed a fantastic building erected for educational purposes by a half-crazy man, and called the Moneyan Institute. It is a centre piece with two rounded ends, not ill-looking in itself; but on the road is a gateway inscribed with fantastic characters, which stand for all the languages in the world.

The "Mission of San Gabriel" is an attractive building, like all those erected by the old Franciscans. The priest's house adjoins the church. We went there for the key, and were told by the handmaiden who showed us round, that we should be expected to deposit " an

alm !" Like the Mission of San Dolores, this is a long
narrow building made of adobe, covered with plaster,
buttressed picturesquely, and, like all the rest, a little
more than a century old. Its long side is on the street.
Its lower wall, or bell tower,— which is not a tower at
all, only a thick wall containing niches for bells,— is next
the priest's house. It is gabled, and has six bells,— one
in the very peak, two a little below, and three more
still lower down, which gives it a sort of pyramidal
air of strength. The buttressed wall ends on the street
corner, with a high external stair built of brick and
adobe, which leads to a gallery for the choir across the
narrow end. Between this stair and the wall some
pepper trees were growing. The whole street was
shaded by their feathery plumes. The graveyard is
behind the church.

Inside there are some old frescos which look like de-
funct wall-paper, with their William Morris's olives and
blues. There are also very fair copies of old Italian pictures of the saints. The principal altar is opposite the
choir and next the bell tower. Above it, in the centre,
Mary with her child is carved and painted ; to the right,
St. Anne ; and to the left, San Joachim. Over Mary is
San Gabriel adorned with a pair of wings ; over Anne is
Anthony of Padua ; and over San Joachin, San Xavier.
These upper carvings with their canopies are exceedingly well cut in wood ; the guide called them *wood-cuts*,
and said they were brought from the city of Mexico.
They strongly resemble those from the old Jesuit Cath-
edral in Arizona, which S. S. Cox has described.

We drove off over a section of a race course to the
great wine and brandy ranch of Mr. Rose, now carried
on in the name of Stern & Rose, the former partner

furnishing additional capital. The orange trees here
are nearly ruined by the scale; and certainly, if California throughout its length and breadth trusts too
little to the spade and too much to irrigation, this
man would seem to have been insane on the subject of irrigation. He walls up a sort of pit about
the root of each tree, and leads the water into it. It
does not seem to drain away, but to stand, and must
ruin the trees. We have all seen the same ruin over-
take an ivy in a flower pot, for the same reason. His
famous avenue, often photographed, and perhaps half a
mile long, consists of old orange trees, every one of
which has been cut back on account of the scale. It
was a deplorable sight.

We paused a moment at his pretty little villa,
and asked leave to see the distilling, and then
went on to the works. Outside, great carts were
standing, heaped with grapes. Vineyards, olive groves,
and orangeries stretched out on every side over
dimpling valleys and crested hills. The view was
picturesque at every point; but I longed to see the
laughing girls empty their baskets into the casks, where
men would trample out the grapes with crimson feet.
We went into the crushing room. Last year one hundred Chinamen were employed merely to pick the
grapes off the stems. To-day a sort of wire basket
catches all the stems and throws them out. I wish I
could see the day when all the *drinking* could be done
by machinery ! The superintendent thought this ma-
chine something very new; but Oswald Crawford
described the same thing in Burgundy some time ago.
When the Emperor of Brazil was at the Centennial, he
was urged to take home some reaping machines. He

shook his head, and said, "My most anxious duty is to *make* work for my people." I have always remembered this to his honour; for although machines must come, yet a liberal thoughtfulness, a Christian sympathy, for working people might well regulate a too rapid substitution. California is no longer a good country for the working man. On all sides I hear the cry, "A man needs to be rich to live here." There is a large unemployed population.

The juice of the grapes on the Rose vineyard runs into eighty casks, each of which holds 2,000 gallons, or 160,000 gallons in all. From this the brandy is distilled. I am amazed at the immense quantity of wine made. This year shows 5,673 acres of vineyards in this county, 53,000,000 pounds of grapes, 2,500,000 gallons of wine, and 300,000 gallons of grape brandy. The wines are mostly light, and I should have been glad to see men drinking them rather than the strong and often adulterated spirits sold over the counters of San Francisco. I have been offered wine in nearly every house I have entered, but nowhere have I seen the wines of the country. I have inquired about this, and my hosts reply, "Oh! *we* know how California wines are made." I can assure them that California wines are made exactly like European wines. They require some additional sugar; and that involves strengthening the percentage of alcohol with their own brandy that the wines may keep, which can hardly be called adulteration. I am told that the number of acres devoted to grapes has not increased for some years; that the yield is forty-eight per cent greater than in 1878, but not forty-eight per cent better. Sonoma, Santa Cruz, Santa Clara, and other counties tell the same story.

The superintendent, seeing that I knew something of household distilling, 'wished to talk with me about orange-flower water, and I promised to send him some receipts for making it. When we came away, they brought us a tray heaped with Malvoisie and sweet-water grapes. The "Mission" grapes are not yet ripe. Mr. Dugdale assures me that the proper name for these is Black Morocco.

Returning, we went through a longer and still longer avenue of oranges. Hundreds of acres are devoted to the fruit by this firm. A thousand acres have lately been planted with vines; and, besides this, the firm take all the grapes the neighbors will sell.

We ran through other orange orchards belonging to a Mr. Titus, who has been much afraid that his neighbor's "scales" would run across the road and attack his fruit. He himself uses far less water than the owners of the diseased plantations.

From hence we drove through a plashing pool of water into the orangery of a Mr. Ford, who emigrated from Dedham, Mass., and came to greet us with the bright women of his household. He gave us ripe oranges, pomegranates, and Chasselas grapes. The crop of oranges was gathered long ago, but in all the orchards some of the finest fruit is left on the trees as a treat to unexpected guests. This ought to be very sweet, and this plantation is celebrated for the quality of its fruit; but truth compels me to state that the grain of this fruit was more like that of a shattuck than an orange.

The Fords have been here six years. Mr. Ford sunk an Artesian well behind his house as soon as he came, and sells "water rights" as well as fruit. His mother, sixty years of age, works as hard as anybody. The rapidity with which everything grows here, the beautiful color of the fruit, tempts and delights the ranchman. The climate and the flowers are so delicious, and so well repay the care which provides water, that all the women are tempted to overwork.

Next we swept round the superb glacis on which stands the house of De Barth Schorb. Schorb came from Baltimore, and has a Spanish wife. Cries of wondering admiration burst from our lips. There is a semi-circle of mountains sweeping the horizon in front of this house, as grand as that of which Pike's Peak forms the centre on the mesa at Colorado Springs; and the foreground is not a brown barren, but a tangled wonder of orange groves and vineyards, green as summer, and glistening in the sun. This range of mountains has been dimly visible for five miles. It now rises with supernatural charm. We cannot bear to turn away. Oh, how much at home the old Spaniards must have found themselves in this mountain country! The Sierra Nevada parted the waters of the Gaudalquiver from those of the Xucar, between the Mediterranean and the Atlantic, before it undertook to divide the San Joaquin from the Sacramento. Every mesa, or valley must have talked to them of the Pyrenees. In Portugal, on the road to Setubal from Palmella, the soil and rocks glow in red, purple, pearl color, and gold. How homelike must have seemed the tall cliffs in Arizona and the Garden of the Gods!

The yellow-top boots, worn to defend the legs from the prickly pear in the old country, had to be replaced here by wooden stirrups of gigantic proportions, which I found as far up as Leadville. Many a sleepy old

fellow, astride his donkey, must have rubbed his eyes
when he first came upon the Mohavè Desert, and wondered if those were the identical cacti and yuccas that
he last saw in Spain, on the Sierra Morena!

Life would not be long enough to look, if landscape
and sunlight and far stretching verdure were always
like that offered to us to-day from the Schorb terrace.
Our way then led through the Wilson estate, owned by
one of the best cultivators of this region, who has married into the Schorb family. About one hundred acres in
oranges here; and we go out of it into the "Wilderness,"
as tangled a maze of wild vines, live-oaks, and alders,
with a sweet spring near, as one could find at this season in the heart of Massachusetts. Here we ate our
lunch of bread and fruit, took out our horses and rested
for an hour before we went on to Passadina. Near Passadina, alas! is the wonderful raisin ranch carried on by
Miss Austin; but I had no time to visit it. None of
us were in the least tired. Our light spring-wagon,
lightly covered, was carried by our two fine horses as
easily as their own harnesses.

I cannot tell how long we were in driving through
this Wilderness. It reminded me not only of many
a summer route in New England, but of a wild drive
along the "benches" of Lake Superior years ago, where
tree was looped to tree by tangled vines, and trunks of
prehistoric age stood sweet and green in the delicious
coolness.

We went from the Wilderness to the high school,
where Mrs. Jenny C. Carr, late Assistant Superintendent
of Schools for the State, is trying an experiment after the
fashion of Quincy, Mass. Her husband, Dr. Carr, was
the actual Superintendent, and made her his deputy.

She was most useful, popular, and admired throughout the State, until political cliques were created to displace her. Then she came here to Passadina,—an Indian word, I believe, which means "key of the mountains." An Indiana colony began a temperance settlement here six years ago, much in the same way that one was begun at Colorado Springs.

Mrs. Carr has travelled with Muir, who is preparing a work on the glaciers of the Western coast, and is supposed to know a great deal about the mountains and the Yosemite. I felt very sorry not to see and talk with her for a longer time. A teacher was lately needed for the high school, and Mrs. Carr fills the place for the present. We drove directly to the school. It was recess, but some of the children went for Mrs. Carr. She at once came out into the sunshine, with a face as strong and cheery as the sun itself. A compact little woman she, in a bright calico dress made with such simplicity as it was a pleasure to see. She did not at all like my brief visit. Had been giving the children a lesson in the geography of Passadina! They had no idea that geography had anything to do with the place they lived in, and were much surprised at being asked to draw a map of the school-yard.

Mrs. Carr has had forty acres of land here under cultivation for the last two years. She has already canned and dried tons of fruit. Never was there a place in which trees were in such a hurry to bear. I wish my New Hampshire cousins could see it. It is well the Spaniards settled here; no other people of that time would have known how to deal with the alkaline soil. Passadina is a vast cultivated plain.

We drove directly through Mrs. Carr's plantations,

filled with all manner of rare trees and vines. Professor
Carr sat at his desk in a library half filled with cabinets.
A nightshade with lovely purple blossoms climbed over
the porch and festooned the eaves. The Professor — a
fine, benevolent looking man — brought us many kinds of
grapes to taste; among others the Zinfanel, looking like
a ruby, half sweet, half sour, from which the finest
clarets are made. We drove on through raisin ranches
and vineyards. The company have brought water
down from the mountains, and every purchase of first-
class land entitles the purchaser to a water right. Proprietors of second-class land must buy this right in
addition.

Vines, oranges, lemons, limes, pomegranates, figs, almonds, English walnut trees, and pepper groves make
this settlement one of the loveliest spots on earth. We
went through charming gardens, by houses bowered in
roses, laurestinus, dacomas, and so on, thirty feet high;
but words mean nothing to one who has never seen it!
We passed the Gilmore place, and another owned by
the nephew of Jewett, who published "Uncle Tom's
Cabin." All along, in addition to the tropical luxuriance, there was a semi-circle of mountains on the
horizon like that in Colorado, but finer in its contrast
with the cultivated mesa and hill-sides. We drove
across the Arrojo Seco or Dead River, with its mighty
hidden beds of lava. Mountains sprang up at the right
as we entered the town at its eastern end, and went
across the Los Angeles river to our boarding place.

I had no intention of going to Santa Barbara unless I
was wanted; so while Nettie and I packed our hand-
bags in order to go out to "Red Roof" for the night, Mr.
Severance telegraphed for me, as Mr. Peabody had sug-

gested. Red Roof stands at a pleasant drive of three miles to the west of the town of Los Angeles. Never saw I a prettier picture than that presented when we crossed the end of the avenue, Mr. Severance mischievously driving on that we might not for a moment suspect that he had anything to do with the lovely place. Our shouts of delight arrested him. Palms, castor-oil plants, bananas, and yuccas skilfully arranged give a far more tropical look to the approach than I have seen anywhere else. The long, one-storeyed house is surrounded by a piazza broad as a room. This is covered by a passion flower, a shell flower, a gigantic wistaria, a dacoma, and cleanthus. Oh! that I could but make these flower names glow and burn for you, in purple, blue, crimson, and gold as they do for me! On each side of the porch magnificent ivies start up, and their giant branches spreading under the roof of the piazza tapestry it with verdure. A hammock hangs in each wing. The centre is furnished as if it were a room, — a privilege conferred by the dry season which treats upholstery gently.

Here we were glad to sit for a little while, enjoying the unwonted environment. It seemed impossible that we could have driven thirty-five miles since morning; and yet when we thought of all we had seen, we might well have been a week on the way.

A door opens into a room, half hall, half parlor, with floor and wainscoting of red wood. A good Corôt stands on an easel; pretty water-colors hang on the walls, and skins cover the floor. Behind this is a large dining-room. To the right are four bedrooms; to the left are the pantries, offices, and so on. The kitchen, opening upon a lemon grove, is in the rear of all this. Upon the central portion of the roof is a single, good-sized sleeping room built for boys, which goes by the name of "the bunk." To this our host's voice summoned us speedily that we might see the mountains in sunset light " before the fog covered them." I laughed to myself as I ran quickly up, for I knew the fog had curled quietly in some time before. It was a superb sight for all that,—the summits canopied in gold and purple. There were guests at dinner; some of the neighbors came in after; and then I wrote out notes of one of the most delightful days of my life.

From Los Angeles, via Wilmington and the Pacific, to Santa Barbara, Sept. 24, 1880.— I heard mocking birds before breakfast, and yesterday one swung on the rope of the hammock while Virginia lay there reading. I rose early. There had been a heavy fog, and steps and roof looked as if there had been a shower. I went about picking unknown flowers, looking at the Chinese umbrella tree, and watching the method of irrigation. I do not believe that any tropical plants are improved by irrigation. I am sure that much of the fruit I saw yesterday would be greatly better if it were simply " cultivated,"— that is to say, well spaded about; but this would probably cost more than water. Mr. S. pays two dollars a day for water.

Soon after breakfast, Mrs. S. and I walked down the block to see my friends the W.'s. They live on a pretty little place, planned a good deal like Red Roof, but less costly and younger. I saw all the children but two. Lulie was to have a "musicale" to-night, to which I had been invited. The neighbors had sent in a dozen watermelons. They had themselves bought a bushel basket of grapes for *ten cents !* "Tell all our

friends," said Mrs. W. laughing, "at what an expense
we entertain."~ How pleasant it was to sit there, seeing
the look of far-away faces in the children's eyes! Safe
at the bottom of a huge trunk, and tied with a blue
ribbon, are the little printed love-letters the father of
this family sent me when he was a boy of six. I have
destroyed many more costly things, but they are safe!
How little I thought then that I should ever see him
a "fruitful olive" in this far-off land. He used to
come shyly behind me and push his little letter into
my pocket, as I sat sewing for my own marriage beside
the sofa where his invalid grandmother lay, full of
interest in my "seam." How clearly rise the dear faces
of that far-off time! Then California was not,— not a
modest woman within the borders of the State: and
now!

We walked home. I helped Mr. S. to gather some
lemons, chiefly that I might say I had done it; and put
up some fine stalks of pampas grass, and one or two
big pomegranates.

Then we went over to the pretty little house built by
Miss B——. It cost, with half an acre of land, and
the windmill which irrigates the garden, just $2,800.
The principal room is a hall running straight through
the house, with three small rooms on each side; three
bedrooms, a parlor, a music room, and a dining-room.
There is a kitchen separate outside, with a loft over it
for the one Chinese servant. A ladder leads up to the
loft from the porch, and this is taken down after the
servant retires for the night, which prevents all uncertainty as to his whereabouts. Two young ladies live
here alone.

We gathered the beautiful "bird of paradise flower"

as we went home. "See how anxious these things are
to do their duty," said Mr. S. as he met me, and showed
me a fig tree about a foot high with three ripe figs
upon it!

After lunch there was nothing for it but to prepare
for departure. I had not seen W. himself yesterday,
so we drove into his yard that I might at least shake
hands with my old correspondent. Opposite his avenue we entered some fine grounds, remarkable for a
great show of Australian flowers. Don't imagine for
a moment that California takes any comfort in her own
flowers, any more than her own wines. Not a bit of
it. She is nothing in her own eyes, if she cannot show
you everything Australia or Japan can boast, from the
cryptomeria to the roc's egg!

In town I found a cordial telegram from Santa Barbara. Mrs. Severance had on her mantels some barnacles from Santa Monica, the prettiest match-safes
that could be devised. I thought of various scientific
friends who would be delighted with the pink and
white things, which are between three and four inches
high and nearly two across, and grow in groups of
three. So I went into all the stores in a vain search
for them, but I "created a demand," as the merchants
say; and next year travellers who don't know what a
barnacle is will reap my harvest.

Santa Barbara, Cal., Sept. 25, 1880.— I think we
waited in Mr. Severance's carry-all, at the dépôt, a full
hour.

Los Angeles is just a century old. It covers six
square miles, has sixteen thousand inhabitants, and was
christened Pueblo de la Reina de los Angeles,—"Town

of the Queen of the Angels,"— which was very soon shortened by Spanish laziness into its present appellation. To my great amazement I find it thirty miles from the mouth of the Los Angeles River, when I had supposed the town was on the Pacific itself. It is in a large valley, with two harbors, Santa Monica and Wilmington; and, with the Sierra in the background, magnificent views offer themselves whichever way you turn. It is the centre of five railways. I think I did not tell you yesterday that we passed the Sierra Madre villa, eighteen hundred feet above the sea, where a delightful hotel is kept for invalids. I am perfectly certain that dyspeptics and many chronic invalids will find the dry season, during which they can sleep and live out of doors, a great advantage here; but I do not think there is a place on this coast fit for people who are sensitive to changes of temperature. The inhabitants will not own it. The difference between morning or evening and noon is very great. Yesterday morning, when I rose, the thermometer was only 40° on the piazza at Red Roof; and when I drove into town after lunch it was 83°! This is a common experience on the whole length of the coast, including Santa Barbara.

We were to leave on the cars for Wilmington, and then take a tug six miles down the river to the steamer. There is great and growing dissatisfaction here with the policy of the Railroad. While our journey was under discussion, a great deal was said about the indifference to public comfort which delayed necessary repairs at Santa Monica, and compelled passengers to go to Wilmington. Last year the Legislature appointed a committee to inquire into railroad abuses. The committee required evidence to be given openly in person, and in consequence no one dared to appear before it; and nothing of consequence was done. The United States has given so much to all the overland roads, that they ought to be compelled to be just in dealing.

Our cars ran down through a sort of delta to Wilmington. From thence we took a tiny tug to a barge anchored six miles away, from which we boarded the steamer for Santa Barbara and San Francisco. We were very crowded, and it was by no means convenient for people with hand baggage. It was very foggy till we got out to sea, and quite rough all the way. A full moon then made everything lovely, and I would have liked to sit up to enjoy it, but the queer long swell of this detestable Pacific kept me on my back. I staggered up now and then to look at the peaks of the Sierra Madre and the Coast Range, garlanded by wreaths of fog that were snowy white.

For the first time since I crossed the Rocky Mountains, I received the utmost courtesy and attention. One of the finest staterooms was put at my disposal. The stewardess was a character. She had gone out to India with Lord and Lady Campbell; sailed between China, Japan, and San Francisco for six years; was then transferred to the Oregon Line, and was now making her first trip South. She did not like it any better than I did; but tried to divert my headache by telling of Chinese gardens, and of a visit from the Mikado, who proposed to her to teach the young princesses English!

At half-past four this morning she brought me a cup of tea, but it was atrocious, and I contrived to dress without its help. She and Nettie followed me out to the wharf, and put me into a carriage for Mrs. Dugdale's boarding-house. I shall not forget the drive through the soft, half lighted dawn, and gardens heavy with mysterious sweetness. I was alone for the first time on my journey.

My ring at the door was answered promptly. I was ill enough to go directly to bed, hoping for sleep, but an old friend was coughing away his life in the next room, and I had to give it up; and after a breakfast which I made small attempt to eat, my room was changed to one on the ground floor. How little I realized, as I looked out of its windows upon the wilderness of flowers, that this day was to bring me into close contact with a tragedy I shall never forget.

My headache did not abate. Several callers came in, and each one asked me if I knew Theodore Glancey, a young Republican from Illinois, who had come here to edit the "Daily Press" through the current campaign. I did not know him, but he professed to know me; had heard me lecture, was coming to see me; had given me a pleasant notice in his paper, and would be in church to-morrow! Mr. Winchester, whom I remembered with his wife at the West Church in Boston, and Mr. Knight, also of Boston, came in with hymn books, order of service, etc., and seemed rather perplexed over my prostrate condition.

I was sure that a good night's sleep would set me up, provided I could get a clear two hours for preparation in the morning. In the course of our talk, it was decided that I should speak of my journey through the country, and of the duties of California people; so I began to think about this, and as I lay, prostrate with pain, the whole thing arranged itself in my mind. I heard each of my visitors speak with affectionate in-

terest of Theodore Glancey, who had only been here
four weeks. I thought a good deal of *his* painful
editorial duty, and unconsciously shaped what I had
to say somewhat for his comfort.

I dare say that in the little story I have to tell of
this faithful "Gift of God," you will all think that I
exaggerate its importance and effect. So you would
have thought if I had written to you on the morning
after the battle of Lexington, and told you of John
Hancock's visit to the parsonage of that little town!
It is in obscure moments that history is made; and
if the inhabitants of Santa Barbara be but faithful to
their duty, there is no reason why the events of this
day shall not constitute the dawn of political regen-
eration, — may not put an end to the reign of force
on this great Western coast.

After dinner Mr. W. came round, with his wife
and a friend, to take me to drive. If anything would
relieve my pain, it was surely the fresh air. So
we went out through the town to the mesa, or high
table-land which commands the Bay. Santa Barbara
sits, like Naples, a queen of the sea. A semi-circle of
superb mountains hems her in. Her Bay is full of
lovely islands, on which are mountains that are high
enough to shut off the terrible trade-winds.

To the right hand and to the left of this Bay the
spurs of the Coast Range shoot out into the sea. A
beach of snowy sand is spread out at her feet, and
tossing waves of laughing blue, which look like broken
sapphires, leap over the snow. It is almost too beautiful to bear. The hills themselves are greener than any
I have seen in California, and there are many groves of
live-oak in the hollows by the sea. How glad I am

I have not missed this sight! Returning, Mr. W. took me first through the grounds of a Mr. Dibbles, who is going to put up on the mesa a superb one-storey house in the Spanish fashion. Its extensive terraces will command both sea and land in a truly royal way. Before I was half satisfied with seeing, we turned and drove to the old Presidio, or residence of an old Spanish governor, where Richard H. Dana once went to a wedding, which he describes in "Two Years Before the Mast."

The house is of adobe, covered with stucco, and the walls are three feet thick. It is built round a court; and the tiled roof is extended over this court so as to protect a wide walk, and is sustained on the inner side by light pillars. In the centre was once a fountain, and opposite to the entrance hall was an archway under the house, through which a carriage might pass from the street to the enclosed court. The wood-work is of red-wood, carved in a true Moorish fashion; and the ceiling has been frescoed by Indian hands. Some modern Goth has colored the red-wood green! The rooms are high and spacious. The whole aspect charmed me.

From this we went to the Santa Barbara Mission, which is larger and finer than any I have seen. It has many shrines with figures carved in wood, such as I have already described. The oddest thing about it is the colored rosettes on the ceiling, which look exactly like old Moorish tiles. Half way up the church a Franciscan, with his gray robe and cape, his girdle of rope, and his rim of yellow hair, was earnestly teaching the catechism to a class of ragged Indian boys. The friar might have stepped out of an old missal, the boys might have served as models to

Murillo, for they were half Spanish,—the words were the purest Castilian. Where was I ? I had never expected to see all this till I lounged, half dreaming, in the courts of the Alhambra!

None of the friars were at leisure to show us the cloisters, where schools are still kept.

As we drove into town, Mr. W. stopped at a drug store to get me some ammonia. He came out instantly with a white face. "Clarence Gray has shot Theodore Glancey," he said, "and they say that Glancey must die."

Alas! all editorial hardships were over now. This friend, so sure to greet me in church to-morrow, I should never see with mortal eyes. No one spoke. I had seen excited groups of men talking at the street corners for the last half hour, but I knew too little of Spanish-Mexican ways to make sure it was unusual. Silently my friends dropped me at my own door, and then, from my horror-stricken host I gleaned what follows.

On the 15th of September, 1880, the Republican State Convention met at Santa Barbara, and Clarence Gray, an Irish lawyer, whose real name is Patrick Mc-Ginnis, with many *aliases*, was nominated for district-attorney. It was a disgraceful nomination, on account of the character of the man; and in alluding to it, September 16th, the "Daily Press" very mildly said: "The charity of our silence is more than he can expect."

That evening Gray met Glancey, and told him that if another word of the sort appeared in the paper the town would not be large enough to hold them both. On the 24th the "Press" had occasion to refer to some delay of the decision of the Supreme Court in regard to the elections of this year; and added that if "no county elections should be held, the Republicans would have this compensation that they would be saved the necessity of defeating their own candidate, for Santa Barbara would not submit to have its county officers chosen from among the *hoodlums* and law-breakers."

A very mild statement this seems to those who are familiar with the courtesies of Western newspapers; and it came out last night. At two o'clock this afternoon, just after Glancey had been warned by a friend of mine with whom he had been talking over the service in the Unitarian church to-morrow, he was attacked by Gray in the street. When the latter showed a pistol, Glancey seized both his wrists, saying, " You shall not shoot an unarmed man," and as another person approached Gray, he left him and turned to enter the Occidental Hotel. Gray fired twice. The first ball shattered Glancey's wrist and then passed through his body near the navel ! Gray was arrested; but after being bailed for five thousand dollars went gaily about town, shaking hands with his hoodlums.

In talking over this matter with my host, the son of a Philadelphia Quaker, he said that the present district-attorney was a shiftless fellow who never put anything through, and that Gray had been nominated because of his business capacity, as the whole county was impatient over the present state of things. " I should have voted for him myself," said Mr. Dugdale, " if Glancey had not pointed out the folly of such a step." This assassination will not make much impression on Eastern people, but it is a very critical thing here, — the first time, I believe, such a cold-blooded murder has occurred in what may be called the quiet New England community of Santa Barbara.

Santa Barbara, Sunday, Sept. 26, 1880. — I went to bed directly after dinner last night, but not before it was certain that Glancey could not live. Gray was a second time arrested; the town was convulsed with excitement, and there was loud talk of lynching. Gray flinched, like the coward that he is, and begged to be put into a dungeon, where the noisy crowd that gathered about the jail doors could not reach him. The fellow is said to have three undivorced wives living, and the poor Irish girl who married him last walked round and round the jail all night, hoping to keep off his enemies.

Before breakfast this morning a circular deeply bordered in black, and bearing the following words, was thrust under every door :—

"THEODORE GLANCEY,

"Editor of the Santa Barbara 'Press,' died this Sunday morning, Sept. 26th, 1880, from a pistol-shot wound inflicted by Clarence Gray. His last words were: 'Tell my friends that I die like a man, — die for a principle, and would not go back on it now if I could.'"

George William Curtis, James Freeman Clarke, and the men who are struggling like them in New England for political purity do not find the cold faces of their party very pleasant; but this poor fellow laid down his life for the cause, and was not ashamed.

And he had known me, he said, "ever since he was born." I wish I could have seen him. Of course I had not slept, much as I needed it. I had been thinking out what I should do, all night.

The Unitarians here have just fitted up a modest little

wooden building, but they had not plastered the walls. When they got my telegram, the staging was all up for the plaster to go on ; but they removed it, replaced the seats, and prepared for a service. It was well filled to-day. I made the whole service a funeral service, every word of which should bear upon and evolve the thought of immortality. My text was from the first chapter of Genesis,— " Without form and void." I tried to show that this was what the world would be without a " Living God"; and that if Death reigned, a " Living God" could not be. I was profoundly moved by the aspect of my audience. Every mortal in it was sad as if for a personal loss, and there were several young mothers in the seats with babies in their arms. The last time I saw that, I think, was in the Lynnfield church, and I remember how the babies crowed now and then, while the green branches of the elms, waved by the breeze, brushed across the windows.

When the service was ended, a lady dressed in black, about sixty years of age, and with a face streaming with tears, came up and took my hand. She was silent for some instants. " You have done me a great deal of good," she said at last. " You do not know me ; you will never see me again, but I felt that I must come and tell you." I begged for her name. She gave it very reluctantly, and added that she was from Illinois. As she turned away, she continued, "I shall never forget one word you said." So it was worth while to lie awake all night, — which I had doubted.

I am sure I never spoke in so hot a place as this little chapel proved to-day.

There was a warm little buzz of welcome and sympathy from those of the audience who lingered, and I went home hoping to sleep. But I had several callers. Among others came a young girl, who wants to preach; but I could not encourage her, for she has not the natural qualifications. No man should aspire to the pulpit without a good voice at the start,—and still less should any woman.

Santa Barbara, Sept. 27, 1880. — This morning Mr. W. came early with Mrs. W. and a guest to drive me about the town; but it was some time before we could do anything except talk over the assassination. Although it was one of the loveliest days possible, a pall seemed to hang over the town. People muttered below their voices at the street corners. Glancey lived nineteen hours. About an hour before his death a letter arrived from his young wife. He had written her about moonlight walks upon the lovely crescent beach. "Soon," she said in this reply, "we shall be walking there together." At this point Glancey said faintly to the lady reading, "Stop." After a pause he motioned that she might go on, and in less than twenty minutes after she had ended he was dead! When I remember that his dying words came close upon this tender greeting, I think they gain an added power. We had to think of all this, because the poor young wife will never see even his dead face. It has been found impossible to embalm the body.

We went first to the beach. The tide, which is said to vary only three feet, is now very high, and we could not get down to the lowest sands. From the beach we drove over to Montecito. Mrs. Eddy was away, to my great regret. Besides being very lovely in themselves, her grounds are nestled in a valley green as emerald, and

have the most charming outlook over the Bay. I am
perfectly sure that there is a great deal of fog in Santa
Barbara, but the residents, who are of course also the
proprietors, steadily deny it. Yet this morning one of
them drew my attention to the islands, whose sides were
wreathed with snowy vapor. "Do look at those mountains," he said, "it is a hundred days since I saw them
as plain as that!" I think the variations of temperature
here quite as great as they are in Los Angeles, though
the trade-winds are cut off by the islands. It was 42°
when I rose yesterday morning, and 87° when I got
home from church!

In ordinary seasons life here must be delicious to
well people. The aborigines thought so, for in 1542
Cabrillo found this the most densely populated part of
the coast. At that time there were forty native towns
within the limits of Santa Barbara County. Like the
harbors on the coast of Maine, this harbor faces the
south with its soft breezes. The Santa Inez range
stretches back of the town parallel to the coast for
seventy miles, and only three miles from it. It is a
wall three thousand feet high, and spurs shoot down to
the sea each side the town, not more than a mile and a
half from each other, and enclose the Bay. Beyond
this Bay, about twenty-five miles to the south, a group
of islands rises, and the mountains upon Santa Rosa,
Santa Cruz, and Anacapa are twenty-five hundred feet
high, and break the bitter chill of the southern trades.
Yet these make themselves felt. Here, as at Los Angeles, people carry wraps, and do not sit out at night.
The white chalky cliffs are rosy red at sunset. A few
foot-hills not hard to climb separate this valley with its
sloping sands from that of Montecito. The upper part

of Montecito is seven hundred feet above the sea, and
overlooks its azure plain.   Here there is a merry
music of waterfalls and shifting shadows of green
vines.   Live-oaks hung with blossoming parasites, and
beautifully rounded hills vary the river, while the ocean
breaks angrily into snowy spray over a few scattered
rocks.   Here the threads of vapor spinning over all the
sky turn to golden meshes, or films of amethyst as the
sun sinks.   Olive, almond, and orange-trees are petted
in shy corners here; but I think they will never be
profitable for market.   It is best honestly to acknowledge cold winds and heavy fogs.   Nothing can be more
beautiful than the approach by sea.   Ten miles away
from the town and about a mile from the shore a perpetual oil-spring rises and floods the ocean surface with
an iridescent calm.   Its odor is distinctly perceptible
on the west side of the town, and the people fancy it is
healthful.   Under the barren plains and lofty mountains
all the way to San Francisco a great stream of petroleum
flows, or a solid bed of asphalt lies.   Between the rivers
Zulia and Calatumbo and the Cordilleras, Mr. Pluma-
cher of Maracaibo, in Venezuela, has lately reported to
the State Department fountains of petroleum mixed
with boiling water, which yield two hundred and forty
gallons an hour.   They are as noisy as steam-engines.
The end of the world is not very near.   Its loving
Maker and Preserver has supplied it altogether too pro-
fusely with fuel and light.

Three hundred feet above the sea stands the old Franciscan Mission, the most beautiful mission on the coast,
and the only one preserved to that order.   It is built
of sandstone and painted or whitened like the old public buildings in Washington.   The nave is two hundred

and forty feet long and forty feet wide, — a proportion
observed in all. Two domes with open belfries surmount towers united by a "curtain," in which is the
main door. To the left is a wing of one hundred
and thirty feet, with a corridor supported on arches
with pillars running the whole length. Here the
faithful friars keep a "college" at work. Three thousand Indians built this mission with its reservoirs,
basins, fountains, and aqueducts. The water from its
cisterns still supplies the whole town. In the towers,
from enormous beams by strips of raw hide, are hung
the five great bells which strike the hours. A rude
figure of the virgin and child is niched into the pedi-
ment above the curtain. In the rear I catch a glimpse
of a belfry surmounted by a cross like that at San
Gabriel. This belfry is made of a single thick wall, and
beneath it is the graveyard with its shattered crosses
and thousands of nameless graves. There is an old
garden brimming over with fragrant bloom, and over
the door which leads from the church to the cemetery
are three human skulls with cross-bones adroitly sunk
in the plaster. Nineteen buildings were once needed
as dormitories for the converts! In 1796, three hundred and twenty-five Indians were baptized, and the
Mission owned two thousand head of cattle and eleven
hundred sheep. A beautiful view of the ocean the
Gray Friars have, as they dreamily pace up and down
the cloisters, and the sailor coming up the Bay sees the
lovely form of church and belfry rising far above the
town. Inside the building are some very barbarous
pictures, — a very odd one of the Last Judgment, a
copy of Orcagna, I think; and over the tomb of the
first Bishop of California hang his jack-boots and the

green-satin hat faced with gold which pleased his simple converts.

After this we drove out from Montecito to see, not the largest grape vine in the world, for that was cut down and sent with its statistics to the Centennial, but the next largest, which is one of its offshoots. A hundred years ago, a Spanish lady came through from Sonora on horseback. At the last moment her lover broke a bough from a vine, with which she might brush away the flies from her steed. She planted it when she dismounted, and at the end of the century it had a girth of four feet and six inches. The offshoot, which is now almost as large, trailed over a trellis, encloses a spacious hall, and last year yielded three tons of grapes.

As we went into town we visited the club and library rooms, which give a little New England air to the place. We tried in vain to find good abalones, or barnacles. We went also to Mr. Ford's studio to look at some interesting sketches in oil of the cañons and missions. He has a very excellent gallery; without making any wild pretensions, his pictures are nicely painted, and there are a great number of them. I found it a very pleasant way to make acquaintance with many parts of the coast that I shall not see. Mr. Ford has a fine collection of fossils and curios. I coveted innocently some of his fulgurites and moss agates.

After dinner, Mr. Knight took me out to Spence's gardens, that I might see the great dépôt for the exportation of pampas grass. The grass is brought in from all the country round, green, and tightly encased in the sheath. This is slit by a woman's hand, and when it is removed, the stalks are laid on the ground for two or three nights and days, and bleached. If they were gathered ripe, they would "shed." Mr. Spence has sent one hundred and fifty thousand stalks to London this year; and Mrs. Spence told me she could open fifteen hundred stalks in a day. She sat under a great fig tree at work. Beside the usual overflow of half tropical flowers, I saw immortelles of wonderfully brilliant and varied hues; and I was introduced for the first time to the slender spires of the *Statice Harfordii*. They are immortal, and look a little like lilies of the valley,— of a lovely violet color, crowded on their stem. When I went into ecstasies over a great bed of English lavender, now out of bloom, and cried out for my linen shelves, Mrs. Spence kindly brought me all she had saved for her own drawers, and insisted on my bringing it away. I bought some pampas grass, of which the part of the stem in flower measured forty-two inches!

I can give no idea of this garden, spread over a level space, where more superb roses were trampled under foot than any New England horticulturist ever saw in his whole life. I went into the barn where they were packing the pampas. The feathery wonder climbed in bales to the very ridge-pole, and fifteen thousand stems were going in one box to New York.

We drove about the town a good deal, to pick up persons to go up to Colonel H.'s ranch to-morrow on a sort of picnic, and so I got a glimpse of many pleasant people and their homes. At the Dugdales' I found Dr. Lincoln and his wife whom I used to know at Jamaica Plain. I had not seen him since we stood together by the death-bed of my dear friend James P. Walker.

Santa Barbara, Sept. 28, 1880.—We started in a light and most convenient omnibus for Colonel H.'s ranch. The road runs parallel with the shore, and a good part of the way between fields of lima beans, which are dried and exported from this country in immense quantities. Mr. H. told me of a small farmer who bought two hundred acres of land for three thousand dollars, and paid for it by the first crop of beans which it produced.

Although Santa Barbara is not a good place in which to raise figs for market, and although it has no crop at all this year, yet it so happens that I have eaten my very sweetest figs here. They were white and brown Smyrna. I think it is the brown Smyrna which should be used, if people mean to plant for a distant market. It is fleshy and dries well, with a rich flavor. The green or white Smyrna fig is a shorter fruit. Mrs. Winchester sent me a basketful procured in the neighborhood, which were so sweet and rich as not to require cream, which is the common way of eating them. They were cracked deeply, and sugared with their own juice.

On the left of the road as we drove to Glen Annie, which is the name of Colonel H.'s place, there is a little lake named for Governor Fenton.

At the little town of Golita, the creeks running inland are salt for many miles, like Charles River, near Boston. As we got a little away from Santa Barbara, the sea breezes brought the odor of petroleum.

When we entered Colonel H.'s ranch, where the acres are counted by the thousand, we passed between vast orchards of olives and almonds. The Santa Barbara olives when pickled are small and very black, but they make a delicious oil. Mr. Cooper, on the next ranch to

Colonel H.'s, devotes his land to olives. The fruit has a bitter tang, but I find that those who eat it long grow very fond of it. A great deal of eloquence was wasted upon me to-day, in the attempt to convince me that I had never tasted the finest of foreign almonds or the purest Lucca oil. I am prepared to admit that there may be some disappointments and some adulterations in food, but I have never yet found reason to believe that a person who knows what good food is, and has the money to buy it, will not be able to do so.

Mrs. H. has also made a very successful experiment in pickling limes.

We got out of the wagon at Mr. H.'s farmhouse, some ten miles from town. On the porch was a bit of stone, pierced by the ocean borer. It looked like a fossil honeycomb. This led to my hearing strange stories of sea urchins and oysters imbedded in rock. The germs are floated into the cells of such a comb, and there they develop. The sea urchins soon perish, but the oyster lives and seems to secrete some acid which enlarges his quarters. He has a very thin shell, and must be near enough to the external surface to get nourishment by thrusting his long foot out.

We walked a little way to the beautiful spot about one thousand feet above. the sea, where Colonel H. has terraced the soil, and once meant to erect a large house. He was prevented, I think, by some lawsuit about his title. The frequent lawsuits about titles that I find on this coast are enough to take the courage out of the boldest pioneer; and the same may be said of the unlucky squatters in Leadville. A mining claim underlies all others. When Colonel

H. bought his ranch, nobody thought of mines or oil in this region, and I believe there was no allusion to either in his deed. The original owner of his ranch is dead, but he has left five or six sons. With some of these Colonel H. has come to terms ; the others refused to sell out this mining claim, and brought a suit against him which would undo the work of twenty years if it should be successful. Whether successful or not, such a suit prevents any sale, and takes the heart out of a ranchman's efforts. It is time California put an end to such nonsense, and made her titles clean and whole.

The site I spoke of commands the shore for thirty miles, and the view, though magnificent, is not just what I should wish to be compelled to see from every window. I would rather walk to it through my garden. The Colonel was an Ohio farmer. In 1853 he brought his sheep into Santa Barbara County, having been two years in driving them across from Ohio ! He sat down on this ridge, was thrilled all through by the ocean view, and resolved to be rich enough some day to buy it. Ten years ago he completed his purchase. Mr. W. went through the nurseries planted just here in a vain search for some late apricots or nectarines. Santa Barbara is so famous for these fruits that I am disappointed not to taste them from the tree, but it is too late. My friend picked me a few strawberries however, which were as sweet as honey, and far more delicious. I want to note this, because I have seen none from market that I considered eatable. They all have a bitter tang, which I suppose they get from the alkaline soil. These Hollister gardens and plantations have given me a new idea of what flowers can be and do. A wall with an arched gateway, covered with the crimson bracts of the *Bougainvillia spectabilis*, was the most magnificent mass of color under this warm sun that I ever saw. Each crimson bract carried a long yellow tube expanding into a corolla; and oh, how wonderful it all was! No green to be seen anywhere, — leaves hidden out of sight.

On and on, through walnut groves we went till we came to the pleasant cottage where Colonel H. actually lives. The broad piazza in front of it looks down to the sea through an oval clearing a mile long. It is planted on its outer border with a double row of eucalyptus and Monterey cypresses, which are intended to keep the cold winds from the walnut and orange groves. Directly in front of the house was a circular bed of gigantic calla lilies, in the very heart of which some mighty plumes of pampas waved. This is a far lovelier spot to live on than the famous "Ridge." We passed the house bowered in roses, and kept on through the cañon till we came to a spot sheltered by large oaks, furnished with prostrate trunks, and lying between two high walls of rock. There was nothing to distinguish it in appearance from many places that I know in New England. I was a good deal disappointed to find that we were not going on to the olive ranch. Mr. H.'s overseer is a Mr. Coffin from Nantucket, who took a great deal of pains to show me the characteristics of the different oaks. Colonel H.'s servant brought us a wheelbarrow load of watermelons, the crimson fragments of which were soon glowing in a dozen places. They were not as sweet as many that I have eaten from the Boston market. In Washington or West Virginia no one would have

dreamed of eating them; but that is the paradise of
melons, — not to say "millions" as the natives do.
We were furnished also with delicious milk and cream.
Just as we were coming away, after a hearty lunch,
Colonel H. appeared in a black velvet suit, and carried me away through his lime, almond, and walnut
groves. There I discovered that a fine fresh almond
tastes no better than a new chestnut. It is at least
two months after it is gathered before it matures and
develops its own special flavor. The same thing is
true of the chestnut and walnut, but not to the same
extent. The lime trees are always in bloom, which
is true in a very limited sense of the lemon, and not
at all of the orange. Colonel H. presented me with a
single spray of orange blossom which was all he could
find on hundreds of trees, and which he insisted must
have bloomed on purpose for me, as its appearance
was most unusual. He loaded several gentlemen with
Persian Cassavas, called here the "spoon melon," which
he wished me to taste.

Colonel H. has still about seventy-five thousand
sheep, only four thousand five hundred of which, however, are on this magnificent ranch. Everywhere as we
entered were live-oak groves covered with slender pointed acorns of vivid green. A funny little woodpecker
makes holes in the thick bark, and studs the trees
with thousands of acorns which he sticks into the
holes. It is supposed that each acorn holds a grub,
and that Master Woodpecker discreetly waits for it to
fatten, and puts it in his own pantry where it need not
fall with the autumn leaf. This ranch is too large to
have the lovely perfectness of the fruit ranches at Los
Angeles. It has a general air of *unfinish*. We passed

herds of cattle winding between the foot-hills and scattered orange groves. Mr. Coffin says they often feed out fifty wagon loads of water-melons to the cattle! If not sweeter than those "fed out" to us, the milk would be none the better. There are three hundred acres of walnuts, and both sweet and sour limes. Upon the lime-trees I found an anomalous fruit which was peculiarly delicious, and of which I could easily have gathered a bushel. The proper fruit is like our pickled lime,— large, with plenty of seeds, and quite often a very thick skin. On the ends of the branches were scattered a great many limes no larger than a nutmeg, with a rind as thin as the thinnest foreign paper, and no seeds at all. I brought away as many as I thought I could use in crossing the continent, for they were ripe and perfectly delicious. I have seen a phenomenon something like this on Northern trees of a wholly different species; but I never saw it anywhere on such a scale.

I asked Colonel H. what "chapparal" was, — for every two people differ in the definition of it. The old Spaniards made rustic chapparal fences, and they are very picturesque. The rods are from four to six inches in diameter, are set close to each other, perfectly erect, and as uneven as a knotted fringe at the top. They frequently grow where they are set. He considers the word equivalent to our "brushwood," and says it does not indicate any special growth. The roots of the thing are large, and sold for firing. "Madera" means "matter" or "material," and seems to correspond to our English word "deal."

When we came near the house, Colonel H. drew my attention to a superb "cloth of gold" rose which nearly covers it, and whose blossoms are counted by thousands, I think. He said it was only eight years old !

Finally we packed ourselves up and came away, — I most unwillingly keeping the whole party waiting while melons and limes and fresh almonds were packed into the carriage for me; but you will guess that it was by no fault of my own. It was a delightful day; yet it does not rival in memory my superb ride from San Gabriel to Passadina. However, I cannot do it justice. To-morrow Theodore Glancey is to be buried; and the next morning I go with the steamer that takes his body to San Francisco, otherwise I could not have had the heart to go exploring to-day,— for with me it was exploring and not picnicking.

When I got home I found that another black-bordered hand-bill, announcing the funeral from the Presbyterian Church, had been thrust under the door.

Santa Barbara, Sept. 29, 1880.— Early this morning Mr. W. drove me into town to purchase supplies for my journey. I did not give up the idea of going to San Francisco by land and in a carriage, until I found that to do it would cost me nearly a hundred dollars, if I were not able to ride all night ! I wish Miss Bird would lend me a little of her spirit; for to that task I felt wholly unequal. The stage coaches travel all night. After the first day's journey I must sleep at an inn, and take a carriage of my own, for only one stage passes in the twenty-four hours. Then I might not find the beds clean, nor the food eatable. It is really a great disappointment; but if it had been spring and the roads fair, I would have done it. It is not probable I should have seen a woman on the whole road. As it is, I take the steamer with to-morrow's dawn ; and I find that Mr. Stearns, proprietor of the "Daily Press," and president of the State Republican Committee, takes the body of the brave Glancey to his wife on the same steamer. She is with her father at Calistoga Springs.

Does Santa Barbara know what has happened to her ? Does she realize that this shot, like the one fired at Concord, should be heard all round the world ? I cannot tell. What has happened has brought me into a very vital connection with the place and people ; yet absorbed as everybody is, it has been impossible to divert interest to shows and scenery.

After I had tried in vain to buy some of the dried figs, prunes, nectarines, and raisins which ought to be for sale in every part of California, we drove again to the Mission, where at my request a young French friar from Bordeaux showed us all the old silver and the robes. Some of the old Spanish embroideries were stiff with gold, and the silver vessels were like well known modern reproductions, threaded on the repoussé with gold. Among them, some very old "olios" demand a word. These are small vials of wrought silver, with a silver spoon attached to the stopper, with which the oil is applied in extreme unction in case of contagious disease. They are not much used ; but one of them held the oil in a beautiful crystal marked with the twelve hours. Opposite the tomb of the first bishop was a strange old picture of the Last Judgment, which I have not described, although I spoke of it on my first visit. The open "mouth of hell" is represented by the gaping jaws of a veritable dragon ready to crunch his prey. Two holes have been cut into the canvas during the last month by mischievous visitors. The friar told me, with tears in his eyes, that a valuable crucifix had lately been stolen. I felt a sincere pity for this graceful young Frenchman, whose heart is in his Order, — an Order which has lost control of every mission on the coast except this. I was sorry that I could not spare time to go through the college. I put out my hand, and thanked him. "Madame, it is I," he said, for he talked English when he found that I hated to talk French, — "Madame, it is I who should be grateful for unusual sympathy."

At home, where I went to pack up my odd collections of mosses, corallines, algæ, and so on, I found an old fisherman with a bushel-basket of barnacles, but none were of the right sort; and some ladies who had heard of the little girl in Canada who wanted "sand from the Pacific," brought sand and shells for her.

After lunch I walked sadly down to the Presbyterian Church, which was soon filled by the indignant and loving friends of Theodore Glancey.

Every clergyman in town took part in the service, which, so far as the speaking was concerned, was of the first excellence; but it grieved me to see how little those who officiated knew the resources of the English Bible. The whole service might have been drawn from the Old Testament in eloquent and suitable words. What was read seemed poor and dull. All the speakers were deeply moved. Mr. Weldon, a resident invalid, once pastor of the society worshipping in this church, made the address, and fully met the fact, that, not so much Clarence Gray, as the whole

State of California, is responsible for Glancey's death; and so, if a jury will agree to convict the wretch, not merely the town but the whole State will be saved. At present, assassination appears a pleasant pastime.[1] The certain punishment of crime is one of the greatest safeguards of society.

When the coffin, covered with flowers, was carried to the hearse, the whole congregation reverently followed. It was then apparent that, beside the audience which filled the church, at least five hundred persons had been silently crowding all the approaches. Chinamen, hoodlums, Mexicans, Spaniards, and all the riffraff lined the sidewalks in their best clothes. They looked sober enough as we passed between them. Every place of business was closed; every carriage in town seemed to follow the hearse. The procession was more than a mile long. When I first came out of the church I was glad to walk slowly through the strange crowd, till the carriage overtook me. The Long Wharf, which juts out to meet the steamers, is half a mile long. It was pathetic to watch the slow march of the mourning people, as they followed the body to the warehouse, where, properly guarded, it will wait until morning. Mr. Winchester drove out upon the beach, where we kept sorrowful silence till the living tide turned.

Never since that morning after the assassination of Abraham Lincoln, when I found myself the only woman on State Street, without knowing how I got there, and without anybody caring whether I was there or not, have I seen a whole population swayed by one emotion, as here in Santa Barbara to-day. God grant it may be to some lasting good!

[1] See the acquittal by disagreement of both Gray and Kalloch, March, 1881.   18

As we drove back into town, I saw a fine old adobe house. The smooth, hard walls, full three feet thick, provide deep window-seats and doorways. The windows are large, and the roof tiled with the usual "bits of split cinnamon." A wide porch covered with passion flowers, cloth-of-gold roses, and jessamine runs across the front of the house. One passion vine fills, I am told, a space two hundred feet long by fifteen wide, — a solid wall of green, starred with purple! The house nestles at the foot of a cliff seamed with ravines, a wagon road wound along the ascent, and near on dizzy heights countless sheep were feeding. In the square yard before the house four century plants were in bloom. The leaves were five feet long. They shaded a plat twelve feet in diameter. From the centre rose a flower-stalk thirty-two feet high, of the usual bluish-green color. Around this column the flower-stalks spring out spirally about ten inches apart. Each is tipped with bluish-green bracts and obscure white flowers.

On each side of these immense plants rose huge daturas, dropping white and purple bells ten inches long by five across; and a great columnar cactus, about twelve feet high, realized the description of Joaquin Miller:

> " At his side a cactus green
> Upheld its lances long and keen,
> Flat-palmed and fierce with lifted spears ;
> One bloom of crimson crowned its head,
> A drop of blood so bright, so red,
> Yet redolent as roses' tears."

I went back to the hotel to dine this last night with the kind friends who have done so much for me. Colonel H. recognized me, and brought me a parcel containing beautiful mosses and arrowy acorns from the live-oak sent by Mr. C. He introduced me to Mrs. H., who did not appear yesterday,—chiefly, I suppose, because she heard I was a preacher; and being one, she fancied I could not be a lady!

I have now seen Santa Barbara, the "loveliest spot upon the coast!" This is said to be a wholly exceptional season, but I must write of what I find.

There are no marked changes of season, so far as I can discover, on any part of the coast. There is only the rainy season and the dry; but it seems to me that each day holds *all* the *four seasons.* The night grows steadily cool from dusk to dawn. You may begin with one blanket and add to it till you have three, and your eider-down quilt! Two blankets are all I need in a Washington winter. At dawn here the thermometer is 42° or less. At noon it is 89°. It only "stays warm" for less than three hours, and in driving very heavy wraps are needed. Fan-palms, oranges, almonds, olives, apricots, pomegranates, peaches, figs, and grapes, as well as apples and pears, grow here; but the former would never be profitable crops within ten miles of town. To raise the semi-tropical fruits people must plant away from the sea.

The pepper trees are lovely beyond describing; geraniums and heliotropes grow to the height of sixteen feet. There are thirty varieties of acacia. It is said one may have open windows all the year round. I have never yet seen any one *sitting* by an open window, and fog is manifest morning and evening.

No one can exaggerate the beauty of the Coast Range, and any one who knows about mountain scenery will understand me when I say that at sunset the peaks turn to amethyst, amber, and ruby. They look translucent, not merely purple, yellow, and red. Thirty miles inland is the Ojai valley, studded with alder, sycamore, and cotton-wood, and covered with magnificent groves of oak. It is one thousand feet above the sea, with pleasant cottages gleaming through the trees. This is a favorite resort for people with bronchitis.

Santa Barbara to San Francisco by sea, Sept. 30, 1880. I lay down but did not undress last night, the arrival of the steamer was such an uncertain thing. I heard the Mission bell strike every hour. At five o'clock, while it still was very dusky, the hack took myself, Dr. Dunning, and Mr. and Mrs. Stearns down to the wharf. The sun rose into a sky flecked with rose-color. The fog lay low, wreathed about the mountain tops, which glowed like gems. The harbor is most lovely; and very beautiful were the heights of the mesa as we floated under them. The most verdant crops are in the bean fields, and perhaps they are the most profitable. I sat a long while on deck watching the fog and the pranks of the gulls. At least a hundred of the latter were playing round the ship, picking up a lunch and balancing themselves on the waves.

How strange it is they should never be sea-sick! They seemed to rendezvous and dance cotillons in the air. They fly backward as a man would chasser.

I do not like this clumsy ocean. It has no salt air, no fine fish, no lively motion. We reached Point Conception, and the wind grew cold.

Then came a low line of beach and some scarp mountains. The coast is very monotonous. At Point Harford, the port of San Luis d'Obispo, we found a mere wharf at the foot of most abrupt rocks. From this

wharf a narrow-gauge road runs sixteen miles into the
hills, passing through several tunnels. We had not
time to go up to the town, and I enjoyed walking back
and forth on the wharf with Mr. Stearns. He thinks
as I do of the importance of Glancey's death to the
whole State, and has a wistful feeling about it, because
Gray really intended to shoot Stearns; and, coward-like,
only turned away from him when he found that he went
armed. As the proprietor of the paper, Gray insisted
that Stearns was responsible. I saw at Dr. Dimmick's
the other day some beautiful Japanese anemones four
feet high. That comes up now because we discussed
the climate, and because Dr. Dimmick is as thoroughly
crippled by rheumatism as if he had lived all his life in
New England.

On board the Orizaba, Oct. 1, 1880.—I had an oppressive headache, and could not sit up much. When I
came on board I had a stateroom to myself; but the
agent, who I am sorry to say is a woman, sent two other
persons into it. The purser swore there was no other
room, but the fatter of the two women made sure she
could never get into the upper berth. She showed more
of the "wisdom of the children of this world" than I
ever possessed. She went to the purser. " Have you a
step-ladder on board?" said she. " No, indeed," said
the astonished man. " Then have you two stout sailors
to lift me into my berth?" Another stateroom was immediately found! The steamer is very full, — the food
is excellent and plentiful. Two tables are set for every
meal. Nowhere in California have I been so comfortable as on these boats. The "Orizaba" is not as large or
as fresh as the "Ancon," but she rolls less and is well

managed in every respect. My first thought morning
and evening is of the silent body on board, a mute pro-
test against the violence of the land borne on a halcyon
sea.

This morning the mountains on shore are three deep.
Bright sunshine lies at their feet, although we sail under
a cloud. Just after passing Point Sur we came upon a
mountain apart from the shore, rising like a pyramid
from the sea. I could not find that it had any name.
Across the Bay of Monterey there was a heavy swell,
and from behind black clouds the sunshine streamed
over distant hills and pastures. Santa Cruz could be
guessed at; how absurd it seemed to be obliged to pass
on to San Francisco before I could reach it! Whoever
wishes to make Santa Barbara a desirable residence, or
to increase the value of its real estate, must put it in
communication with the rest of the world. A town
which one can only approach or leave once a week, and
then by nothing but the slowest of comfortable steamers, will never attract a very spirited class of citizens.

The approach to the Golden Gate was beautiful, and
we sailed out of a golden sea in lovely sunset light, into
the harbor of San Francisco covered with black fog. So
little did anybody expect me, that not a soul came to the
door when the carriage drove up!

San Francisco, California, Oct. 2, 1880. — I found
thirty letters awaiting my arrival, among them one
which would have enabled me to go to the Yosemite if
it had only been written according to promise.

At night we all went to the Carnival. It was the
last night, and although painful anxieties connected
with the health of those dearest to me would have

kept me at home, it was something, everybody said, not to be missed.

Everybody was right for once. In the first place there was a procession across the stage of the great hall, where the Mechanics' Fair was held, consisting of all the groups clad, I may truly say, in gold and silver and precious stones. It marched to stirring music. Certainly there must have been from eight hundred to a thousand persons in this procession, all superbly dressed for their various parts! In Californian vernacular there were two thousand. The amount of money spent on these costumes must have been enormous. They were all perfectly modest and in excellent taste. I saw only one absurd group, and that was the Egyptian. Nothing could have been worse. The affair opened by an exhibition of the Olympic Club. The costume or "tights" of this club is not flesh-color but white, which gives a very statuesque effect to their performances. The whole magnificent procession seated in an amphitheatre at the rear of the stage, acted as spectators to their pleasant feats. It was easy to imagine one's self in an old Greek theatre waiting for a gladiatorial combat. It was truly a superb sight, which drew down thunders of applause when the curtain rose. Some of the pyramids of legs and arms were painful to contemplate; nor do I think any good comes of one man's standing on his head till he is black and holding another on the soles of his feet. The club had been an important part in the opening procession, and it was curious, as it crossed the stage, to see some of the performers turning somersaults in the air from the shoulders of others.

The training is perfect. If all these men only knew

and obeyed the moral law as they know and obey the physical!

Only two of the tableaux challenged special admiration. Guido's "Aurora" was very well got up; but a Mrs. Holmes personated "Venus rising from the sea" in the most exquisite manner. Her drapery was snowy and perfectly modest, as might be guessed from the fact that she walked about the hall in it, leaning on her husband's arm, after the entertainment was over. Her beauty would make her a fit companion for the new Hermes at Olympia. The shell in which she rose opened gradually, and colored lights were thrown upon it, which while her own attitude was changing made a variety of charming pictures.

San Francisco, Oct. 3, 1880. — I went to the North Beach, and, perhaps for lack of a guide, found no wonderful surprises. My Washington letters are greatly dejected on account of the last news from Maine. I expected it, but I expect also that Maine will go for Garfield. How small an appreciation of peace and comfort must those people have, who consent to Government patronage!

San Francisco, Oct. 4, 1880. — To-day I visited Mrs. S. at Menlo Park. This morning I tried the resources of the "White House," which is I suppose the best dressmaking and "ready-made" shop on this coast. I bought a warm ulster made in Berlin for seven dollars, and had it fitted to my figure for one dollar more.

I got a boy to bring my baggage to the dépôt, as I expect to go on to Santa Cruz as soon as a brief visit to Mrs. S. is over. Warned by previous experiences, I brought the morning's paper to the dépôt, and asked for a through ticket to Santa Cruz with a stop-over at Menlo. The man positively refused to sell it, and concealed from me the fact that I could go on in the way I desired by the narrow-gauge road. He was so rude in answering and not answering my questions that I sent my sweet-mannered daughter to him, to try if she would be more fortunate. He was quite as rude to her, and then we took our seats and waited patiently for Cousin Henry to join us.

Menlo Park is the aristocratic suburb of San Francisco, where many of her wealthy merchants have built houses like those of Brookline near Boston, or of Irvington on the Hudson, only on an infinitely more pretentious scale.

We ran out through some pretty little suburban towns for perhaps three quarters of an hour, — a nearer estimate of its distance from San Francisco I cannot give, for when I asked, every one said, "I don't know," and I cannot find it on map or gazetteer. We stopped at Fair Oaks, and the train was in such haste that I could not get off safely, and Nettie hardly did so. Captain K. came to the rescue, and the train was again stopped a hundred yards beyond. A beach wagon with two comfortable horses was waiting for us. The town consists of large estates in a great "live-oak barren," as they say at the West. Each is neatly fenced, and the roads are excellent. Each proprietor, with the aid of irrigation, keeps a half-acre or so of lawn about his house, bright and green; but the outlying fields through which the long avenues wind look like well-shaven wheat fields. The live-oak, covered with moss or ivy, the eucalyptus, with its bluish leaves and long red rags of fluttering bark, the candelabra pine, and the Monterey cypress make these fields verdant. ~ The flower-beds are nearer the houses, and from them roses, verbenas, and heliotropes overflow. There is no way to describe the abundance of flowers here, nor the wealth of color carried by climbing and creeping vines. Mrs. S. was born in Alabama, and met us on her porch with sweet Southern courtesy, and showed us herself to our separate rooms, where we found all the luxury of a Parisian bed-chamber. When I came down again I went through a long billiard room to a library fitted up with carved furniture from Venice, which has grown dark through the changes of three hundred years. When we went to dinner we returned through the billiard-room, crossed the wide hall, and entered a long and elegant dining-room, where a table laid with fruits and flowers and an abundant dinner, served item by item by a white-gloved butler, kept up the graceful foreign illusion.

I wish that old furniture could talk ; I think it would express a dissatisfied astonishment at its change of location.

Menlo Park, Oct. 5, 1880. — Obliged to stay here some twenty hours longer than I intended, on account of the discourteous stupidity of the railroad agent. I went down to the office this morning and telegraphed to Santa Cruz that I would arrive to-morrow. Then we drove about among the various plantations, all charming ; but, perhaps on account of the limited lawns, much less finished than our Brookline gardens. It amazes me to see so many people raising thirty different kinds of flowers, and not knowing the names of ten. I have already been introduced to six or eight kinds of "shell-flower," each totally distinct from the other. "Better fifty years of Europe than a cycle of Cathay." Among others, we drove into the grounds of a Mrs. Rathbone. Although she was not at home, we got out of the carriage and went in to see the house, which was built after that used by the British Legation at the French Exposition.

The hall and stairway are hung with fine plaided India mattings, held in place by delicate black-walnut mouldings. Furs covered the floor. The reception-room to the left was furnished with rich embroidered velvet, and a curtain of crimson velvet embroidered with a rose-tree in profuse bearing, which Mrs. Rathbone brought from Paris, makes a portière leading to the dining-room. On the dining-room side it is lined with a lovely bit of Beauvais tapestry. Above stairs there is a beautiful room called the glass-room. It runs the whole length of the central building, which projects in front of the wings. It has a window at each end, and is glazed all across the front in three bays, with deep box-seats. These windows are screened half-way up with a transparent linen bunting embroidered in faint colors. All the accessories are elegant and exquisite. These people have immense wealth and no children. Having finished and furnished this house, they desire new worlds to conquer, and want to sell it.

Mrs. S. has two hundred and fifty acres here; two hundred are in wheat, and these in this year of abundance will not pay the expenses of cultivation. So she stores the crop. Only large ranchmen can make money if Nature continues to be so bountiful. In the lovely sunset light I walked over the estate and across to a little cottage surrounded by fruit-trees, where one of Mrs. S.'s daughters lived for a while after her marriage.

It was a pleasant little house, but looked dreary because it had no lawn. Wheat-straw was spread over the dusty soil.

Menlo Park to Santa Cruz, Oct. 6, 1880.—After breakfast my daughter returned to San Francisco and I went to drive with Mrs. S. We passed through long avenues bordered by immense live-oaks. On Mrs. S.'s own lawn I observed fine young sequoias growing. They are lovely green cones, full of life and vigor. The " big trees" remind me, when I look at their foliage, of extinct dandies, with a single lock of hair straggling over a bald pate. We saw Mr. Flood's place from a great distance. The avenue seemed half a mile long; and after spending one million on his house, he has bought so much land that no one can guess how many acres he owns. At the dépôt the agent refused to sell me a ticket any farther than Pajaro, and could not tell me how many miles it was to Santa Cruz, nor when I should arrive there !

What was my amazement on entering the train to see Mr. Stearns there. I had to look a good many times before I could believe it ; but I was very glad, as I could hear, through him, something of the funeral at Calistoga. He found the wife of Glancey a delicate invalid, overwhelmed with grief, and so young as only now to be giving promise of what she might hereafter become. It must have gone hard with him to have to tell her the whole story, including Gray's fierce pursuit of himself, which only ended when Mr. Stearns's friends sent him pistols and insisted on his carrying them. Mrs. Stearns went with him, and they delivered to her Theodore's last written words. What can any human being say to a woman afflicted like this poor young wife? The home funeral showed how much Glancey was beloved and respected. A great company followed the body to a lovely spot in the cemetery, nine miles from the town. Mr. Stearns showed me a sweet, tender, little note from Mrs. Glancey, addressed to the people of Santa Barbara, thanking them for their sympathy. He was now on his way to Santa Cruz in search of an editor to take Glancey's place. He promises to see me again there. He found he should have to stay on at Pajaro, and gave me his own ticket to my destination,—so I had no more trouble with railroad agents.

At first we went through wide wheat fields, dotted with live-oak, and through a very level country. At Pajaro we ran through charming valleys and green ravines, till we came to Soquel, the most English-looking cluster of cottages, on a sea-beach. There is still a larger group at a distance from the road. Still skirting at the slowest possible rate the lovely bay of Monterey, we came at last to Santa Cruz! We have been more than two hours making the twenty miles.

I have come to Santa Cruz to see the woman whom Brook Farm remembers as Georgiana B. Did any one ever see her magnificent eyes, flashing with indignation or glowing with smothered feeling, and find it possible to forget her? For many years she has been Mrs. K. of Santa Cruz. She is one of those brave, strong women, with whom one may differ at many points and yet hold a sweet, firm relation to her until death. In her half-French, half-English veins she carries the blood of the brave, eccentric Princes of Condé, mixed with a more cultured and quiet stream flowing from the English gentry. She planned all my Southern tour for me, and planned it well.

Mrs. K.'s servant was at the dépôt, expecting his mistress as well as myself. She had been suddenly called to the Jesuit College of Santa Clara, at San José, where her youngest son is at school. John found no one but myself, and speedily drove me to the house, where a charming young Chinaman let me in, and I found no mortal beside. I sat down by a cosey wood fire to read; my host soon came in, bright and genial, and excused his wife's absence. If California were not full of romance, the romance of Richard K.'s life would probably have been written years ago. He came to New York from Staffordshire, and shipped on a whaler in 1843, going round the Cape and bringing up in the Sandwich Islands, from whence he sailed for Vancouver's.

It is not very easy to guess what this journey was like nearly forty years ago. While the officers of the vessel were merry-making in their own way, Mr. K. and five others deserted. They put off in a whale-boat without food or water, and when they tried to land were attacked by unfriendly savages. After thirty-six hours spent without water they landed, but only delayed long enough to fill their keg, as unfriendly foot-marks surrounded the spring. A terrible storm swamped the boat, and three of the men were drowned. The others, thrown upon a sand-spit, ate the bodies of a sea-gull and a porpoise that had been killed by the storm. Their boat was snagged on the other side of this spit, and putting off to the mainland they found blackberries, which quenched hunger and thirst. The first Indian whom they met stole from them the few articles which had been intended for barter.

From a friendly village they learned that the jargon which described an American was " Boston Tillicum." The Indians at this point took the boat, provided the three men with food, and then set them to work to build their chief a " Boston house." In two weeks they had built a cedar house, twenty by thirty feet, and were then kindly guided across the country to Chenook and Astoria. This was in 1845, and three months after one of the men went back and exchanged a good rifle for the boat they had left behind. He took it overland to Columbia, the Indians helping to make the portages.

This whale-boat served as a pilot-boat on the Columbia for many years.

Mr. K. went to work at once in a tannery, having stumbled on some curriers' tools, and soon had enough to do. The next spring, some capitalists agreed to start him in a tannery above the falls; but just then a dispute began about the north-western boundary. The capitalists wished to withdraw, and offered him a fine horse and an outfit for California. Mr. K. accepted the offer, and started with a large party of Canadians and half-breeds, who soon broke up into separate companies. Being warned on the way of recent attacks of the Rouge River Indians, they travelled safely till they got news of the Mexican war, in the Sacramento Valley. At Sutter's Fort, K. was prostrated by chills and fevers; and an old mountaineer giving him sixty grains of calomel at a dose, he nearly lost his life. He was carried on an ox-cart to the river, and there taken on board the " launch " about to carry wheat for the Russian Government to Yerba Buena. He was kept alive by a little tea, till he found a United States sloop at the foot of Montgomery Street, in what is now San Francisco, and was kindly cared for. When he was convalescent, an order for rations at the Sonama barracks saved him all further trouble, until he regained his strength. After he had fulfilled promises to those who had protected him, Mr. K. bought a small valley in sight of North Beach, and set up a tannery of his own. Here he worked up a few hides and deer skins, — peeling his "bark" from live-oaks standing near the "Presidio." To crush the bark, he took stones from a grist-mill on Clay Street, and his tools were made by a blacksmith !

Judge Blackburn, of Santa Cruz, coaxed him away from this primitive work to dress hides for him in Scott's Valley, in the winter of 1847-8. Then and there the gold fever broke out. Mr. K. went to the mines; made three thousand dollars in three weeks; made a great deal more in trade; followed Frémont and Dr. Corey to Merced; made about thirty-six thousand dollars in a few months, and lost it in as many weeks.

By this time he had learned that nothing was so steadily profitable as well paid labor. He opened his yard in Santa Cruz in 1850, and in 1855 enlarged his firm, and with fine water-power proceeded to make the leather which is now well known on the Atlantic coast by his stamp.

An ardent advocate of good schools, religious freedom, and "black Republicanism," when this last meant something forcible, he justified his English birth by a flower-garden as lovely as the glades of Devon could show,— skilfully concealing the barren soil by borders of vivid green.

After she left Brook Farm, Miss B. devoted herself to the prisoners at Sing Sing; taught colored people in Missouri at a time when to teach might mean to die; and finally took charge of a colored school in West Chester, Pa. I think the pleasantest things I ever heard of Margaret Fuller were the accounts Mrs. K. has given me of Margaret's kindness to her, — steadily continued, with real assistance nobly rendered in emergencies. I hope Mrs. K. will live to write out her own "reminiscences." Not many women could write so charming a book; for she came in contact with many remarkable people.

At about eight o'clock she and her daughter reached home, and after half an hour's lively talk I was very glad to go to bed.

Santa Cruz, Oct. 7, 1880. — Ora drove me down to the beach, where we stood awhile, and then rode along the sand, looking at the beautiful Bay, to which the encircling mountains add the charm of the Riviera. Coming back I saw on the sand, just above the beach where it was a little loose, beds of what look like a parti-colored pink verbena, and we got out to pick the flowers. They were exquisitely fragrant; the breath of lilacs is in them. The people call them the "beach verbena," but the true name I could not hear. We drove to Branci-Forte, and from the heights of Ocean Avenue, which runs along the spur where the river enters the Bay, we got a wholly different glimpse of sea and land.

Fifty years after Columbus discovered America, Cabrillo sailed North, exploring this coast. When he reached Santa Cruz, he fell into ecstasies because here for the first time he found mountains covered with

19

trees! He called the Cape after his viceroy, Mendocino, and by that name it is still known.

In 1578 Sir Francis Drake came, and him, too, the forests astounded. In 1602 Viscayno began to talk about "rose-trees and arable lands."

All this was before the Mayflower came into Plymouth Bay; and during this time the Jesuits worked hard further to the south, and dotted the coast with pretty Missions built by native hands. Of the fanatical Society of Jesus, it was always the most disinterested and genuine part that went into exile to do the work of pioneers.

When the Jesuits were banished in 1767, the Franciscans came in a more adventurous mood; and so, in 1769, cattle and houses were sent as far as San Diego by land, while provisions, tools, and officers came by sea. The priests did not intend to invite emigration,— only to educate the natives themselves. They meant to go on to Monterey; but they went thither by land, and the description of Viscayno had been written at sea, — so they went on and on till they stumbled upon Santa Cruz. "It was a pleasure," writes Father Cressé when they had crossed the San Lorenzo, "to see the herbs and rose-bushes of Castile!" Redwood and sycamore were cut down to permit the cattle to pass.

All the existing Missions sent contributions to the new town at Santa Cruz, when the cross was erected here in 1791. They built a church one hundred and thirteen feet long, thirty wide, and twenty-six high. The adobe walls were five feet thick, and the Indians burned tiles for the floor.

At this time Captain Cook was travelling through the Southern Seas, and John Ledyard of Connecticut

was with him. The Spanish Government wrote to
the people at Yerba Buena, and told them not to let
Ledyard land; but however he did it, he managed
to learn so much that when he went to see Jefferson
in Paris, and told him about California, he excited
an interest in the country which Jefferson roused
himself to transfer to Washington, and which has
been steadily growing ever since. The Indians were
even then almost as delicate as the Hindus, whom
a man may kill by a sharp slap on the chest.
Their work was like the work of other pioneers,
yet they died at the rate of fifty-four to three
hundred and eighty-eight in a single year. It is
said this Mission had once a great treasure, beside
its three thousand head of cattle and its countless
sheep. We hear of golden chalices, and of a priest's
vestment worth twelve hundred dollars. Grain was
ground by hand in a mortar. There were no vegetables.
The beams of the old Mission Church were hewn and
sawed by hand. In 1825 five hundred people from
the United States were on the California coast, and two
hundred of them at Santa Cruz.

In 1836, Graham of Kentucky assisted one Alva-
rado to organize an insurrection against the Spanish
Governor. The Governor fled; but the Mexican Government proceeded to recognize the insurgents! This
had not been expected, and in 1840 the frightened
conspirators rose against Graham. There came then a
dreadful time of confusion, which led to claims against
Mexico, — the Mexican Indemnity, as you have heard it
called; and of this, a few years after, Graham received
thirty-six thousand dollars! It was only three years
later that Mr. K. came and worked in a small tan-

yard in Scott's Valley, with Paul Sweet. He had eight
oval vats made of logs. The bark was ground by a
large wooden wheel at the rate of half a cord a day;
and five hundred skins were dressed in this way in a
year! Santa Cruz makes me think a little of the ocean
drive at Newport. It has not the Neapolitan charm of
Santa Barbara, but looks out to sea in the boldest way.

Santa Cruz, Oct. 8, 1880. — Last evening we went to
hear Clara Foltz, a young lawyer and wife in San Francisco, who has excited a great deal of sympathy on
account of her vigorous efforts to support herself and
four children, under such circumstances as most try the
souls of women. She was to make a campaign address
for the Republican committee. It was said to be a capital audience that gathered to hear her, yet it only half
filled the small Opera House, and the *hoodlums* in the
gallery kept up a constant cat-calling. She is a bright
and rather pretty blonde, and her address would have
been a very fair one for any provincial orator of her
age; but I demand more than this of any woman who
comes before people. I did not like the popular hits
which brought down the house; and her voice, which
would have filled the auditorium in her usual parlor
tone, she lifted into an unpleasant screech.

She is still quite young, and capable of far better
things. If she had started on a high moral ground, I
am sure her audience would have risen to the occasion.
She came in to see me after her address, and I found
her very pleasant in private. Something led to our
talking of the low order of morals prevailing in the
State, and the possible influence of the women who are
getting into public life. I spoke of a woman in a cer-

tain town of whom I thought I had reason to complain, and was told that she only kept her place because she was the mistress of one of the men she served! A great many men in Southern California employed in female high schools, if I may believe what I am told, have used their position to corrupt the habits of their pupils! Why not employ women?

I spoke to Mr. Stearns at the meeting last night. He has found a man brave enough to take Theodore Glancey's position, and goes back to Santa Barbara to-morrow.

Santa Cruz, California, Oct. 8, 1880. — This morning Mrs. K. and I drove along the cliffs for several miles. The mountains meet the sea with a charm not to be described. We talked a good deal of the condition of education in the town. There is some disagreeable scandal connected with the school committee, and there is the usual talk about the abuse of pupils by male teachers all through the State. A very simple way to remedy this evil is to employ women to teach girls in the high schools. If they are not to be found here, there are many such women in New England as Miss Cleveland and Miss Austin; and there are those with failing health, to whom the mere change would be complete restoration. Beautiful is the sunshine, beautiful the rippling streams which dart down to the sea, beautiful the green coverts filled by nurseries and orchards of all the semi-tropical fruits. I cannot think these last will prosper, — the climate is too cold.

The Pajaro Valley has a soil said to be inexhaustible, after a cultivation of twenty-five years. The most beautiful thing I have seen in the country is Mr.

K.'s garden, which does not give a sign of the arid soil, which spoils so many others. Where there can be no lawn the paths and beds have a green border, which gives it the look of Devonshire. The town has a fine bathing-beach of clean white sand. The wild-flowers show by their species a cooler climate than any I have visited. I see buttercups, clematis, anemones, barberries, lupins, clover, primroses, convolvuli, and azaleas, with an abundance of ferns. These, either the same species or species closely allied, creep up to Boston Neck, Cambridge Bridge, and the Brookline Meadows, — to say nothing of Middlesex Fells.

There is a mountain near, of what the New Yorkers call *stink-stone*, — that is sand or limestone saturated with petroleum. There was at one time a factory for extracting the oil. About six miles away, on the Railroad just built, lies a big-tree grove, where General Frémont once had his camp. There are half-a-dozen fine trees, and one three hundred feet high and twenty in diameter. A few years ago there was a great excitement over columns, capitals, and other architectural wonders found on a Mr. Locke's ranch. Some of these wonderful formations are now bedded in Mr. K.'s garden. There is little to astonish us in the fact that they were mistaken for pre-historic ruins. The most prominent industry in Santa Cruz is that of the tan-yard. Lumber, lime, and powder are sent from this county to the markets of the East.

The powder-works must sell at a high profit. They are situated in a most lovely valley, where it is impossible to dream of slaughter; and, although every now and then they most foolishly blow themselves up, the California Powder Works are said to be on a paying basis!

Santa Cruz has the beginning of a library, to which the ladies have added a free reading-room. There is also, thank God! the beginning of a temperance movement. I say this without believing in the least in pledges, total abstinence, and the like, except as the necessary but inefficient means of beginning a good work, — a means imposed by ignorance and a quick conscience.

Everywhere throughout this beautiful world, alcohol is largely provided by natural processes. The juice of some kinds of palms, of all kinds of citrons, of the peach and many berries, turns to alcohol when these fruits ripen, or whenever they are allowed to stand when ripe. The Peruvian finds maté in the stems of his cactus; the Esquimaux, in piles of beach berries. There are many possible circumstances in which life cannot be preserved, so far as we know, except by the use of alcohol. It seems to me, therefore, that it forms part of the Divine plan, and that the only effectual way to secure temperance is to teach self-control instead of legislating abstinence. No restraint which comes from without is worth a straw except in a few painful cases. The restraint which is to save us comes from a manly exercise of the will; and we must begin at the beginning.

The stomach is to a great extent exactly what we make it. Little babies must be *fed*, not *crammed*. Over-eating must be branded as shameful; and, above all, the women of the whole world must cease prating about the burden of housekeeping, the trouble of daily cooking, and the impossibility of baking bread and pies for their families. I know no more frequent cause of drunkenness than the bad cooking of ignorant women. Hunger ceases to be hunger when the stomach is abused, and becomes a diseased craving for support. Drunkenness abounds in all hard-worked communities, chiefly because these communities are likewise imperfectly fed. I know that I saved one high-born drunkard in Canada simply by giving him good coffee and hot oysters whenever he came for them, even if it were in the middle of the night. If he had gone to any public eating-room he would have gone into temptation.

One other thing is needed, — that the punishment for drinking should be made disgraceful. Whenever a man is found drunk I think he should be set in the stocks, or flogged. He is no longer a man; he has made himself a brute, and should not be comfortably fed and lodged at the public expense. Still further, men should be compelled to pay the full penalty of any crime committed in drunkenness. Murder is murder, and robbery robbery, and arson arson, — whether the guilty creature be drunk or not.

In these ways the law can help us, and in no other. I feel at liberty to say these things, because I have never offered alcoholic liquor as a beverage, and because I have never refrained from using it when disease seemed to point to it as a natural remedy.

I cannot say much about the Unitarian church in Santa Cruz. Great sacrifices have been made for it, but its frame of gold seems to rest on feet of clay. I do not believe in building churches in any hope that Spiritualists, Universalists, Christians, and Unitarians may settle into a homogeneous whole. If I were a young preacher I would take my life in my hand. I would walk all the way to some spirit-starved place East or West, if I could not afford to ride. When I got there, if I had not money to hire a hall, I would preach on the hill-side or in the open square. The doctrine of God's love and man's good-will appeals to the common and the cultivated alike, and I believe whoever yields these a firm faith, and takes the risk, will find his reward.

In the afternoon we drove to Soquel, the loveliest little nook on the coast. A few cottages, built as a summer resort for the people of San José, are clustered under the great oak-trees. We drove further on, to the beach, which I passed as I came into Santa Cruz, and which has a little settlement of thirty or forty houses close on the sea, and is called Camp Capitola. On the sparkling sand, under the glowing sun, it seemed to me more like some little watering-place on the British channel than any of our pretentious American resorts.

We came home in a most remarkable sunset. The sun went down in a firmament full of lightly flecked clouds. It sank at last behind a band of dark gray cloud five or six times its own width, which gave no evidence of unequal character; yet unequal it must have been, for the golden orb was crossed by three black bands, and glowed with refulgence between.

Santa Cruz, Oct. 9, 1880. — This morning we went down town and bought "water drops." These are transparent pebbles of silica and quartz, colored by various minerals, and about the size of a large scarlet pea. They are all nearly of the same size, and are gathered with great pains on a pretty beach a few miles away. I bought some limpets and sea-sand for Agnes Strickland's little grandniece, and some brilliant corallines, — red, green, gray, and purple. The latter, I am sorry to say, fell to pieces before we got home.

I have spent a good part of the day in reading Mrs. K.'s autobiography, one of the most fascinating memoirs that ever came to my hand. I could give you one or two charming stories out of it, if I did not most sincerely desire that she should finish and print it herself. After lunch, Ora and I went to Moore's beach, — partly to pick up pebbles, and partly to see three arches eaten out of the cliff by the restless, overbearing waves, and called "natural bridges" here, although they are bridges that lead nowhere. Ora thought we had better go to the lighthouse and see whether Miss Hecox might not have some barnacles for sale. This is one of the pleasantest visits I have made in California. We danced away over the beautiful road and in the clear air. At the gate we fastened our horses, and when we went into the house were shown into a sort of private kitchen.

There Miss Hecox came to meet us. She is the daughter of the keeper, a woman about twenty-eight years old. She is supposed to have had a fall in infancy, which occasioned, first, convulsions; and then a paralysis of one side. Many a child would have been soured by her fate, but Laura soon began to take pleasure in the study of shells, until she is quite an authority on this coast, and very useful to many more famous collectors by exchanging or forwarding what they want. Through the kindness of such persons she has accumulated a pretty museum, which her father has been proud to set up. It is the only trace of luxury in the simple house. She had just received the seed-vessel of the Egyptian lotus, labelled "betel-nut" by some odd mistake, and was so grateful to have the label corrected that she gave me some pretty shells. She has a sweet, frank, intelligent face, which makes one forget her misfortune ; and the recollection of her useful and busy life, several miles from any town, will always rest in my mind as a pleasant contrast to the lives of many women whom I know, whom nothing short of London or Paris can furnish with occupation.

Santa Cruz, Oct. 10. — It is a sorrowful Sunday to me. If I had not been full of employment it would have been unendurable. The " treasure " that we hold in precious little earthen vessels in Buffalo we have nearly lost, and the letter which should have come to reassure me is missing.

Directly after breakfast Mr. K. started for a vineyard in the Zeyante valley, which he wished me to see, and to which he had no time to carry me except to-day. As the Unitarian church is closed, I had nothing to leave.

We had a strong, spirited, young horse. The road, though pleasant, was neither remarkably interesting nor characteristic until we got high into the mountains. We passed through some fine woods which would alone have repaid me for the drive. Pine, redwood, and chestnut-oak, how magnificent they were ! Each was seeking the sky, shooting up, up, — without a branch. A good deal more impressive, however, are our Eastern groves, where the bulk of the trees is realized because the spread of the branches is commensurate with it.

I shall never forget my first view of this vineyard. A dozen or twenty hills, all pitched toward each other in the sharpest angles, accessible to their tops, but accessible with difficulty, make a cup in the mountains, lined with the yellow-green verdure of the grape. The

vine is not trained here, as at Los Angeles and Passadina, but sprawls along the ground. In the intervening
hollows, almost out of sight, lofty cedars and red-wood
rise and shut it all in. The first look like the deodars
of the Himàlas, so grand and dark they rise. There
were a few huts, barns, and "sample-rooms," but not a
dog, a horse, or a man in sight. No sign of man's work
either! Angels themselves might be tending the vines
for all one could guess, and yet the lifted eye travelled
over hundreds of acres.

In the three ranches nearest to me there were
more than a thousand acres. Four hundred and sixty
of them belong to the vineyard I have driven twenty
miles to see. The first purchaser paid forty thousand dollars for this spot, and spent twenty thousand
dollars on it. When he broke down it was offered
by the local bank, to which it was mortgaged, for twelve
thousand dollars. Mr. K. wanted it, but could find
no one to go into the purchase with him. I think it
cost the present possessor no more than six thousand.
He is a Frenchman, who made ten thousand gallons of
red and white Burgundy last year, and will make twenty
thousand this year. This vineyard is placed like the
famous vineyards near Oporto, where the best port is
made. It is very much sheltered, yet ice frequently
forms at night.

We wandered up and down, tasting very sour grapes!
There was a kind of Catawba grape, wholly without
seeds, that I thought might make a sort of Sultana
raisin. None of the Muscats were ripe. We climbed
the hill until we stood under some superb live-oaks,
ankle deep in loose soil, and in the midst of underbrush composed of chaparral and laurestinus. Chap-

arral here is supposed to indicate an evergreen oak, but
this was in blossom. It bore obscure greenish flowers,
which had nevertheless a decided effect when seen from
a distance. Where each of these had gone to seed was
a pinch of downy white fluff. Roses, escholtzia, a lovely
pink and white flower growing in clusters at the axils
of bare stalks, and bright scarlet primroses, darting in
twos and threes from a bunch of dark leaves, enamelled
the slopes. Seven miles away a hazy scallop showed
the crescent of mountains which encloses the Bay. Beyond these was the swelling ocean.

"In a clear day," began Mr. K., — but I had hardly
patience to hear. It is what they all say in California,
and never yet has there been a clear day! Of course I
cannot tell what will come after winter rains, but I like
the summer flower and the autumn grain to get a little
sunshine. It is impossible that grapes should be allowed to grow so entirely hidden by leaves, unless they
need to be sheltered from the chill of night and fog.
We walked a quarter of a mile to a fig orchard, but the
"time of figs was not yet!" All around, apple trees
were bending under their burdens. Their tawny or
russet cheeks kissed each other as closely as if they had
been the berries of a bunch of grapes. I tasted, but
the fruit had neither sweetness nor body.

Edith asked me when I came away to "eat grapes"
for her. I am afraid I cannot oblige her, unless I find
some better fruit! As we draw nearer to the house a
man and a dog were visible, and we were cordially invited to share the proprietor's dinner. He is keeping
bachelor's hall, and of course I did not expect any refinement of cleanliness. Yet I was astonished at what
I found. The house is a pleasant one. I saw only

a parlor, dining-room, and kitchen. There were no
signs of restricted means, and there were articles of
all sorts in these three rooms which, properly cared for
and arranged and well dried, might have made a little
Paradise! It seemed as if no woman ever could have
lived there, and yet the host only said his wife was
"away." Neither sun nor air seemed ever to be let in,
for not only had the dust been long neglected, but it
was so damp as to cling in flakes to carpet and furniture, giving a thoroughly unwholesome impression.

The dinner consisted of roast beef, potatoes, and baked
beans, followed by apple-pie. Nothing need have been
better, had it been cleanly cooked and served on a clean
cloth. Behind the master's chair stood the cook and
waiter, — a Chinaman, who was only the dirtier because he wore white linen. When told to give me a
clean plate, he deftly polished it with the tail of his
blouse! As I was allowed to help myself, I deposited
my slender bit of pie safely upon a slice of bread! I
never inquire into what goes on out of my sight, but
what takes place before my eyes is sometimes a little too
much for me. I was not surprised to find this gentleman drinking freely of his own wines at dinner. Such
a dinner could hardly have been swallowed without
alcohol in some form. But I must not forget to say
that he was wholly ignorant of his servant's substitute
for a napkin, and I would not mention the thing except
to show that although orderly the Chinese are very far
from clean. We had not a particle of fruit on the
table! I made a feint of eating, for the Burgundy was
too heavy for me to drink.

We did not get away till we had been carried through
a series of very dirty wine houses, and invited to taste

every kind of wine. It was red and white Burgundy,
Muscat, and dry Catawba. The dry Catawba is a wholesome wine. After we had tasted, I observed that my
host turned the remnant in my glass back into the cask.
I am afraid he would not have been much shocked at
the want of that napkin. Thrifty citizen! We drove
away to the Big Trees I wrote about, and oh how lovely
it all was! Laurel, madrona, or live-oak, stood garlanded with honeysuckle on each 'side of us! There
was a thicket of snowberry, white with clustered fruit.
There were the two kinds of tar-weed plants bearing
brilliant yellow blossoms, whose species I cannot even
guess. Both are black and gummy, looking as if
smeared with tar, and they give women and sheep a
great deal of trouble. The tall bushy kind is said to
indicate a rich soil; that which clings to the ground, a
barren hope.

We drove by the old tannery once kept by Paul
Sweet. When Mr. K. first came to it, great grizzly
bears, each weighing from eight hundred to a thousand
pounds, used to steal into the cattle-yard every night.
On one occasion one of these creatures caught a calf by
the nape of the neck, and leaped a tall fence. A revol-
ver was fired, but the animal dropped the dead calf and
escaped. The next day they followed the bear with
hounds, and took him.

One day Paul met a grizzly bear with cubs, in the
wood. She caught him by the waistband, plunged into
a hollow, dug a large hole in the sand, and buried Paul
out of sight. After a while the tanner worked his way
up to the surface, but Mistress Grizzly was watching.
She darted forward, and snugly tucked him in with two
or three strokes of her big paw. This time Paul was

more wary. The sand was loose, and after the creature had gone off to her cubs, he crawled home entirely un-hurt.

> "This is the tale was told to me,
> And he may believe who can."

It was quite evident that Mr. K. believed it.

Just here I saw great spikes of purple sage, and a huge heath-like plant whose stout spike, or spadix, was cov-ered with bright red and yellow blossoms, funnel-shaped. The natives call it "red-hot poker;" and it was re-freshing to get even so much of an answer to my in-quiries. The road was full of ground-squirrels which darted across like lightning, and in the long furze of the fields might be mistaken for a covey of quail scuttling off. A great many larks, linnets, bluebirds, and yellow-birds made merry over our heads. Mr. K. acknowledges that there are very few singing birds. The chestnut-oak has a large eatable acorn. There were magnifi-cent ferns under the oaks. A little while ago Mr. K. sent to Vick for a new decorative plant, and the man sent out a fern which grows wild all about the K. stables! The Zeyante is a branch of the San Lo-renzo. Roses seemed to be scattered everywhere, — red, white, yellow, — so large and so healthy looking, and so fragrant!

After a long drive through woods which gradually increased in thickness, where gigantic shafts pierced the sky, we drove into a well cleared grove and found ourselves surrounded by the sequoia. The ground cov-ered with the annual deposits of the trees was clean and hard, and the trunks rose so high as wholly to shut out the rays of the declining sun. The trees looked much smaller than they are, as usual; but the diameter of the finest is twenty-eight feet, and its height two hundred and ninety-six feet, seventy feet having been blown off the top in a tremendous gale. The hollow near the base formed a home for a man and his wife all one winter. They lived here to make shingles. The space is sixteen feet in the clear. They cut two windows and a chimney, and all these are now nearly filled in with bark. Before the grove was graded as a summer resort, a man once rode into this tree on horseback; but the floor is now too high for that.

Outside another tree was a curious knot, which looked exactly as if a brown bear were trying to climb into a hole. You can see the tail between the legs, the rounded back, the shoulders and haunches. The head appears to have been plunged into the trunk of the tree.

I have never seen a finer tree than the largest. The trunk turns spirally, so as to be entirely useless as timber, but it is perfectly upright. The cards of visitors are tacked on to the trunks of all the sequoias in this grove, so as to make it look like an advertising parade. On my complaining of this, I was told that a gentleman in the neighborhood had had these cards all removed at his own cost during the last spring! The grove includes a picnic-ground, a beer-stand, a small hotel, and a tannery, which was used in 1845. Square tanks were cut in the trunks of giant trees. I should think each one might hold a single hide. The narrow-gauge road to San Francisco runs up to the grove, and the prosperity of the pretty place was destroyed for this year by an accident which occurred when this road first opened. Fifteen persons were killed one quiet Sunday. Near by, charmingly placed, is the little town of Felton.

At the tannery, when the gold mines "broke out" in 1845, a saw-mill was in process of erection. The mining fever put a stop to it, property changed hands, and the trees are preserved for posterity.

The phrase "broke out" is very significant. Mr. K. made a fortune in two years, and in six months had not a cent to show for it. I find it a common experience. I have yet to see the first mining adventurer who is any richer for his efforts; and the Bonanza Kings do not enjoy their money, and do not know what to do with their accumulations.

As we were exhausted with hunger we asked for refreshments, but not a morsel of food nor a drop of beer or lemonade could be had. Mr. K. could not find a cigar! It is very well that our friend at the vineyard was hospitably inclined.

We drove sharply down hill, on going out of the grove, to the banks of the San Lorenzo, which we forded. Pausing to let the horse drink in the middle of the stream, I saw what I shall never forget. Not a stir of life on the lofty bluffs from which I had lately gazed my fill; not a stir on the broad river, flecked with amber lights, as it made its way round a few intrusive boulders. The sharply pitched banks were set with serried pines, with redwood, and with chesnut-oaks, which seem to recover by miracle when the tanners have pulled off their bark. These trees rise too erect to arch in the stream, which, about one hundred feet in width, lay bathed in sunlight. The shadows coquetted on its surface. In the stillness I could hear a droning fly.

We drove out through an immense ranch where a great deal of timber had been cut. The owner lost the whole by his foolish betting at a single horse-race.

Here the narrow-gauge railway, tunnelling the hills and running in and out the curves like a snake, began to attract my attention. It is adventurous, like all narrow-gauges, and was sometimes above and sometimes below us. It brings passengers from San Francisco to Santa Cruz in three and a half hours, and is the road that the broad-gauge agent ought honestly to have told me of when I started from Menlo Park.

Next we came upon the California Powder Company's group of buildings, hidden under groves of trees at the bottom of a bowl-shaped depression in the hills. I cannot describe the charming road which, after curling midway about the hills, wound through the cañon shaded by superb trees, watered by the tanners' teams, beset by quail and overrun with squirrels, and finally brought us back to town. Below us, in the hollow, was the railway, hidden by thick-clustering tree-tops. Above us, mighty forests on the summits shut out the light. We came past Mrs. Farnham's old farm, across the old peach and fig orchards of the Mission, by the new frame-building of the Sisters of Charity; and, after a drive of twenty-five miles or more, were very glad of our dinner.

Santa Cruz, Oct. 11, 1880. — When I got home last night I found very distressing letters from my invalids. This morning I was obliged to answer them; it was out of my power last night. After I had done so, I went out to calm my spirit in Mr. K.'s beautiful garden. Here are many flowering shrubs that I never saw before. Laurustinus, and daphne with great white blooms as large as lilacs, scent the air. Roses, verbenas, the true myrtle, every variety of fuchsia, violets, pansies, and periwinkle are all in bloom. Then the Norfolk

Island pine with great lateral branches, and the Monterey cypress in solid cones of green, shade the beautiful lawn. Near the cypress, and almost identical with it in effect, is a cedar, the seed of which was sent from Jerusalem. The botanist discovers differences. I do not think either is the cedar of Lebanon. No trimming could make a close cone out of the majestic swaying deodar. Then there are cacti, huge and prickly; century-plants with the mighty columns set with blossoms not yet fruited, and Australian hemp. A fish-pond is on each side the arbor; and in the rear, behind a green hedge, are the vegetable garden and the orchard.

A Spanish woman came to see me, to talk about some lace work I am to have done. Another person came to get the names of some school-books.

After lunch we went down into the "street," which, except that there are tropical looking flowers and vines in the second storey, might be any village street in New England; but it takes a great while to do anything here. I could not get photographs of the neighboring scenery. I went to see a Spaniard who was reported to have curios, cut out of onyx, and marine "tear-drops." He showed us all sorts of extraordinary things, — picture-frames, tables, boxes, and a few beautiful stones. Everybody remembers the Mexican onyx shown at the Centennial, with its veins of cream-color and tender green, with here and there a compact of orange-brown clay. It is really a kind of stalagmite, and is wrought into very large articles here.

The courtesy of these Spaniards is delightful; but it did not prevent our Señor from smoking as he sputtered away to me, first in Spanish and then in French.

I was ashamed of all the trouble I made him, and had to buy a few pebbles. I was in his house, he retorted, and it was at my disposal: I must see everything. I think there was garlic everywhere. The odor seemed to distil from the onyx! We went out through the kitchen, where it seemed to be lying on the floor and in the sink, and to be stewing over the fire, and then into an outer shed to see some of the larger pieces of onyx. I bought some note-paper and some drugs, and some fine linen for the Spanish needle-work.

Ora then drove me up to the highest terrace on the north of the town, where in the midst of desolation Judge Logan has built a house. I went to look at varieties of needlework, of which Mrs. Logan could show me many. I remained entranced by the ocean view. Ocean, beach, and town, mountain heights and meadow slopes, lay lovely in the radiant sunshine. Why is it not Mentone? The lazy water is far more like an inland sea than the enfolding ocean. Almond and olive trees keep up the illusion, but I think this bay is too cold for the graceful feathery plumes and purple clusters of the white-pepper.

From this charming spot we went to the Mission. In the ruined old adobe building, whose naked timbers are still worth seeing, they have cleared away the accumulations of stable and workshop, and show well vitrified tiles, manufactured and put down by the Indians under the old floors. Here I looked over the old Spanish registers carefully kept and beautifully written, which tell of the conversions, the marriages, the births, baptisms, and deaths, and record the small gossip concerning cattle and crops. The priest in attendance was a young Irishman who could not

read a word of them. He showed us some fine embroidered vestments which came up here from Peru,
and which are probably three hundred years old; and a
superbly embroidered white satin cloth in gold and silver, made to cover the sacred chalice. It was strange
to see how much fresher all these things were than the
very finest made during the last thirty years. We saw
also a very old picture from Peru, which seemed to be
a Spanish copy of a Carlo Dolci. Three thousand Indians lie in the old Jesuit church-yard.

When this particular Mission was founded in 1791,
Salazar and Lopez came from Santa Clara to start it.
They brought thirty cows, five yoke of oxen, fourteen
bulls, twenty steers, and nine horses; from San Dolores five other yoke of oxen, and from Mount Carmel
seven mules. So prosperous were all these Missions
then! The nineteenth century has not taken possession
of the Spanish race, only of an isolated minister or professor here and there upon Spanish soil. To penetrate a
Spanish-Mexican town is to modern civilization much
like what D'Albertis found in New Guinea, as com-
pared with Algeria or Barbary. Here they built a
church one hundred and twelve feet long, twenty-nine
feet wide, and twenty-six feet high, with walls five feet
thick; they set out ten hundred and twenty-two fruit-
trees and twelve hundred vines! At the end of twenty-
three years they had thirty-three hundred head of cattle,
thirty-five hundred sheep, six hundred horses, twenty-
five mules, and forty-six hogs.

The church had once a store of costly decorations,
which were not wasted on a race so fond of color and
glitter as the natives of this coast. Beside the brilliant
chasubles and robes, there was a golden chalice worth

six hundred dollars, and another worth three hundred and twenty dollars. A beautiful melodious old Spanish bell now lies broken in the court-yard.

In 1819 this Mission put up a house for widows and children, with two wings. Its possessions reached inland for three leagues, and stretched eleven leagues along the shore.

In the evening we went to the opera-house, which seems like a little village theatre, quite neat and pretty, to hear Newton Booth, late Governor of California, and Mr. Esty, of San Francisco, discuss the political situation. Both spoke in an earnest, noble, and convincing way, from as high a plane as I have ever heard anywhere. Governor Booth's eloquence impressed me very much.

I am struck here with the low estimate put upon physicians. Very few women in California seem to have any faith in the purity of men. I do not mean only those women who have been born here, but those who once knew a different state of things at the East as well. It troubles me to hear them talk. I feel a pitiful contempt for men who make a habit of talking against women. How can I help feeling the same for women who make a habit of talking against men? The two sexes make one race, — come clean from the hand of God. They need, and why should they revile, each other? I hear the women on all sides of me say openly that all the physicians here connive at unchastity in men and women; that any one who undertook to do otherwise would be driven out of practice in a week. No one believes me when I say that not one of honorable and regular standing at the East would dare to do so. They "know better."

Santa Cruz, Oct. 12, 1880.—After dinner Mrs. K. took me to see Dr. Andersen, a good botanist, who instantly translated my "scarlet horn" on the hill-side into "Californian primrose," and showed me a large collection of Pacific algæ beautifully kept. As, however, I had already seen most of these in Santa Barbara, the principal interest of his collection centred in delightful specimens from Key West, sent by a Mrs. Curtis. Among them the most bewitching was a little creature no bigger than the head of a large pin, and looking greatly like a microscopic mushroom. This was white, brown, or sea-green, according to its age. His best collectors were women. He showed me also fine fossils from the Sierras, and beautiful specimens of red and black pipe-clay. The clay can be cut like putty, when it is first brought in, but grows very hard in time. It is odd that this should be true of so many stones as well.

I found in one of Dr. Andersen's books the true name of the nelumbrium, or lotus, which I had wanted for Laura Hecox. A Miss Lennebacker, a school-teacher here, who is distinguished as a scientific collector, came in. She promised to send me a collection of algæ.

Mrs. K. was kind enough to drive me to the lighthouse. We saw Mrs. Hecox first, and she said that after I went away, and Laura looked at my card, she knew that I must be the mother of "Alaska Dall," and was vexed that she had not done more to please me. I think you children may have been a little impatient sometimes of attentions shown you for my sake. Nothing, however, pleases me more than those that are now offered me for yours! Both of you have "turned the tables" upon me these many years. Laura was quite delighted that I had brought back the label for her, and we parted with regret, after I had written out for her a short description of the nelumbrium, and of the areca for which it had been mistaken.

We drove a mile or two further, over the lovely cliff. The azure of the sea was not broken by a single white-cap. The Carmel mountains might have been cut out of moonstone, so lucent did they rise against the pearly horizon. The cliffs were precipitous. Lovely little islands, snowy-white, rose near the shore, the favorite perch for the sea-fowl. Against these the sapphire waves playfully tossed, broke, and retreated in rivulets of foam. They were not in earnest. The Pacific tide was down. Here and there the wind and water had eaten out a projecting cliff till it formed a most *un*-natural bridge. At Moore's beach we saw the three arches full of sunlight, with gulls flying in and out. We dallied longer than we had any excuse. Very reluctant am I to leave this charming spot, where the kindness of those who permitted me to come to them when they were un-der the shadow of a great grief has made every moment refreshing. Here, first, have I truly made acquaintance with the Pacific Ocean.

We went back to Dr. Andersen's that I might look through his collection of ferns. We surprised him at his studies, for he belongs to one of the Chautauqua classes in history. I think these classes, suggested by the Boston "Society to Encourage Studies at Home," have a roman-tic interest for their members, because they are all ex-pected to be busied with the same books and subject at the same hour, although it is probable that this does not always happen. A chart of the city of Rome, just made in colored chalks, lay open on the table and attracted my attention. It was the hour for the Doctor's Roman lesson. Miss Lennebacker also was at work. The Atlantic coast seemed so very near that in a moment my eyes filled with homesick tears. Anna Ticknor ought to be a proud and happy woman.

At home I found a telegram bringing the news of the death of Benjamin Peirce, and all through the evening rose before me that magnificent head with its lambent eyes. I do not like my friends to survive their finest powers, so I shall not mourn for him, — only keep him safe in tender memory "so long as we both do live." He would not have been the great mathematician that he was if he had not also been a great poet. I have had no higher delight in life than to hear him discuss the great themes which interested him: his thoughts gushed like spring torrents. And on the Executive Board of the Association for the Promotion of Social Science, it was a great triumph for me to sit between Peirce and Agassiz, and see the first turn from his mathematics, and the second from his paleontology, to discuss the education of woman and educational suffrage, or rise to welcome Mary Carpenter, fresh from India; Florence Lees, from the ambulances of the Franco-Prussian war; or Mrs. Leonard, from the Woman's Prison at Sherborn.

Mrs. K. gathered a few of her friends and neighbors together this evening, and a good many excellent stories were told. Ora told of her attempts to get a school and hoodwink committees (who were not of the slightest use unless they could be hoodwinked!) in Virginia City. After she got a school in Carson she dismissed a boy, who persisted in robbing the miners. He would take two bits at a time out of their pockets after they went to sleep in their bunks! But the committee could not stand his dismissal!

Then we talked of Salt Lake; and, *apropos* of one of my stories, Mr. K., who is not much over sixty years old, told how in his early life he had seen a man *sell his wife* in the town square! There was a toll-gate near the town, not ten miles from Birmingham, where the farmers paid toll on their cattle as they drove them through to market. With some dim idea of conforming to law, or custom at least, the husband drove his wife through the toll-gate and put her up at auction where he sold his cattle. The readers of the "College, Market, and Court" will remember what point I made of the fact that the local governments in England have never interfered to prevent this scandal. Interested as I had always been in the matter, I had never before seen a person who had been eye-witness to such a sale.

Santa Cruz to Monterey, Cal., Oct. 13, 1880. — This was the day I was to leave Santa Cruz, and very reluctantly I went. At ten this morning Mr. K. came up with his spirited colt to give me the greatest treat possible, — a farewell drive up the grade. That means six miles up the San Lorenzo valley, under the magnificent redwoods which I saw on Sunday. What leafy coverts hundreds of feet below me! What serried ranks of pines and cedars a thousand feet above! There is just danger enough of being whirled off the edge of the road as one drives, and dropped into the iron jaw of the narrow-gauge, to keep one's blood hot. Blue-jays screeched from every tree-top. Thousands of tiny yellow-birds whistled, and thick as flies in August the squirrels scurried from under the wheels they had not the wit to avoid.

My companion told me a great deal about the un-

happy life of Mrs. Farnham on this coast. He did
his utmost to prevent her marriage with the dissipated wretch who was her second husband, and although she rejected his counsel, he was her loyal friend
to the end. On one occasion when this man had left her
at Santa Cruz, and gone away breathing out threatenings
and slaughter against her and all her possessions, at a
time when there were no public conveyances, Mr. K.
harnessed his team, took Mrs. Farnham in, and ran a
neck-and-neck race with her lawful protector to San
Francisco, eighty miles away.

I wish I knew the country well enough to describe
this drive with the fierce eloquence with which it was
rehearsed to me. They were out two nights. The poor
woman lay asleep on a bear-skin in the bottom of the
wagon, while Mr. K., having shaved his beard and put on
a Spanish hat, was able to pass the desperado without
recognition. He won the race by five hours, which Mrs.
Farnham employed in transferring her books and threat-
ened property from her lodgings to a Santa Cruz schooner
at anchor in the Bay. Much good did it do! Her
husband found her before the schooner sailed, and
coaxed her into returning to share his fate. This
woman was as great in capacity for self-delusion as
in her wise foresight for mankind, and in her spirit
of general philanthropy. Perhaps the present generation will not be able to recall her great work at Sing
Sing, nor Margaret Fuller's interest in it.

Dr. Andersen came and brought me some algæ;
so did Mrs. Bailey. Both found me walking in the
garden, beautiful with its evergreens, its trout-ponds,
and its sundial. I am very loath to leave it, for
I shall never see such another. Dear to my heart

as are the tangled alleys of Ashton, they can show no tropical grace, no languid charm of constant slow surprises. What fascinates me in this spot is the supreme tact with which Mr. K. has outwitted Nature. Mother Earth has been forced to hide her bare and dusty body.

At half-past three Dick came to drive Ora and myself to the beach. A little steamer from San Francisco runs every week down the coast as far as Santa Barbara. It seemed better to use my pass on this boat to Monterey than to go through the mountains to Pajaro, and yet I could not bear to give up a last glimpse of the Pajaro valley, where there are one hundred and fifty thousand acres of the richest land in the world. I whizzed through it so unconsciously while I talked with Mr. Stearns about Theodore Glancey, and the spirit which justifies murder and assassination in every corner of California, that I shall always feel as if I had seen it in a dream.

At four o'clock this little steamer came panting into the Bay. It looked like a crazy water-beetle. Not a hundred feet long, it seemed as narrow as a knife when it cut the waves of the lovely azure Bay. I congratulated myself in silence that the Bay was so calm, that the strong breeze which would not allow the boat to keep up her sails was only a "Pacific Trade." Two hours were to take us across, and we made a hasty survey of her accommodations. It seemed impossible mortals should be expected to sit on the narrow slanting benches. Perhaps Ora thought I was cruel not to look up a berth, but I was only intent on fresh air.

How shall I describe our voyage? The narrow boat could not ride even half a Pacific "roller," far less a whole wave. The sea struck us sidewise, and each time the boat careened so, that in describing a frightful arc our masts seemed truly to sweep the sea. I held on with both hands; and a poor little woman, emigrating with her husband and two children to Santa Barbara, was wild and white with fright. I should certainly have been frightened at such a performance on any other sea, but in my mind I likened our water-bug to a raft, and remembered what Lord Collingwood had said of that. The husband of the emigrant said that the furious Aeger of the Bay of Fundy had never frightened his wife, and she had always felt as if she loved the sea, until the slow, steady swell of the Pacific, cut by our razor-like keel, drove the life-blood back to her heart. For myself, I felt for the moment in perfect health. I had neither headache nor nausea; and every time we dipped down and our passengers began their varied antics, I was tempted to indulge in a merry laugh not at all suited to my sober years.

We were all glad when the bracing of a cable told us we were near our port. The fog covered Point Piños, so we could not calculate our distance, yet the moon and Jupiter made a strong effort to act as guides. Long before we landed we heard the firing of guns. I did not believe it was in honor of our sorry vessel with its sorrier crew; so as soon as I got out on the wharf I cried, "What are those guns going off for?"

"Well, it's the Republicans," said the driver of the hotel wagon, and his very tone told that *he* was on the wrong side. "They've got news about Ohio, I reckon!"

"Nonsense," said I, "everybody has always known that Ohio was Republican; it must be for Indiana," and so indeed it proved. We have saved Indiana by a majority of five thousand, and may that comfort the faithful servants of the country, who have been shaking in their shoes ever since Maine showed us how much mischief could be done by the personal ambition of one man.

We dropped some of our passengers at a mysterious old adobe house, with a double piazza and a corral. There was no sign of welcome or light until the driver's whip had started a panel in the outer door, and a dark-lantern appeared in the distance. Then rushing over the rickety roads, over heavy coast sands or dunes, and under a superb oak-grove, which was so like that I had driven under at Old Fort, in Beaufort, that I could hardly believe my senses, we drove up to the doors of the El Monte. Lights streamed forth from every window. We were ushered into a great square hall, with a fire of oak logs on an old Virginia hearth. There were only three or four people in the house, and when we had thoroughly warmed ourselves by the great blazing fire, we went to bed.

Monterey, Oct. 14, 1880. — We rose early, and found that the hotel stands in the midst of one hundred and six acres of live-oaks. Some of them, perhaps the greater part, are several hundred years old. They are so twisted by the trade-winds, that they remind me of old cypresses or stone-pines. Often a single tree throws all its foliage to one side, making a long arch over the carriage-road after a fashion that would have delighted Calame.

This hotel is built by the railway kings out of their own pockets, and far in advance of any actual need. If they desired to be reimbursed there would be no hope for them, but fortunately they do not. The money the

United States Government gave to the Transcontinental Railway project it will get back in time, through
such improvements. The kings are ambitious to create
here the finest watering-place in the world, and I think
they may succeed.

The El Monte is built after an Eastlake pattern.
It is three hundred and eighty-five feet in length with
wings, and it is one hundred and fifteen deep. It has
a central tower and three floors, including the attic. It
is more like Dr. Pierce's Invalid Hotel in Buffalo than
any Eastern affair, but is much larger. There are parlors, billiard-rooms, and corridors on the first floor, and
the great hall which received us last night is also the
office. It contains on this floor twenty-eight suites of
rooms, each with a bath-room. The second storey has
forty-eight suites,— and so on. There are three towers,
the central one eighty feet high. Twelve hundred English walnut-trees have been planted in the park, and it
has a railway station of its own.

The beach is a quarter of a mile away, and is connected with the house by drives and walks. There is a
race-course, and a little lake where children can safely
row about. After exactly such a breakfast as Delmonico
would offer, a sort of fare that I always designate as
"starvation rations," we hired a spring-wagon with two
horses, and drove off to Mount Carmel. The road is
uphill all the way, shaded with magnificent oaks, and
here and there with walnuts. At last the Carmel
Range came into view, height above height, glowing,
lucent, opaline, in the sun. The Carmel River flows
at its base toward the sea; and I suppose, although my
travelling map does not show it, that the Carmel is a
spur of Mount Diablo. The valley of the Carmel has

a rich black soil, and is said to be the best dairy land in the State. Several thousands of acres here belong to the Athertons of Menlo Park.

We see the picturesque and lovely towers of the Mission, standing clean and clear upon a hill, long before we get to the church, passing through a valley planted by the Jesuits more than a hundred years ago. It is strange how far back a century seems to throw things in this Spanish dominion! If I were to say a building was two hundred and fifty years old in Plymouth County, the time would not seem so far away as one hundred will make it here. The old pear-orchard hangs full of brilliant red and yellow fruit. When we pick it, it is as void of flavor as the apples of the Dead Sea, and I suppose for the same alkaline reason. The man who has charge of the orchard took a twenty-five cent toll toward the repair of the dear old church, which I should have been glad to quadruple.

We lumbered through the gateway into a rough field, from which we could overlook hundreds of acres once covered by buildings which Indian hands erected, and of which the ruins are an involuntary tribute to the intelligence and artistic skill of the natives.

This church, by far the prettiest and most elaborate of the Missions, is in fact the most ruinous. It is the only one I have seen in which no service could possibly be held ; and, as we know, the churches at San Gabriel and Santa Barbara are in constant use. This Mission at Mount Carmel is called San Carlos, and it was built in 1770 by the famous Junipero Serra. It is a great deal like the old cathedral at Salamanca in its general look, and its walls slope outward at the base, just enough to make them look safe and solid. In its church-yard lie the remains of fifteen of the early governors of the State, and in the church is the grave of the great Christian apostle Junipero.

I have heard people talk as if the early history of these Missions had been only one long story of fraud and cruelty on the part of the priests, but it could not have been so. The grandchildren of the natives who built this church have a traditionary love for its founder. The chancel is full of recent graves; and only last week a very old Indian from the hills was buried, at his own request, close to Father Junipero. An unfailing spring of pure water runs through this Mission, and the Padres took advantage of it. Here, in 1826, were raised the first potatoes ever seen in California. At that time the Fathers had ninety thousand cattle, fifty thousand sheep, two thousand horses, as many calves, and three hundred and seventy yoke of oxen, forty thousand dollars in silver, and merchandise to a greater amount. Ten years later the Mexican government confiscated the whole !

The Mount Carmel Mission is built of sandstone, covered, where needful, with a fine and firm cement. The wall-curtain, which contains the principal entrance, has a large belfry-tower to the left, surmounted by a dome. On the top of this is an iron cross, of lovely Moorish arabesque. The bells were approached by an outside stone stair built into the walls, and the roof of a baptistery just beyond. To the right of the curtain is a two-storeyed stone tower, enclosing a circular stairway with port-holes for guns. It is accessible still to the very top, and was evidently built for defence alone. Over the great door is a sort of rose-window, surrounded with fine mouldings,— an evidence of very great skill in building. It is slightly out of the perpendicular, and must have been so in the beginning. Inside the great door we find two or three feet of earth, covering the tiles which once made the floor; and the whole interior is filled with the graves of those Indians who have desired to lie there, since the body of its founder was discovered at the foot of the high altar. Many have been brought from the recesses of the Sierra. Some bodies had been very lately interred, and a shingle at each end serves for head and foot stones.

The vestibule is separated from the nave by a flattened arch of cut stone, just ready to fall. The whole roof is gone, and its broken arches are replaced by rude rafters which must have been put in to support the thatch after the quaint old tiles had fallen. On the sides the windows are set in deep embrasures, but small and square like those in King's Chapel. They were never glazed, only barred. On the left of the entrance behind the belfry is the loveliest little baptistery, with an arched roof and a font. I was never tired of looking at it. It seems to be built in the thickness of the wall; and what might be called a continuation of this, running half-way up the nave, still holds the bodies of the old Franciscans in the close embrace of indestructible cements. They were buried standing, and a second tier of funeral-cells, built against the first, stops half-way, with an unfinished vault, and makes an awkward break in the wall. Behind this, close to the outside belfry-stairs, was a sort of closet to be entered from the open air, which the Padres called "a receiving tomb,"— and here the body stood in state, while preparations were made to wall it in.

Half-way up the nave, against the opposite wall, is the pulpit, reached by a stone stair, and behind it a large "tiring room," still accessible and well protected. The altar still keeps its place; and the chancel has the same beautiful grained arch as the baptistery. Between the pulpit and the chancel, to the left, is a large plain chapel, still roofed in, and often used.

What chiefly impresses me in the whole building is the excellence of the Indian work. The whole form of the building is so familiar to me that I feel sure the old Fathers must have had both a picture and a plan for the natives to work from,— engraved, perhaps, in some old Spanish work on church architecture. The outside stair, leading to the belfry, is so skilfully set in as to add greatly to the beauty of the wall. How home-like all this region must have seemed to these first comers! Three hundred yards away are a row of small square vats, nicely finished in cement, each large enough to hold a single hide. A tannery was the necessary adjunct of a Mission in those days, and the monks of that time were neither indolent nor thriftless.

In 1602, in the reign of Philip III., Viscayno first sailed into this lovely bay, and set up a cross at the head of a ravine, or *chine*, clothed with cypresses. The spot was named for the then existing Count of Monterey, who was Viceroy of Mexico. Here Viscayno intended at first to build a church, but it was one hundred and sixty-six years before another white foot pressed the soil. In the fall of 1769 the Governor of California came over-land from San Diego and set up another cross.

In 1770, Junipero Serra came hither by sea, landed on the day of Pentecost, and celebrated High Mass.

From this time the town grew till it became the capital and principal port of the territory, not only under Spanish rule, but for a long time under the Mexican, and even after the United States took possession.

It was in 1850, I believe, that San José became the capital; and Monterey then fell to building " Castles in Spain," the only kind of building that went on till the bonanza kings began the hotel a year or more ago.

The Bay of Monterey, famous for its heavy rollers, and for a safe anchorage which could accommodate all the navies of the world, is twenty-eight miles across its mouth; and the Salinas River enters it a little nearer Santa Cruz than Monterey. The beautiful Mission stands near the mouth of the river Carmel, surrounded by vast heaps of adobe, — the ruins of what were once barracks, dormitories, school-rooms, convents, and the like. Its beautiful orchards and vegetable gardens are still green.

The blue of the sea; the translucent mountain domes; the glittering heaps of snowy sand; Point Lobos, a long rocky point, like the Gurnet, rushing out to sea; the distorted cypresses, so like the stone-pines of the Riviera, — make up a landscape which, for sunny charm, must be unequalled on this continent, as it seems to me.

Here and there, within the Mission walls, are the stone-heaps of the "Avenger," piled above the nameless graves of assassins, as in the old Hebrew days. Here, at last, is added to enchanting sunlight and enticing shore that charm of old association which teems from the Lida of Venice or Genoa.

We mount our wagon, and drive under the eaves of the keeper's cottage to ask for some fresh water and some bright-colored pears of Sodom. They were brought by a bare-footed Spanish maid, whose straight black hair hung over her eyes, as if she had been a Shetland pony.

Then we swept away to the left, over lovely slopes, under overhanging oak and gnarled cypress, where the "water-drops" the sea-nymphs shake from their hair turn to agate and crystal. Here we paused under a tree to see whether our eyes would ever tire, whether indeed we should be able to leave the delicious spot. The blue main, like a great floor of *lapis-lazuli*, met the overhanging vault of sparkling sapphire in a long line of soft invisible color. To the right, the deep shadow of the hills; and to the left, some low rocks, saucily set in sputtering foam, broke the serene charm.

I sent the driver down to the beach to find shells and pebbles for Isabel. The guide-book is always telling me what wonderful things are accessible at *low tide !* But a low tide I have never yet found in California.

All along the points the United States Coast Survey has set up its triangular standards. One of these, on a very lofty point, was surrounded by a group of men, and I hoped to find some officers I knew. They turned out to be some Portuguese sailors watching for a whale ! Whales are very common here; sharks also drift into the Bay. Court-yards are paved with the vertebrae of whales. Side-walks are curbed by their mighty jaws. More than once we drove round gigantic skulls, and skeletons grinned at us from the shop windows.

We drove by a Chinese fishing ground, where a Celestial village occupies itself with catching and drying

tomcod to export to China. Next came two whale-
boats, manned and waiting; and in a moment more we
were rushing through heavy groves of trees, choked by
mighty fallen limbs, by underbrush cut out from the
newly opened carriage-road, and by trunks that the
storms had prostrated, till we came to Cypress Point.

And here I must confess my sins. When Mr. Kirby
showed me the Jerusalem cedar and the Monterey
cypress trained and trimmed into stiff cones in his
front yard, as if Mr. Turveydrop had been head gardener, I utterly refused to believe that either was akin
to the great deodar of the Himàlas, whose picture is so
often sold as that of the cedars of Lebanon. But here
I saw the cypress in its home, bearing its foliage in
mighty shelving layers, bending defiant to the trade-
wind, — stony, arrogant, and monumental. The thing
looked more probable, and I felt that if the story were
not true it ought to be.

There is a very curious limitation to the growth of
the cypress all along the shore, which I should be glad
to understand. It is easily propagated in public squares
or gardens, yet here it has never crossed the road! The
cypress was always between my carriage and the sea.
Toward the hills, live-oaks were frequently interspersed
with pines, but never a cypress. The common people
say the line is very distinctly marked.

A little way on we passed Seal Rocks, on which the
stupid lubbers were clambering up and down, as if for
a marine circus to amuse the tomcods. The acrobat
generally rolls over and falls with an ugly splash.

Then we came to Moss Beach, where oddly dressed
collectors were picking up corallines,— pink, white, and
green. Here I stopped for a while to gather small lim-

pets and prettily rounded bits of abalone which the waves had polished.

With what words shall I render the glory of sea and sky? All language seems too poor. On the Eastern coast I could never have had such color or such brilliancy except united to a degree of heat that would have made both unendurable.

Carmel and Santa Cruz jut out from the Diablo to enclose the Bay. From Cypress Point, gay autumn flowers straggle in and out the tangled trunks and underbrush. On the Gabilan Range, serrated ridges, feathered with pines, melt into the filmy horizon. The foam crawled along the silvery beach, and seemed to gnaw away at the rocky points. Here and there a schooner was stranded; it seemed "a painted ship upon a painted ocean." The quail ran out to the very sands, thick as the blades of dry beach-grass, — the tamest creatures I ever saw of the name. The Sierra of Santa Lucia drooped — brown, barren, velvety — to the shore. The Moro rose into the still firmament like a lifted finger, warning us of dangers under the angry crags. The waves broke at the feet of enormous sand dunes, whose snowy sides, tufted and freckled with juniper, promised wealth to all the glass-factories in America. Just beyond me a jutting crag met a rocky isle. Partly between them rose the mighty crest of the incoming tide. Again and again I saw it, — the reflected sunlight breaking from the water itself, as it was held again and again like a sapphire in the air, before it fell and was shivered into a thousand glowing fragments.

We turned away from the lighthouse here, and drove briskly into the famous shades of the Pacific Grove. This is a place like the well known Ocean Grove near

New York. A hundred acres well cleared are filled with neat cottages, and there is an amphitheatre with seats for five thousand people. It is about three miles from Monterey, and commands a charming sea-view. We sat down in the porch of a deserted cottage to eat our sandwiches and drink some mineral water out of a rusty tin dipper, while our driver went away ostensibly to "feed his horse."

I have not wanted to spoil your enjoyment of this delightful drive by telling you how uneasy I had been all through it. The horse looked sick to me when we started, and the driver, who owned the team, abused him from the very beginning. I interfered several times, but was told the creature had got the "devil" in him and must have it "whipped out!" He had been biting all the horses in the corral before he was harnessed. What I should have done if this had happened on a New England road you can guess, but here I felt at the mercy of the driver. In getting into the wagon in the morning my foot went through the bottom. Having satisfied myself that extreme care might prevent a broken ankle, I became critical, and investigated the condition of the "team."

The near horse was restive from the first, and his sides bore traces of a recent severe flogging. Our driver claimed to be a Virginian, nephew of the man for whom the town of Martinsburg was named. He seemed a pleasant fellow enough, but told more than he knew; and, when the horse refused to drink, declared that he "would give him fits." When we stopped, the creature panted so violently that I felt very uncomfortable. As soon as we had finished our lunch, Ora

strayed along the sea, and I went in search of the
stables which were at some distance across the road.
There I found the Virginian trying to bleed his best
horse, but he could accomplish nothing, — the lancet
did not draw. I insisted on an exchange of horses,
but there was not a horse within three miles. His
head was then tied up; gunpowder and water were
given him; his owner declared him well; and, because
I knew I had not strength to walk to town, we got in
and drove back to the village. There the words, "Where
will you go, Ma'am?" were answered pretty sharply by
these others : "Straight to your stables to get another
horse."

The driver dropped us at a Spanish fisherman's little
cot upon the shore. Perhaps he had heard me say how
sorry I was to give up going to the lighthouse on account of the horse. I had expected to find there some
mosses and water-drops on sale. At all events my
Spanish fish-wife showed me finer specimens than any
ever bought at the Moro. She swam out to an island
six miles from shore this very morning, carrying a
netted lap-bag in front of her, and seizing the great
branches of the algæ as she encountered them. This vigorous creature washes them clean of all adhesive matter,
leaves them in soak in pure water over night, and then
presses them in dryers made of the largest newspapers.
Some of the branches were eighteen inches long, and
had to be bent in the middle to be pressed. True films
of woven hair they seemed, just lightly flushed with
rose-color, purple, and green. The most delicate lace-
work is not more captivating than these mosses treated
in this way. The fish-wife assured me that they would
neither break nor wrinkle, and she rolled mine up in their

newspaper driers as carelessly as if they had been Breton scarfs. If I had wholly believed her I would have invested largely; but I remembered my corallines.

This woman had on her mantel a large glass jar of water-drops, the very finest I had seen. She would not sell any; and if I had been wholly up to California manners, I suppose I should have taken some and left ample payment behind. As my heart was quite willing I must be responsible for the sin; yet I felt a little ashamed of the overt act! What a queer state of things it is, if you stop to think of it! She could easily have replaced them, for I have no doubt they are to go to New York next "steamer day!" Have I ever told you how odd it seems that all business matters here should still be regulated by "steamer day," just as they were when these vessels were the only means of communication with the East? Money is called in, notes are given, and accounts are all settled with reference to this bi-monthly occasion. If that is not Spanish, I do not know what is!

From the trig little fish-wife we drove with a fresh horse to the Catholic Church. It was built in 1794, and has a pretty baptistery, a little like that at San Carlos. On the walls hang some old pictures brought from Carmel when the Government took possession of it in 1835. Two heavy, solid silver candlesticks, about seven feet high, stood each side the altar, and in front, mounted on a lofty silver rod, was a silver crucifix gilded.

If I had not been so upset by the sight of the lancet and the suffering horse, I should have looked up vestments and curios; but I do not think I lost much, and I had not the heart for it. We drove about in search of shells and photographs, but could find neither. We were delighted with the dead-alive old places; and at last took possession of an open studio, sent out for the proprietor who was lunching somewhere on garlic and tomatoes, and really bought *one* photograph of Mount Carmel! Rambling stone walls topped with turf, adobe walls roofed in with tiles, ran about the town in inexplicable ways. No wonder so many Spaniards have taken natural wash-outs for castle walls, and undermined them in search of treasure! A ruined adobe looks exactly like a wash-out, and, in fact, it is one. The old Spanish houses have two storeys surrounded by pillared porches. They run round a square court in most cases, and the inclosed space is a half-tropical garden. I would have liked to go into one of these courtyards, for through an arched carriage-way I saw flowers and fountains and scarlet curtains gleaming in the sun.

We saw the building which served as headquarters for Frémont. The first Constitution of California, a far better state paper than the last, was signed by William M. Ginn and thirty-nine others, in 1849,— signed in a long, low, white-washed building of two storeys. This is made like the nest of the mason-bee, — being a long series of separate cells. As there are no active little grubs to eat a way through, each cell is entered from an outside gallery.

There are several "zinc houses" in town,— a thing I never saw before. The plates fit closely together, and they are said to be serviceable. They were sent from England.

A lady who has written about California, after a two-years' residence, says the poor Spaniards are clean! If

I were to express my mind after a two-months' experience, I should say that the word *filthy* was inadequate to any conception of the condition of their
houses. The truth probably is that the Spaniards are
just like other people, — sometimes tidy and sometimes
not.

A little way out of town we were shown a spot off
shore where the corvette was wrecked that had once
taken Bonaparte away from Elba.

We had hardly reached the hotel when we heard that
our poor horse was dead. I wrote till dinner, and then
sat down by a big oak-fire to read. I had a captivating
book. I do not know, in literature, two more charming
love-stories than those of " Cesare Donato " and " Lord
Brackenbury."

Monterey, Oct. 15, 1880. — After breakfast we were
shown through the hotel and into the tower, where, over
the heads of the live-oaks, we caught the gleaming
of the distant sea. A vista should be cut from the
hotel to the silver sands. Our driver told us yesterday,
as he jerked us over the shocking roads, that in a
week two hundred men would be here at work, and
thirty miles of perfect macadamized road would be finished before another season, with hot and cold and
Turkish baths on the beach, bowling-alleys and all
the etceteras of sea-side resorts. The house is beautifully built. All the panelling is exquisitely grooved
and moulded. It is furnished and finished in a manner
that would not suit the Pacific shore for half a century,
if the inhabitants had to be taxed to bring it about.
And here you will perhaps permit me to say that I
have never seen men successful in forestalling time or

Providence. When I lived in Canada thirty-five years
ago, the gentlemen at the head of the Educational
Department were men of culture and enterprise. Under their auspices Canada imported the finest school
apparatus in the world, and undertook in her normal
and model schools to lead the way to its use. But she
could not import intelligent teachers or an educated
public; and the treasures grew dusty in the national
storehouse. When I returned to the United States I
found Massachusetts wholly without various charts and
models easy to be had in Canada. I sent back to To-
ronto, and was proudly allowed to purchase the specimens I wanted; and Massachusetts has never since
needed any prompting of that sort. The apparatus here
at Monterey is intended for a public that does not yet
exist. Will the heirs of the present proprietors feel pride
enough in the project to keep it up at their expense?

The tiled fire-places filled with blazing logs are a
delight to our eyes. The rooms lately occupied by President Hayes are no finer than all the rest. Indeed, there
is little choice of rooms, except that some look out upon
a lovely little circular lawn planted with tropical plants
and sheltered by majestic trees, and that a few have
bath-rooms attached.

This hotel, as well as all the improvements in the
town, were undertaken by the bonanza kings, who own
the Central and Southern Pacific Railways, and who are
supremely indifferent to justice and comfort in all that
concerns those roads. Two of them are Governor Stanford and Charles Crocker, Recently, in celebrating his
own golden wedding, Governor Stanford said: —

"We are the people who know how to use either wealth
or poverty. I can remember the time when a tent to cook

in and a tent to sleep in constituted my sole earthly possessions; and my wife and I had to lie very still when it
rained, because there was a tin pan between us to catch the
drippings from the canvas."

I do not know Governor Stanford, but as regards
bonanza kings in general, I could not endorse his
statement. It is not to be expected that the millions
which have been "shovelled up" should be put to wise
uses, and as a rule they are not. The sudden rise of
purse-proud and uncultivated families seems in many
places not only to extinguish the old wholesome New
England element, but to thrust some of the kindest and
wisest entirely out of sight.

It is curious that either covetousness or pride should
lead men to such an undertaking as this at Monterey,
which will be of incalculable benefit to the discontented
working classes for a time, and it may be a great pleasure and profit to the travelling public. In this way the
gold, which energy has extorted from the Sierras, will be
forced into circulation. Can it be a solid growth or a
lasting benefit? It does not seem proper to set experiments of luxury like this side by side with the building
of Western or Transcontinental railways. An Illinois
farmer, once showing me thousands of acres of corn that
it was impossible to send to market, at the same time
speaking of the need of railroads, said: "Do you wonder
that we are ready to lie for them, go in debt for them,
nay, even steal for them, if that would build them?"

While you ponder the question, the following facts
are suggestive. I arrived at evening and went away
on the second day just after breakfast. My bill was
made out for the *whole* of the day of departure! I
wanted a ticket for San Francisco, with a "stop-over"

for San José. A through ticket to San Francisco, about one hundred and twenty miles away, could be had for $3.50. If I took a "stop-over" for San José, about half way there, it cost $5.50; for it is the present policy of the road to force every traveller either to San Francisco or Monterey, and to ignore what lies between! The hotel is to be kept open all the winter at a loss, and of course the cheap fare which entices the visitor must serve both ways. After a little inquiry I bought a ticket to San José for $1.75, and found that by paying the same price from San José to San Francisco I could accomplish my object. Certainly it was not necessary for the "heathen Chinee" to emigrate to California to instruct her citizens in "ways that are dark"!

I have not said a word about the climate of Monterey, because I have not thought of it since I came. We have not been out after dark, but mornings and evenings have been very cold. Ora has had plenty of employment in running after my shawl, and I have no doubt that the variations are as great as at Santa Cruz. Mrs. K. has suffered severely there, and declares that "neuralgia and rheumatism are to be had there in stock and on demand." Certainly I never saw so many sufferers from both as in this boasted land,— not so much among people who have come here for their health as among those who have lived here for thirty or forty years. The number of invalids in California is a great drawback to the pleasure of travel. I don't mean to complain of them, poor souls! but when a person goes abroad for rest or health, it is just as unwise to go intentionally into a family of invalids as it is to group insane people by the hundred and expect them to get well. Both are insanitary experiments.

There is a special dépôt near the hotel, and thither we went. Opposite to it is a superb oak, twisted and knotted into the very fashion of an old olive. We passed great dome-like sand-dunes between us and the sea, freckled with a low juniper bush. Tar-weed lighted our way with its golden stars. The heavenly blue of the sea melted into a long unbroken horizon of silver fog woven thin, yet close enough to hide the other side of the Bay. Then came wheat fields and stacks of straw, waiting, I suppose, to go to the paper-mill at Stockton. Wise farmers lay this straw thickly over their orchards and door-yards to keep down the clouds of dust. We came upon the dry bed of a river full of green grass, glowing like an emerald against the silver sand-dunes.

When we reached Castroville a bright little fellow entered the car, dressed as a gentleman's son might be. He was nevertheless a beggar. Not more than ten years old, he had already lost one arm by an accident. His cards of solicitation which he laid on our laps were quite elegantly printed. That was some sentimentalist's pet charity! How much better to put him in the way of an education and make him independent! The gentlemen all gave him money, — the ladies did not. I thought I saw the boy puzzling over this, and I wanted to tell him that it happened because the few ladies in the car had thought pretty seriously on such subjects.

At Salma, where there is a good deal of salt marsh, the dry lagoons were full of a short crimson grass, which sent a warm glow across the landscape. Out of it here and there pricked skeleton trees as white as snow. Their naked arms looked pitiful.

We passed through one tunnel after leaving Monterey, and I believe it is the only one on this road. The nar-

row-gauge road through the mountains to Santa Cruz is
full of them.   There is a little town named San Juan
somewhere about here to which I wished to find my
way, but no one would tell me how to go to it.   I have
already told you how impossible it is to get any answer
to my questions.   The railway men cannot tell you
about connections, know nothing in short beyond their
own sections, not even enough to tell you where to
apply for information.   People you meet know nothing
which does not interest them for some personal reason.
From Salma we ran on through a lovely valley, with
Mount Diablo on one side and the foot-hills on the
other, as far as Coyote.   There the scenery begins to resemble that at Menlo Park nearer to San Francisco.
Wide fields of grain or scattered groves of superb oaks,
looking like overgrown apple orchards, diversified the
surface of a wide spreading plain.

At San José I parted from Ora with regret.   She
has been a charming travelling companion, whom I
would gladly take with me on a longer journey.   I
had come to San José to meet a friend whom I had
not seen for more than thirty years.   Charlotte H.
was my next door neighbor in Portsmouth when my
young Professor was a baby.   It was her hands that
dressed for him his first Christmas-tree, and hung it
among other things with the famous Fairweather diamonds.   I remember as if it were yesterday how forlorn I felt, when she came in to tell me she was going
West.   Those were the heart-searching yet somewhat
dreary days of Brook Farm; and, filled with a desire to
try a new life, Charlotte had written to her far-away
cousin, Mr. Ripley.   George Ripley had by this time
found out that the disciples of Fourier were men and

women like their neighbors, and not angels in disguise; he had seen that wherever men associated together the obvious evils of social life would appear; so he did little in the failing hours of Brook Farm to tempt my Charlotte away. Still he told her of a Western experiment in a more prosperous State, and thither my bright young neighbor went and found after a time her fate. I knew that she had married, had children, and was the wife of a prosperous fruit grower in Michigan. Imagine my astonishment, when I reached California, to find her two grown daughters studying Froebel with Miss Marvœdel, and to receive a warm invitation to visit her in San José!

I found myself apparently unexpected. I had pre-paid a telegram to Mrs. M. last night, and when I found no one at the dépôt did not like to hurry away, lest Charlotte should come for me and be disappointed; so I waited till the very last, and then took a hack. I was to go to Mission Street, but the driver declared there was no such street in town. In my utter ignorance of people and things, I thought it best to drive to a bank. The cashier came out bare-headed, directory in hand, and gave a sharp rebuke to the driver, who trotted off with such indefinite energy that I half expected to find Mission Street in the next town. It was, however, on the outskirts, about two miles from the Court House. They call San José the Garden City. It seemed very flat, and I drove everywhere through streets lined with trees.

The Court House I have spoken of is, after the capitol at Sacramento, the finest building in the State. The top of the dome, which surmounts it in true State-house fashion, is one hundred and fifteen feet from the floor, and its architecture is Roman Corinthian,—if any one knows exactly what that is! San José is the county seat of Santa Clara, situated in a beautiful valley. It is said to be extremely healthy and well suited to lung diseases. That was what induced Charlotte's husband to come here. I cannot well understand why a fruit grower, who has passed the greater part of his life in the open air, should be in danger of lung trouble.

Arrived at the house, after what seemed a very long drive, I found myself warmly welcomed. My friend had grown handsome with the passing years, and it was pleasant to look in her motherly face. No telegram had been received.

For some months the little hall in which the Unitarians worship has been closed, and almost the first question asked was whether I would be willing to fill the pulpit on Sunday.

After lunch Charlotte and I drove over to Santa Clara, stopping at a newspaper office on the way to insert a notice of the promised service. Santa Clara is five miles from Mr. M.'s house and three miles from the Court House. A beautiful Alameda, or road planted with three rows of trees, mostly aged willows, connects the two. The Santa Clara Mission was the first settlement, and led to that of San José.

We went this afternoon to Eberhardt's tan-yard. Last week he had sent Mr. K. some lovely white goatskins, which I thought would make pretty presents for some of my Eastern friends. I had a letter of introduction. We found a beautiful tan-yard, but no Mr. Eberhardt. The foreman showed me the goat-skins. There were hundreds of them laid up in sulphur in a dark outhouse, but I could not find one as well dressed

as those I had seen at Santa Cruz. Mr. K.'s tan-yard
is a perfect poem: I always meant to go to it with
himself, but I never did. Everything is exquisitely
clean and in perfect order, and there is a quiet but faithful oversight of the comfort of the men, who are boarded
in the yard.

We drove over to Santa Clara through the business
streets, looking exactly like those of any American town
of fifteen thousand inhabitants. The houses stand
separately in gardens, which have a look like those in
Central New York. Some of the estates occupy a whole
block. At last we came to the Alameda. This triple
row of trees running for two miles was originally planted
to give the padres a shaded walk from the old Mission
to a new church and convent in San José; and not that
only,—the friar who proposed it thought it might break
the rush of the half crazy hordes of buffalo and cattle
which swept over the valley in those days, to the great
alarm of the wayfarer. His brethren laughed at the
idea; but the gentle hearted Indians heard the talk, and
soon set the broad road with three lines of willow twigs
from a neighboring brook. Many of these have since
been replaced by poplars and oaks, so as to form a
boulevard, on which are the finest residences in San
José. Many of the farmers' fields are bordered by tall
poplars, a fashion that I like. It cannot be pretended
that they injure the fields by shading them, but they
must suck up a great deal of moisture.

In the evening a Mrs. Watkins, who I am told is a
candidate for election to the Legislature, came to see me.
Last year, at the last moment, she put her name upon
the Republican ticket for the School Board. The man
elected was a very popular man, many years a resident

here; yet he had not a dozen more votes than Mrs. Watkins, who seems a remarkably bright, clear headed woman.

As to the Legislature, every one knows how sincerely I believe that women must work for and attain to suffrage before social life will have any chance of harmonious development. But I do not wish any woman to accept office until she can do so with the cordial consent of men. I do not feel in the least in a hurry about suffrage. I know it is coming, and I want women to work steadily and sensibly for it, because such work is in itself educational. The delay of woman suffrage for a decade will not do half so much harm as the conferring of it while the bulk of our women are indifferent, indolent, or unprepared.

San José, Oct. 16, 1880. — Late last evening I received a few encouraging words from Calcutta. They have been long delayed, but you will know what relief they give.

I am sorry I was not here on the fourteenth, when the news from Vermont, Indiana, and Ohio came in. Then paraded the finest torch-light procession which San José ever saw. Every man of character and position turned out. Mr. M. himself carried a torch. While I was in Santa Cruz the Democrats wrote "329" on every shutter and flag-pole. Mystic numbers these, which were supposed to destroy Garfield's character at a glance. Mr. K.'s wrath rose high, and he uttered some sharp threat. They did better here. The Republicans carried the mystic figures as a badge of honor on banner and blaze!

After lunch Charlotte took me two or three miles away to Rock's Nursery, where I went to see some won-

derful cherry trees, two years old, which will be bearing
next year. Rock, who is a German, was just going to
the city, and could not give us his personal attention. I
was much surprised to hear him say that the frost had
already come, and that the last two nights had destroyed
his vines. Pumpkins and tomatoes certainly looked
black enough, but unless tomatoes can be better than
any I have seen in the State, they will not be much of
a loss to anybody. The dahlias were still bright, and
the young cherry and plum trees showed a wonderful
growth. Some Hungarian prunes were drying on a
board. The green-houses were nearly empty, but still
held some large scarlet begonias.

We went next to Fox's, — a garden famous for rare
Australian plants. We found his glass houses full of
ferns, orchids, and palms. I saw a green vine of great
extent, thickly covered with a bright orange plum, about
an inch and a half long, without suspecting I had ever
seen it before. It was a passion-flower, and Mr. Fox
gathered some of the fruit for me. The skin was very
thin and half empty. What it held was a table-spoon-
ful of white meringue, as light as if it had just been
beaten. At the heart was half a tea-spoonful of brilliant red currant jelly with four apple seeds in it. The
whole thing was a little less acid than the confectioner
would have made it. I wonder if anything ever was
made on this planet of which some hint does not exist
in Nature? Mr. Fox says that the climate of Japan is
very bad for fruit growers, and that the Japs have to
pet every seed vessel that matures there into something
eatable. They eat a great many of these passiflors.
The fruit of the camellia looks like a small green
apple. It had split open on one side and showed some

dark seeds. The tough green rind was as hard as the burr of the horse chestnut.

Mr. Fox is an Englishman, and a bachelor, and was one of the very last to employ Chinese labor. His answer, when I asked him why he did it, is worth recording. " I could not find honest and faithful laborers," he replied. "My men went away every Sunday and came back drunk. They shirked whenever I was out of sight. The Chinaman sticks to his work, does as he is told, and however he may steal at other times, touches nothing of mine while his contract with me lasts."

This is in accordance with my own conviction that honest and faithful workers have nothing to fear from the competition of any race. Throughout California there is the greatest outcry on the subject of labor and wages, — an outcry with which I feel no sympathy. A woman cannot get up to speak in a social science meeting, without raving fanatically against capitalists. The popular outcry against the Chinese is an outcry against low wages. Let no man complain to me of this till he can show me a piece of really well-done mechanical work, something that I have not seen for years until I went to Salt Lake City. In Boston, workingmen used to come to me with petitions for an eight-hour law. I never signed them. I used to tell them plainly that once or twice in my life I had had to support myself, and that I never could do it without eighteen hours' work in a day. There is only one way to pay for labor that is fair, and that is to pay by the hour. Work is wholesome, far more wholesome than leisure, for most men. It is educational, and develops human faculties far more rapidly than books alone. The time must come when political economists will understand this.

It happened to me once to have a new zinc roof put on the house in which I was living. At the close of three working days, there was still about two hours' work to do to finish the roof, and a storm was approaching. I offered extra payment to the men, to induce them to go on, as each one of them would have gone on if he had been working for himself. Not one would stay, — the "Union" would not allow it. The storm came, and drenched everything in the two upper stories — bedding, books, carpets, pictures — which it was impossible to remove. I worked hard and unavailingly against the flood all night. At last the work was done. I paid an intelligent expert five dollars to go over it and see that nothing had been neglected. He assured me that it was all right, and I proceeded to refinish the interior. The first storm that came after, saturated one ceiling till a part of it fell. I sent an honest hodman up to examine again. On the upright of the French roof half-a-dozen slates were missing. They still lay on the zinc above, with the nails beside them, which should have been driven in. My "expert" did not see that! If I employ a plumber to replace a pipe, I have to put on my hood and shawl, and stand by until the work is covered in. If I do not, a smaller or lighter pipe than that I have ordered and shall pay for will certainly go in. While these things last I cannot feel much sympathy for the laborer; and all through California I find people complaining of these and still worse outrages.

Mr. Fox gave us some fine pampas; but the principal pleasure I derived from my visit to his garden came from making acquaintance with a great many seed vessels that never mature on the Atlantic coast.

We looked through all the shops for photographs.

We could find nothing but stereoscopic views, which would not answer my purpose.

Then we hitched the horse and went to the convent of the Sacred Heart. It was after hours, but the sweet-tempered woman who was cleaning the lodge went in search of a Spanish sister watering the lawn with a hose, *pour passer le temps*, as she herself said, — amusing herself, "because on Saturdays there was not a corner indoors safe from brush and broom." She carried us through the pleasant hall, into long grape arbors, by shrines with fountains, through a delicious pepper grove, which last winter's frost had done much to injure, and last into a tempting vegetable garden. When I exclaimed at some *ripe* tomatoes, the first I had seen in California, she called the French gardener and ordered him to gather some for me, "bien mûr." Charlotte laughed because I would not put the dusty things in my pocket; but the Spanish sister approved, and said I must have been "bred in a convent." The kindly woman at the gate brought a piece of brown paper. We parted with pleasant words and a message from the sister to "our ladies" in Washington.

Our last errand was at the newspaper office, for by some oversight Mrs. M.'s notice of the expected Sunday service had not appeared. Imagine her surprise to find in to-day's paper an advertisement like this : —

"If Mr. M. will call at the Western Union telegraph office, he will find a telegram from Monterey."

That was my missing telegram, which had been twice inquired for, and which the operator knew perfectly well where to deliver! Surely we may put that among the "oddities of travel!"

We had intended to drive into General Neigla's grounds, but it was too dark. The famous Normal School building here was burned down a year ago; we drove round the new one in process of erection, and through some of the prettiest streets. Many long streets are shaded by Lombardy poplars stiff and tall. Except that the exuberance of vegetation is so great, and that the houses are all of wood, the upper part of Franklin Street in Buffalo is a good sample of the town. You must imagine half-a-dozen such streets crossing each other at right angles.

San José, Oct. 17, 1880. — The Sunday paper was faithful to its duty. There was an unwonted air of Sabbath quiet in the streets as I rode down to Unity Hall. I have become so accustomed to military reviews, street pageants, and other commotions on Sunday, that the quiet seemed strange. It was a pleasant, attentive audience, and every seat was full in spite of the late notice. If the announcement had come out yesterday, I think there would have been more than the hall could accommodate. I spoke on "God in the world."

Almost every one remained after the service to welcome me. A great many persons whom I did not know inquired after friends of yours and mine at the East. They were all cordially delighted to see each other, and glad to have the church open. There had been no service since June, and yet I did not feel as if any one of them was prepared to make any great sacrifice for the church. Why is it, I wonder, that in California people will pay for everything willingly except a minister?

In the midst of the crowd was Mrs. V. I have spoken to you of her as of a young woman with a family of children, struggling to support herself and them by the practice of law in San Francisco. I was amazed to find her here, but she said she had heard in the city that I was to preach, and came to take her chance. She was almost the first to crowd her way to the platform, and then delivered herself in this mysterious way: "I am so glad I came I want to thank you. You do not know, and I have not time to tell you, what makes this service a very important thing to me. It will impress all the remainder of my life."

A young architect came up to tell me that I had started a new train of thought for him, and he was going away to follow it out. I hope he did. I went home with a lovely bunch of flowers in my hand. I smelt lemon verbena in all the gardens. It grows twenty feet high here, and perfumes all the air.

Mr. and Mrs. S. and Mrs. Watkins came home with us to lunch. Mrs. S. said the church had held one hundred and fifty-three sociables lately in as many months. What they earn in this way goes, I believe, to the current expenses. It is also their way of having a good time, and I cannot consider that those who engage in it make any sacrifice. She said she had never lived anywhere where the women tried to improve themselves, and were as active, as in California. I very gladly acknowledge that wherever there is a nucleus of New England women in California, I have found them exerting themselves in a truly remarkable way. I am greatly interested in the work which the Chautauqua Society is doing for both men and women. The classes for study at home were started at the lake meetings by a Mr. Vincent, who has written some of the text-books in use. There are many subjects open, and the members of the classes, if faithful,

study the same lessons at the same hour all over the
United States. This gives a touch of sentiment to the
affair, which loses nothing when we remember that
streams which flow into the Atlantic, as well as the
great Ohio flowing into the Gulf of Mexico, have their
source at this fountain head of knowledge.

One thing I *am* sure of, and must say, and that is
that I never was in a country where the law makes
such victims of women as in California. It is difficult to account for it, unless by the exceedingly corrupt influence exercised by the women at the first.
I must say this very explicitly, because when Mrs.
Stow brought me her book on the Probate Laws of California I would not buy it; and I told her very plainly
that I thought her emotions had so confused her statement that it was practically useless. As I am brought
face to face with the facts here, I cannot only excuse
this, but I wonder that any woman keeps her senses
under the indignities which widows are called to endure.
If the climate made this country a paradise, which it
does not, these laws would make it a hell to any intelligent woman.

The other day, as Charlotte and I were driving home,
a tradesman stepped up and asked her if she would sign
a petition to the leading shop-keepers asking them to
close their places of business on the Sabbath day. " You
see," he continued, " times are hard; decent people don't
want to go where the Sundays are so noisy. Eastern
men who have money don't want to settle. We 've got
to do it." I am afraid that my argument is not much
nobler than his.

Mrs. Watkins was the wife of a man of property. In
his last years he bought all his property in her name,

thinking to make her administration of the estate a simple matter. On the contrary, after his death the court required her to prove that these purchases were made with her own money!

This house in which I write was bought with Charlotte's money, — money inherited from her father in Portsmouth, N. H. The deeds were made out and the purchase registered in her name. The attorney who did it never whispered one word by which her husband could guess that this would not make the property hers. Fortunately her only son was bred to the law, and when he came home on a visit he told his father the deeds were not worth the paper they were written on! As soon as this son can spare time to attend to it, Charlotte is to deed all the property back to her husband, and then *he* is to deed it back to her, with the absurd clause added that he does it for "love and affection." In other words he is compelled to give a reason for leaving his wife in possession of her own property! This done, *she* will not be required to show *ante-conjugal* possession.

I have never known anything so base as the manner in which the courts swallow up small properties, if I except my experience in the District of Columbia, where, in the absence of a will, a woman is the lawful prey of all sorts of sharks. Here the wife has half the " community property " if a husband dies without a will, but cannot dispose of a dime during his life; while *he* can give it or will it all away from her! A pretty state of things!

San José, Oct. 18, 1880. — As I stood dressing in front of the window, I think a hundred birds flew out of the great Monterey cyprus in front of it. The tree is about thirty-five feet high.

The S.'s were so kind as to send me their carriage and a horse this morning. This last made a team with Charlotte's, and as soon as breakfast was over we all went to " Alum Rock." This is a small cañon about six miles from town, in which there are various mineral springs. There are soda, alum, and sulphur waters, and a spring of sulphur and iron. This last makes a black pool called the " Devil's inkstand," which smells and tastes like rotten eggs. A large brook, wasted to a thread at this moment, runs through the cañon. The springs are on the very margin of it, on the sides of the cañon, or dripping from the rock above. In one or two instances I thought the water as good as Congress water. I was glad to go to this spot, as I shall not see the geysers, and it is really interesting to find a clear stream close to and yet undefiled by these chemical abominations, which, spurting up to the surface within a few inches of one another, must certainly spring from widely separated sources.

The road rose steadily all the way from San José. The cañon is tufted with live-oak and with poplar turned to a golden yellow. Both are garlanded with poison ivy, which is now a brilliant scarlet. It looked exactly like October at home. This cañon has been bought as a city reservation, and now serves as a park to San José. The road to it is planted on both sides with trees.

We found a graceful young Spaniard there with his gun. He brought down some buck-eyes, a sort of horse chestnut, and desired me to wear them for " good luck." He had killed a ground squirrel, and showed me the pretty mottled creature with its hollow cheeks. · When we got down to the little inn where we watered our horses he was there before us, and offered us each a glass of wine, which we did not accept. I shall long remember this delightful morning. I find the sunshine here as delicious as at Stockton; but we always encounter fog and chill before we get home at night.

Yesterday Mr. M. showed me a gopher he had just trapped. It looked like a short, thick, brown rat. Its tusks overlapped, and its cheeks were lined with a soft, short fur. Mr. M. loses trees by the creature daily, and his own traps are of little use unless his neighbors will set them also. He digs deep, sets his trap in the ground, covers it with a shingle to prevent the earth from falling in, and then fills in and smooths the surface.

We then had some talk about the yellow scale, a microscopic turtle with six legs, a beak, and antennæ, which is destroying plums, pears, and cherries all through this valley. Mr. M. has owned this farm four years, and has sold his fruit on the trees hitherto. Now this cannot be done, for the yellow scale not only sucks the juice but poisons the trees. The inferior fruit is picked and sold below the cost of production, as opportunity occurs. Professor Comstock is to come out next summer to investigate this on the part of the Smithsonian. It would be well if Professor Riley could do it also, for so far the scourge is undescribed. I observe that Mr. M. disputes such statements as the observers have so far published, and I see that it will take more than one season for the best entomologist to understand all the conditions. The California people are accustomed to think that farming here need encounter no obstacles; but the destruction of orange and nut trees at the south, and of large plum, cherry, and pear orchards at the north, from such causes as this must in time convince them of the contrary.

Here as elsewhere prosperity is to depend on intelligence and industry. I have known three successive crops of vegetables raised in eastern Massachusetts in one season, and that is all that can be done here. Farmers borrow a great deal of money here in California who would not dare to do it in the Eastern States ; and I rather think those who lend money would be more willing, other things being equal, to risk it here. I believe the same sum would go as far in New England as in California, especially if employed in the high cultivation of ten-acre farms. The rapid and showy growth of fields and orchards is not only an encouragement but a temptation, and fruit-growers seem wholly to ignore the deficient flavors.

Times of trial have certainly begun. As I have gone from shop to shop buying inlaid woods, ornaments of abalone, and bits of Japanese bronze or lacquer, I have been offered some very rare things at very low prices, the dealers saying that they had no hope of selling in these bad times, and no expectation that the times would soon mend. Now that men are beginning to work instead of speculating at the Stock Board, they will have little money to spend in needless ways. I think that people at the East do not generally understand why it is worth while to buy Japanese articles here. The principal Japanese dealer in San Francisco is an Englishman, who has lived long in Japan and has personal relations with all the modern factories. Not only so, but he understands the value of antiques and where to obtain them. Twice a month a steamer goes to Japan

23

from San Francisco, and orders can be sent thither as easily, and goods received in return as promptly, as between New York and Liverpool. I wish the Japs would keep to their old work, — the work for which we especially value them; but they are deliberately spoiling their own markets by all the shabby tricks of trade they have learned from Western nations. At the shop I speak of I not only found Professor Marsh, of Yale College, buying up old bronze, but some very well known English collectors, with whom I had also travelled in Utah.

After lunch we drove over to Mr. Pierce's place in Santa Clara. As Mrs. Hayes and the President were driven through it, I suppose it is thought one of the finest plantations. Mr. Pierce was an Eastern miner, and now raises a great many grapes, which he sells to the vintners, but does not himself attempt to crush. The house is without pretension. It is surrounded by beautiful flowers and fruit, but there is nothing picturesque or especially attractive in the arrangements. There is always something delightful in these vines, fuller of leaves than fruit, and the fig trees sending their crumpled shadows across the path.

From the plantation we went to the Jesuit College and the old Santa Clara Mission church, which has been so deftly enclosed that one has hard work to find it. The Jesuits have screened the old adobe walls with modern clap-boards. Within it has been well kept, and probably gives a better idea of what these chapels originally looked like than any I have seen. The carvings of saints and angels came from older churches in Mexico. They were finely enamelled once, and precisely resemble those now in the National Museum and brought from the far older cathedral in Arizona. It is asserted here that these Mexican carvings were made by Indian pupils. I should have doubted this entirely but for a curiously carved wooden tabernacle, painted in white and gilded, which the Indians here carved for the first altar at Santa Clara. It is still preserved, though no longer used to enshrine the host. On it was a vine with grapes, ears of Indian corn as a symbol of the wafer, and all the sacred implements of the crucifixion. On this the arrangement of the symbols spoke for itself, for although exceedingly well done it was not in the least European. The ceiling is very carefully ornamented with full-sized figures of some of the saints, which are really ambitious. The walls are six feet thick. The vestments and reliquaries especially belonging to this Mission are kept at a small chapel in the mountains nearer to some native towns, where a service is held every Sunday.

We were not allowed to go into the college, because a recitation was going on ; but we looked at the beautiful gardens and playing fountains, enclosed by the college buildings, as well as the great cross opposite. It is thirty-three feet high, and was planted by the Indians a hundred years ago.

As we drove home we went through the famous grounds of General Neigla. The moss drips from the branches of its live-oaks. The cyprus boughs brushed my face as we swept through the old avenues. Although a dreary place to live in, because it is so hidden by the unpruned growth of years, it is most attractive. The vineyards are immense, and as they are a steady source of income are kept in much better order than the house or grounds. The General makes a great deal of brandy on the spot. I could not help thinking how lovely the whole place would look in the bright sunshine, with a jolly crowd of Italian vintagers. The fog, however, had descended upon us before we entered the grounds.

San José to San Francisco, Oct. 19, 1880. — At eight o'clock this morning Mr. M. drove Edith and myself to the cars. It was hot and misty, and he said they must be having a norther at San Francisco, which brought all the fog down here. After a quiet, uneventful journey through a valley studded with live-oak, we got home safely. There I found various bewildering invitations; among others one for a reception at Professor H.'s in Berkeley, which his wife had been deferring until my return. They had all taken it into their heads that I must certainly come home yesterday. Then the wonderful news that Theodore Wynkoop was in town with his mother, to leave in the Japanese steamer at noon on his way to the Presbyterian missions in Japan, China, and Hindustan, offered me a chance of direct communication with my husband, and obliged me to go to the Palace Hotel. We went out to Berkeley as before, and dined with Professor Stearns. At eight o'clock we went up to the H.'s, where we were most cordially received, and met a large University company.

I do not consider any private entertainment open to remark, but two points struck me this evening which it ought not to wound any one if I allude to. The first is the surprising fact that all the professors congregated in one room and all their wives in the other, and that there was no general conversation of interest, as one ought to expect at a University gathering. I remember that Cambridge parties used to present the same extraordinary spectacle when I was a young girl, but we considered it a trace of provincial barbarism, and set ourselves to correct it. The entirely separate lives led by the men and women in California is a most painful thing in the society on this coast. I seem to have lived for months without any proper social opportunities; and this dissociation, which if not natural to new countries is certainly a universal fact throughout the West, must be broken down before anything like graceful and cultivated society can arise.

The other point is the entire absence of fruit from our entertainment of ices and cake. There were a few grapes, but they served for decoration only. I mention this because I certainly never ate so little fruit in any two months of my life as in these last two spent in the very midst of what ought to be a California harvest. At Mr. M.'s, although he was a fruit-grower, there was little left; but I greatly enjoyed and freely ate while there a sort of prune, with red flesh, which had half dried upon the tree.

I do not allude to these things captiously or from any personal motive, only my physician ordered me here that I might eat fruit freely, — especially grapes. This has not been possible so far as the table of my boarding house is concerned, and when I buy it for myself it withers in the basket and tempts nothing but the eye. Other travellers might need it more than I, and encounter a similar disappointment.

I met at this pleasant gathering a Mr. Gompertz, who is instructor in Spanish, who has passed a great deal of time in Mexico, who knew Maximilian, and who is as much excited as I am over the discoveries Dr. Charnay may possibly make in Yucatan. I talked over with him the matters relating to the Mission churches, and promised to meet him to-morrow morning at the library, when he will give me a catalogue of the library of Señor Don José Fernando Ramirez, one of the ministers of Maximilian, whose books are now for sale in London. No collection has ever offered to scholars so large a number of Aztec and other native grammars.

The weather is most exhausting. I cannot find out what a norther is, except that it is a hot wind from the deserts of Humboldt and Arizona, which scorches the plants and burns one side of every tree as if it were a devouring flame. Between trade-winds and northers this vicinity seems to have a hard time.

Berkeley University to San Francisco, Oct. 20, 1880.— At ten I went to the library. Last evening Mr. Gompertz told me that some of the Jesuit Fathers alluded to the fact, or to what my friend Professor Larkin asserts to be the fact, that the Chinese peons in Lima could make themselves understood by the Aztecs in the absence of interpreters. He talked of the spheres of silver given to Cortez, and said that he had traced them as far as the grandson of Columbus, and believed them to be now at the University of Salamanca. Besides the catalogue of the Ramirez library, he brought me a cigar case of modern Aztec manufacture, presented to him by one of his pupils in the City of Mexico. It represents a grape-vine heavily fruited running over a chased surface. He showed me also a masonic badge made in repoussé by the same workman.

I asked him also the meaning of the great cap of heavy leather which protects the Spanish stirrup. He said it was very necessary to defend the wearer against the "cats' claws" which he must encounter in the mountains, and that most of the peasants wore leather jackets for the same reason. I naturally looked perplexed; and then he explained that "cats' claws" were the spines of a large cactus which work into the flesh. In Peru the stirrups are made of orange-wood, which is still more impervious.

He then brought me the great folios of Humboldt and Bonpland, and the nine volumes of Lord Kingsborough, that I might examine the plates thoroughly afresh, and especially that I might see the *colored* plates in Lord Kingsborough's books while my mind still retained a vivid impression of the Mission frescos. N. thought I might just as well have waited till I got to New York to look at all these, but my determination had its reward. The problem of the peculiar colors used in these churches is solved at last; and very simple it is, although they do look as if William Morris or Walter Crane had presided over the achievement. The Indians painted the roof and carving with their own vegetable colors, which they had used for centuries in their public buildings before Cortez ever came to the country. The colors in Lord Kingsborough's superb book are *facsimiles* of what I see in the churches here, — dull magenta, red, olive, and a dark blue, like the first stain of some black inks. What these are any one can easily ascertain who has access to a copy of Lord Kingsborough with colored plates. I am not sure that I ever saw the colored plates before. Only two hundred such copies, hand painted, were ever finished.

Oddly enough looked the wreaths of flowers which decorate the walls at Santa Clara in such colors. There is a circle of cherubic heads on that ceiling also which seems to link together the figures of several of the prophets, — a more ambitious design than I had known the Indians to undertake.

In a representation of a Mexican manuscript at Dresden, in Lord Kingsborough's book, there is shown the hanging of a black prisoner. He is a negro, and strangely enough holds in his hands a red cross of the Christian shape. I could not ascertain its age.

Mr. Stearns was occupied the first part of the morning, so Mr. Gompertz acted as my guide. I do not like to say anything about the University, because I have been able to give so little time to it. It still seems to an Eastern eye in the very infancy of its work.

The museums must in time become most wonderful collections. The close neighborhood of a most remarkable fossil and mining region of course contributes remarkable specimens of various kinds. It is a very pleasant thing that two of the fathers-in-law of professors employed have given two of the new buildings. Mr. Toland erected the medical college; Mr. Harmon, of Oakland, put up the gymnasium; and Mr. H. D. Bacon, in November, 1877, gave a valuable collection of paintings and sculpture, a library of several thousand volumes, and twenty-five thousand dollars in money to the University, on condition that the State should also give twenty-five thousand dollars toward the construction of a gallery and library room. Such a library, able to hold ninety thousand volumes, and a gallery thirty-eight feet wide by ninety feet long, will be ready for use at the beginning of 1881. Mr. Lick has provided for the erection and equipment of an observatory, which will be built on Mount Hamilton. Several chairs are

filled by graduates of the University, which seems to
me a very bad plan at this early date. The separate
sitting-rooms and reading-rooms for the two sexes
seemed ludicrously insufficient. The Assembly Room, in
which the classes in rhetoric are held, has the portraits
of benefactors and presidents upon its walls, and also
the fine folio photographs of the Yosemite. The best
recitation-room is that in which President Le Conte
lectures on physical science. In the laboratory they
were using kerosene stoves under their retorts, and
seemed greatly in need of many things they do not
possess.

There was a great deal of noise in the halls. Order
and silence in passing up and down are not required. I
have never encountered that state of things in a college
intended for both sexes, and I am not pleased with the
consequences. There is not a State in the Union where
gentle and courteous restraints should be so much insisted upon as in this, at every opportunity. Neither is
any order observed in seating pupils in the class-rooms.
An alphabetical order would mix the two sexes in a
natural and easy way. The girls were generally huddled into one corner, with a sort of indecorous consciousness. I do not know how this is managed in other
mixed colleges, for nothing ever occurred in my visits to
them which obliged me to think about it. I do know,
however, that in most of them each pupil keeps one
seat for the entire term, which could not happen here.

I went with Mr. Stearns to Professor Rising's chemical laboratory, and then to the museum. In the latter
place I saw a live rattlesnake of a very scarce variety.
Its imbricated coat was most beautifully colored in a
way we often see in pictures, but seldom now-a-days in

the specimen. The creature kept up a perpetual hiss. In the lecture-room a professor was hanging a portable and pliable black-board which I had not happened to see before. I found in the museum a very fine carving from China, which looked so Mexican that I could hardly believe it Oriental. Among the sections of wood I saw one of the Yucca palm, which has so odd an effect in the Mohavè Desert. In talking of the Big Trees and comparing the bark of the sequoia with that of the redwood, I told Professor Jackson that I felt sure the age of the sequoia had not been properly estimated. In a climate which produces two or three crops a year of most vegetables, there is nothing to prevent the formation of more than one ring in twelve months; and I wish the age of some recently planted sequoias could be tested by cutting down one known to be about twenty years old. Professor Jackson thought there was a good deal to sustain my view. He said that he had often found crowded and obscure rings interposed between the well-defined growths. The bark of the redwood is darker than that of the sequoia and more compact.

I saw here many specimens of lava in various stages of decomposition. I have never before realized, what I must have heard, that the color of black lava changes first by the oxidation of the iron in it, and next by its being bleached or washed out. Professor Jackson is anxious to get specimens of slag. I did not offer him my own samples of these beautiful "accidents," but I told him what furnaces in Colorado had yielded me the finest. Under the microscope I saw some tiny sections of granite. In a bubble of air in a cavity in the quartz I saw a perfect cube of salt. Professor Hilgard's own cabinet, consisting of twelve thousand specimens of plants, is open to the use of the students, — an act of great generosity on his part. The widow of the late ornithologist, Grayson, has given a rare work to the University, consisting of one hundred and sixty-three pictures of Mexican birds. These are drawn and painted to the life, and there is said to be a duplicate set in the Smithsonian. This collection was made for the Academy of Arts and Sciences in Mexico at the instance of Maximilian, but the contract was rescinded at his death.

The collections of pottery and Indian implements are of course good. So are those of fossils obtained from the various surveys. There is a superb collection of ores.

Coming home to lunch, Mr. Stearns showed me some eatable pine-seeds, used by the Indians for kidney diseases with excellent results. They are the size and shape of an ordinary olive stone. When cut across, they are so full of oil as to seem translucent. They are of a pinkish-brown color, and the taste is very sweet, with a slight flavor of turpentine.

After lunch Miss S. and myself went over to the Deaf, Dumb, and Blind Asylum. The superintendent, Dr. Wilkinson, stands very high in general esteem; but it seems to me impossible wisely to unite inmates of such different needs in one institution. The interests of either class would furnish one man with occupation for his whole life. The schools are only open in the morning; so all I could do was to examine the buildings. Some time since the institution was partly destroyed by fire. The new buildings not yet finished are of common brick put together with white mortar, and, although admirably laid, are about as ugly on the exterior as anything I ever saw. Within they are nearly perfect. The ventilation is admirable. In the dormitory for growing pupils, each has a bedroom neatly furnished. The partitions do not reach to the ceilings, and there is a six-inch ventilating tube discharging fresh air in each corner, and four others in the centre. The gas is burned in a cavity in the fire-proof walls, and shut off from the rooms by a pane of glass, so that it really aids ventilation. No drains from the wash-basins open into sewers, but their contents fall into hoppers, with a current of air crossing them; and the hoppers are trapped. The little children have a safe swimming bath in which they can frolic. The older ones use separate tubs. There is a fire-escape enclosed in a sort of circular tower at the end of each new build-ing. There is a gas-burner in every fireplace to aid ven-tilation by starting an upward current of air if needed. In the kitchen the walls are finished with pure white tiles, far above the point at which it is possible to spat-ter them. The wood-work is white cedar finely pol-ished. The dusty character of the soil and the fact that many new buildings are going up made the floors a little dusty; but everything else was spotless.

Dr. Wilkinson has lately had a little cottage erected for himself. It is of redwood well oiled, and the in-dented margins of the sheathing are painted vermilion. The effect is very pretty.

We made a call on Mrs. Wilkinson as we came back. Her library is panelled with redwood. This is filled first with corn-starch which absorbs the natural oil. It is then finished with shellac. This method was new to me, but it has produced a charming effect. We started for San Francisco almost immediately after our return, and were too tired to admire the lovely warm mist which the norther drove back over the Bay.

San Francisco, Oct. 21, 1880. — Have been packing blankets at the Mission mills. A good California blanket can be bought at the East, but I wished to carry home a few colored ones of a quality no longer made, and which have been on hand since 1876. I packed with them some cheap Japanese toys, but these can be better bought at the East. Marsh, the English dealer under the Palace Hotel, receives annually a quantity of very cheap Japanese toys for Christmas. He says the patterns are never repeated, which makes me feel as if I should like to have a choice of his importations every year. I bought of him a little Banko teapot of unglazed stone-ware for twenty-five cents. It is made of two lotus leaves, and tamped over a wooden model. The lower part is bent up in the shape of a butter-boat till it breaks on each side, showing the inner texture of the leaf. The stem is bent round so as to make a firm stand, and then carried up to form a handle. Where the stem was cut off, the pores of the interior structure show plainly. The cover is made of a smaller leaf, the stem being bent so as to form a knob. All the veins and textures are perfect. It is seldom that the most costly article is so satisfactory in an artistic sense.

San Francisco, Oct. 22, 1880. — Yesterday the papers gave the details of a most awful murder. The murderer is the son of a Second Advent minister in Gorham, Maine. He married a young girl from Shrewsbury, Mass., about ten years ago. About three years since he took a younger sister of his wife as his mistress, although she was almost a child. The wife knew this, and allowed it; at least she made no open complaint. This sister the unhappy man has now murdered. His excuse is that he could not otherwise prevent her marriage to a scoundrel! The girl, according to his own story, allowed him to suffocate her with his hands. If she had made any resistance, he could hardly have done it in a house filled with lodgers. The murderer gave himself up at once, confessed his crime, and says he is glad to give his life to save her from the fate in store for her. The case is so extraordinary that I could not help telling you of it. I do not give the names; for it seems to me that the three parties to this crime must all have been insane, and that we ought to protect all those akin to them from the terrible dishonor of it. Cannot Maine and Massachusetts take better care of their children than this? How hopeless life seems when we are compelled to look into such a mäelstrom!

I can find no inlaid woods for you. They must be bought in the Yosemite Valley, and are very costly there. Out on the confines of the town I found a German at work in colored marquetry. I shall try to get a specimen of his work, but I would rather have the woods of the natural color. His veneers are inconceivably thin. After they are cut, paper is pasted on the back to strengthen them, and they are then applied to furniture or panels.

If ever you come to this part of the world bring all the woollen wear you are likely to want. All such things are very dear, and I hardly know how to supply myself for my journey home.

San Francisco, Oct. 23, 1880. — I begin to feel, with great disappointment, that I must not wait for my son's arrival. The wife of Captain B., his friend and companion, arrives to-night, and N. had gone for flowers to decorate her rooms when I went to a lunch at the Palace Hotel. There were six ladies present beside myself, and every one of them had a bad cold ! Among them was Mrs. Williams, the daughter of James the novelist, and the talk was very brilliant at times. The drama and Sarah Bernhardt came up for discussion. Mrs. Williams has seen the best actors of this century on both continents. One person coolly asserted that it was impossible to find a good actress who was not also an impure woman !

I have been reading the new novel called " A Sailor's Sweetheart." I think the author must write exclusively for people without imagination. I found the story too painful to pursue.

San Francisco, Oct. 24, 1880. — We wanted to drive over the hills after church to-day, as my days are getting to be very few; but it did not seem clear enough, so we went up California Street on the cable, and after we had gone as far as the steam dummy would take us, beyond the cable, we walked over the sand toward the Presidio. As we danced up and down over the hills which make up California Street, the fog lifted or shut down, and the glimpses of the Bay were perfectly delicious. I do not wonder that San Francisco people adore their Bay ; that is, if they can ever get a chance to see it !

We came back a good deal tossed by the wind, and went to dine with Miss N. This is my last Sunday in San Francisco, and I was glad to spend it with her, as I had also spent the first, for her sweet Sunday courtesies have added greatly to my pleasure. Her friend, Mr. S., had just arrived from Los Angeles, as much puzzled by the fibrous stem of the yucca palm as ever I had been.

Our dinner consisted of tomato soup, shrimp salad, roast duck with green peas, Ratafia ice, strawberries, and a bunch of flaming tokays that weighed three and a half pounds! The strawberries were most beautiful to look at. Each one looked like a rosy peach; but if any New England girl had put one into her mouth with her eyes shut, I am sure she would never have thought of a strawberry. They are sweet and they are sour, but they are not fragrant; and they have a disagreeable, bitter tang which I never tasted in any other fruit East or West. The flaming tokays are beautiful to look at, but they are not here a proper table grape. One might sheathe a *bidarka* with the skin of them, it is so thick.

"The Tender Recollections of Irene M'Gillicuddy" was spoken of to-day. The author was connected with the London "Times," and married to a young wife whom he idolized. Both became converted to the ascetic views of an evangelical brotherhood. They were compelled to separate, and gave up their wealth to the common purse. They were then sent abroad on beneficent missions. It ended in utter scepticism of everything good on the man's part; but the sorest thing of all was that they were actually in San Rafael at the same time and did not meet. She was a servant in a family there, and he went for a day on some brotherhood errand.

Of course I do not know whether this story is true, but I could tell as strange a one that *is* true of our friend Sir James R. Is it not inconceivable that men should reject the loving kindness of the Almighty Father, and submit to these tyrannies called "brotherhoods" in the way they do?

San Francisco, Oct. 25, 1880. — I went down to Mr.
Horace Davis's office this morning to complete my financial arrangements. Whenever I go there I allow myself
the indulgence of a special growl over the climate. Mr.
Davis's cashier is a Massachusetts man, and we find
ourselves privately entirely agreed as to the comparative
merits of east winds and trades.

Then I went with N. and Mrs. B. to the end of Geary
Street to see the interior working of the Geary Street
cable. Everything in the dépôt was in beautiful order,
as it might be in a lady's storeroom. The gentleman in
charge told us that the whole patent as applied to the
San Francisco roads has never been used elsewhere, and
it has only been three years in use here. What a change
it has made! The hills, before inaccessible, are now the
most desirable locations in town. There are cable cars
in Cincinnati and at Niagara, but these are worked by
windlasses alone, and there is no stopping after you
start till you get to the end of the journey. The windlasses here are moved by steam. The cables are of steel,
filled and fined by sawdust and tar. Then between the
rails there is a middle slot, in which the cable runs, and
the brake of the dummy has an iron " grip," which fast-
ens on the cable and moves up or down with it; whenever the conductor looses this "grip" the car stops, and
this is done at each of the cross-streets which terrace
the hill. Part of this I have told you before.

The whole afternoon has been spent in turning my
gold into Treasury notes and going to the Mission Mills
the third time for my bills of lading. I should like to
have taken home a pretty bit of gold ore, but I could
buy it cheaper in New York.

While I was in Santa Cruz I read a book which asserted that the San Francisco joss-houses were Buddhist temples. Recollecting what I had myself seen, this seemed incredible, so I decided to ask the question of some educated Chinaman. The vice-consul was the most accessible person. I was to have gone to him this afternoon, but when the hour came, I was so utterly weary that Mr. W. offered to go and make the inquiry in my stead. The vice-consul, who is a very cultivated man, asserted most positively that there is not and never has been a single public Buddhist shrine in California; and, in order to convince Mr. W., sent for several of the inferior officers and questioned them in his presence. At one time a rich tea merchant came over on business, and a small private Buddhist shrine was set up in the Globe Hotel for his use. "Very few Buddhists ever come to this country," said the vice-consul, with his nose in the air. In the only interview I ever had with this man, I was shocked at the contempt he showed for the lower classes of his own countrymen, and at the entire absence of any religious faith in himself. All educated Chinese seem to be like him. There is something touching in the dependent trustfulness of the lower classes, and in their faithfulness to any duties assumed. So far as I have been able to observe here, I can echo Miss Bird's statement that we have done great harm to both Japanese and Chinese by our contact with them. They have lost all their own faith, and esteem it a proof of intellect to deny God and immortality, because no "people of education" at the West now believe in either! Whoso shall deceive "one of these little ones that believe," it were better for him of a truth "that a mill-stone were hung about his neck, and that he were cast into the depths of the sea."

After tea I went to the Chinese quarter and finally to the Chinese theatre with Mr. C. There is one thing which must strike every European in the Chinese life here, and that is the indifference of this people to observation. No curtain ever hangs over a Chinese window; and at night, when the lamps are lighted within, it is very interesting to stand and look in, if one can persuade oneself that it is not impertinent. I have come to the conclusion that it would be foolish to attribute such sensitiveness as we feel to any of the Chinese whom I have met. We walked about the narrow alleys as before, and looked into the barbers' shops. Men and women have their hair put up once a week, and sleep on bamboo pillows, which prevent any disarrangement. The men ply their trade deftly; their customers appear to go to sleep under their hands. The sleek appearance of the hair is due to a bandoline, made from what they sell in the Chinese shops under the name of "shavings." These are probably made of some large soap-wort; they are as thin as foreign letter-paper, and look a little like slippery elm. It is the best thing I ever saw of the sort, for it keeps every hair in place as if it were glued; but as it is quite as stiff as glue, I think the hair must be badly broken by it. The fluffiest puffs keep a permanent shape, when treated with this. The long queue of the men is finished by plaiting into it a knot of coarse sewing silk, which hangs down like a tassel or fringe.

Late as it was, the markets were full of customers. I have observed that Chinese servants always eat all the good things they have access to, and by so doing they grow more human and attractive-looking. The use of many things still eaten by the better classes is only the trace left by a diseased or morbid appetite, which great

poverty has engendered. Those who think this people
do not eat filthy things should walk through the Chinese
end of Dupont Street at a late hour. A tailor's shop
which we passed was open, and twenty or thirty men at
work in it. Mr. C. says these shops are open all night,
and he thinks the masters employ two gangs of workmen; but it is difficult to understand the need of this.
Three storeys of the building were lighted.

The most interesting shops were those of the apothe-
caries. They are as neat as wax, and it is evident that
the system of drugs gives way now and then to a system
of magic! Here lizards, toads, newts, and herbs that
look malicious are dried, pounded, and mixed with great
care. The prescriptions are pounded and mixed in full
sight of the customer. Gilded dragons hung on the
walls, and I saw a man swallow some powdered gold
leaf in some liquid. The very same disgusting remedies
for female diseases are given here that are given to the
poor whites under the incantations of the Voodoos in
West Virginia. The most mysterious remedies appeared
to fall to the lot of those who wore the grandest dresses!
Mr. C. wanted me to talk with a Chinese woman, who
is his tenant; so we went into a small house, where the
smoke was so thick that I did not for a few moments
perceive that I was in an opium den. Tsui-zan, or
Susan, as my companion called her, was not at home,
and the woman who kept watch would not answer a
question. She looked stupid, and to all inquiries reiterated, "No sabe, no sabe." She reminded me of the
lower class of negroes at the South, who reiterate
"dunno" in precisely the same way. Two men who
were smoking lay on wretched calico-covered couches.
They seemed too stupid to see; but one of them, who

was on a double couch, moved a little and invited my
companion to lie down. The stalls in which the couches
were, occupied more than half the depth of the house.
The space in front was nearly empty. It held a chair
for the watcher, a wash-stand with water and towels,
and a few pots of flowers, which must have had a hard
struggle for life.

We went across the street to the theatre. Two short
flights of stairs led us past a police officer and a Chinese
door-keeper. There was nothing outside to indicate a
public building. The Chinaman could speak no English,
and the fees were paid by each person carrying a silver
half-dollar in his hand. There was no need to ask questions or receive change. Just above the door-keeper
was a cheap colored calico curtain, the two lower corners of which were pinned back *bias*. This left a triangular open space, near the stair, and too low down to
create a draught, by which the audience went up and
down noiselessly. There was neither door nor vestibule,
and no loud word was permitted after one crossed the
threshold. As soon as I passed this bit of calico I was
in the theatre.

Imagine a large, bare auditorium finished in white-
wash and white paint, with two galleries and a stage.
There is no scenery, no drop-curtain ; and two ordinary
doors at the back of the stage serve for entrance and
exit. There is no interest or decoration to draw the
eyes from the performers themselves. The pit held
certainly three hundred persons seated ; and back of it,
the space usually given up to boxes was crammed by
people standing, among whom at first I also stood.
This arrangement, I believe, is precisely that which
obtained in London in Dr. Johnson's time.

Far up on the white-washed wall and over the stage was a portrait; underneath, the words —

"KOM QUAI YUEN,"

on a tablet. In connection with the portrait, which was, however, only another representation of Kar Quon, I thought the inscription might designate a dramatic author, or perhaps the name of a play; but it turned out to be the name of the theatre, — "The Gold Cinnamon Garden." The theatres are named as ours are; and beside that they take annually the name of the troop that opens the performances of the year.

It is pleasant to think of The Gold Cinnamon Garden; what fragrance might not have delighted me could I have read it at the first! On each side of the tablet was a gilded scroll about two feet long; from a dragon's mouth in the centre of this came out a lighted gas-jet, and these two gave all the light the players had, — a few scattered jets here and there in the house only serving to make darkness visible. There was no such thing as a chandelier. Mottoes, or possibly the names of plays, hung against the wall on red, blue, and purple paper. At each end of the stage were two very elaborate paper lanterns not lighted. They had little balconies round about, which were quite full of figures of men and animals, beautifully cut and colored; and as the whole lantern was about five feet long, it must be quite effective when lighted. There were no carpets on the stage. At the back of it, a little fenced off from the players by a few rails, half-a-dozen men were playing on noisy jingling instruments, — forcibly reminding the spectator of a child's first efforts on a tin kettle. Their dresses were more shabby than those of the com-

monest coolie on the street. I could not *see* that any
one of them "led the discords;" and you may write it
down that in China music means noise,—rhythmic
perhaps, but not in the least melodious.

Just in front of the musicians was a chair arrayed in
crimson and gold, with a mat before it. When we entered the theatre, an emperor sat in this chair,—an
emperor of the Tartar line,—in a costume stiff with
gold thread and embroidery. On his head-dress every kind of ball and flag seemed to flutter in company
with two long feathers bent down the back, and about
four feet in length. Something like the general effect
of this head-dress may be seen in any insane asylum.
A woman whose hair was hidden under a close mandarin's cap, and who wore for the rest a beautiful bri-
dal dress of white and gold, was talking earnestly to
him. The theatre was crammed from floor to ceiling.
There was not a fly stirring. A Chinese shoe never
creaks.

Finding that we could not see properly, my companion put some money into the usher's hand, and he
then led the way up a rickety stair and behind the
gallery seats, through a passage so narrow that our
clothes touched the whitened wall on each side, to a
stage box with four wooden chairs in it. Here we
overlooked both stage and auditorium. I might go
oftener to our own theatres, if I could be as well ac-
commodated!

Every performance begins at two P. M., and does not
close till after midnight. In the afternoon loose women
are admitted. In the evening, only those who are
"kept." There were some lovely children in the wood-
en pen which was divided from mine by a red cotton

curtain. I stooped over and asked the mother who the portly emperor in the big chair was, but she answered only by the everlasting "no sabe." Her stiffened hair was done up in numberless bows, very much as it was once worn by European women. It had been gummed till it looked as if every bow was made of steel.

The most perfect stillness reigned throughout the house. The audience evidently came to listen. Last week I had heard of a play in which a baby was born on the stage, and the midwife, while she dressed the babe in Chinese fashion, told the story of the amour which had given birth to it. I should have been so excited by the whole thing, that I do not think even that would have embarrassed me. But to-night the play was much purer and far more amusing than a French comedy; and for fear I should forget it, let me add that there was no offensive untidiness nor any disagreeable odor, except an occasional whiff of opium from the pipes of the musicians, who did not seem to be forbidden their creature comforts so long as they diligently continued to madden us with their discords.

Of course I had largely to guess at the story, and whether I guessed right or wrong my guesses will help to the understanding of the stage method. A young girl, hating the lover to whom she had been sold or married, escaped to the emperor, and kneeling at his feet piteously implored his intercession. He gave the whole matter over to the courts. He seemed to fall in love with the girl at once; and after he had sent off to summon the judges, they knelt down together and invoked the favor of Heaven, — and, if I might judge from wild motions and dim visions, they invoked something very like the Tao-ist powers of evil. At this

moment the deserted lover rushed upon the stage. He
was a prince, and came surrounded by a military guard.
After violent and most telling gesticulations on his
part, the stage suddenly filled with characters superbly
dressed and each wearing a mask. Among them was a
frog, about five feet high, who turned somersaults, and
who was killed three or four times over, but who
always came to life again in the most surprising manner. It seemed as if the masked characters were on
the side of the emperor, by the vigor with which the
prince's guard pursued them. The frog was admirably
made and inflated, and exactly like the real creature,
except that he had a long tail in the middle of his
back. Every now and then the prince would catch
hold of this in a most insulting way, and flap him
down on the floor with it, where he lay dead and as flat
as a sheet of paper. Hardly could his enemy turn his
back before he found some way to regain life and inflate
his ribs, and began to frisk round, tripping up the heels
of each warrior at a critical moment with the most entertaining malice, but only to be reduced to death
and nothingness again on the first opportunity. Of the
indescribable movement and gayety of this whole scene
I can give you no idea.

Then the two parties appeared before the judge, who, if
I guessed right, gave a decision against the lover, who
bowed submission backward as he went out of court.
No sooner had the court adjourned than the masks re-
appeared; the frog whispered something to the lover
which seemed to drive him crazy, for he tore the sealed
decision of the judge away from the court messenger,
and took a seat in the judge's chair, where all in a moment he seemed to become the judge himself, and forged

another order in his own favor. The court messenger, arrested by magic, had been standing all this while bereft of his senses, just as the document was torn from his hand. Into its clasp the false judge now delicately insinuated his own order, and off went the messenger with it. In a moment the stage was filled. The emperor was in his chair; he rose eagerly to receive the order, looked at it with amazement, and tore it up in a frenzy of indignation, scattering the pieces to the four winds. At this moment the girl came forward, tore off her mandarin's cap and cloak, and made a long oration to the lover. It was quite eloquent. She had clearly detected his perfidy, and was charging him with it.

A low murmur of approbation ran through the house, and the actors threw themselves on their faces and touched their foreheads to the floor in acknowledgment. I saw boys creeping noiselessly through the audience carrying baskets of figs and grapes on their heads. My attention was distracted for the moment, and when I turned again to the stage there was a complete mêlée. All parties were engaged in a free fight, and the frog was industriously tripping up the performers on both sides. I was sorry not to stay to the end, for I should like to have seen somebody even with that frog, and it must have been "on the cards."

This play will go on an entire week. The fabrics used for the costumes were very superb. The whole "get up," however, reminded me of the "Mandans" and their sorcerers as Paul Kane and Catlin used to describe them. The lances of the soldiers had each a scalp-lock attached to them, and the chief magician had the true medicine-man air. The judge was quite a venerable figure, with a white mask and a long white beard. It occurred to me that the frog might be made of silk, sustained by whalebones that suddenly collapsed. The whole play was acted with indescribable spirit, so far as I saw it.

San Francisco, Oct. 26, 1880. — I took N. and Mrs. B. to look at Japanese curios; went to find the bit of marquetry ordered for you, and bought some "Franklin Squares" to read on the overland journey. I went with Mr. W. to look at old bronzes, but found nothing good. I meant to go into the Chinese quarter again, but the joss-houses were not open this afternoon, nor have they been lighted this evening.

San Francisco, Oct. 27, 1880. — We went out to make calls; and Miss C. told us about the great Chinese funeral which passed her house while I was at Santa Cruz. There were five or six barouches filled with hired mourners, dressed and turbaned with white, who howled as they went along. The hearse came next, — the white horses trapped with black. At least a hundred carriages followed; and from the windows the Chinamen threw narrow strips of paper with a well gilded circle in the centre. In the old religious services money was thrown to the poor, and I fancied that this might be a mimetic relic of the old way; but the servants said "it was to buy the man's soul back from the devil." "He ver rich," said Tsing, "but much bad. They throw to keep off devil. He got him; been after him much years!" During my absence Netty was invited by a friend to go to the house during the funeral hours. The priest, a benevolent looking old man, sat at the head of the coffin with a book. The women, clothed in white, sat howling on the floor. The street in front of the house was filled with tables covered with food. After the ceremony was over this was taken back to the butcher and sold at half price. Under the State religion the oblations offered to ancestors were finally divided among the poor. Looking at this matter on all sides then, I find that this was a Tao-ist service; for any other class of the Chinese the devil does not exist.

Miss M. is really sorry to have me go away. She has not told me all she wants to about the undisguised vice of the towns. Beside the obscene writing on the school fences and the seduction of pupils by teachers, she assured me that to her own knowledge there were brothels in town open to boys of twelve! I should think this could hardly have happened before since the days of Aristophanes; but I have heard the same story from other quarters.

I have said as little as possible about the great evils incident to adventurous life, which have crystallized here. When M. and A. told me that they had left California and gone East because they could not bring their children up in purity, I felt as if they ought to have stayed and compelled purity. But, alas! I also should have fled from the evil to come. What I can scarce bear to hear of I certainly would not have endured.

Poor Miss M. is much exercised over the deacons and church members who run the houses in Dupont Street, and in wondering why the police never think it worth while to descend on the Montgomery Street "hells," but must always organize startling expeditions into Chinatown. So, to tell the truth, am I.

I found to-day at Shreve's a collection of bronze buttons from old sword-hilts that was very fine.

San Francisco, Oct. 28, 1880.— To-day we took the long-talked-of drive over the hills. It had been deferred and deferred in pursuit of a clear day until the very last hour had come, and still it was not clear. The smoke driven down from the Oregon woods by the norther was still hanging over the Bay, and great white wreaths of fog were rolling up from the sea. At first we rode over bleak sand-dunes, looking back over a still bleaker town. Then we got glimpses of sea and rock between black mist and white fog, each partly lifted. Then came hills covered with sage-brush and lupin, green with last night's showers, — for the rain has actually begun, and one would think the fog might go. In the conservatory at the park we found the blue lotus and the magnificent victoria regia in bloom. As we came out, a flock of quail darted up at our feet. We were late at lunch ; but Mr. C. had checked my trunk, and Cousin Henry had sent tickets for the Stock Exchange.

After lunch I went down to the Chinese theatre on an errand with Mr. W. The colors over the stage were much more brilliant than at night, and the war of "discords" was just beginning. As we came back through the quarter I saw that the shops were full of new goods, and so were the markets. Betel-nuts with strips of white cocoa-nut enclosed in a horn of coca-leaf were exposed for sale, and looked very fresh and tempting. Not so the half-putrid rats and rabbits, or the dried Chinese oysters. The men were sprinkling the stale stock !

I have not said much to you about the Chinese ques-

tion.   I do not know that I have anything to say, for
you would not believe what I could tell you.   You
would think that I had been deceived, or that being a
woman I had not known how to approach this subject.
I have no sympathy whatever with the outcry against
them as laborers.   As fast as they get possession of
the small manufactures they raise the price of their labor, until the American has no occasion to dread the
competition.   If they work more steadily, skilfully, or
faithfully, let him go and do likewise.

If the Chinese will come to this country to live
above ground, and accept our laws to the extent of
doing nothing in contravention of them, I do not see
any possible way of shutting them out.   But it is wholly
impossible to allow them to exist in a quarter of their
own, fouler than the well remembered Ghetto, and
subject to no sanitary regulations.   It has been said
that Chinatown has been cleaned out; but no one will
pretend that its sewers have been repaired, its underground caverns filled in, its loathsome invalids taken to
good hospitals, or its opium dens burned out.   Until these
things are done it cannot be clean ; and this can never be
done until San Francisco is ready to subject itself entirely to the legal and sanitary reformer.   So long as the
men of San Francisco are unwilling to close their own
houses of assignation, their gambling dens, and their
brothels, they have no power, either human or divine,
to close those of the Chinese.   If they will not stop
drinking on every street-corner, they will hardly undertake to drag the opium-eater from his quiet den.   So
far as I can hear, no municipal power has ever interfered to check the sale of unwholesome food, to empty
overcrowded houses, to release the victims of the "last

chance," to prevent the daily murder of female or mal-
formed children, to check polygamous intercourse, or to
bring the murders and assassinations of the "quarter"
under the cognizance of our own courts.

There are no Chinese women employed as servants
among the families in San Francisco. Those that are
brought over are *sold* as servants among their own country people, — a thing to which our law is surely competent to put an end. This leads, as soon as they are
old enough to a life of prostitution. The women are
strangely like each other. It is difficult to recognize
them; and they all look like the old enamelled London
doll with wooden joints that you will remember seeing
among my old toys, — you are too young ever to have
played with one yourself. Strange to say, just such
faces are to be found among ourselves; and many more
— even to the oblique eye — are to be seen among the
Spanish women on this coast.

As servants I think I could never endure this people. Their noiselessness would be a nightmare to me.
I should never feel secure from their observation. I
should never feel confidence in their cleanliness. If
one could take a very young child and bring it up, the
inherited habit of obedience and the sense of order
might make a good foundation for training.

I have seen only one first-class servant in the country, although I have seen many equal to the average
Irish or German servant. The one I speak of was
Tong, the cook and launder at Mrs. K.'s in Santa Cruz.
Ora is herself a first-rate housekeeper, — a qualification
so rare among young Western women as to be worth
mentioning gratefully. Tong was not only clean, but
he was *observant* to a purpose. The Chinese are so

quiet that they are not thought to observe, but their dexterity as burglars and assassins shows that the half-closed lids cover watching eyes. The first day I was at Santa Cruz, I declined a fine salad on the ground that I could not eat garlic. When his mistress put out garlic the next day, Tong would not allow it to lie on his dish,—"Lady no eat onion," he said. The day I left, it was desirable to give me a specially delicate dessert, that I might remember the well-kept table where I, who relish so few things, had always relished all. Ice-cream was proposed; but no,— "Lady like whip;" and whipped cream it had to be. Tong was superstitious; and when the shadow of death hung over the family, he wished to leave. Compelled by his father to stay at advanced wages, he was never again quite happy. After I went to El Monte I was greatly disgusted by the poor cooking of the French and Spanish cooks at the hotel. I sent back word to Tong that nobody cooked as well as he, and it quite cheered him up.

Horace Davis tells us that in 1878 there were in this country one hundred and fifty thousand adult male Chinese, and that in California they form one third of the adult male population! Nowhere have I found them so obvious an evil as in San Francisco. In smaller towns, on the sea-shore or the farm, it is more difficult for them to keep up their own ways; and even a proper diet alters the character. The missionaries tell me that there are well constituted Christian families in the Chinese quarter. I meant to investigate the matter, for I find it hard to believe.

I suppose you know how these people come. There are here six emigration companies. Wealthy Hong

Kong merchants send their agents into the most desperate and crowded districts, to allure the poorest by the promise of high wages. The laborer mortgages himself, and perhaps a wife and children, for the repayment of his passage money. He is consigned to one of the six companies, and that one receives the net proceeds of his labor till the debt is paid. This sort of thing has occurred in North Carolina since the war, and has been widely denounced. Is it any. less dangerous on the Pacific Coast?

It is supposed that there are six thousand Chinese women in California. We know what class would follow such men. Mr. Davis says their emigration is conducted by the Hip Yee Tong, — a society strong enough to defy our laws. It need not be very strong to do that! I believe there is no law against fornication in the State; if there is, it is defied on every street. The Chinese are governed by their own laws, secret tribunals, and police. They put offenders to death without interference. If there had been a proper respect for law *per se* in California this could never have happened twice. It seems to me that whenever the State of California is prepared to enforce her own laws, the emigration of the Chinese will necessarily cease; and these laws should be enforced, if necessary, by the help of the United States army. One third of the adult male population cannot be braved by the municipal courts alone. If, as I am told, the laws of California are as yet inadequate to the demand the dilemma makes, then they can be made so. California, in my judgment, has the remedy in her own hands. When she is in earnest, she will use it.

I do not know why I wanted to go to the Stock Exchange. It has a sort of historic significance, however,

25

in connection with the development of the State, as well as with the enormous fortunes which now rule its material prosperity. The crowd of hungry gamblers about the door attracted my attention yesterday, and made me apply for a ticket. The Exchange is a fine stone building. The interior is an amphitheatre with a gallery, which cannot be entered without a permit. Above the chair are two finely carved bears, and a cartouche holding a group of miners. The Goddess of Liberty is just over the desk. The floor is divided into two parts; one is for the Stock Board. The seats on this Board are still thought to be worth about twenty thousand dollars each, and a tax is paid annually on this valuation. The seats in the rear of these may be hired by reporters or speculators. There are telephones everywhere, and also a great gong in front of the gallery which strikes at a touch of the "caller's" foot. When the Board are in session, all bids are sent to the desk, where an officer named the "caller" cries them. In open session, such as I saw this afternoon, each man "cries" his own bid, and the wildest confusion prevails. They were doing it when we went in, and picking each other's pockets of kerchiefs, cigars, and the like as they crowded up. This was called a jest, but it interested me to see that the small morals of the place were in keeping with the large interests. The rules are very strict. If a man is suspected of "selling short" they run up the bids, and at any cost he must make his sales good. If a man cries "taken" he is held to his bargain, or must forfeit his chair. The gallery has a beautiful bronze rail, ornamented with alternate bulls and bears. I am sorry I have not seen the Board in session, but this little glimpse of boyish disorder was better than nothing.

On my way home Mr. W. took me to the Safe Deposit Company. The basement is very showily fitted up. A gigantic warder in gold bronze presides over each section. I was a good deal surprised to find that what I had supposed to be slabs of wrought stone on the outside of the building were only slabs of cast iron! It has been my last day in San Francisco, and I have been "thinking up."

I once did some shopping in the Bonaparte carriage, in Baltimore, and, as I was in very plain traveller's dress, was amused to see what a degree of attention the gold lace on the liveries secured from strangers. For the last ten years any lady shopping with strange merchants in Boston or New York would have cause to consider her dress. She could not help discovering that it saved some time to dress like a lady who could buy real lace and diamonds if she chose! I have never been anywhere where this seemed so important as in San Francisco. The shopmen are not discriminating. In New York my plain English tweed and hand-carved buttons of solid pearl would have secured respectful attention. Here the tweed is only a woollen dress, and the buttons so much smoked pearl!

The new Mint is on Mission Street. I passed it on my way to the marquetry factory. The basement is built of granite, but the two upper storeys are of a blue-gray free-stone, from an island between Vancouver's Island and the West coast. Oddly enough, it is British stone.

I do not know why San Francisco should be any more cosmopolitan than New York, but certainly in walking the streets one seems to hear every language but English. I wish I could give you any idea of the flat and

only half articulate sounds made by the Chinese when
they talk. I can imitate them exactly with my lips, but
I do not know how to represent them with letters. I
should have supposed this manner of talking peculiar
to the uneducated classes, if I had not encountered it at
the theatre.

We went to take tea with Dr. Stebbins, and saw the
two babies, handsome as Greek gods, splashing in their
evening bath. I am very sorry to say farewell to this
lovely family, but of the church I know absolutely
nothing. I have come into no contact with it.

For the first time in my life, I believe, I am writing
when I have nothing to say. I think it is because it is
the last night, and I do not like to go to bed.

San Francisco to Stockton, Oct. 29, 1880. — This morning I saw something like a sunrise. I sat watching a
golden globe on the horizon for more than an hour, absorbed in thought and stupidly expecting it to rise. It
did not, and I was not surprised at the delay, till the
glowing clouds broke far above and let the real day-god
through. Then there were two suns, and I discovered
that the first was a reflection on the Bay from the rear
of the clouds, which must have been very close to the
earth. No one was up, save Mr. C., who kindly went
with me to the station, when I had eaten my dreary,
uncomfortable breakfast. Lovely indeed was the Bay
when we crossed it. It was not clear of fog, but the
mist was pellucid with opaline tints, and a light haze
lifted and settled alternately over all the lovely rocks
and wooded hills, and at last hid the Golden Gate.

I started this morning, as you know, for Stockton, because San Francisco makes the apex of an isosceles tri-

angle, and the line connecting Stockton with Sacramento is its base, and a ticket to the East may be used *via* Stockton, or to Sacramento direct. I should not have known this if my cousins had not written to bribe me to pass my last night with them, by the promise of such a lunch basket as my dear Minnie's hands know how to pack. I cannot be thankful enough that this arrangement has been carried out, for if we never meet again I shall have the lovely memory of these last hours, and Minnie's careful provision will make my good health on the way a certainty. Food bought at the stopping places *en route* only means starvation and failing strength to me.

We had hardly started before we came upon fields where they were burning the wheat stubble. A watchman was beating out the fire here and there. The smoke was so purple that it reminded me of that which has been conflicting for the last few days with the white fog in the Bay. A gentleman on the cars said this last undoubtedly came from the tule swamps, which they are now burning off. This grass is so stout that it will burn several feet below the surface of the soil, which its ashes greatly enriches. I saw wagon-loads of tule at San José, and was told that the nursery men use it when they pack their trees.

When I took my "stop over" for Stockton from the conductor, he asked me in a mysterious manner for my post-office address, and endorsed "Washington, D. C." on my ticket. This was a new freak, of which I could get no explanation; but as I had no evil intentions I did not allow it to disturb me. "It was the company's orders!"

All along the road were superb flaunting orange pop-

pies, very much deeper in color than any I had seen
in the summer.   They do not wait for rain any more
than the scarlet primroses at Santa Cruz, but come
with the autumn.   I wonder what people at the East,
who think California a perfect paradise, would say
to the half-dozen remedies for catarrh which were
hawked through the train!   A good many eucalyptus
trees, planted in groves, which I was sure I had
never seen, suggested to me that I must be travelling a
new road.   So at San Leandro I inquired.   The afternoon train from Oakland to Stockton goes to Lathrop
by the Southern Pacific on its way to Los Angeles.
This morning I took what is called the "old road
to Sacramento," and go through to Stockton without
change.   Very suddenly, I found myself among the
mountains.   Oh, how beautiful they are !   I do not
wonder at the way Californians love their country,
while I am among the hills.   Just now they have a
tender surface like olive-green velvet, quilted down here
and there by valleys, with an occasional oasis of vivid
green, revealing a hidden spring.   We came upon a long
sluice, carrying water to feed a flour-mill.   Beautiful
creepers and flowering vines were growing under the
ties, and completely festooning the sluice as far as the
eye could reach, and economizing dust and moisture in
a charming way.   In the spring, something very like a
river must flow through these foot-hills.   Then came live-
oak groves, wheat fields to the farthest horizon, brick-
yards, and at last great vans filled with firewood, each
dragged by six mules.   Out of the hills little streaks of
white smoke curl here and there, and the shadows fly,
changing the charm each moment.   At Altamont the
sheep tracks begin again, and the hill-sides are checked

by the tramp of thousands of tiny feet. If a mathematician had done it, the lines would not be more even than they seem at this distance.

It is amusing to see how the half-trained Spanish children behave on the train. Two magnificent creatures, with eyes like a great cow's, and hair hanging over their eyes as if they were Norwegian ponies, have been playing with the cup and faucet ever since we started. Just here a gray-haired man went to the ice tank, waited for the children to move, and then deliberately washed off the marks of dirty fingers from the cup, and rinsed it two or three times before he drank. He must have been very thirsty to drink at all, under the circumstances. The children, neither of them over nine, flew to their mother in a rage. Their faces were scarlet, and the soft vowels and aspirates fairly sputtered from their lips, as they complained of the "insult!"

When we are passing through a grain country, the villages are little more than a post-office, a railroad dépôt, and a hotel as clean and as big as a band-box. So it seemed at Tracy and at Banta. Wide grain-fields, a green and tangled wilderness, and then Stockton came into sight.

My cousin's carriage was waiting for me, and very soon I clasped my dear Minnie in my arms, and the four dogs clasped me. I am sorry to say that none of the latter are as well bred as Mr. M.'s dog at San José. When I first sat down in Charlotte's parlor, Tiny sprang into my lap, apparently to try an experiment. That led me to tell the story of the neglected stable-dog here, who gave me the whole passion of his outraged heart, and seemed to take great pleasure in showing the parlor pets that *he* had a friend. Of course I acknowledged

that the embraces of this broken-hearted creature, which
I had not the courage to repel, were extremely incon-
venient. "Well," said Mr. M., "you need not hold
Tiny a moment longer than you like. He will never
get into your lap again if you forbid him." I did not in
the least believe this, but I put the spaniel down, looked
at him seriously, and said, "Tiny, go away, and never
get into my lap again." The pretty creature looked
at me a moment, then walked away, and during the
week that I remained made no further attempt to attract my notice.

In the evening Mr. Belden, whom I had met at Calaveras, came to talk over fossils, Indian remains, and
missions, which may very well seem to you like related
subjects! I drew plans of Mount Carmel, and he
sketched for me obsidian spear-heads and skin-scrapers,
blocked or serrated in unusual ways. I am to examine
and name some plants for him, and he is to send me a
bit of gold ore and some fragments of lava from the
Dead River. Just as he was going away, we had a few
interesting words about the crimson " snow-plant"
which was presented to Mrs. Hayes at Summit in a
block of snow. Mr. Belden says this plant grows just
where the snow melts, but never in it. It is fragile
like the " Indian pipe," but can be preserved in snow
for a long while. The specimens shown to General
Grant and Mrs. Hayes were brought a long distance,
and were merely set into the block of snow to keep
them fresh. This, however, the authorities did not
explain.

Stockton to Sacramento, Oct. 30, 1880. — These are the
last words I shall write in California, and I dedicate

them to my Cousin Minnie. I wish that every careless young girl I know could look into this spotless home and see this serene, lovely woman, capable of the highest converse, of far more than ordinary beauty, of graceful and delicate toilette, who is nevertheless a perfect house-keeper; whom I have more than once detected at work on the kitchen fire, and who gives the last touches as well as the first thought to every dish that comes to her table. When I first saw her running down to the gate in her snowy dress to welcome the stranger, she made me think of "The Wife" in the "Sketch Book," which I committed to memory with much enthusiasm when I was a school-girl. But Irving's picture is a bit of sickly sentimentalism beside the actual fact which I have found at Stockton. No man living ever did anything to deserve such a home as she makes; and more than any other words in our English tongue do those of Thomas Carlyle describe her: —

"I have seen no human intelligence that so genuinely pervaded every fibre of the human existence it belonged to. From the baking of a loaf or the darning of a stocking up to comporting herself in the highest scenes or most intricate emergencies, all was insight, veracity, and graceful success. Her own fine, modest composure and presence of mind never in any greatest other presence forsook her!"

These words should not be written if I did not know that whatever discomfort may suffuse her cheeks when she reads them will be more than offset by the inspiration which any mention of such a creature must impart to every thoughtful young wife. It is my bitterest thought in leaving California that I may not only never again see her, but most probably never again encounter her like.

I had a quiet run over fields of stubble to Sacramento. Into the cars came half-a-dozen Highlanders in grand costume, and every one a little "tight," after some sort of a Caledonian celebration at Stockton. One of them, — a tall, upright fellow, with hair as white as snow, — stepped up to me, the only woman in the car, and said : "Now, if you 're a Yankee girl, and wanting to marry a Scotchman, take care ! You 'll never get a divorce ; a Scotchman will stick to you."

On the opposite seat to mine was an Irishman in the same hilarious plight. "Gloria in Excelsis !" said he, jumping up and explaining to the Highlander with a confidential nod, " That means 'glory in the highest;' and if *you* 're a Scotchman, it 's an Irishman *I* am ; and not a fig would I give for the whole of ye." My white-haired hero in philibeg, plaid, heron's feather, and cairngorm, regarded the Irishman with a supreme contempt it is impossible to put on paper, and walked into the smoking-car. Two or three times afterward he paraded himself and his dress for our benefit ; and every time the Irishman pulled at his mantle, turned him half round, and compelled him to shake hands violently. The Highlander showed the dignified tranquillity with which a big dog usually endures the assaults of a little one. The matter is worth recording, because in more than six months of lonely travel it is the only thing I have heard or seen that could possibly give a woman annoyance ; although I have been struck ever since I passed the Rocky Mountains with the entire absence of those thoughtful courtesies which make a woman comfortable at the East.

The cars are full of lithographed copies of Garfield's letter to Morey, several representatives huddling over it, and putting their heads together in the vain hope of writing or doing something concerning it before election. The papers are full of accounts of a Chinese primary meeting at which there was an attempt to move for higher wages, and the arguments were *wooden stools* flung at each other's heads! The Chinese may be pretty safely left to their own devices. Subjected to United States law, all the perplexing problems which concern them will soon settle themselves.

The conductors on these trains have no inclination to help a lady. They have far more time than the porters, but ask one of them to lift a parcel and he says, "I will send some one;" and that is the end of it.

My dear Minnie gave all this morning, and perhaps many others which I do not guess, to fitting me out for the next five days. A heavy but delicious provision is the result. I hired the boy who brought in the baggage checks to carry my basket round to the overland train when we reached Sacramento. Fortunately the porter of the Silver Palace was off duty; so I found my way to my berth, dropped my valises on the floor, and went to the office to pay for it. The manager of the office at the Oakland Ferry told me most distinctly that I could engage and pay for my sleeping car to Council Bluffs, here. This is entirely untrue. I can only pay half way, — to Ogden.

Last night was very cold at Stockton. I sat by Minnie's fire contentedly until I came away. Here I find the thermometer at 89°, and with the beautiful reaches of the river in sight it is hard to remember that it is not summer. Sacramento is planted with poplars like San José, but by maple, elm, and sycamore as well. The city has been twice destroyed by fire and once by

flood, but since 1854 has steadily gained in prosperity.
It is of course one of the railway and steamer centres,
and has entered somewhat largely into manufactures.
Its pretty homes are surrounded by semi-tropical gardens, which stretch away to cultivated farms, or sheep
and cattle ranches, till all these are lost to sight at the
base of snow-capped mountains or on the brink of land-
locked bays. The State House crowns the perfectly
level city, as that of Boston crowns its triple hills. The
top of the dome is three hundred feet above the first
floor, and the front wall is three hundred and twenty
feet long. It is situated on a third and upper terrace
of a beautiful park, and is chiefly remarkable in its interior for the lovely decorations of California woods,
especially the laurel. I had nearly two hours in the
town as the train was delayed.

At Rocklin we found an old negress from Tennessee holding up cockles of grapes, the very best I have
seen. They were sweet muscats, and as solid as dam-
sons. She is trying to earn money to get back to
Tennessee, where she thinks that she has children still.
Here, too, are the quarries from which are cut the immense slabs of granite in the pavement of the Palace
Hotel. The Round House with twenty-eight stalls is
built of the same beautiful stone, and here we took an
extra engine to begin the ascent of the Sierra.

Newcastle, the great fruit-growing town, has oranges
growing in the open air, and curious boulders in her
fields that look like great stone beehives.

I have only six people in my sleeping car, and seem
likely to make my journey East with a degree of comfort which will be in strong contrast to that of my journey out.

In this company is Mr. G., late English vice-consul at Tokio, and Mr. Basil Hall Chamberlain, who will be remembered gratefully by all the readers of Miss Bird's "Japan." The latter is a professor in the naval school at Tokio. In speaking of Melbourne and the wonderful administration of its public offices, Mr. Chamberlain introduced me to a person who had been there nine years. He said that in the revolving dome of the post-office building there a man was seated in such a way that as it turned he could oversee every clerk perfectly, and every man works with the knowledge of this. Mr. Chamberlain praised the California fruits, and then excused himself by saying that Japanese fruits were so poor that whatever was received from California seemed delicious. He thought the Japanese would not eat the passiflor if they had plenty of plums. The hot and rainy seasons coincide in Japan; therefore all fruit gets soaked, and turns out flavorless.

Mr. Chamberlain showed a warm desire to see the United States. He wished he could have started earlier so as to see the autumn foliage in its glory. I then told him of a white satin *Fuk-sa*, or royal napkin, to be thrown over princely gifts when they were carried through the street in the time of the Daimio and his feudal barons. I had bought it in San Francisco. It was of white satin, embroidered in gold and colors, and covered with autumn leaves. It was said to be two hundred years old, and suggested to me that the autumn foliage must be very brilliant in Japan. "Yes," said my friend, "the Japanese adore autumn leaves. They dwarf the very brightest trees they can find, and plant them in their door-yards. Their little shrubberies are really a blaze of glory."

I have fallen on a jewel of a porter. He heats my coffee. He keeps my basket in a cool place; and when I said to-night, " Plato, do you think it necessary to let down that upper berth ?" "Madam," said he, "I don't think it necessary to do nothing to inconvenience you!" Do you suppose I can be the same person who was treated with such persistent and ignominious disrespect on my way out ?

From Reno to the Palisades, Oct. 31, 1880. — Some very eccentric travellers from Boston got into the cars at Carson in the night. This morning the ladies told us they had been to the Consolidated Virginia City and California bonanza mines, and described the excessive heat in the shafts, two thousand four hundred and fifty feet below the surface, where hot springs fill the air with steam. The miners work naked and only a few hours at a time, receiving immense wages. The whole party had taken cold.

There are so few of us in the car that we have a delightfully luxurious time. Our peace seemed very likely to be disturbed to-day, but our porter was equal to the occasion. At one of the small stations communicating with the mining regions, there darted in upon us a most unsavory party of Spanish Americans. Father and mother, an oldest son about twenty-one, and four children made themselves visible. They were covered with dirty diamonds and wound about with conspicuous gold cables. They could not speak much English, but advanced gesticulating wildly with money in their hands, shouting, " For sleep! How much? This car not full ?" Plato swept down upon them like a thundercloud, wisely ignoring the inquiry, and with a most unchristian disregard of the porter in the rear. "Back!" shouted he; "room there! Porter! *here's fees.*" I shall always wonder why the creature did it. The party swept out, leaving the door open. Plato opened the windows and went to shut the door, remarking with rare perspicacity, "'Pears like them people always lived in barns!"

The English gentlemen and myself sat on the rear platform all day to look at the Palisades. The Palisades are perpendicular rocky walls on the Humboldt River, beginning about five hundred and eighty miles from San Francisco. My companions said they looked like the Scotch crags, but Mr. Chamberlain thought them more like craters of extinct volcanoes on the Spanish Sierras. They were painted richly with yellow and purple lichens, reflected brightly in the broad river rounding through the valley. We saw a long, low horizon with the outline of mountains just against the sky. Sunlight was over and under them all, and seemed to come out of the very heart of one peak of glowing amethyst. Five Mile Cañon lifted hundreds of pinnacles into the air, all hung with shifting, rosy clouds.

Mr. Chamberlain says the climate of Japan is very exhausting, and that all brain work soon tells on the constitution there. Both he and the vice-consul are going home to recruit.

Never did I see feathered game so thick as it is all along the way, and it is as tame as possible. We travelled yesterday through thickets of laurel studded with vivid crimson berries, and the snort of our engine started thousands of quail as we came. I ought to have enlarged a little on the Forty Mile Desert, beyond Humboldt, when I came over. Extending from

Colorado to the Cascades, it was strewn with the
dead bodies of men and animals, in the days when
emigrant wagons made their slow way across the
continent. There is no water fit to drink the whole
way; it is too dry and hot to hurry cattle over, and
many herds were lost here and many trains bewildered
in those trying days. About half way over it, emigrants were distracted by a mirage, which was so constant that it has given its name to a railroad station.
In this neighborhood, or beyond it, a hot spring bursts
out at the foot of the mountains, and vast beds of salt
are found. This salt the bonanza mines ship in large
quantities. If the traveller be quick to observe, or if
he stay long enough to discover the true character of
these plains of death, he will be tempted to forgive the
railway a great many sins. The levels are strewn with
black basaltic masses, as if Pluto had ·bombarded the
plain in person.

Salt Lake, onward, Nov. 1, 1880. — I rise very early
to take advantage of the almost daily pause for freight
trains to pass at six in the morning. In this way I get
a complete bath comfortably before any one else stirs.
Pluto winks at my endeavor, and the dressing-room is
always clean and ready. Then I take a hot cup of
Minnie's mocha and go out into the sunrise, which
was to-day most lovely. We were coming in sight
of Salt Lake, and Antelope Island rose like one fair
mass of opal from a translucent field. I cannot tell you
what it costs me to give up my second visit to this
valley. If I positively knew what is most probable,
— namely, that I shall never look on the Wasatch
again; that I shall never go up the cañon of the

American Fork, — I think I should break down and weep.

> " When over dizzy heights we go,
>   One soft hand blinds our eyes ;
>   The other leads us safe and slow, —
>   O Love of God, most wise !"

and blessed forever be that soft hand !

This is the cañon that made such an impression on Charles Kingsley. He preferred it to the Yosemite. From the point where the Utah Southern leaves you, you take a narrow-gauge railway sixteen miles nearer heaven. These cars only move up this sixteen miles at the rate of six miles an hour; for there is a steady grade of two hundred feet, and at one point it increases to two hundred and ninety-six. The valley is about one hundred feet wide, a brook falling from rock to rock all the way. The walls of dark-red and brown granite are wonderfully contorted, as if they had been fused upon the spot. At one point a hole through a crag shows a luminous circle of blue heaven. They call it " The Devil's Eye," with some inward consciousness I suppose that this is what they ought to encounter; but it is the eye of God himself for an instant made visible to loving hearts. Toward the end of the cañon is the old mill, — a ruin amid dense trees and rippling water, green bushes and bold rocks. This is the steepest railroad grade in the world; and when you start to go back the engine is detached, and like a live creature, without a signal, the little train starts on its return, which it has several times accomplished in forty minutes. But, alas ! I lingered too long by the Pacific. The snow has already fallen in the mountains, and the wise people tell us that this is to be a winter of terrible severity.

Just here the Wasatch range is magnificent, the finest I have seen in my whole journey. It rises clear cut and intensely blue.

With great regret I parted from our English companions, who are on their way to Salt Lake City. Before they went they introduced a young Japanese, the educated agent in New York of the Tokio Manufacturing Company. I had in my bag a beautiful little bronze button an inch long. It represents a blade of grass, with its flower stalk, a swaying spray of golden bloom, a cricket climbing the blade, and two silver daisies peeping out beneath. It is very old, and I hoped Shugio would know something about it, but he did not.

When later I went to the rear to look at Weber Cañon, I found two Englishmen, who had got on at Salt Lake, in full possession of my camp-stools and territory. Of these the first was a wealthy, retired army man, travelling with his servant; the second, a Mr. C. from West Broomwich, who has just been round Cape Horn on a voyage of recovery from a severe accident in a colliery of which he was superintendent.

Do you remember how you remonstrated because I would take this journey in the summer? I cannot tell you how glad I am that I came just when I did, for these cañons seem cold and dreary now. How well I remember their delicate beauty three months ago! Now yellow lichens embroider the gray and barren rock, scarlet vines creep along the crevices, and purple and yellow broom waves mist-like along the valley. Now that the soft green of the deciduous foliage has fallen away, a delicate fringe of pine trees shows itself against the sky at the top of the ravine. Peak over peak the wave-swept summits are lifted. In Echo Cañon the red needle-like rocks rise against the blue in such bleak contrast, that it seems as if I had never seen them before. All along the way a crust of ice crackles, and streaks of snow fleck the nearer summits.

My Englishmen talked of early marriages. E. M. said that the expensive club-life of England discouraged them, by accustoming young men of moderate means to a life of extreme luxury. You know how often I have said the same thing of our clubs. If we could begin again to be hospitable, not to the indiscriminate travelling public, but to our near friends, as our grandmothers were, nobody would want a club.

Castle Rock reminded E. M. of the abbey at Glastonbury, which he described. He said the legend told how Joseph of Arimathea had wandered weary to Glastonbury, and planted there his staff of thorn. It is still there, and blooms at Christmas in perpetual miraculous attestation!

The clouds are heavy. There is plenty of snow somewhere, and curious chimney-pot rocks project over the ravine. I took care of a sleeping baby through the travellers' dinner hour, and let the tired mother get a mouthful of fresh air. Power to help in such ways is one of the blessings shut into my dear Minnie's basket.

A miner from the Bell Mine in Montana showed me some charming specimens. He gave me some big garnets and smoky quartz. He is carrying to New York the most beautiful piece of copper and silver ore that I ever saw; it is part of a layer about four inches thick, perfectly homogeneous, and sparkling with the deepest amethystine hue. Both the upper and under surface of this layer is thickly frosted with pure silver. Out of its purple bed yellow pyrites rise like blossoms of gold.

I have a very kind porter on this train also. Plato took pains to speak to him in my behalf at Ogden; but he lives in perpetual fear of the railway inspector. The Union Pacific will not allow its porters to keep so much as a tin dipper for the convenience of a sick or dying passenger, and spies come in at every important station. I suppose I ought to write the "Pullman Co." instead of the "Union Pacific." Quick confusion to them and their unrighteous gains!

We are in a fine car, carefully kept; but then there are only four of us, — refined people who do not scatter our leavings, so that Jack has an easy time. I am the only lady, and have the dressing-room entirely to myself. But for Minnie's basket I should fare badly. Jack has no dipper to heat water in, and I drink my coffee cold.

Nov. 2, 1880. — *En route.* At sunrise one of the mountain peaks — Elko, I think — showed itself mirage fashion, lifted high into the air on a sea of mist. Alkali covered the plains as thickly as two inches of snow would have done. Thin streaks of snow continue visible on the distant ranges. They are probably five hundred or six hundred feet wide, but look to us as if laid on by a paint brush. Elko, one of the most beautiful cloud-mountains in the world, has a snowy cloud nightcap all ready to drop over its head.

Just as all seemed going at its best, our pace slackened till the cars fairly crept. Before night-fall we were three hours behind time, and excessively tired of one another. The cause of it all was a freight train lately wrecked. We skated round it as we could on temporary rails, and then waited for a dozen

delayed freight trains to get off the side track. A
wreck is like the Day of Judgment,— it reveals the
inmost heart of things. Such a mess! Fruit jars
for the canning factories on the Pacific Coast, lamp
chimneys for the miners, mirrors, flour barrels, tin
sheathing, car wheels, and in the midst the fire set by
the overturned engine still spreading and smouldering in
our track. We have begun to pass through snow-sheds.
Medicine Bow Range rose against a pale, cold, blue sky,
mottled with white and silver. The Elko was superb,
showing ravines filled with snow during the last twenty-
four hours, and glittering in the sunlight. Words are
useless to whoever has not seen such a sight; but the
weakest words will plunge whoever has seen it into
a trance of delight. Gray, castellated clouds mocked
the mountains, and rose against a black sky to the east.
To the northwest a whole continent seemed to stretch;
meadows fleeced with snow receded, breathing light; and
beyond an icy shore islands of the blest floated in a blue
sea.

E. M. has talked a great deal to-day of his travels in
Europe. He has received from repeated visits such an
impression of the unhealthfulness of Rome that he
would neither go there himself nor allow his family to
do so. In Naples it has been necessary to build hotels
on the ridge far out of town. Monaco is an earthly
paradise; but no one who will not gamble is allowed to
remain in it: he himself had been ordered out of the
town!

At night-fall a single silver star shone on an amber
sky between deep purple bars. We breakfasted at
twelve, having been delayed four hours. There was
much dissatisfaction among the passengers, who thought,

rationally enough, that we ought not to have waited for the regular breakfast-station. We were at a full pause for more than an hour on account of the freight. Of course, my basket stood between me and discontent; but why could not those freight trains have waited for ours?

Nov. 3, 1880. — *En route.* No time was gained last night. I think I should have been less weary if I had walked the distance than by the slow crawl of the railway coach. This morning I saw several travellers reading "The Light of Asia!" Cattle were all round us; but it is now too cold for the sociable little prairie dogs, or their downy guests the "Turveydrop" owls. One may even hope that the rattlesnake is coiled up peacefully for the winter. We passed several hundred sheep marshalled by a drover on horseback. He had the high Spanish saddle and stirrups, and was waiting by the track for his freight cars to come. On one side of us we saw the stubble, and on the other the green springing blades of winter wheat. Planted trees began to break the monotony.

At Cheyenne, at noon, we heard that Garfield was elected, and that New Jersey and Connecticut had gone Republican! For these two States we proposed an honorary torch-light procession. How I rejoice over this I cannot say. Certain I am that any other result would have plunged us, practically speaking, into a civil war, although it is not likely that the struggle could have continued long. The Southern members of the last Congress may thank their own folly for the fact of this overwhelming vote. Besides this, Garfield's election is due to the strength of the Hayes Cabinet, — a strength

which has never been equalled since the first hours of
the Republic; to the dignity and delicacy of President
Hayes; to the loving matronly presence in the White
House; and last, but not least, to the steady sale of " The
Fool's Errand." Perhaps you will not recognize all the
factors I name; but I am sure that Judge Tourgée ought
to be the happiest man in the United States.

It will be remembered how easily at Council Bluffs
my baggage was to be rechecked in the cars! As we
arrived, worn out, too late for our various Eastern
trains, I had not even this small comfort. The man
who came with the checks had forgotten those of the
" Canada Southern;" and although, in consequence of
the delay, my ticket would have been good on any road
that I chose to follow, my baggage was allowed no such
advantage, — a distinction without a difference, as I
thought. I retained my porter by an extra fee, for it
was eleven at night when we arrived. He went with
me to the baggage room, and I checked the baggage
myself; and we then went to the Telegraph office
where I telegraphed to Quincy, Illinois. I wished to
telegraph the hour of my arrival, but the railroad agent
at this most important railway station in the whole
world knew nothing about through trains; and, although
he was not in the least busy, he coolly refused to look
this up. "I could not go till morning any way, and I
must wait!"

Council Bluffs to Burlington, Iowa, Nov. 4, 1880. — I
was obliged to pass the night at the Railway Hotel, a
much poorer establishment than would dare to exist if
this were still the day of stage coaches. A room fifteen
feet by eight and about twenty feet high received me.

One window, of a single narrow pane, ran up to the ceiling and lighted this charming bower. It was un-curtained, and I pinned up Mr. Chamberlain's parting present — my English wrap — as a screen, and pro-ceeded to repack my hand baggage. Here I had to part with Minnie's still precious basket. After we left the Central Pacific it went into various unsavory places, and received rather rough treatment at the hands of the porter. I gave it to a cheery chambermaid, who assisted me to supply the deficiency of a quart ewer and a towel as large as a pocket kerchief. All through the West the toilet towels appear to cost about ten cents apiece! This girl prejudiced me at first by coming to wait on me with a newspaper in her hand. When will servants learn that in order to prepossess they must answer a call with no interest apparent except in the needed service! I sympathized in the girl's ardent desire "to know about the elections;" but why not know this also?

I took out of the basket some dried fruit and a little pot of spiced and pickled figs, which I am bringing to you. My chicken jelly, my delicious Westphalia ham, my fresh bread and butter, and my superb coffee were already at an end. My bureau drawers were full of the débris of the last traveller's bag. This I emptied into the hall opposite my door. There was no bell. They are calsomining the entire house; the halls are full of litter, and the carpets are everywhere trodden with lime and color. I could find no public parlor, and never should have got my hand baggage to my chamber if it had not been for the kindness of my new Japanese friend. After I went to bed there was a grand torch-light procession at Omaha in honor of Garfield. I should have liked to hear the speaking, but it rained far too heavily for me to cross the river. This morning the man who sells tickets over the Burlington and Quincy road assured me in the most unprincipled way that the 8.40 train would take me through without a stop! To complete the illusion he checked my baggage through to Quincy. Then I bought some Eastern papers, got into the car, and proceeded to have a "good time!"

In a speech at Mentor, Garfield bears fit testimony to the great and good influence exercised by Oberlin in the politics of this country. It is the first time so eminent a man has done his whole duty in this respect. Whenever Western men come to the front, the fact must be more and more recognized. I have read "Figs and Thistles" with great delight. The president of the college, in this book, who takes the church-service out of the hands of the pastor when the war breaks out, is Finney of Oberlin. Never shall I forget the prayers he made, as I knelt beside him in his parlor, when all our hearts were sore because of Andrew Johnson. Finney impeached him, item by item, before the Great White Throne he believed in, and then he went on in a burst of impatience,— "But why should we tell these things unto Thee, O Lord? Thou knowest them better than we can; and Thou knowest also how to bring out of his ignorance and contumacy far better and nobler things than would be the natural fruit or man's wisdom and obedience!" It was as if he challenged the Almighty, or would put him on his mettle!

All along our way grass, alder, and willow are starting into leaf, as if the first days of spring had come. The cars have been very uncomfortable. There was no

Pullman. Hot stoves on one side and cold draughts on the other. Near me was a stout German, who dandled a little girl of two years and a boy who was not four upon his knee. The girl amused herself by repeatedly pulling her father's watch from his pocket with a merry jerk. The boy held two bits of paper. They looked like railway passes, and he asked continually, " Papa, what is the letter on my paper ? What does it say, papa ?" At last the father spoke : " It says, Howard is to go to the junction, and there they will throw him out." It was pretty to see the look of undoubting love and trust which the boy lifted to his father. "What for ?" he asked brightly, with no sign of a shadow on his fair brow. " Aren't you a Garfielder ?" said the father with a terrific frown. " Yes, I *are* a Garfielder !" shouted the boy gaily. " Mamma said I was to be a Garfielder, and I ARE !" " And what did *I* tell you ?" pursued the father. The boy paused, and at last shook his head. " You don't remember what *I* say !" said the man ; but at that moment we reached the junction, and the whole party were " thrown out."

Rain, rain, and wide fields followed.

Toward nightfall two boys came into the car. They were between nineteen and twenty-one, both drunk, dirty, and profane. I think you know what my feeling is about profane or obscene language. I have a constitutional horror of both, and could commit a crime, I think, without losing as much self-respect as I should do if either crossed my lips. Yet I am often compelled to acknowledge in these far lands that the use of oaths is a mere habit, showing the want of education and the entire absence of natural refinement, but proving nothing worse. The older of these two boys was help-

ing the other off to some mining country. He warmed
his feet, tucked him into the seat, and then resumed
some conversation which their entrance had interrupted,
in tones husky with drink : —

"Damn my soul, Jem, you 're doing the right thing,
and I 'll tell you why. Before ever I saw you, there
was a man came here with a wife and four children.
By Jesus! that feller never made twenty-five cents a
day! Warn't that rough on a married man? And I do
hope your girl 's a good one, — that 's all, Jem. Well,
this feller came to me, and I said, 'I 've got just one
dollar and twenty-five cents in this world, and I 'll give
you the dollar;' and I did. 'By God!' says he, 'won't
the old girl laugh when she sees that?' And he went
away. I took the twenty-five cents, and drank brandy
till I could n't think. You would n't suppose I could
carry three pints, would you, Jem? but I did."

Spitting, swearing, chewing, he rattled on till the
bell rang and he huddled off the train, almost too late.
The object of his interest was too far gone to answer.
A very little care in early youth would have changed
that fellow's whole history.

On this train, all the conveniences of travel have
proved positive nuisances. I soon learned that it never
connects with the Quincy road.

Burlington to Quincy, Nov. 5, 1880. — At 10.30 last
night we ran into Burlington, a town of thirty thousand
inhabitants now. As it was raining and I had no rub-
bers, having wholly forgotten in these last three months
that it ever did rain anywhere, I went to the only hotel
which sent down an omnibus. It was the B., and the
floor of the vehicle was as deep in dirt as the street.

It is many years since I have seen so untidy a room
as that into which the clerk ushered me after I had
drunk a cup of sour milk ! I had dined on a few walnuts ! A path had been swept—perhaps by the skirts of
some hapless inmate — from the bedside to the door ;
but no broom had ever gone under the bed since the
carpet was put down. I could get no additional water
or towels, and it was difficult to conjecture when the
tumbler was last washed. The rest may be guessed!
The "premeditated poverty" of many darns diversified
the bed linen ; but that constituted a real claim to my
respect. I am glad to have the opportunity to say that
I have not seen an untidy *bed* since I left home ; and
that indicates a great change east as well as *west* of the
Mississippi in the last twenty years.

I had a good night's sleep. For breakfast this morning I got some *hot* milk (I am quite sure it would not have
been safe to boil it), two small bits of tongue, and two
pasty buckwheat cakes,—price seventy-five cents !

In spite of the landlord's assertion that the trains
never left the dépôt till forty minutes after the advertised hour, I went to the station on time. After my experience of yesterday I do not feel like trusting anybody ; but the landlord was right. At the last moment
my valise gave way, but I bargained successfully with
the news-boy for a piece of rope. The thing cost ninety-
nine cents when I started, and has travelled nearly six
thousand miles ; so peace be to its remains, which I
shall inter at Quincy.

Burlington stands in a lovely situation. From its tall
bluff it looks down into the glowing bosom of the river.
In the meadows everything is starting as if it were early
spring. I find a great change in the faces of the people

in the car, when I compare them with those west of
Omaha. They show a New England descent, and are
of a strong and manly type, in marked contrast to the
worn out, anxious countenances in the mining and oil
regions. Whenever the basis of a man's life is expectation rather than labor, he shares the lot of Tantalus, and
shows it on his forehead.

At Dallas I got another lovely river view. The winter wheat is starting, and from one cottage window the
Stars and Stripes were waving for Garfield. The orchards here are planted as I like to see them, with a
row of trees outside the fence. Wheat! wheat! but it
does not burst all warehouse bonds, as it did in California. The towns have Massachusetts names. We
were on the Illinois side of the river. All the men
on the car were reading the local papers. The "Hawk-
eye" is headed with the "Elephant of 1884,"—crushing
its Republican way across the continent. I wish we
could get an extension of the presidential term before
that election. Of the four years to which our President
is elected, one at least is generally wasted in getting
new men into place, and filibustering with enemies. If
the term were eight years instead of four, this unsettled
state of things would occupy no more time, and the
country would gain in peace and quietness. Politicians
wear the anxious look and heart of all gamblers.

Very unintentionally, I read the heading of a newspaper column over the shoulder of my forward neighbor:
"A better feeling to be derived from local news than
from election returns." The stupid editor did not guess
that local prosperity grows or dwindles in sympathy
with the election returns!

Beautiful horses were at the dépôt in Mendon. It is

like a lovely New England town. The clothes hanging
on the lines gave me real pleasure. Not since I crossed
the mountains on my way out have I seen any that were
really washed!

J. V. B. met me at Quincy. He goes to Chicago to-
morrow night, and wants me to fill his place here. I
am too tired; I would rather go to Chicago with him;
so he will telegraph to all available points. There
were twelve letters on the study table. The despair
with which I looked at them suggested that I had not
gained much beside endless pleasure from my long
journey.

Quincy, Ill., Nov. 6, 1880. — We drove about the town
this morning. It has not changed much since 1866. It
has a fine stone court-house, but in its undrained lower
storey, among foul odors, where gas must always burn,
it imprisons all culprits awaiting trial. Of what use
is all our boasted knowledge if such things must
be? Graham Bell's new spectrophone reveals the existence of invisible spectral bands which speak in music
with the voice of light. Darkness visible or invisible
responds in discord dire, and discord in a human life
means sin.

A new Presbyterian church has arisen on the ashes
of the one burned just when it was completed. The
upper end of Main Street looks as State Street used to
look in Newburyport, and presupposes a good deal of
wealth. We drove to Sunset Bluff. The beautiful
river, the gay trees, their loose leaves fluttering down,
the bay with its ice sheds, and green wheat-fields beyond a barred gate made a lovely picture. V. has gone;
we hoped for telegrams to the very last, but no helpful

one came. I have been receiving kindness ever since last May, and have had very few opportunities to do anything for others; so I must not grumble.

Quincy, Nov. 7, 1880.—The Sunday-school and church are in excellent condition, and their minister is respected as he should be. My own audience was not more than half as large as it was in 1866, owing perhaps to the fact that the service was not advertised; but I also think the parish has grown smaller. I held but one service, which many people were kind enough to regret. It was very pleasant to find persons here who could recall my visit in 1866, and several who remembered with pleasure Mr. Dall's visit in 1841,—thirty-nine years ago!

Quincy to Chicago, Nov. 8, 1880. — This night I started in reality for home. I had a delightful Pullman, so well lighted that I occupied myself until a late hour in reading up my newspaper and magazine mail. I was a good deal entertained by two tradesmen who sat near and talked to each other for hours about the various ways in which they hid their political views from their customers! The worst point of the whole was that they were not in the least aware of anything degrading in the story, but rehearsed it in the best of spirits.

Chicago, Nov. 9, 1880. — Never did I see so glorious a sunrise as that which greeted me when I drew the curtain. A seraph's wing thickly feathered in dark gray stretched from the horizon to the zenith. Soon every feather was touched with crimson. This faded, and the shoulder and extreme tip glowed with flame. Then bars of gold crossed the plumes, and at last the whole thing contracted and floated, devoured of effulgent light.

V. met me the moment the cars stopped, swept me into a carriage and carried me away to breakfast. We had a good talk, and I supplied myself with reading.

The cars ran out of Chicago along a boulevard. Then came the rear of the pretty houses on Prairie Avenue, and a noble view of the Lake. Then a low stone wall, a little park, and a Lincoln monument. A queer group of wooden houses, painted yellow and standing high on wooden piles which were painted stone-color, had a very odd effect. High steps led up to them. Then new public buildings, flower-beds, and garden walks just laid out, and long stretches of meadow shaded with oak. At Michigan City there were pretty hills and blue laughing water. The farms slope to the south and look over the golden sunset. In order to meet my train I got off at the junction outside Detroit. The conductor gave a boy my bags, and told him to show me the way to the Canada Southern. No sooner was the little wretch out of the conductor's sight than he dropped my bags, and telling me the dépôt was a block off round the corner, he disappeared. I was left in scriptural "outer darkness," but did not make it worse by gnashing my teeth! I inquired again of the brakeman, and made my way over the rubbish, cutting up a good pair of boots. I bought my ticket over this Canada Southern to look at the changes effected in twenty-five years, — knowing very well it was the least convenient route. Of course, therefore, I did not originally intend to go over it in the dark!

Buffalo, Nov. 10, 1880. — I slept soundly till 4.30, shared a cab with three sportsmen and as many guns, and in a short fifteen minutes felt the arms of those I love best in the world about me.

CONCLUSION.

Boston, Sept. 1, 1881. — When a year ago I stood in the streets of Santa Barbara, thrilling with horror at the thought that a mad greed for office should cut down a true and useful man who had gone thither to do what he could to insure the election of James A. Garfield, I felt as if I were in the midst of barbarians ; and, although I ought to have known better, I regarded California for the moment as an exceptional State, for whose salvation a special effort must be made. Little did I imagine that the same lust of power was to strike down the chief magistrate in the Capital of the nation, before a year should end. Theodore Glancey, fighting for Garfield, but with a brave and determined purpose to secure purity in politics, died for the very cause that will have made a martyr of our true-hearted President, *whether he lives or dies,* — for Garfield's strong body must feel the consequences of the assassin's malice to his last hour, as that of our beloved Massachusetts Senator felt the weight of a coward's cane. Those who have read the preceding pages will have read to little purpose, if they do not understand to some extent the state of society I have tried to describe.

I shall also have made small impression, if, under the weight of anxiety still felt throughout our country, my readers have no desire to know whether Clarence Gray was convicted. In the month of March, 1881, this criminal was acquitted in Santa Barbara by the disagreement of the jury. While the panel was going on, Gray was allowed to challenge juror after juror, on the ground that he had been prejudiced against him by listening to the address delivered at Glancey's funeral. That address dropped Gray out of sight: it was a solemn impeachment of the State of California. Her daily papers bear steady witness to the fact that the reign of violence is not ended. Assassinations have been common in California, as on all frontiers; but they have not been common in Santa Barbara, where the irresponsible part of the population is very small, and where there has existed for several years all the security of a New England country town.

The people by their attorney, Charles T. Jones, of Sacramento, appealed from the decision of the first trial; and on the 23d of March Gray left Santa Barbara in charge of the sheriff, to be tried a second time, before Judge Head, at Redwood City, San Mateo County. Mr. Jones's management of the case is said to have been masterly, and Gray was convicted of murder in the second degree, and sentenced to twenty years in the State Prison.

Had the verdict been as to murder in the *first* degree, capital punishment would have been doubtful; yet nothing less than this could make the needed impression on the lawless part of the community. Santa Barbara congratulates itself, however; for conviction is rare in such cases, and the Press took the strange ground that this brutal murder was not unprovoked! The San Mateo County "Journal" sets a good example to some Eastern papers, when it prints the following words:—

" Theodore Glancey died not for himself, but for the people. He was killed in defence of their rights, not his own. To sustain the freedom of the American press is not the duty of one man, but the duty of all citizens. It is they that are interested in this principle far more than he. The truth that Theodore Glancey asserted by his death was worth more to the country than his life, even had he the will and force of a hundred men. Great principles have ever made martyrs of men; and as the blood of the martyr is the seed of the new principle, so death alone brings it to full harvest."

Let us rewrite this paragraph for a greater man, and with slightly different circumstances in view: —

" President Garfield suffers not for himself, but for the people. He was attacked while defending constitutional rights, not personal issues. To sustain the dignity and purity of the chief magistracy is not the duty of one man, but of all citizens. It is the country that is interested in the issue far more than the President. The political honesty which he vindicates by every pang he suffers is worth far more to his country than his life. Great principles have ever made martyrs of men ; and as the blood of the martyr is the seed of the new principle, let us make sure that in this case his long agony brings it to full harvest."

And what is this harvest? — for it is the same for the obscure editor on the shore of the Pacific and the President borne into office six months ago, by a popular ovation which thrilled the country from ocean to ocean. *It is the triumph of civil-service reform.* This will make the lives of public men safe, will diminish the pressure upon public officers, and will give us statesmen where we have had politicians.

The "terrors of the law" have long since ceased to be "terrors." An unworthy governor may pardon Clarence Gray. If our beloved President recovers, Guiteau, who has a hundred times confessed that he *meant to murder*, will not meet a murderer's doom.

To purify politics, by the establishment of civil examinations, and to drain our national city so that the life of the meanest citizen, as well as that of the chief magistrate, shall be safe, have long been the first two duties of Congress. From this moment they are the *evident* duties. Let the two Houses see to it that they are speedily fulfilled.

When Lincoln was assassinated, for the first time in the history of the world all nations held their breath and together listened at one moment for one sound, — to the bell which tolled out the mournful story of his death. Since the second of July, by reason of the same marvellous "girdle" with which human invention has invested the earth, the whole civilized world has waited at the bedside of one suffering man.

Whatever this may have done for Europe, it has made the citizens of the United States one people in a new and special sense. It has developed their faith in the unseen and spiritual. It has made selfish men disinterested, rude men courteous, arbitrary men humble, and rash men cautious. It would seem as if for the moment the selfish greed of the politician had received a death-blow.

Lincoln, Mass., Sept. 20, 1881. — In my own mind, every page of this book is as inextricably linked to the memory of Garfield, as every hour passed in Santa Barbara was interwoven with that of Glancey.

The bickering of the colleges, the intrigue of the markets, and the want of equity in the courts do what they can to destroy our faith in human nature; but no sooner does a great emergency arise than the true key-note of humanity is touched, and men rise to the level of our ideal.

If out of the whole world I could have chosen a President for the United States, I would have chosen James A. Garfield. That a convention of delegates would nominate him never suggested itself to my wildest hope. Filled with fresh expectation because of that nomination, I travelled westward. In California I encountered the perplexities which followed the publication of the forged letter to Morey, and which led to the defeat of Horace Davis, — one of the best Representatives ever sent from the West coast to Washington. I lingered there amid rockets and torch-light processions, and came homeward through the joyous acclamations which greeted the rescued States. I dropped my pen, while Pennsylvania Avenue resounded to the tread of eight thousand troops, and echoed the pæan of victory.

My final glimpse of that glowing and heroic face was taken later just before I left Washington, when in his last public address our President set the advantages of a liberal education before the graduating class of the Deaf Mute College. It was the pencil of the proof-reader which dropped from my startled hand, when "the shot heard round the world" was fired on the second of July. On that morning the President, starting for Williams College, intended also to go on to Worcester as the guest of Senator Hoar, and while there to go with him to the Cemetery of the little town of Lincoln, from whence the father of Garfield had emigrated to Ohio. He was to stand for the first time on the grave of his ancestors.

When I heard of this, I also determined to make that pilgrimage; but the long anxieties of the watch which

I shared with the whole nation drove the thought for a while from my mind.

On the nineteenth of September, still hoping against hope, I came up hither to pass the night. Seated on the very summit of its county, nested amid green hills, with more than thirty spires dotting the horizon, the night spent in Lincoln was uninvaded by the "passing bell." Unsuspicious I went out to greet the dawn of this new day, and over the dewy grass to the gate of the Cemetery.

Directly opposite to me as I entered, and between me and the massive monument consecrated to the descendants of "Hoare, Sheriff of Gloucester," I saw the name —

ABRAM GEARFIELD.

My tears rose, as well as the proud quick thought that in the hero's veins ran the blood of Massachusetts.

At this moment a lady came out of a house at the bottom of the hill, far beyond ordinary ear-shot. She waved the morning paper from her outstretched hand, and evidently sought to attract our attention. We turned silently and faced her. On the still air of the morning, which no breath of bird or hum of insect stirred, came to us distinctly one word, — "DEAD!"

NOTE.

If any readers have followed this journal with interest, they will perhaps wish to ask a few questions to which this postscript is intended to furnish the reply. Everything was said to prevent me from going to California in summer, and to divert my purpose of going alone. I was warned continually of the great discomfort to be expected, and the constitutional disturbance to be feared from alkaline dust and water. I had no choice, for if I did not go in summer and go alone, I could not go at all; but looking back with grateful pleasure, I am perfectly content with the result. In crossing the plains, we had rain nearly every night, and did not suffer from the dust at all.

On my return I was congratulated by every one, because I seemed to have accomplished a great deal for the length of my stay. If I did so, it was because I went alone, and was not detained by the plans or ailments of others. That I kept the power to travel was largely due to the kindness of friends, who received me into their houses, and, by surrounding me with the best possible conditions, kept me as strong as it was possible to be. But these friends were not strangers to whom I presented only a traveller's claim : the ties which united us had been knit long before I ever thought to see the sun set over the Pacific. In the early life of California it was necessary that every family should receive the traveller, and he was welcome because he broke a silence which has ceased to exist. Now the throng of visitors throws every resident back on the instinct of self-preservation, and the traveller may go everywhere to a public house, which he can make comfortable if he does not find it so.

I have dwelt with emphasis on the discourtesy of railway officials and the discomforts of the much boasted railway travel because no one prepared me for them, and because the United States contributed so largely to the building of the overland railways that travellers have a right to expect what they do not find.

That the facts do not owe their existence to my imagination the reader will believe, if he consider that at the moment I am writing these lines the United States Government is sending a Commissioner to the west coast to look after its interests. It is rumored that the proprietors of the Southern overland route have built that road to defeat the ends of justice, and to deprive the Government of its lawful royalty on the freight transported by the Northern. I could not help seeing that the only persons whose comfort was considered by the railways were political powers, and that their eyes were persistently blinded. A woman without a vote, and not known as an influence in any other way, was not likely to be considered.

I not only gained time by going alone, but I was constantly thrown into travelling parties which would have been inaccessible to two persons. The travellers in the summer season are chiefly English gentry, and of most of those I met I have made more than a mere acquaintance.

It was the earnest desire of my Western friends that I should stay through the winter. It was most fortunate that I did not, for it has been a winter of unparalleled disaster. The rains have been strenuous ; the lovely Mormon ranches of the Sacramento Valley have been flooded out of sight ; a pretty little watering place near Santa Cruz, and several mountain towns where I lingered have been washed off the face of the earth ; freight despatched from New York in January had not reached Stockton in April, — and for all this I do not think the spring flowers would have compensated me. The rain which usually averages twelve inches has this season been a little more than twenty-five. Property, crops, and cattle have suffered. Nor is California prosperous according to the opinions of her residents. From the moment that I first saw what is called hydraulic mining, it seemed to me that the State would have to interfere to check its legitimate consequences. The overflow of the Sacramento, which has broken its levees, is the result of the shoaling of a river filled to the brim with the débris of the hills. In the same way the harbor of San Francisco, perhaps the finest in the world, is fast filling up. The bonanza mines once brought in a revenue of two to three millions a month. Now the stocks are assessed about a million a month. This is depressing, and everybody talks of hard times.

I think it very probable that some of my readers will be annoyed at the persistency with which I have criticised the climate of San Francisco and of California generally. I do this for the same reason that I have spoken of the discomforts of railroad travel, because I was not myself prepared for the fogs, or the daily alternations of temperature, or the fact that in California rheumatism and neuralgia are "kept in stock," by anything I had ever read in books of travel.

When I was in Utah I was told by all the authorities, and by the common people, that the Mormon church never made any attempt to proselyte within the United States, and that converts coming from any part of the United States always bore their own expenses. The papers of this week report that forty Mormon missionaries in Omaha are bound to the mines in Colorado, and as many more are mentioned as having gone to Chattanooga. I have seen both items repeated, with the information that the parties are bound for the mines in Wales and Cornwall ; and I hope that the latter is the truth. The paragraphs have set me wondering whether proselyting to polygamy within the limits of the United States could be prevented if it were attempted. In Wales and Cornwall even Mormonism may find a mission.

WASHINGTON, October, 1881.

INDEX.

University Press: John Wilson & Son, Cambridge